Mark Perlman

THE RELUCTANT SOLDIER

Historical Novel

To: Dave

Mark Perlman

11-11-23

www.thereluctantsoldier.com

ISBN 979-8-36-002027-1

Cover and interior design by Kirsten Navin, www.kirstennavin.com

Cover photographs courtesy: Samuel Branch on Unsplash, Wikimedia Commons, Library of Congress, Creative Commons, National Archives

• Table of Contents •

List of Significant Non-Fictional Characters*

Josephine Baker: (1906-1975) African-American dancer and singer who immigrated to Paris, France in 1925. Virgil developed a thirty-year friendship with one of France's most celebrated performing artists and human rights activist.

Sylvia Beach: (1887-1962) New Jersey native who emigrated to Paris, France early in her life. She founded Shakespeare and Company, the famous bookstore. She befriended Virgil (alias, Joshua) for three decades. Sylvia introduced him to several famous literary personalities.

Eugene Bullard: (1895-1961) African-American Renaissance man. Boxer, World War One pilot, and infantryman for France. Musician, club manager, and owner. Civil Rights activist later in life upon his return to American. Friend of Virgil (Joshua) and his wife, Christina. He introduced Virgil to Paris' High Society.

Hamilton Fish III: (1888-1991) Raised by a well-known patrician family from New York. Soldier, Republican Congressman, and founder of the Order of Lafayette. He was Virgil's commanding officer of Company K in the First World War. He also assisted Virgil with his legal defense for murder in 1956.

Ernest Hemingway: (1899-1961) Famous American journalist, writer and adventurist. Met Virgil (Joshua) through Sylvia Beach while living in Paris.

Marie-Louise de Nonancourt: (1891-1952) Renowned owner of the House of Delamotte and Laurent-Perrier Champagne companies. She employed Virgil (Joshua) and Christina. She also helped Virgil with his run-ins with the Gestapo.

Madame "Billy" Saccadato: (1901-1974) Madam of L'Etoile de Kléber brothel in Paris. Although many of her clients were German, she also helped the French Resistance. Billy nursed Virgil (Joshua) after he was wounded on a mission that killed his wife's cousin.

List of Significant Fictional Characters

Virgil Lincoln Carpenter: (1891-1973) Alias Joshua Clément. Story's central character. His life story is told through his 'eyes' (a fictional memoir) until the time of his death.

Beatrice (McBride) Carpenter: (1896-1921) First wife of Virgil Carpenter.

Mildred "Millie" Carpenter: (1890-1977) Elder sister of Virgil. Mother to Paulette and Vera.

Mary Carpenter: (1893-1909) Younger sister of Virgil. Dies of illness at age sixteen.

Maria (Ramos) Carpenter: (1897-1972) Third and last wife of Virgil.

Christina (Peretti) Clément: (1891-1944) Second wife of Virgil, aka Joshua Clément. He met his Corsican love in France during World War One.

Alexa (Pietra) Clément: (1926-2011) Daughter of Joshua Clément (aka Virgil) and Christina.

Paul Clément: (1928-1952) Son of Joshua and Christina.

Mr. Hitchcock: (1871-1928) Fredericksburg Banker and benefactor to Virgil Carpenter.

Mason Jenkins: (1956-) Great nephew of Virgil. Son of Vera and Charles Jenkins. Wrote story of Virgil and the Carpenter ancestry based on his meetings with his great uncle, diaries, and interviews with relatives and friends.

Kadid Kolda: (1895-1975) Youngest son of Chief Kolda of Senegal. Befriends Virgil while both are recuperating during the Great War. They remain friends while Virgil makes a new home in France.

Captain (Inspector) Le Van: (1882-1944) French liaison officer to Virgil's combat unit (369th Infantry Regiment). Befriended Virgil when he returned to Paris in 1922.

Sergeant Marshall: (1883-1954) Sergeant Major in Virgil's Company K during World War One.

Thomas Peretti: (1895-1944) Cousin of Christina (Peretti) Clément. He recruited Joshua to become a French Resistance Fighter while Joshua is on the run from the Gestapo.

Attorney Foster Reynolds: (1909-1993) With the help of Virgil's niece, Paulette, and his former Captain, Hamilton Fish III, attorney Reynolds defended Virgil against a decades old murder charge.

Maggie Stephans: (1901-1975) Woman who helped Virgil escape from a crime scene. She testified on his behalf over three decades later.

The real-life personalities incorporated in this novel are depicted in a historical perspective and had no actual interaction with any of the fictional characters.

*This book is dedicated to the brave men of
the 369th U.S. Infantry Regiment during World War One.
They truly earned their nickname, the "Harlem Hellfighters."*

• Acknowledgements •

First and foremost, I want to thank my wife, Elaine for her support of this arduous journey for more than a dozen years. She pushed me to complete this book, even when I wanted to give up. My children, Alysha and Aaron assisted me in formatting my manuscript and other technical issues than I confess, am incompetent to master. My friends Seymour and Rhonda, provided suggestions and literary resources in order to keep this project on track. One of their references was Marcia Bradley, of Sarah Lawrence College in Bronxville, New York. She helped me correct grammatical errors and guided me into the realities of publication. Also, I'd like to thank Jane Lassner, my neighbor. She made several suggestions to the content that I incorporated.

The personnel of the archives department at Virginia Military Institute were very hospitable and helpful when I visited there in 2017.

The French Military Archives at Château de Vincennes, provided the needed research materials I needed regarding the American Expeditionary Force and the French Army, especially their interaction with the Harlem Hellfighters Regiment.

Karen Corinne Herceg was my English editor. She is a poet, editor and author. She now resides in France. Karen was instrumental with the grammar, punctuation, and dialog formatting of the book. Also, she assisted me with the publication process, literary resources and links to resources and communities that speak French in North America.

Lastly, without Johan Brag, my friend and neighbor, this book would never have been published in French. He worked the English manuscript and basic French translation into a lucid, accurate, and realistic French adaptation. Also, Johan provided expertise with the French language, geography and culture.

• Prologue •

My name is Mason Jenkins. I am the great nephew of this book's protagonist, Virgil Lincoln Carpenter. I am your storyteller for the first two chapters of the book. The balance of this story will be told through the "eyes and voice" of Virgil. He had the foresight to leave a pile of his diaries, and I had the great fortune of meeting him and listening to the story of his remarkable life shortly before he died in 1973. I took the poetic liberty of filling in the blanks of his life and dialog with the help of his friends, family and research. I also embellished and expanded on people, places, and things as I interpreted them from his notes and telling.

My great uncle lived an extraordinary life spanning from 1891 to 1973. He lived, fought, and loved in France much of his life from 1918 to 1919, and then from 1922 to 1955. Virgil returned to America to live out the balance of his life. His daughter, Alexa, had married and moved to Italy, and visited her father every year for a month. I got to know her well. She was a great source of information about her father. I did not have the same opportunity to meet Paul, his son, due to his untimely death in 1952 at the age of twenty-four. The title of this historic novel is "The Reluctant Soldier." You will learn why as you read about his life and times. He fought in two World Wars. In the Great War, he was a member of the 369th U.S. Infantry Regiment, an all-Negro Regiment, except for the higher-ranking officers. The regiment's *nom de guerre* was the "Harlem Hellfighters." This unit was assigned to elements of the French Fourth Army. A handful of Negro regiments actually fighting, were assigned to French units. This was a political compromise in the then segregated American Expeditionary Army.

In World War Two, he reluctantly fought with the French Resistance. I could have coined the book's title, "The Reluctant Warrior;" you can decide if I made a good choice. My Great Uncle Virgil was thrice married: to an African-American, then to a Corsican in France and, finally, to a lady from Puerto Rico living in New York.

Virgil belonged to the Negro race. Growing up in Virginia in the late nineteenth and early twentieth centuries was by definition, a hard scrapple life. As discriminatory as that time and place was, Virgil grew up in a loving family in Fredericksburg where his imagination took him to far off lands and times. For a Negro in the South growing up over a hundred years ago, he led a substantial and very unconventional life.

Virgil Carpenter did not plan it that way. As with most plans, they melt away upon the onslaught of life, like battle plans when the first sounds of war are heard. He struggled with the decisions he made and the choices thrust upon him during his turbulent life and events. Did he plan to return to France and stay for more than three decades? No, but much of his story is based on those halcyon years — the jazz era of the 1920's, the years of growing national anxiety of the 1930's, and the Occupation years from 1940 to 1944.

He is buried in Fredericksburg at the Old Shiloh Baptist Church Cemetery, formerly for "Coloreds." An American flag stands testament to his devotion and courage. A wreath adorns his stone every Christmas season. I visit it when I can. I did that a lot while I attended Virginia Military Institute, and when I returned to teach there. I place a penny on the stone and a French Tri-Color flag next to the Stars and Stripes.

Chapter One

"And All That"

An early morning mist hung over the Blue Ridge Mountains like a blanket of snow as I began my run, or more accurately stated, a fast jog from Red's Tavern in Lexington up Route Eleven until I reached the Maury River. At age sixty-two, I was in good shape except for hypertension, but I demanded a lot from my sexagenarian body today. A fast jog equal to almost ten miles was the order of the day. I hoped to complete it in about ninety minutes, and then have breakfast with my wife, Gracie.

I slowed my pace as I took in the sights and sounds of Jordan's Point, a tree dense island in the middle of the river. The poplars and oaks were in full bloom on this hazy early May morning. It had rained the night before making my pace more intrepid, but my eyes took in all of nature's bounty. I journeyed on alone.

This was familiar ground for me. I ran here and all the way to the Appalachian Waters Scenic Byway over forty years ago as a "rat," or lowly freshman, at Virginia Military Institute or VMI, as it is known. I usually ran alone, reflecting on what seemed the distant past of my troubled youth, the challenge of fitting into the rigors at VMI, or my future as a Negro man in a changing America. Sometimes I ran with a brother rat, Wesley Browning, or Brownie. He hailed from Norfolk, Virginia. Brownie was tall and lanky with an infectious smile and an even temper. He helped balance my moody ups and downs. I knew he would have an easy time commanding troops into battle. I would meet up with Brownie several times after we graduated, including the Desert Storm Campaign and in Iraq, a dozen years later.

More than a half hour passed since I left the tavern. I was now on Route 631, a bucolic two-lane road that runs along the river. The road was lined with plush Virginia farmland, and miles of split rail fences. I was close enough to hear the river despite the noise of passing cars. At times Route 631, locally referred to as Furr's Mill Road, ran so close to the river that I could look down and see the light of the rising sun skip off the rock-strewn water. The road turned into the river and crossed over it at Gould Creek. I stopped there, halfway into my morning's arduous exercise.

Truth be told, I was glad to catch my breath. Looking down from the road to the meandering waters, I thought about what I was going to say to my colleagues, cadets, or "keydets," the term used at VMI for student/soldier, and my family tonight, as I bid farewell to VMI after forty-three years of service. The last nine years I had been the head of the history department and, today, history was foremost in my thoughts. Maybe this run would put me in the right frame of mind.

I went a little further then returned over the bridge and down the same local sun swept roads. As I headed back towards Lexington, I ran into one of my students, Colleen McDaniels, from Wayne, Pennsylvania. She was a second classman, a junior, of average build, with red hair and deep blue eyes that seemed to search for simple truth. I found her to be an engaged and vocal student. She stood out in this semester's class, "The American Experience in the Great War." Colleen recognized me. I continued to labor up the hill.

She hailed me with, "Colonel, Colonel Jenkins, you're up early on this beautiful Saturday morning."

I picked up my pace, then I replied, "Yes, Ms. McDaniels, a great day for mind, body and soul. How are things with you?"

"Do you mind if I run back to VMI with you? I have no classes this morning," she replied, then added, "Now that I will be a first classman in the fall, I plan to spend some time at Ft. Lee this summer. I would like to develop my skills with the Bradleys and the Abrams technologies. What do you think, Sir?"

I was trying very hard to keep pace with her. I called out, "Very ambitious of you. I have high hopes for you. You are a fine keydet;

now slow down a bit, please!" I took a deep breath and continued, "Plan on commanding with the armored branch, right?"

"Yes Sir" she exclaimed. "Now that women can command in armored cavalry, I plan to be in the thick of it, just like you in Desert Storm."

We kept a decent pace, but I know Colleen was handicapping me. She was waiting for an answer, but I said nothing. My thoughts were reflected back to a rainy night in February 1991 when we ran into a Russian made T-72 tank commanded by the Iraqis. The T-72 was the best they had. My lead Abrams was coming down a reverse slope when the enemy was backing out of its protective bunker. My heart was racing. I knew there was going to be a firefight between my tank platoon and several T-72s. I took a deep breath as my navigator spotted it for a heat-seeking round. "Fire," I bellowed like a wounded animal. Next came the Sabot "dart." It penetrated the T-72 under the turret and blew it off. It was destroyed.

"Colonel, you are very quiet; big day for you, correct, Sir?" asked McDaniels. We finally made it back to VMI.

"Oh, I'm sorry, my mind drifted for a bit. When you said Desert Storm, it took me back to my first 'kill' on the night of February 25. I have no doubt that you will be a better commander than I. God willing, you may never have to use deadly force," I said, as I tried to hide my exhaustion.

She thanked me; we saluted and Colleen ran back to her barracks. I walked home to my wife, Gracie. It was an effort to climb the seven steps to the front door of the old federal brick colonial we called home since 2008. Before the screen door shut, Grace called out from the kitchen. "Mason, set yourself down for breakfast. Did you run clear to Richmond?"

"I'm headed for the shower, woman, I must have lost a few pounds along the way the last two hours," I replied while laboring up to the bathroom.

Gracie had just turned sixty. She was proud in allowing the gray to remain in her hair. At five feet eight inches and about 135 pounds, she reminded me of Cecily Tyson. We'd come full circle. I met her forty years ago when I was a first classman at VMI, and she was a junior at Washington and Lee. We met at Duck's Tavern in town one Saturday evening. I was with two of my fellow rats at the bar popping down shots of Jack Daniels when I spotted her. Grace was with a few coeds at a table in the corner. When two of her mates went to the restroom, I summoned up the courage to walk the thirty feet to introduce myself. I waited until she looked in my direction and then said, "Why haven't I seen you here before? I'm certain I would have spotted you even in the dark."

Gracie kept her eyes down, starring at her glass. She took a long sip of what appeared to be a mixed drink and replied, "Are you cadets always this forward?" Her friends had returned, and she looked to them for affirmation.

"Not sure of the entire corps, but I felt compelled to introduce myself," I stated.

She looked up at me directly now and said, "From what I can tell you have not completed your mission. Name, rank and serial number?" Grace smiled as her friends giggled.

"Sorry, pardon me ladies, Mason Jenkins, first classman at VMI, from Hempstead, New York, at your service," I quipped, as I focused on her hazel eyes.

A conversation ensued between drinks in the smoke laden tavern. We stepped outside after the noise and cigarette smoke overpowered our conversation. A two-year courtship followed, then we married in 1981 while I was stationed in Texas.

As I sat down to enjoy Gracie's omelet and hash browns, she asked, "Mason, big day for you honey. Parade, dinner affair in your honor. What are you goin' to speak about? Got a speech prepared? Can I see it?"

I played around with the hash browns as Gracie, hands on her hips, waited for my response.

"Well, I have nothing much on paper yet," I replied.

"You have to get dressed for the parade soon and before you know it, time will be your enemy," she reminded me, "but I know you are always prepared." She gave me a wink while she poured coffee for both of us.

I fixed my coffee, took a long sip and answered, "Gracie, I would not be inclined to self-indulge other than to reminisce about VMI then and now and on my thoughts of being part of the facility. Since this year is the hundredth anniversary of the end of the Great War, I'd thought I would talk more about my Great Uncle Virgil and the impact he had on my life. What do you think?"

"Mason," she exclaimed, "you have been fixin' to publish that damn book about him for months now. What's going on with it?"

Looking subdued, I replied, "I should be finished, including the revisions and editing, by the end of the summer. Most of my progress has been made over the last year."

"I expect you'll show me your edited version very soon. Anyway, I know you will give an impressive speech tonight," she replied.

I took great pains to make sure my uniform was perfect, but my true judge was Gracie. She examined me from all sides and from top to bottom. She gave me a thumbs up, then we kissed and commenced to walk to the parade ground escorted by one keydet from each class.

We approached the viewing stands. My eye caught General Sinclair, our Superintendent at VMI. He came over to us and said, "Colonel, Grace, can I have the pleasure of sitting next to you?"

"General, you would honor us. It is a fine-looking day!" I snapped back enthusiastically.

The general was a man of few words, but he seemed to be an active listener. Short, with a dark complexion, he graduated from VMI five years after me. He was deployed with the First Armored Division during Desert Storm and made two tours in Iraq during the post 9/11 attack.

My older, ailing brother, Paul, made the trip from upstate New York, with his wife Alma. He had suffered from a mild heart attack a few months ago. Our three children were coming to the parade and staying in town for the weekend. Virgil, our eldest, was flying in from Boston with his wife, Keisha, and their two kids, Henry and Shayna. Mary, our middle child, was recently divorced. She was coming with her younger sister, Vera, and Vera's husband, Ken, and their kids, Rachel and Kisha, by car from Philadelphia. We told them to meet us at the parade stand by 3:30 p.m. They all made work and school sacrifices in order to be here. That made Gracie and I very happy.

The 4:00 p.m. hour approached. The corps of keydets formed up for the dress parade. Forty years did not diminish my excitement for this tradition. Each company in their dress grays turned with precision to salute me. I held Gracie's hand while saluting back. Admittedly, I soaked it all in, thinking I had come a long way from joy riding along Hempstead Turnpike at midnight.

The General turned to Gracie and me and, in a hushed voice said, "We are proud of you and Grace, and your service to country and corps."

"Thank you, Sir," I replied. I continued to salute and smile nervously.

It was over in about an hour. Mary recorded it all on her iPad, while Virgil and Vera were preoccupied with their kids. The entire family took pictures with the general, a few colleagues and several of the keydets, including the captain of keydets. We toured the campus for about an hour; the bulk of the tour would be done tomorrow.

At about 7:00 p.m., Gracie and I headed over to Crozet Hall for the reception and dinner. For me, it all went by like a blur, as we met and received well wishes from the attendees. After a quick hour or so, I found myself on the dais with the general, several dignitaries, and a few VMI trustees. General Sinclair was speaking and would be the one introducing me. For some reason, maybe influenced by the scotch I consumed, I fell into a reverie — I was back in 1991, in Iraq.

Early in the morning of the 25th of February, our "Spearhead" Division penetrated about eighty kilometers into Iraqi territory. We were protecting our right flank, moving two armored brigades up front and one in reserve, close by. Abrams, Bradleys, Apaches, service and supply vehicles all moved under a windblown, cloudy night sky. Even in the desert, the sand can change in density, so our lead tanks needed to keep a constant pace. My platoon of five tanks, including a Bradley, was set in a diamond formation. We could smell the burning rubber, steel, and composite materials as elements of our division engaged the 806th Brigade of the Twenty-Sixth Iraqi Armored Division. I had confidence with the superior Chobham armor, shell range, optics, technology, and our Abrams crew – damn we had one hell of a fighting machine! My commanding officer, a "bird" colonel, gave the order to light up the sky with tracers at 2500 meters. Our satellite navigation systems were out of service, so we relied on compasses and an inertial device in a Fuchs recon vehicle as guides.

During the time my unit was traversing a reverse slope, a T-72 took aim at the Abrams on my left and hit it, blowing out its port track. Before I could give the order, Jack Turley, my gunner, targeted the enemy at six hundred meters.

I ordered a Sabot dart projectile fired from both tanks. Instantly I yelled, "gunner, sabot, tank." It blew off the turret of the T-72 that first engaged us.

Even at night, with the cool air circulating in the tank, we were sweating, adrenaline pumping, and hearts racing as we engaged more T-72s and BMP fighting vehicles, similar to our Bradley. Additional elements of our division moved into support. Apache and Black-hawk helicopters provided the needed air power. Our Bradley took over coordination of deploying local assets while I maneuvered my tanks per First Battalion orders. My first concern was with my disabled Abrams.

All of a sudden, I was snapped out of my daydream by loud applause that finally penetrated my reverie. Colonel Allison, seated next to me, gave me a nudge and said, "Mason, you're up."

I composed myself hoping no one noticed I had been in "La La Land," and went over to General Sinclair to thank him for the introduction.

I got up to the podium. I blew a kiss to my family seated up front. With my hands gripping the podium, I welcomed all the digni-taries, colleagues, guests, staff and most of all, the corps attending. I focused in on the middle of the assembled, then I proceeded to address them.

"Over the past few days, I have reflected on what I would say to you. Would it be about my school days here, or my deployments to hostile areas or my privilege teaching and then leading the depart-ment at VMI for close to a decade? Truth be told, the stories of my rat days here would have been most humorous. On one occasion, two of my fellow rats and I varnished several first classmen's inner soles. I laughed for years after that prank. I could regale you with more such stories. But I'd rather spend my time with you honoring a man who, besides my parents, was the most influential person in my

young life before VMI. I was a rebellious teen growing up in Hempstead, New York back in the early seventies. I hung around a group
that made poor decisions, and poor choices with poor consequences.
Although my parents provided a good home, a proper education,
guidance and love, I had it in my genetic code somehow to be a
'rebel without a cause.' I was going nowhere fast and could have
amounted to nothing much or even worse.

One day after a joy ride incident while I was just a sophomore
in high school, my mother insisted that I visit my great uncle who
was convalescing at the local hospital after suffering a heart attack.
I walked down the hospital corridors past nurses in their starched
uniforms, doctors with white smocks, orderlies with mops, and
gurneys with patients being pushed along. I finally made it to room
546 on the cardiac floor. The bed near the window was occupied by
Virgil Lincoln Carpenter, my great uncle. I had not seen him for
over a year, when he had attended my mother's birthday party. He
was assisted with a cane then. As I came close, I could see his white
hair had receded, and he looked thinner from what I could tell of
him under the sheets. He took a deep labored breath, and without turning to me said, 'Who sent you, your mother? Was it your
mother, Mason?'

'Yes, Uncle Virgil,' I replied hesitatingly.

'Well, I hear tell that you're not taking advantage of the gifts you
have, son,' he commented as he looked out the window.

'What gifts?' I asked him.

'Pray tell, Mason, the gifts of a solid family, good education, and
progress for your race these past twenty-odd years. You're wasting
your God given talents, wasting your place on this earth,' he lamented as he motioned to the window. 'A storm is coming, where will you
be, what will you do?'

I stood dumbfounded. 'Uncle Virgil,' I replied, 'it's sunny out
today.' I was thinking he was disoriented or senile. 'I don't see a
storm comin'.'

'Come over here Mason, hold my hand,' he declared.

His grip was still strong, stronger than I would have thought. He
pulled me closer and whispered, 'A storm is coming – it always does.
A storm of cultural changes, upheaval, conflict, and violence; just

like over this Vietnam War. You are in conflict
down you want to be somebody, but you need th
dence in yourself to break free and be your ow

He let go of my hand as he finished speak·
Over the following days, weeks, and month
learned of his life, his times, his trials, his heroism, an
I had no idea about his life and how much his story would .
my own, being young and self-absorbed. But what he shared with
me prior to his passing would change me forever.

Virgil Lincoln Carpenter was a reluctant warrior. He fought with
the 369th Infantry Regiment during World War One. You may
know that unit as the Harlem Hellfighters. At that time, General
Pershing assigned the regiment to the French Fourth Army. This
amalgamation was a way to satisfy some sentiment at home for
Negroes to fight yet remain a segregated American Expeditionary
Army. He later resettled in France, Paris to be specific, after a deadly
altercation in Virginia, leaving his teaching profession, family,
friends and America behind. He assisted in solving a series of political assassinations with his detective mentor during the twenties.
His first wife, Beatrice, and their newborn son, died shortly after
he returned from the war; I think it was in 1922. Uncle Virgil also
fought as a Resistance fighter in Paris during the Second World
War. His second wife, a Corsican woman he met during his time in
France in 1918, died by the hands of the German occupiers. Yes, he
was a reluctant warrior, a great man, an unsung hero to whom I owe
so much. I am completing his biography that I began twenty years
ago. It reads like a memoir. While I remember and reflect on the
hundredth anniversary of the 'war to end all wars,' I will celebrate
a man I have come to know well through his diaries, and the short
time I had the privilege to spend with him.

I want to thank my wife, Gracie, for all her love and support
over these thirty-eight years. I am also very proud of my children
and the joy I have with my grandchildren. On behalf of my family
and me, I would like to tell you all that it was my sincere honor
and privilege to serve my country, VMI, and the corps of keydets.
God bless and good fortune to you all," I summoned with a breaking voice. The assembled audience rose up and applauded. I like to

that I weathered the "storm!" It was a challenge expressing heartfelt sentiments that day.

The next morning the family met at the Wingate Hotel where everyone was staying. We had breakfast there while planning our Sunday. Our first stop was the George C. Marshall Museum on the VMI campus. Marshall was arguably the most famous alumnus at VMI. My friend, the museum director, opened it up just for us. He escorted us through the hallways and exhibits. My grandkids, well at least Henry, were fascinated by the weapons and uniforms. The director commented on many of the First and Second World War posters. We really liked the Uncle Sam and the Tuskegee airman posters soliciting war bonds. After the special tour, we visited the barracks I lived in forty plus years ago. A new section was built after I graduated. I lived in the middle section near the "sally port" corner. I showed them all four floors, which represented each year at VMI, starting with the rat class on the fourth floor.

Vera asked, "Did the rooms look the same back then?"

I replied, "Besides the much-improved technology and females residing here, not a significant change."

After a visit to the new gym facility, Cormack Hall, and the auditorium, we stopped by the statue of General Stonewall Jackson, once an instructor at the college before the Civil War.

My son, Virgil, spoke up, "What did you think of him, Dad?"

"Early on I had conflicting views. I mean I appreciated his skills as a great field tactician and aggressive leader. He was a complex man, a man of unyielding discipline. He held grudges and had some very weird personal habits like eating a lot of lemons and elevating his arm to keep 'an equal flow of blood.' I only wish he had fought on the Union side," I remarked.

"What about now, Dad?" asked Virgil.

I turned my eyes away from the sun shining brightly through the highly polished window and answered, "My views have not much changed. I do appreciate his teaching skills more now."

Later that day, we took in the local sights and cuisine of Lexington. We had dinner at the Southern Inn on South Main. I had the liver and onions, not popular with the family, but a favorite of mine. Before long, the kids and grandchildren had to leave. Paul and Alma left at sunset. Gracie and I felt very lucky that everyone was able to be together this weekend. That evening, I sat on the porch gazing up at a multitude of star configurations in a clear, calm sky and thought about my future. Monday would start a new chapter for me.

Chapter Two

Hempstead to Harlem

I remember the date like one remembered where they were and what they were doing when they heard President Kennedy was shot or when the Challenger Shuttle exploded. It was September 27, 1973 when my great uncle, Virgil Lincoln Carpenter, died. No news announcements, no headlines, just a gut-wrenching phone ringing at five a.m. It woke me up immediately. I knew instinctively what the call was about: my Great Uncle Virgil had succumbed to old age. The death of his first wife did not kill him. The death of his newborn son did not kill him. World War One, World War Two, the death of his second wife, the death of his second son, and being a fugitive, had not killed him. I like to think that he finally just gave in to the twentieth century. Simply, his time had passed.

I could hear my mother on the phone, mostly listening, interrupting with a word or short phrase. She did not wake me. I would be getting up by 7:00 a.m., and the two hours would make no difference to the deceased.

The rain drizzled down my bedroom window as dawn broke. It was Friday, just another day at Hempstead High, in my senior year. I knocked on my parents' door at about 6:30. I heard mom respond, already downstairs, calling out from the kitchen, "Mason, come down. I have sad news for you."

Entering the small white and cream-colored kitchen appointed with appliances from the local Sears store, I found Dad stirring his coffee, creating a whirlpool in the cup, as Mom turned to me with a coffee cup in her hand. I broke her concentration by blurting out, "It's about Uncle Virgil. He died this morning, right?" She gazed at me through weary, sad eyes.

Mom, or Vera by name, had aged well for her forty-eight years. She grew up in Queens, New York, went to CCNY, the City College, after the war, where she met my father, Charles. Both became educators. They prefer that designation to teacher. Mom taught elementary school, while Dad taught at the high school in Hempstead, Long Island. Vera had a light complexion for her race, hazel eyes, and a cropped afro hairstyle peppered with streaks of grey. At five feet nine inches and about one hundred forty pounds, she was even more imposing with her high heels, her sharp intellect notwithstanding. My dad, Charles, never known as Charlie nor Chuck, taught chemistry and was an assistant football coach. I was devoid of talent in both these areas. Dad was a bit paunchy with a lot of grey on his balding crown. He had fought in World War Two, known as "the war," as a mechanic for the Tuskegee airmen unit in Europe. He had gone to college under the new GI Bill. It was his ticket out of menial work, and he took advantage of it.

"You heard the call come in?" asked Mom.

"Yes, ma'am. Calls at 5:00 a.m. can only mean a baby is born or someone died," I remarked, while I helped myself to some orange juice.

"We need to go to the Presbyterian Hospital and then to the funeral home in Harlem after school," Mom stated with a resolute tone.

"Can you help us with the obituary, Son?" asked Dad. I nodded yes. "Also, Alexa is arriving with her husband, Phillipe, from Italy tomorrow afternoon. We'll pick them up at JFK Airport," added Dad.

Alexa was Virgil's daughter by his second wife, Christina Peretti, the Corsican woman he first met in 1918, while fighting in France. They lived in Milan, Italy.

After school, we took the Long Island Railroad to Pennsylvania Station. The rain streaked along the moving train car windows like slow motion bullets. When we arrived at Penn, it was rush hour. The mass of moving bodies helped obscure the drab and depressing décor that was the "new" Penn Station. I heard the old one had much more class. I hoped the same fate did not befall Grand Central Station. New York was in bad financial shape from what my parents said, so I think that had a significant impact upon any so-called new improvements. I felt bad for the several panhandlers positioned in strategic places begging for change. Most were Black men of all ages, desperate and alone amongst a sea of humanity.

We took a very crowded Number One subway train up to the hospital located by 168th Street and Broadway. We did not get a seat until the 96th Street Station. I was not a fan of strap hanging. After shaking out our wet umbrellas, we were inside the formidable edifice of medicine and healing by 6:15 p.m. We were escorted to the morgue by Doctor Patel, a resident doctor who was one of the cardiac physicians caring for my great uncle. He stated that Virgil died from congestive heart failure. The last time I visited him was on the 25th, a Wednesday, after school. I recall the last thing he told me as I was leaving: "Mason, prepare yourself for a life well lived. Be fierce, but humble. God be with you. See you soon." I didn't realize it then, but the times I spent with him would change my life.

My parents identified Virgil as I stayed outside the holding area, preferring to remember him in life. The times I spent with him over the last couple of years changed me, as it turned out. We then went to the Weldon Funeral Home on 116th Street. We took a yellow cab and arrived by 7:30 p.m. We were greeted by what I assumed was one of the funeral directors. A young man with a cropped afro, slim of build, with a thin mustache extended his hand and said, "Welcome; my sincere condolences to you and your family. My name is Rodney Carter. I've been with Weldon's for eight years. I hope this rain will stop soon. Let me take your umbrellas, please. Do you want some coffee or water?" he asked as he motioned for us to follow him. We declined, then made our way to his office, a small space for four people. There were pictures of Dr. Martin Luther King and U.S. Representative Adam Clayton Powell, Jr. behind his desk. The light-ing set a somber tone. I assumed that this was by design.

Mr. Carter took some time to ask us about Virgil's family and, most importantly, Virgil himself. Before he could forge ahead with the arrangements, my father leaned forward and said, "Our uncle wanted to have a wake in the city he lived in and loved. He has family coming from Italy. He wanted his remains be transported by rail to his final resting place in Fredericksburg, Virginia to the family plot. Can you accommodate us?"

The director leaned back in his well-worn leather chair, tugged at his waxed mustache and replied, "Mr. Jenkins, this request is unusual, but we can make all the arrangements. I will need to know details for the wake. I can work out logistics with the railroad and funeral home you want in Virginia."

My parents and Mr. Carter spent another hour on the wake times, casket choice, and other related matters before we left. My dad gave him all the documents including the death certificate, social security card, visa, and a life insurance policy. There had been a few conflicting issues to clarify. My great uncle's alias was Joshua Lamont Clément. He had to change his identity when he escaped from America as a wanted fugitive after killing a man near Fredericksburg in self- defense in 1922. He bribed a merchant ship captain in New York and made his way back to France. He told me the story shortly before his death.

The next day Dad picked up Alexa and Phillipe at the Air Italia terminal at JFK. He went alone in our family's well maintained 1969 Oldsmobile in order to make sure there was enough room for the luggage and passengers. They arrived at our modest home late in the afternoon, a short ride to Hempstead. Mom and I hurried out to greet our Italian relatives. Alexa was about the same age as Mom. She was even lighter in color with auburn hair that was pulled back and tied in a bun. She wore a navy-blue dress and a strand of pearls. She let the men retrieve the baggage as she approached us.

Without hesitation, she kissed us on each cheek and slowly said, "It is so wonderful to see you even on this sad occasion."

She continued in English with a native French accent that was a bit difficult to understand, as she gazed at us admiringly and said, "You both look magnificent! And you, Mason, so tall and grown up. I love your home — it stands very impressive in brick and with a nice portico. C'est manifique!"

I took a bag from Phillipe while Mom remarked on Alexa's outfit that clearly evidenced European chic.

"Oui, yes, my Phillipe, please meet Vera and Mason," she said.

He kissed us in the same way as his wife; a European custom. He was a bit older than Alexa, maybe by six or seven years. He was only about five feet seven inches tall, trim with long greying hair and a trimmed mustache. His accent was slightly less pronounced than his wife's, but still challenging to my ears.

We waited for my older brother, Phillip, to come from Schenectady. He was an engineer at the General Electric facility there. He was almost ten years older than me, and still single. He had graduated from Hofstra University in 1968. At dinner we talked about our common bond, Virgil, and stories that were new to me, and some I had heard before. We also talked about French, Italian and American politics, especially, the current Vietnam War.

The newspaper printed Uncle Virgil's obituary. I helped author it. It read as follows: "Virgil Lincoln Carpenter passed away on September twenty-seventh after a long illness. He was eighty-two years of age. He is survived by his daughter, Alexa, her husband, Phillipe, and two grandchildren, who live in Italy. He is also survived by several nieces and nephews in New York, Washington, D.C., and Virginia. Born in Fredericksburg, Virginia in 1891, he later immigrated to France in 1922. Virgil returned to America in 1956. Carpenter fought in World War One with the rank of sergeant. He was wounded several times and gassed late in the war. Mr. Carpenter's first wife, Beatrice and his infant son, died in childbirth in 1921. He was married to Christina Peretti from 1925 until her untimely death in 1944 as a result of her heroic participation with the French Resistance in Paris. They had two children, Alexa and Paul. Mr. Carpenter taught French at the Cathedral High School in Manhattan for several years. In 1962, he married Maria Ramos who recently predeceased him. He will be waked on September twenty-ninth at the Weldon Funeral Home, 343 East 116th Street, New York City, from 2:00 to 4:00 p.m. and from 7:00 to 9:00 p.m. His remains will be transported to Fredericksburg, Virginia, and burial will take place at the Old Shiloh Baptist Church."

All six of us piled into the reliable Oldsmobile. It was cramped, but Dad assured us that the trip to Harlem at midday would be swift. As we made our way across the Triborough Bridge to Manhattan, traffic going crosstown proved to be more arduous than he'd suspected, even at that time of day. However, we made it to the funeral home with time to spare, parking notwithstanding. We were greeted by Carter, the director. He welcomed us with a firm two-handed greeting, then he remarked, "I hope your trip was easy on you." Without waiting for a reply, he led us to where Uncle Virgil was laid out and then left us.

Each one of us spent time privately with Virgil. When it was my turn, I knelt down, closed my eyes and thought about the time I had seen him at the hospital. His stories of another era, another land, seemed a fiction, but they were all too real. His recollection of those times had been vivid as he related them to me. Alexa followed me at the casket. She stayed by him the longest. I could hear her whispering something in French. Then she made the sign of the cross and kissed him.

The afternoon wake brought a mix of former colleagues from Cathedral High School as well as a few former students. Old men from his Harlem neighborhood sauntered or hobbled in. Several of them, including those in wheelchairs, introduced themselves as former veterans of the famous Harlem Hellfighters unit that Uncle Virgil had belonged to. I wondered if they knew who he really was, given his complicated history and the alias he had taken. This handful of vets congregated in the back and as my father would say, "predicted the past." If so, they had a lot of predicting to do.

Alexa admitted to mom that she was heartbroken for not visiting her father more often after he left France. Mom consoled her as a teacher would console a student. I was aware there had been some hard feelings between father and daughter due to the untimely death of Paul, brother to her, and son to Virgil, in 1952. He was an alcoholic who was killed in a single car crash.

The evening wake was pretty much the same, a mix of former colleagues, students, friends, and a few army buddies. The procession made its way past us. Soon an old man said to me, "Son, my condolences to you. I knew Virgil Carpenter when he was a reluctant warrior. He was my sergeant in France."

I didn't catch his name, but I did trail him with my eyes as he sat in the last seat in the next to the last row. He appeared very average looking with the exception of a fancy walking cane with a carved handle, and a black suit that seemed too small for him. I excused myself from the family at about 8:45 p.m., after a prayer by the pastor. I went over to the gentleman with the cane and asked if I could have a few minutes of his time.

"I'm sorry, but I did not catch your name, Sir," I admitted.

"Otis Ellison. You must be Mason Jenkins, Vera's son," he remarked.

I nodded and continued "How did you know Virgil?"

Mr. Ellison rose and started to make his way to the anteroom, motioning for me to follow. We sat in a couple of high-back chairs along a back wall. "I joined the New York Fifteenth Colored Regiment with Virgil shortly after war was declared in 1917," he began. "We joined for different reasons. For me, I joined at the urging of band leader James Reese Europe. He was a force of nature and helped Colonel Hayward build up the regiment. Virgil joined out of a sense of guilt. His college students were leaving and enlisting. We served in the same company. It was months of diggin' ditches, marchin,' training,' putting up with 'nigger this' and 'nigger that,' 'boy this' and 'boy that,' until we were kicked over to the French Fourth Army by Black Jack Pershing, a year after we enlisted. I guess the policy of segregation trumped his own feelings," he explained, his hands resting on the cane handle.

I followed up by asking, "Why did you call him a reluctant warrior?"

Mr. Ellison shifted in the tufted arm chair and replied, "Well son, he never was keen on fightin'. He was the most educated colored man I'd ever come across. You know he was a professor when he joined the regiment. Yes son, he was like a Black Woodrow Wilson!"

He starred down at his cane for a moment and went on. "Virgil was not a casual lover nor a drunkin' fighter from what I could tell. He was a God fearin' man whose intellect tempered any killer instinct regardless of the blood, shellin' and stench of the front lines. A strange thing happened when his buddy Parker, Emmet Parker, died near Séchault. You know where that place is son?"

I think it is a small town not too far from Rheims, from what I heard," I murmured.

"Yes, a speck on the map, a one road hamlet in the middle of nowhere, but we kicked the Germans' ass there. Parker's death affected Virgil to the point of his realization that death was like a stranger to smile at, not run from. He then assumed he would not get out alive." Mr. Ellison leaned forward a bit on his cane, his eyes staring into the distance as if he were watching the story unfold before him.

The next morning outside Séchault," he continued, "Virgil was assigned to lead a patrol to knock out a Boche machine gun nest before the battalion made its assault," Mr. Ellison could see that I was distracted by Mom's hand waving for me to come over. I gave her a ten-finger sign for ten more minutes. She nodded and acquiesced to my request.

Mr. Ellison picked up where he left off. "Virgil possessed a calmness of purpose as if he could see it play out in his mind. He told us that we were goin' to crawl past our partially cut wire, fifteen minutes before our artillery barrage was to commence. Two of us were to proceed to a destroyed barn about two hundred yards from our lines, using a grenade rifle and a Chauchat automatic weapon to distract the Boche. Virgil and Harry Barnes were to crawl along a gully on the flank while the others proceeded on the right flank, past the barn. Virgil did not care much for the French Chitchat as it jammed too much, especially in wet weather. He carried an American pistol, 1903 Springfield rifle, and a mix of French and German trench grenades."

I listened with rapt attention. Mr. Ellison looked at his Timex watch and hurried on. "At dawn, our artillery opened up with fog shells so we could move out with some protection. Then the French '75s,' field artillery, pounded the German lines. We had a few larger cannons for shrapnel and high explosives. It was only a fifteen- or twenty-minute barrage, but it was all hellfire and flame. The whole battalion went over. From what was left of the barn's second floor, I could see Virgil and Harry as the fog began to clear. They were almost within grenade distance from the Boche machine gun nest. I was not the only one to spot them. Harry was hit in the arm and leg; he immediately collapsed. Emmett Parker made a suicidal charge at the enemy with grenades in both hands. After seeing this sacrifice, Virgil let out a guttural yell, 'BAY-O-NETS, fix BAY-O-NETS!' He ran his raggedy ass to a nearby stone wall, bullets whizzing by him. He hurled two German trench grenades into the nest and ran at it with pistol in hand."

Mr. Ellison inhaled deeply, then continued. "In the end, he knocked off several Boche. One Maxim machine gun was destroyed, but he salvaged the other and started firing away at the enemy. He held his position until some of the boys from 'C' Company reinforced him. He was 'hell on wheels' that day. Virgil was carried off wounded in the face and body. It took a long time for him to recover. He didn't join us again until the Armistice. We'll, I guess that's all the time we have for now, son. I hope the story brought you closer to him. It's time to clear out." He smiled as I helped him up from his relaxed position.

Before I returned to my family, I asked. "Where do you live?"

"I'd like to see you or at least phone you," I requested.

He put on his coat and pointed to the registry, "It's there, my address is on the sign in registry. Look me up, son," he smiled warmly at me, then he departed.

Most of the faces I saw were now a blur to me, but Otis Ellison was a man to be remembered. I ran his story through my mind again and again imagining it while I looked out the rear window of the Oldsmobile on the way home.

All these years later, I still visit my great uncle's grave, giving care to it and reflecting on all the wisdom he imparted to me.

The headstone on my great uncle's grave reads: Virgil Lincoln Carpenter, 1891 to 1973, First Sergeant Company K, 369th U.S. Infantry Regiment, World War One. Father, Husband, Educator and Warrior.

Now his story...

Chapter Three

Enter the Carpenters

I could have been named Virgil Mason or Virgil Wood for that matter, but my grandfather's master preferred the name Carpenter. From what my grandmother often told me; it suited my father. I never met my grandfather. He remained with his ne'er-do-well master and owner after his wife, Ruth, and their son, Charles, were sold to a new slave owner in the town of Fredericksburg, Virginia in the early years of the Civil War. Charles would become my father. My grandfather, Joshua, was born about 1840, we think, near Charlottesville, Virginia. He worked on a small plantation there, home to a family by the sur name of Phelps. The master's wife was named Pauline, and they had three children, two girls and one son.

Granny Ruth described the master as a middle aged, tall and wiry man with a Scottish bloodline. He would quote scripture while inflicting severe discipline on his slaves for what he deemed as infractions or dereliction of work. His wife was a self-described aristocrat and social climber. She adored her children to the brink of spoiling them, and defied her husband whenever she could. She was fond of having the musically inclined servants play for her children and friends on a regular basis. She would reward the "darkies," as she described the servants, with extra food, especially on Sundays. Her children tolerated the help except for the youngest, Katie. She was an independent soul with a personality that discounted one's color as a reason to put up social barriers. She played with several of the slave children. They would go off to a part of the hay shed that became a girls' sanctuary. They pretended that they lived in the north of Scotland, on a sheep farm.

Granny recalled that there were about ten or twelve slaves on the property. One male and one female were the "inside niggers." Ruth worked the fields and inside the house when needed. The earliest picture of her and my father was taken in 1873, in Fredericksburg during the era of Reconstruction, at a local studio on Caroline Street. The six by six-inch photo was sepia toned with no one smiling, as was the Victorian tradition for the time. Ruth was dressed in a white linen dress adorned with a dark waist belt. She was thirty-two at the time, but she already possessed some white hair and noticeable lines around her dark, deep eyes. My father, Charles, at age fifteen, looked more like a man of twenty. Tall at almost six feet, he appeared to be very protective of his widowed mother. Ruth's second husband and their daughter, born in 1870, died of typhoid the following year. The same studio took a "death" picture of the child. It was morbidly popular at the time.

Ruth worked as a seamstress and domestic in town. She was also left a small inheritance from Rufus, her second husband. It came from a five-hundred-dollar life insurance policy, some livestock and a gold watch. She could not locate Joshua after the war. She did not know where he was destined to go when she and Charles were sold. He may have wandered north because, she did not find him at the Phelps's homestead. Only four freed slaves remained at the plantation. I dreamt of him hitching train rides to Chicago or St. Louis. He was a carpenter and stonemason. Joshua built and maintained the buildings and equipment for Master Phelps. Granny Ruth would paint a verbal picture of Joshua as a broad-shouldered man with coal-colored eyes and a broad nose. She would tease him about his "bull" sized nose, including his snorting when he was up in a sweat or just mad. His hands were like oversized mitts. He was very proud of his work. Occasionally, he would be loaned out to local Whites for his skills.

In December of 1862, shortly after the Union Army, under General Burnside, bombarded and destroyed much of Fredericksburg. Many White slave owners fled the city, slaves in tow. Ruth, with her young son, then only age four, seized her opportunity on a Sunday while the remaining masters were attending church. She ran down to the destroyed railroad bridge and, with only a carpetbag of worldly goods, hoisted her son, into a pontoon boat with other slaves on board. They crossed the unusually calm Rappahannock River with scores of fellow slaves to where the Union Army awaited on the north side of the river.

Upon reaching shore they were met by "Bluecoats" with Hardee hats. These were men of the "Iron Brigade," storied soldiers from the Great Lakes region. The hats were their distinguishing feature. They were broad-rimmed black hats. Now in the custody of Lincoln's soldiers, these slaves were free from bondage.

Ruth traveled with the army, now commanded by General "Fightin'" Joe Hooker. She repaired many a trouser, blouse, and coat for Union officers and infantry. She did not care for the prostitutes that hung around the camps, like fish catching a ride with a shark. She avoided them at all costs except for one that befriended her and her son. Her name was Amanda, a crossbreed, not uncommon during slavery. Amanda was orphaned at age fourteen and traveled with Hooker's army a year later. She was a seamstress and "comfort" woman. She had access to tobacco, coffee, chocolate and other niceties due to the erotic comfort she gave to men far from home with death a clinging companion. Amanda would give some of her hard-earned merchandise to Ruth. Granny said that Amanda was an elegant beauty and a "right smart person for no proper schooling."

Eventually, Ruth and Charles made their way north to the nation's capital just before the Battle of Gettysburg. They lived in D.C. until 1866. She had met Rufus after the war. He was working as a plasterer and also spent time burying the Union dead across the Potomac River at Arlington, the former home of Robert E. Lee. They moved to Fredericksburg because Rufus could find a lot of work rebuilding the town. Ruth also had many former clients there.

They settled in Darbytown, a Negro enclave south of the town's train bridge, near Lafayette Street. Their house was on Charles Street. It was a small white brick clad structure with a room for a boarder. The home was also appointed with a new outhouse and well. Granny would tell me about one of her clients, a Mrs. Mabel Hodges. She was a widow who lived on William Street. She was about sixty. Her son died in a Union prison somewhere in Chicago. Her daughter moved to Richmond with her husband. Mrs. Hodges treated Granny like any White woman. They would talk for many hours while Granny made quilts and sewed. Mabel and her daughter volunteered at a Confederate hospital in town from 1864 to the war's end. She told Granny about the horrors and suffering sustained by the soldiers. The hospital had so little in the way of resources. Limbs would be sawed off and stacked like cordwood outside the hospital, not an encouraging sight. Negro men would bury the deceased and limbs in large pits. When Mrs. Hodges passed away, she bequeathed a thousand dollars to Granny, a handsome amount at the time.

Ruth and Rufus joined the Shiloh Baptist Church, at the old site, when they settled in Fredericksburg. This historic church for Negroes was located on Sophia Street, next to the river. Before the war, Mr. George Rowe, a White minister, had to oversee the congregation. Dr. J.D. Harris, an African-American physician, came to town and pastored the church members. Baptisms took place in the river just above the railroad bridge. My father went to school in the basement of the church. A few dozen boys and girls attended from the town and surrounding areas. Dad met his future wife at the school, Anne Malone. She was the daughter of Elijah and Mildred Malone. They were freed Blacks before the war due to the benevolence of their master and mistress. Elijah owned a hardware store on William Street, in an area called Liberty Town, not far from the slave auction block and holding area on Charles Street.

In 1877, they were married in the same Shiloh church with Dr. Harris presiding. They honeymooned at Washington D.C. in time for the inauguration of our nineteenth President, Rutherford B. Hayes. Shortly thereafter, Reconstruction ended and new repressive times swept across the South. The Jim Crow era had begun, along with the birth of the Ku Klux Klan.

Dad worked in Elijah's store and pretty much managed things as time wore on. Dad was a hard drinker, an affliction that us children and our mother had to endure. Mother and father bought a small house in Darbytown, off Lafayette Street, with the help of a down payment from Granny. They could not have children for some time. There were a few stillbirths. Then finally in 1890, my sister, Millie, was born. I came a year later, and Mary was born in 1893.

I was baptized by the Reverend James E. Brown. He came from Chesterfield, Virginia. There was a split in the congregation that finally went to court shortly before I was born. The congregation ministered by Reverend Robinson held services at the Revere Shop. Our family remained with the "old" Shiloh Church. The building collapsed due to water damage over time in 1885. A new church was built in 1890 due to the leadership of our pastor. Reverend Brown continued to minister until 1905.

Millie and I went to school in Fredericksburg a few blocks from the church. It was established in 1884 for us coloreds. My first memory, oddly enough, was a parade on the Fourth of July in 1895. Mom took Millie, Mary, and me down to Caroline Street. I was fascinated by the bands and Confederate veterans marching down the street, accompanied by fire wagons and a few horse-drawn floats. I also recall the fervor and excitement when war was declared in 1898. American flags were everywhere. It was also the year our family was in turmoil. My father had a love affair with a customer of his store. She was much younger, about twelve years younger than him. Her husband had been abusing her, and she found a vulnerable man who wanted excitement and romance as a diversion from whisky. Mother eventually discovered this and kicked father out. He stayed at a boarding house in Liberty Town for ten months before mother took him back. He promised to be counseled by our pastor. He did swear off women but kept whisky as his constant friend.

My father and I were never that close, but he did teach me how to fish and ride a quarter horse. We would go catfishing on the Rappahannock on Sundays after church, weather permitting. Sometimes Millie would tag along. She did not want to bait the hook. Other than that, she liked to fish while cooling her feet in the water. When I was eleven, I would help Dad at the store on Saturdays. I was responsible for counting the inventory and polishing up the leather goods. I liked talking to the customers, including a few old timers who would pass the days playing checkers by the wood stove or out on the porch. One of them, Jake, was the body servant to General Wheeler, a revered cavalry officer in Lee's army. He also served under General Schaeffer in the recent Spanish-American War. Jake told amazing stories of his travels with General Jeb Stuart's cavalry from Virginia to Maryland to Gettysburg.

In 1904, when I was thirteen, Elijah Malone died. The store passed to my father. This elevated status increased his dependence on whisky. Millie and I helped as much as we could, considering our schooling. With all of Dad's shortcomings, he did want us to have a good education and a better life. That same year, a Black man, no older than eighteen, was lynched outside of town, near the battle-field cemetery. He was accused of harboring a love interest with a White girl of sixteen. That was enough for a lynching. A group of Black town leaders, and even a few Whites, marched in protest. But it was to no avail, as police broke up the march and no murderer was found. No one would have been convicted then, anyway.

The local newspaper decried the invitation of Booker T. Washington, a prominent Black educator, to Teddy Roosevelt's White House. Blacks were now able to hold federal civil service positions. We were proud and had hoped a new era in race relations was forthcoming.

Some days after school, and more often in the lazy days of summer, Millie, Mary, and I would walk down to Lafayette Street to the Civil War Cemetery across from the Sunken Road. It was on a hill. Beautiful flowering trees spotted the garden of white grave markers and monuments honoring Union dead from Maine to Michigan and villages and cities in-between. I found it incredible that row upon row of Bluecoats would march up the hill near Marye Street only to be mowed down like a sickle does to wheat. Confederates would be lined up behind a stone wall up on the heights with musket and cannon. It was a bad day for the Army of the Potomac and its hapless leader, General Burnside.

The three of us would read many marker inscriptions to find the youngest and oldest who had died. Occasionally, we would see visitors, mostly old and some very old, gather around a single grave marker. Some knelt, some stood, and nearly all prayed. Flowers or wreaths adorned some of the graves, even forty plus years after this costly battle.

1905 marked my first year at the new Normal and Industrial Institute for Coloreds. It was a marked improvement over the school built twenty years prior near the Mount Zion Baptist Church. I was a freshman at the school and adapted well to the academic curriculum.

One muggy day in April, I was walking from school to the church for choir practice when I saw the rare sight of a horseless carriage backfiring. The loud noise spooked two horses pulling a loaded wagon. The wagon bolted down Caroline Street toward a young girl wearing a light blue, linen dress and holding a doll. Without thinking, I ran across the street and pushed her out of harm's way. Other than her dress in need of a good washing, she was not injured. Her father ran out of a tobacco shop tending to her cries. As the situation settled down, the father, now composed, thanked me heartily. The crowd that had gathered pointed to me as her hero. After a trip to the drug store for a soda as my reward, I found out that the girl's father was the president of one of the town's banks. The girl, Adeline, was only seven years of age. Her father asked me about my family and my schooling. He took a genuine interest in me, unusual for such a powerful man. I did not make it to choir practice that day. I guess due to the banker's influence, my heroics made the local news. I became a celebrity for a time until, like many such events, memories fade except for those affected.

I earned high marks in school, and I participated in the debate club and played third base for the baseball team. In my junior year, our team was challenged by the town's high school for Whites. The game was played nearby at the University of Mary Washington. A big crowd, segregated by skin color, attended to support their favorite sons. Police and town elders made sure that racial tensions were kept to a civil level. A partially cloudy but warm May afternoon welcomed us as this rare competition commenced at four o'clock. The first three innings were a pitching duel. In the fourth inning we opened it up with three runs, including a double I belted off the fence. The score held at 3-0 until the bottom of the seventh when their pitcher hit a two-run homer. We scored another run in the ninth. The score stood at 4-2 with the rivals batting in their last attempt. Their centerfielder singled, stole second and moved to third on a sacrifice fly. With one out, he scored on a single. The next batter struck out. With two outs, the man on first stole second after a controversial call by the umpire. The game was stopped for ten minutes as a ruckus developed, bottles littered the field, and police ousted some spectators, almost all coloreds. With the sun setting and tension rising, our pitcher threw a curve ball that was hit into foul territory. It was caught. We prevailed 4-3! The police and hired private enforcers cleared the two factions before dark.

We subdued our elation in fear of retribution until we reached the farmhouse of our pitcher, Samuel. Several of us engaged in horse-play until Sam's mother promptly made us retreat to the barn, cleats and all. Sam uncovered a handle of whisky, Jim Beam to be specific, he had hidden under a water barrel. The contents were consumed until we staggered and stammered.

Elijah, our quick handed third baseman, broke the incoherent utterings suggesting that our best Negro ball players could compete against the likes of Ty Cobb, Christy Mathewson, Cy Young, and Nap Lajoie. We spent the remaining time together imagining a game between rivals of color.

In 1908 Millie graduated. We were very proud. That summer was also notable as the banker who befriended me paid a visit to our modest home. His horse-drawn cab waited on the street. My parents invited our important guest, Mr. Hitchcock, for tea and cake. After some nervous small talk, our guest asked me about my plans upon graduating high school. I looked at my parents and stated that I probably would take over the family hardware business. It was a response my father wanted, but I really had my heart on higher education. However, we could not afford college, because much of our money had been siphoned off for father's whiskey and some large medical bills for Mary, who had become increasingly ill of late.

Mr. Hitchcock, a man younger than his position may have suggested, sat back on the worn but very comfortable armchair. He took a sip of tea in one hand and gently replaced the cup on the saucer. Then, while indenting the brim of his fedora that he held in his lap, he said, "Mr. Carpenter, I am eternally grateful for the quick thinking and heroism displayed by your young man when he risked his life to save Adeline. My wife and I feel strongly that we want to demonstrate our appreciation by supporting Virgil's college expenses."

My father, now intrigued to be in a man-to-man discussion, asked, "What exactly do you mean?"

It appeared that Mr. Hitchcock had it all figured out as he readily explained. "We would like to pay for Virgil's tuition and room costs for the college of his choice. We will pay for each year he maintains at least a 'B' average."

My father turned to me and asked for my opinion. I, with some hesitation, stated that my heart was set to go to college and be a teacher or professor.

"How about the store?" Dad bemoaned as he bit into another piece of cake.

Mom, looking to de-escalate the moment, asked Mr. Hitchcock if he would like more tea.

"My dream may never be fulfilled, but can I be faulted for pursuing it?" I exclaimed, my voice cracking a bit.

My father rose from the sofa and thanked Mr. Hitchcock for coming and making such a generous offer. He told the banker that he would think on it. Over the next several days, Mother and Millie worked on Dad to the point of distraction. Since he could find no peace, he finally relented. Maybe the wastefulness of the family's finances changed his mind, but he took credit for the change of heart.

I applied to Hampton Institute by the Chesapeake Bay, near Norfolk. In May of my senior year, I was accepted, thanks to my grades, and some key references from the banker and our pastor. The summer days of my senior year were halcyon days. Baseball, fishing, preparing for college, and working at the store took up all my time. At a church sponsored picnic, I met Althea Robinson, a daughter of our Darbytown barber. She was a junior at our high school. On that breezeless, muggy, July afternoon, we talked for a long while under a poplar tree close to the river. Althea was slender, brown eyed and had black wavy hair she wore in a ponytail. She had an infectious laugh; in short, she was a "catch." Her ivory-colored taffeta dress showed off her womanly figure.

We became inseparable. We went to D.W. Griffith movies, just the two of us. We would also picnic at Old Mill Park, near the river, that was secluded enough for young lovers to be private. One evening, after spooning for a long time, Althea let me make advances. She let out a moan that I had not expected, so we discreetly buttoned up in case anyone came upon us. I was a novice at love making, probably more so than Althea. We did have "relations," and we felt so alive. We made love in the park behind Hazel Run Stream, the Civil War battlefield, and several other unorthodox venues. Luckily, we were never caught, and she never got pregnant.

Finally, Indian summer had arrived, and I bade farewell to my family, friends, pastor, Mr. Hitchcock, and especially, Althea. We promised to write often and see each other for the holidays.

Chapter 4

Before the Storm

Althea, a few close friends, and my family, bade me fare-well at the Fredericksburg Train Station. Mary could not come, as she was very ill. A local midwife nurse and friend of our family saw after her. The train approached as the sun rose high enough to burn off the remaining clouds. The sound of pistons churning was more pronounced as the iron horse slowed. The soot from the coal lingered and settled down on our clothing like black snow. We hugged as it was time for me to board. Mother and Millie had streams of soot-colored tears rolling down their sullen faces. However, the joy of going to college on behalf of the family was overshadowed by what fate may befall Mary, the angel of the family.

The ride to Hampton was uneventful. Sitting in the back, as required in this era of "Jim Crow," seemed normal by habit. I took a carriage to the Institute with another passenger. He was an Indian from what I could tell. He introduced himself as William Strong Bow, a member of the Cheyenne tribe and a freshman at the Insti-tute. I should not have been surprised, as the college had been admitting Indians for over thirty years. William wore a black suit that was too small for his muscular body. He also wore a bowler hat that did not hide his midnight black ponytail. Soon, we struck up a conversation. I did most of the talking, while William listening and toyed with his hat, while we bumped along the cobblestone roads.

After orientation, I made my way to the dormitory. It was a brick and iron building that had rooms accommodating two to four men.

I was fortunate to be assigned to a two-bed dorm room. While I was unpacking, my roommate staggered in, burdened with suitcases and other paraphernalia. He unloaded his bags. This enthusiastic lad reached out, shook my hand and said, "I'm Roscoe Bullock from Wilmington, 'Noth' Carolina, but my friends just call me Buster."

Buster had a heavy southern, Negro accent; not that I spoke the King's English. Buster was an acquired taste. He was over six feet tall, but hardly a hundred-fifty pounds. His suit seemed like a hand-me-down. It was too short, and made him appear somewhat comical. Buster stripped down to his essentials. He was all muscle. He parted his black, wavy hair down the middle, a growing fad at the time.

The routine of college life set in by late summer. The breeze from the Hampton River and the Chesapeake Bay alleviated the unusual heat if one was lucky enough to be outside near the water. My course load was heavy, but the classrooms were more problematic. Ninety-degree heat outside, felt like a hundred degrees in class. I studied Latin, English literature, European history, French, chemistry, and algebra. I was up to the task in all my subjects except chemistry. My chemistry professor was an older White man who relished wearing his black frock while demonstrating magical experimental outcomes with electricity or compound mixtures. I struggled, but I was able to maintain a C+ grade in this class. I almost destroyed part of the chemistry lab when I reversed the mixture of two compounds over a running burner. I was a marked man after that!

I returned home for the Thanksgiving holiday. My father met me at the station with the buckboard. We exchanged small talk on the way, but I knew that the pall of Mary's health weighed on everyone. The family put on festive faces in preparation for the big dinner. I went to Mary's bedroom. The windows were open slightly as full light invaded her space. She was surrounded by dolls, flowers and family pictures.

I bent over and whispered, "Mary, my angel, I am so happy to see you."

She labored to kiss me and remarked, "Why Virgil, you look the college man! Please tell me about Hampton."

Mary was coughing intermittently as I regaled her with my challenges and new experiences. She occasionally coughed up blood; a combination of consumption and pneumonia was a deadly duo for most. We would see what God had in store for our Mary. I was not optimistic.

Just prior to Christmas, I received a telegram to hurry home. Mary was dying. I arrived on the twenty-third, after sunset. We held vigil in her room and recounted fond memories. The next morning, I entered Mary's bedroom alone, before everyone was stirring. She was awake, calm, and very alert, considering her physical state. She summoned for me to come close.

"Virgil, promise me that you will press on and make me proud of you as I look down on you from heaven. Do you believe in heaven?" she asked, as she gripped my arm.

"If there is a God, there is a heaven, and you, my girl, will be greeted with open arms, but that will be years and years from now," I labored to say.

Mary just touched my cheek and looked toward the light filled window. At about three o'clock that afternoon, our pastor arrived. At 5:15 p.m. she passed away. The trials and tribulations of this world were left to us. We laid her to rest at the Old Shiloh Church Cemetery on the second day of the New Year. The church was at capacity with family, neighbors, friends, and some White folk, including the Hitchcock family, my benefactors.

I returned to school and prayed for Mary at the Memorial Chapel. I sat under the "Emancipation Oak" on a windswept, but sunny January afternoon, and reflected on her shortened life. The oak was given its name because it was believed that one of the first readings of Lincoln's Emancipation Proclamation was read under the tree in 1862. It was also where the school's first teacher, a freed slave, Mary Peake, taught escaped slaves during the Civil War under the protection of the Union Army.

I buried myself in studies and athletics. I took time every week to write to Althea. The return letters came less and less frequently as spring arrived. I completed my freshman year an A minus student. Upon returning home, I found out that Althea left town for Washington, DC with an older man! My first love left a "Dear John" letter as my parting gift.

The combination of Mary's death and Althea's departure left me in a funk that summer of 1910. I worked at Dad's hardware store and did little else. I called on my benefactor, Mr. Hitchcock, on a Sunday afternoon in June. I had been to his large Victorian home twice before, even using the front door! On this occasion, the house was adorned with lighter hues, replacing the royal blue and maroon colors that had seemed to overwhelm the home's size and grace. Adeline, the daughter whose life I saved about five years ago, was now twelve, a girl in her formative years. She greeted me wearing a Gibson style white dress, and a matching white ribbon that held up her long blonde hair. I showed the family my grades and spent almost two hours going over my year at school, while Mrs. Hitchcock prepared iced mint tea and cakes for all. They had come to Mary's funeral and shared our grief. Neither race nor class seemed to divide us.

I also spent a lot of time that summer at granny's farm outside of town. Rows upon rows of corn greeted me. As I had done in past years, I removed about a hundred square feet of corn with a sickle and lay upon the ground, looking up at the azure sky. I could spend hours there dreaming, remembering, "predicting the past" and foretelling my future. The walls around my "castle" were like stone walls keeping the dragons out. This would always be my special place in both body and spirit.

I returned to Hampton as an all-knowing sophomore. We had our largest class of women since co-ed enrollment began in 1901. The women lived at Virginia-Cleveland Hall. The "Gibson style" invaded the campus in a large way. The girls seemed more liberated in these narrow, modern getups.

I decided to major in English and American literature with a minor in European history. My favorite course was The State of the Major Religions in the Twentieth Century. One of my professors urged me to join the debate club. He said that I was a natural debater. I was not sure if that was a compliment. One topic we debated was Booker T. Washington's approach to Negro rights and integration into American society. He was arguably the most popular alumnus at the Hampton Institute. Almost fifty years after the Emancipation Proclamation, I argued for a more vigorous approach to equal justice and equal opportunity.

My able opponent, Jacob Johnson, from Manassas, Virginia, stood firmly with Washington's "go slow" approach. Admittedly, his delivery was more elegant. His words came out with a lyrical cadence. I urged the packed audience to consider that there can be no traction without friction. We must demonstrate our gifts both intellectually and physically. The post-Civil War Amendments to the Constitution must be tested in the courts until "separate but equal" was abandoned. I became a minor celebrity after that contentious debate.

Shortly thereafter, I noticed a smart looking coed outside Memorial Chapel one cold Sunday morning. I introduced myself. She said that she knew me from the debates. She went by Gail, short for Abigail Bethany Simpson from Annapolis, Maryland. She was decked out in the typical Gibson attire of the day, with a braided black overcoat, white scarf, and an Edwardian Sunday hat adorned with several flowers and a lethally long pin.

We became good friends and cerebral soulmates. We went boating on the Hampton River, or the bay, with the approach of warmer weather. She seemed perpetually shy, almost standoffish, so I did not pursue any romantic attempts until school was almost over. We were boating on the waters near Shore Road. I pressed for a kiss. Gail responded meekly, no pull back, but no resounding embrace. I did not know what to make of this neutral response, so I pulled back and started a conversation.

During the summer of 1911, we wrote letters to each other several times a week. I got permission to travel to Annapolis to visit Gail in mid-August for three days. Her family was not of the poor lot, but not blessed with an abundance of material goods either. Their home was a modest, white, wood clad, and brick structure located on a small lot close to the Potomac River, about a mile from the Naval Academy.

Gail's father worked at the Academy as a grounds supervisor. Her mother died of typhoid in 1903. Her father remarried in 1906. Gail and her stepmother had mutual respect, if not love. I was allowed to stay in the guest room once occupied by Gail's older brother, Vincent, who had moved to Detroit. He worked as a foreman at the Ford Motor Company. It was a venerable position for a Negro.

On my last day there, Gail and I picnicked on the banks of the Potomac. The sun was setting over the lazy river. Orange and gold hues glittered off the calm waters, and the sun loomed larger and larger as it set. I pressed up against her lips and got the same reaction as before.

I was blunt now and asked, "I guess you are not attracted to me?"

She withdrew into her thoughts for what seemed to be one long minute. Then she confessed, "Virgil, it is not you. I have been attracted to you more than any other man, but I mean, well this is damn hard to say."

I exhorted her to be frank and promised that I would be sympathetic. "I like women, I mean I am not romantically attracted to men. That's the ugly truth. I am an aberration of nature — not a positive thing for a Negro woman. Does that repel you?" she asked.

I admitted that I was stunned and privately embarrassed by my naiveté. All I could summon up was, "Gail, I hope we can remain friends."

She hugged me and begged me to pledge this admission a secret until death. I kissed her on her forehead and agreed. It was truly the summer of my discontent!

I entered my junior year more enlightened by how much I did not know. I spent large amounts of quiet time under the Emancipation Oak when the weather permitted. I strengthened my bonds with Will Strong Bow, and I began to frequent the "Wigwam," the Indian dormitory, as the semester passed. At this time, the government was trying to Americanize the Indian tribes. There are always the unintended consequences of an unnatural action. For one, Indian customs and ways of life began to diminish. Discrimination and segregation still befell the modern Indian regardless of his attire, haircut, or education.

Meanwhile, when 1912 arrived, the country was abuzz with intrigue about President Taft's feud with his former mentor, Teddy Roosevelt. Taft was too conservative for Teddy's liking. The problem was that Taft was not Teddy; not like a son following in his father's footsteps. "TR" was not pleased.

On a sunny April day, I set sail in a small rented boat on the Hampton River. I rowed out and cast my rod into the river's murky depths. I soon noticed a larger vessel coming toward me. I waved my arms to no avail. Within twenty feet from my small craft, I jumped overboard to escape a deadly fate. The boat splintered in half as I looked back, swimming a few hundred feet to shore. I had no doubt that an injustice was perpetrated due to my skin color. Now that I was safely on land, I silently thanked my father for teaching me how to swim. Paying for the boat was my major concern. I reported this incident to my dean and the police. I had no illusion about receiving justice. I nevertheless reported it for the record. I had to work at the Institute's laundry for many months, and use my savings, to pay for the sunken vessel.

The year at school ended with my election as captain of the debate club and captain of the baseball team. My position was centerfielder. I roamed the outfield with authority. I had batted .357 that season, usually batting in third position. I had dated from time to time, but nothing serious. A young White woman began conversations with me. She worked at the smoke shop I frequented on Pembroke Avenue, near the downtown area. It was one of the few integrated retailers in town. Her name was Tiffany. She had a dark complexion, with black hair coiffed up and pinned under a smart, small Edwardian style hat. She tucked her white blouse inside a simple, ankle length dress, and carried on in great detail about the changes in women's clothing. Tiffany also talked about the history of her heirloom alabaster brooch worn above her heart. Without making much eye contact, I selected some small cigars from Panama. She was a working-class girl, maybe eighteen, living in town with her large Italian family. I guess my light Negro skin color made me more tolerable to the White patrons. I never got too close to her. I did not want an excuse to be hung from a nearby tree. This was a fate that befell too many Negro men who socialized with White women in Jim Crow South. The photos of the stripped naked men, with admiring Christians standing nearby, was enough warning for me to behave.

I returned home in June of 1912. I helped my father at the store. His long history with whiskey was catching up with him. He appeared older than his middle age years. He was a dull blade compared to a decade ago. I think that the premature death of Mary caused him to console himself with a bottle even more than before.

I followed the national political conventions with a newfound passion for politics. Unhappy that the Republican delegates at the Chicago affair did not nominate Teddy Roosevelt, the progressive wing of the party held their own convention in the Windy City to nominate the bespeckled and toothy Teddy, thus splitting the party of Lincoln. The Dems nominated a relative newcomer, a first term Governor from New Jersey, and former President of Princeton College, Woodrow Wilson. He grew up in Staunton, Virginia, about a hundred miles west of where I lived. I was a Roosevelt man, but I feared that Wilson would be the beneficiary of the Republican rift.

My free time was spent fishing the Rappahannock River and horseback riding with my sister Millie. She had introduced me to her friend, Constance, known as Connie. She was attractive, tall, and with pondering brown eyes. Connie had the whitest smile, aesthetically marred by a large space between her front teeth. We dated, mostly in a small group of four or six friends. We frequented the new movie house, always relegated to sitting in the rear. We were enthralled with "Dr. Jekyll and Mr. Hyde" and "Cleopatra" to name a few.

I returned to Hampton Institute as a senior. Due to my high academic ranking, I was selected to instruct a freshman class in English literature. Volunteering as a tutor to several high school students at the local segregated school, I was able to earn more money. One night in October, Bill Strong Bow and I witnessed three "pale faces" beating up a Negro man outside a local tavern. We did not know the cause of this assault, but the victim barely escaped with his life. We caught up with him as he staggered into an alley. We nursed him for a good part of an hour. He was about thirty, slim with glasses, now broken. Sam, as he told us, bumped into one of the men. His apology did not satisfy this man. He recruited a couple of allies from the tavern then fists flew Sam's way.

We returned to Bill's dorm very upset by this turn of events. We devised a plan for vigilante justice. We enlisted two more fellow classmates in order to execute our plan of attack. Warren Albert, a lanky, fast cohort and I set upon the tavern on a moonless night around 1:00 a.m. We made our way to its alley. We set a fire near a rear door then skedaddled. Strong Bow and one of his Cherokee chums "borrowed" two bicycles. They tossed smoke bombs into the glass pane while riding past the tavern. We caused quite a lot of mayhem there according to the local paper. No one was injured, but the tavern was damaged. It had a long-time reputation as a place where Jim Crow supporters congregated. Maybe our scheme was misguided, but it felt good.

Two weeks later, Woodrow Wilson beat his two notable adversaries to become the twenty-eighth, President. Virginia voted Democratic, and Wilson became the first southern President in many decades. He had similar progressive ideas as Roosevelt, but he was not a champion of my race. In fact, in his administration, civil service jobs, once a haven for Negroes, began to lose their viability for people of color.

Graduation finally arrived on a partly cloudy, windless, and warm day in May of 1913. My immediate family and a few friends from Fredericksburg attended. The Hitchcock family also attended. I graduated *summa cum laude*. My mentor got his money's worth. The Institute's choir and quartet, directed by Dr. R. Nathaniel Dett, got top billing and a standing ovation at the ceremony. This choir performed internationally at London, Vienna, Berlin, and Paris, to name a few cities. It was a thrill for all the attendees.

I spent the summer working two jobs so I could enroll at the City College of New York in Harlem. I was set on getting my Master's degree in English literature. My father was in failing health. Knowing that I was not going to fill his shoes at the store, he promoted his lumberyard supervisor, who had been with my father for fifteen years.

On Labor Day weekend my family saw me off at the Fredericksburg train station. The farewell was emotional, holding both sadness and joy for my life's next chapter. Millie caught me during a quiet moment and whispered loud enough not to be drowned out by the noise of the trains, "Now behave yourself in New York. Show those Yanks what stuff you are made from. Make us proud. The racism is subtler up north, but it permeates society like this coal soot," she warned.

The train whistles pierced the breezeless air as I waited to reply.

"Millie, I had no idea you were so cosmopolitan. How do you know so much about New York?"

Fixated on the train's entrance to the station, she replied, "I read a lot, you know, *New York Times*, NAACP publications, and DuBois's writings."

"I'll take your advice and learn the ropes," I replied, as I fumbled to locate my ticket.

I found an apartment on Broadway and 130th Street, close to the college and within sight of Grant's Tomb, near the Hudson River. The apartment was small, and bleak, but clean. I soon advertised for a roommate as the rent was out of my league. After two unsuccessful interviews, I met a man who intrigued me. He was a clarinet player at the Clef Club. He introduced himself as Howard "Smooth-tone" Butler. He was a native Harlemite, in his late twenties, with slicked backed wavy hair, brown eyes and lips that had an easy relationship with the tool of his trade.

Howard and I became fast friends. He showed me around town, by foot, cab, train and subway. He took me to the typical tourist spots; the Statue of Liberty, the Woolworth Building, Wall Street, Chinatown and the Brooklyn Bridge, and many others. My favorite was Battery Park, where I could see the waterway comings and goings of the city. Howard also took me to many jazz clubs, burlesque shows, sometimes with dates, and we spent memorable days at Coney Island. The amusement park was a true melting pot of the races and cultures mingling and having fun. He also introduced me to the Clef Club's bandleader, James R. Europe. He was a force of nature. Tall, serious, with "bug" eyes, he commanded the room. He assembled a ragtime and jazz orchestra that was matchless. I frequented the club on many occasions. I met Noble Sissle and many other band members. Although I had a heavy course load, teaching nineteenth century English literature to a freshman class mix of men and women from several races, I still found time to earn spending money as a waiter at the Clef Club on weekends.

It turns out, bandleader Europe was recently married. "Willie," his wife, and Jim lived at 67 West 131st Street near Lenox Avenue. They were our neighbors.

We ran into them from time to time. One evening I attended

a dance performance by the renowned couple, Vernon and Irene Castle at their own club, "Sans Souci," located at Broadway and 42nd Street. Smooth-Tone told me that the orchestra would be performing at Hampton Institute.

Although my schedule did not permit me to attend, I gave Howard tips regarding the Institute and the city. While sipping Scotch and water, I was entertained by the Castles dancing the Tango, Turkey Trot, and their famous "Castle Walk." It was well known that Europe and the Castles performed for the well-healed in Manhattan, like Mrs. Stuyvesant Fish. She was the matriarch of the patrician and political dynasty in New York. They also played at their Newport, Rhode Island and Hampton, New York mansions. In addition to these private, society gigs, they performed at the Palace, Hammerstein's Victoria theaters, and even at Carnegie Hall to a mixed-race audience.

I returned home for Christmas. It was a welcome break. I brought presents from the city and, in turn, received Virginia peanuts, new shoes, and two woolen scarves. Millie and I rode horseback to Tappahannock. We saw several automobiles and trucks along the way. Blacksmith shops were now becoming gasoline service stations. A transportation revolution was unfolding before me.

In late June of 1914, I read about the assassination of Archduke Ferdinand and his wife, Sophie of Austria, by a member of Serbia's Black Hand separatist organization. I didn't think much of the repercussions of this event. But by July, Germany and the Austro-Hungarian Empires threatened war with Serbia while Russia and France backed little Serbia. Countries lined up for war, and on August fourth, German armies invaded neutral Belgium. This move brought the British Empire, as a protector of Belgium, by treaty, on the side of the Allies.

Classes began the next month. By September, Germany was on the verge of entering Paris. The French government evacuated the Capital. Germany also defeated a Russian army in the epic battle called Tannenberg, near Prussia. All looked bleak for the Allies. One of my students, a Negro from North Jersey, volunteered to join the French Army as an ambulance driver. By late fall, the Allies pushed the weary Germans back to Northern France. Each side tried to outflank each other. This only resulted in a stalemate, creating miles and miles of defensive trenches in order to protect the combatants from bullets and bombs.

One December evening, while I was waiting tables at the Clef, Howard introduced me to Beatrice McBride. She worked there as a coat check girl a few evenings a week while also working full time as a nurse's aide at the Presbyterian Hospital. We started to date at the beginning of 1915. She lived at Amsterdam Avenue and 145th Street with her family. Beatrice, or Bea, was a natural beauty wearing no makeup except for ruby red lipstick. She was very feminine, but she had a self-reliant personality. Bea had a confidence I found refreshing. I tried to impress her with my new-found artist friends. We took the subway to the Manhattan Casino at 155th Street and Eighth Avenue to see Europe and his orchestra play ragtime and jazz favorites. We went to see the Castles at their midtown club just before it closed, due to a lack of exit doors. The Triangle Shirtwaist Factory fire in 1911, which killed almost one hundred and fifty workers, mostly women, stirred up public and worker safety support in this progressive city. I had read about it while I was at college. Women jumped from over a hundred feet to the unforgiving pavement; some on fire, and all perished. The owners were exonerated. They could afford good lawyers.

Bea persuaded me to listen to A. Philip Randolph's soap box speeches. He made his pitch on the corner of 135th Street and Lenox, near home. He was a devout socialist who set up shop in the city several years ago. His wife was a friend of the famous Madame C.J. Walker. She made fame and fortune selling and servicing hair restoration products to Negro women through a network of thousands of her sales agents. Bea met Randolph's wife at a Walker salon. As the saying goes, it's a small world. Randolph did not turn me into a Socialist. Some of his soap box rants made a few good points, but he did not take into consideration the evolution of capitalism by the electorate, nor did he concede that mankind is primarily motivated by self-interest, property rights, and ambition. Equal opportunity is what we needed to fight for, not equal results. Bea was to my way of thinking...most of the time.

I remembered that Madame Walker had attended the Eighth

Biennial Convention for the National Association of Colored Women at Hampton Institute, in July of 1912. I was back home, and I did not have the privilege of attending. The Institute's brass band played for the convention, and Booker T. Washington gave a keynote speech at the Newport News Navy Yard. Madame Walker was very charismatic, a "mover and shaker." Brought up dirt poor and semi-literate, even by Negro standards, she was undeterred, ambitious and had a keen business sense.

By the time I received my Master's degree, Bea and I were engaged to be married. I obtained a position with the City College of New York to instruct English literature and Rhetoric. We were married in May of 1916 at the Abyssinian Baptist Church in Harlem. Europe was slaughtering itself, but the world still turned. We traveled to my family and took part in another marriage ceremony at the Old Shiloh Church. My sister Millie and Adeline Hitchcock were two of Bea's bridesmaids. Bea wore a simple white gown with beading and a long Edwardian style veil. My family and friends gave Bea and I a warm send off to Bermuda for our honeymoon. Shortly after arriving, we soon became aware of the war preparations the island made, being a British holding. We found the people there friendly, dressed casually, but smart. Surf and sand consumed most of our time. We chartered a small vessel to go fishing on the high seas. Bea caught a Bonito. It weighed about ten to twelve pounds, and looked like a small tuna with silvery scales. After two hours, I landed a Wahoo fish. It was a sleek, long specimen weighing about twenty pounds and four feet long. These fish have a lot of fight; it was hard work! Our time there was like being in paradise.

During the summer of 1916, Bea and I fixed up an apartment we rented near CCNY, at Broadway and 128th Street. It was a relatively new five-story building. We were on the fourth floor, looking north into Harlem. My professorship began in September, teaching four classes to freshmen and sophomores. I also began to explore a PhD. The buzz of the Great War and whether America would enter it permeated most discussions. Wilson's pledge to keep America out of the war appealed to many voters during the heated presidential campaign. Even the sinking of the Lusitania the year before did not force Wilson's hand. Teddy Roosevelt led the charge denouncing Wilson's tepid response to Germany's aggression on the high seas. Wilson did approve of an officer preparedness program located in Plattsburg, New York. More and more of my students answered the call to volunteer with the French for ambulance or pilot service. Even a few women volunteered as nurses or canteen workers.

One afternoon, Bea stopped by CCNY to tell me that Madame Walker opened up her new flagship salon at 108-110 West 136th Street, near Lenox Avenue. She opened it with the fanfare of Europe's music, of course. The following Saturday, she took me there. It was jaw-dropping! Number 108 was the home of Madame Walker's daughter, A'Lelia, and Number 110 was the salon. A grand piano and other musical instruments adorned the brownstone. The elder Walker was one of the two or three richest Negro women in the country. She was a true American success story and an icon. Some of her clients wanted hair thickening or straightening as well as skin care products. The straightening strategy was controversial. Some Negro leaders and newspapers decried it as a demeaning way to mimic their White suppressors, an attempt to fit into White society by unkinking their hair. To Walker's credit, she did not advertise this methodology. Her focus was on improving the beauty of the Negro female.

One a late summer morning after church, I darted into the Democratic campaign headquarters in Harlem while Bea went to visit her family. Signs of President Wilson saying "He Kept US Out of War" were in clear sight. Support for him had waned in the Negro communities across the land since his administration re-segregated the civil service. Also, the number of Negroes in the administration had dwindled. We had hoped for more from the self-proclaimed Progressive, but his Southern roots grew deep. He was self-righteous and uncompromising. The volunteers at the headquarters offered a Booker T. Washington, "go along to get along" approach, to defend Wilson. It seemed "getting along" was more important to them than winning the war.

I started a conversation with a new volunteer while he was departing the campus. This heavy set, jovial fellow named Carl, hailed from Syracuse. He moved to New York to further his education at CCNY. I asked him why he was abandoning his schooling.

As he sat on a wooden bench sipping some cooled off coffee, books at his side, Carl replied, "Professor Carpenter, I have been torn by this decision. My family does not want me to go. I prefer not to go. A Germany dominated Europe may not affect me or my race, but there are my brothers from Africa fighting for France and freedom. I'm prepared to help my race here in America or in Europe. Does this make sense?"

I did not answer immediately. I stared down at his books. Summoning up a response as Carl took another sip of his coffee, I replied, "You have made your deliberation. This is a big sacrifice in time and possibly life or limb. I just want to make sure it is not just for adventure nor for glory."

We parted with an understanding of each other. It did make me wonder about my own future, my commitments, and my manhood.

On April 6, 1917, America declared war on the Central Powers after unrestricted U-boat attacks and the infamous Zimmerman telegram. In this missive, Germany promised Mexico parts of the U.S. if Mexico attacked us and Germany won the war. The British intercepted this telegram and dutifully delivered it to a reluctant Wilson. Within days, recruiting stations were set up all over the city. The Negro press debated our race's position. One of its prominent leaders, E.B. DuBois, urged us to participate in order to show the White dominated society that we would do our part and fight like any other red-blooded American. Black leaders urged the administration to establish a Negro officers camp, and to utilize the soldiers in combat, not just as laborers or stevedores.

A high percentage of my male students, Black and White, volunteered or were drafted into service. James Europe began to recruit men for the newly revived New York Fifteenth National Guard. It was a Negro unit headed by Colonel William Hayward, a prominent New Yorker with connections to the governor. The colonel wanted Jim to lead the regiment's band, and he wanted a fighting unit.

Bea and I were swept up in the fervor watching Europe's ragtime band marching up and down Harlem. It was a novel recruiting tool. NCOs of the regiment were there to enlist new recruits. With the semester coming to an end, more and more under and upper classmen left to join the armed services. The Fifteenth Regiment tried to join the Forty Second "Rainbow" Division, but the commander was told that "Black is not a color of the rainbow."

Teaching seemed to be less relevant with the world in turmoil and America gearing up for the fight. Bea and I argued often about my joining the army. Our emotions boiled over. I told her that I could not face my future children knowing that I could have done my part for my country and my race but had backed down. It wasn't an option for me to just talk and not take action. After two contentious months, Bea finally relented. I enlisted, promising to return to her ... alive.

Chapter Five

Into the Unknown

Howard Butler accompanied me to the regiment's impro-
vised armory, a rented building located at 131st and 132nd
Streets and Seventh Avenue, the former Lafayette Dance
Hall. I was greeted first by Lieutenant Charles W. Filmore, one of
the few Negro officers of the regiment, and a Spanish-American
War veteran. After some interviewing by one of the sergeants, I
was examined by a doctor and dentist. I was sworn in just as Lieutenant James Reese Europe appeared. He had just finished a parade
on Lenox Avenue to drum up recruiting, when he noticed me and
asked, "Virgil, does Beatrice know you're here?"

I straightened up even though I was still dressing and responded,
"Yes, yes, Sir. Bea was reluctant, but she knows me all too well."

With his arms folded, Europe asked, "Sworn in?"

As I responded, "Yes, Sir," he darted off to the drill area and said,
"That's good. Give my regards to your lovely wife."

I was assigned to Company "K" of the Third Battalion. This
battalion was commanded by Captain Louis B. Chandler, and the
company was led by none other than the famous Hamilton Fish,
Jr. He was a football star at Harvard, and his family was a political dynasty. His grandfather served as Secretary of State for President Ulysses S. Grant. The family was connected with the Dutch
Stuyvesants through marriage. Fish's cousin, also named Hamilton,
was a sergeant of Company "L" of Roosevelt's legendary "Rough
Riders." Roosevelt formed a voluntary infantry regiment at the start

of the war with Spain. It's *nom de guerre* was Roosevelt's Rough Riders. Fish was the first American soldier killed in action during the war with Spain in Cuba. Later on, Teddy Roosevelt called it "That Splendid Little War."

I enlisted as a private, a good place to start for a civilian. I was given a uniform, but no rifle or helmet. The captain told us that Colonel Hayward was working on this issue. We drilled on the streets of Harlem and occasionally at Olympic Field nearby. The colonel was able to secure some rifles from gun clubs. The War Department would send more weapons once the regiment was officially recognized as a fully formed unit. Finally, we received the standard M1903 Springfield .30-06 rifle. It was a five-round, bolt-action weapon, and very reliable.

On May 13 we began our journey to Camp Whitman near Peekskill, New York. I felt better for having made love to Bea the night before my unit deployed. She saw me off at the armory on that Sunday morning. My wife had optimism for both of us. At least she relieved some of my guilt. The Third Battalion, the Machine Gun Company, and Europe's band marched to "Onward Christian Soldiers." We took trains at 60th Street and the New York Central railyards after we marched down Riverside Avenue, past Grant's Tomb. When we arrived at camp, we had to construct facilities, and a lot of the personal items were missing. We also lacked enough rifles, but we persisted and drilled, marched and worked all day. We swam at the local stream that cut across the camp, even though the water was bone chilling. Otis Ellison, my buddy from East Harlem, and I relieved ourselves in the stream just before we departed. That was what we thought of Camp Whitman.

After two long weeks, we decamped from our meager accommodations and took part in a Memorial Day parade. We marched down Riverside Avenue, running parallel to the Hudson River. The band played "Battle Hymn of the Republic" while we passed Grant's Tomb to the roar of the crowd.

Bea and I spent my few days on leave like tourists. We picnicked at Van Cortlandt Park, in the Bronx, and made love somewhere underneath an outcropping of rocks. After this impromptu display of affection, she said, "I missed you. When do you leave again? I read about the horrendous casualties on both sides. How long can this carnage continue?"

Dressing in a hurry, I replied, "Don't know. This whole affair is a pox on humanity. Hopefully America will be the deciding factor. Russia is in turmoil which is not good for the Allies. I need to get back to the battalion by Saturday."

Bea knelt down next to me and said, "We need to wait till you come back from France for us to start a family. Don't you agree?"

"Yes," I agreed. "I assumed that is what you wanted. It would not be fair to you and our child if I did not return. Our colonel has impressed upon the War Department through his contacts that our regiment is a fighting unit, not a labor detail, but who knows?"

Bea was able to take two days off from her job. We managed to visit the Lower East Side sampling pickles and other Jewish delicacies at the Yonah Schimmel Knishery on Houston Street. We also had lunch in Chinatown at a nondescript eatery on Mott Street. Then we strolled down Mulberry Street in Little Italy, but we felt a thousand eyes upon us, so we left for more hospitable turf. The next day we went to the Bronx Zoo, a "jungle" in the middle of the Bronx, that opened in late 1899. The diversity of animal life was overwhelming. We saw exotic birds and reptiles, and the chimps and gorillas were fascinating. If only we could go to Africa one day! Later on, we toured the American Museum of Natural History, located across Central Park at West 79th Street. The exhibits of antiquities from Egypt, Greece, Rome, the Far East, and the Americas were so much to take in, we ran out of time before we could see it all. We had dinner at Sophie's on Lenox Avenue. The pork butt and collard greens were the best in the city!

Bea was able to leave work early on Friday so we could go to Coney Island. We had precious little time together. I made a mistake when I downed a couple of Nathan's hot dogs with a Coca-Cola before going on the rollercoaster ride. I unceremoniously vomited while I wobbled off the ride. Luckily, I left the contents on the ground and not on my clothing. Bea laughed and laughed, undaunted by my tribulations.

That evening we laid in bed talking about "what if" and what may happen with our future. We made the most of our fleeting time together. On Saturday, I dressed in my uniform, and promised her that I would write often and keep my diaries going as best I could.

While the Fifteenth was eager to fight over in France, race relations hit a minefield in July of 1917. The Twenty-Fourth Infantry Regiment, a Negro unit that served admirably during the Spanish-American War and the Philippine Insurrection clashed with White police and citizens while stationed in Houston. Elements of its Third Battalion "mutinied" in order to retaliate against police brutality and overt discrimination. There were about sixteen deaths. Sixty-four members of the battalion were court martialed. Thirteen were immediately executed. Black activists questioned why Negroes should help fight in France while they were considered second class citizens at home. *The Crisis*, a paper published by Eugene B. DuBois, saw this as an opportunity for his race to unite, support the war effort, and show race patriotism in order to gain more inclusion once the war was over.

To add insult to injury, a riot of immense proportions broke out the same month in East St. Louis. Negro workers, making employment inroads to businesses across the river there, sparked racial hatred. At least forty Negroes were killed, and much of the housing stock in the Negro enclave of East St. Louis was destroyed. This event caused an orderly protest march in New York City. Almost 10,000 marchers participated, including Madame C.J. Walker, Adam Clayton Powell, other notable Negro leaders, in addition to a number of White supporters. They also marched to get the attention of President Wilson. The community wanted him to sign an anti-lynching law. About fifty to a hundred Negroes were lynched every year, including women and children. Ultimately, the President did nothing other than wanting to "make the world safe for democracy." I watched from my apartment. I could see Black Boy Scouts handing out fliers to the public standing along Fifth Avenue. Men dressed in black, and women protesters in white, marched down the famous Fifth Avenue led by mounted police.

On July 16, we deployed to Camp Whitman, again. I ran into Vertner Tandy, the first Negro officer assigned to the regiment. He was arguably the best of his race as an architect in America. He designed the new, Mediterranean stucco style mansion for Madame

C.J. Walker in Irvington, New York. He was a Southerner and Cornell graduate. Bespeckled and balding, with a cherubic face, Vertner was impressive in his officer's uniform complete with the Sam Browne belt.

The battalion hosted a series of "stunt" nights: social, musical, and dancing events at the improved camp. Most of the time, we drilled and marched, again and again. We decamped on the fifteenth of August and proceeded to Fort Dix in rural New Jersey. The battalion was led by Major Ed Dayton, one of our White field grade officers. We were there for construction and guard duty. The regiment's band also joined us. Captain "Ham" Fish joined Company K upon our arrival. I did carpentry, as I learned this skill while growing up at my father's lumber and hardware store.

On October 8, the Second and Third Battalions went to Camp Wadsworth in Spartanburg, South Carolina. We all knew that the town did not want us there. Negroes with weapons was not their idea of Jim Crow. Colonel Hayward assembled the regiment and gave a speech. He told us that our race was duty bound to show restraint in the face of taunts and hostility, and to not retaliate in any way. He stated that any bad press about the unit would diminish our chance for combat. The camp included the New Yorkers from the Twenty-Seventh Infantry Division and the Seventh Infantry Regiment — the "Silk Stocking" Regiment. They were headquartered on Manhattan's East Side and had a long-storied history dating back to the Civil War. Many of the soldiers came from prominent families, hence their *nom de guerre*.

Our accommodations were poor, the ground was usually muddy, and we had to construct much of the hygienic facilities. Some of the men came down with the flu; doctors and nurses were kept very busy.

It was not too long before a racial incident happened. A few town thugs beat up on a Black private who happened to be bold enough to walk on the wrong side of the street. White soldiers of the Silk-Stocking Regiment retaliated and boycotted the White establishments. That just stirred up more animosity between the soldiers and the townsfolk. They did not take to Northerners disturbing their social order.

Toward the latter part of October, our last and most disturbing racial conflict occurred. A rumor circulated that two of our men were lynched. The colonel acted quickly, and he had his driver rush him to the police station in town. Hayward bolted in. To the surprise of the police, the colonel noticed that the jail cell was occupied with the two missing men. According to the police chief, they were detained for safekeeping. While that was going on, Noble Sissle, one of our bandleaders, went into the hotel to buy a newspaper per the advice of a White soldier from New York. Although there were White soldiers in the lobby with their campaign hats on, the hotel owner knocked Sissle's hat off from behind. He started to rant and beat Sissle with the rationalization that Noble did not show respect by leaving his hat on. Soldiers started to gather in defense of the wounded Sissle when Lieutenant Europe stepped in. He commanded everyone's attention, told the men to stand down, and berated the hotel owner. These incidents finally made their way to the brass in Washington. So, on October 24, we moved out of camp to the singing of "Over There" by elements of the Twenty-Seventh Division lining our passage.

On the 26th, we arrived at Camp Mills near Garden City, New York. I was receiving letters from Bea on a delayed but consistent basis. All my letters had to be reviewed and censored. Bea was spending a lot of time with her family. A young woman alone in an apartment in the city was not recommended. Some of our squad played poker whenever we could. But cigarettes and cards were a poor substitute for female companionship. After two days at the camp, several of us ran into men from Alabama's 167th Regiment. They were mostly engineers and pioneers. They berated us with the typical words of hatred. We did not yield; in fact, more men of our company supported us. The Southerners backed down.

At the end of October, we divided up into four separate armories across the city. Because this move was short lived, I did not have time to see Bea for a much-anticipated night's stay at our lonesome apartment. On November 8, we paraded down Manhattan while being reviewed by General Hoyle, Commander of the Army's Eastern Department. Other military and public dignitaries saluted and cheered us. As usual, the regiment's band played several popular patriotic tunes. With much haste, we boarded the Grand Republic steamer for Hoboken. We all knew the next journey would be to cross the Atlantic's chilly waters. We would be the first Negro regiment to arrive in France. I wrote my last stateside letters to Bea and my parents:

> *Dearest Bea:*
> *My love for you is boundless. We have a long life ahead of us.*
> *I do not underestimate the hardships ahead of us. With that*
> *in mind, I hope to contribute to our race for future generations*
> *to come. Please pray for me, and excuse me if I cannot write to*
> *you as much as I would like. Hold me tight in your thoughts*
> *and dreams.*

Then I added the following:

> *"I say fortune the way I feel it.*
> *You have raised the summit*
> *That mt waiting will have to cross*
> *When tomorrow is no longer there."*
> *My love, Virgil*

To my parents I wrote:

> *Dear Mother and Father:*
> *This may be my last letter to you for a while. I hope you are*
> *all feeling well. Give my love to Millie, and please put some*
> *flowers on Mary's grave for me. I will need to become a brave*
> *and courageous soldier, a man that will contribute to our race*
> *now and into the future. Pray for me as I will pray for you*
> *all. Know this, whether I come back on two feet, wounded, or*
> *dead, I fulfilled my destiny on behalf of the greater good.*
> *Love Always,*
> *Virgil*

On November 11, we boarded our ship at night, the Pocahontas, in Hoboken Harbor to minimize any spying. A few hundred miles out, the ill-fated ship blew a piston rod. We had to return! We spent the next three weeks at Camp Merritt in New Jersey while the ship was in repair. All we did was exercise, drill and march in the damp, foggy November weather. There were many who went "AWOL."

Some went to their families, and some just went to have a good time. I managed to get a pass for several hours. My buddies and I only had time to go to a local club known for jazz, booze, and sensuous singers. We drank too much. Otis stayed behind with a woman he danced with all night. When we returned, our sergeant made us clean latrines the next day. In a more serious incident, one of the sergeants killed a private over two dollars at cards. We called him "Zulu" based upon his self-described heritage. He was subsequently court martialed and sent to prison.

Finally, on December 2, we boarded the ship again. There was a coal fire shortly thereafter. We began to feel cursed! We had to stay on board while the coalers shoveled the coal into the boilers to empty the burning bunker. I gave my letter for Bea to Nurse Amy Olney. She was an angel, getting our letters to our loved ones.

With the fire out, we departed the harbor again on December 13. Not far out, we collided with a British tanker! Colonel Hayward was so incensed, that he demanded the ship's personnel, and some of our skilled soldiers repair the damaged plates at sea. With that accomplished, we sailed finally with a convoy on the fourteenth. We drilled, exercised, and took target practice on ship. I wrote to Bea and the family while at sea, and kept up with my diary. We "polluted" the Atlantic by peeing overboard. On the day after Christmas, the convoy split, with our regiment going to the harbor port of Brest, France. We arrived at Brest without a U-boat incident on New Year's Day, 1918.

We were about to step foot on a foreign shore, in the midst of a death struggle as a nation. I thought, could we make a difference to this country and mine? I lit a borrowed cigar. Staring into the void, I let the ash blow in the wind.

Chapter Six

Children of France

We disembarked the cursed Pocahontas on New Year's Day. Some of our men were still seasick, and some had the measles. We marched down the muddy cobblestone streets of Brest. Stevedores, longshoremen and laborers, mostly Negroes from the United States and colonial countries, seemed unaffected by our arrival. The mood of the French was somber regardless of the American flags on display. Women dressed in black, and old men and children scurried about with a common dour expression. Younger children coped by playing games, even in the unkindly weather. A few ladies, not out of their teens, waved and strolled along our tedious route. They faded from sight as we were nearing our camp.

We boarded a train bound for St. Nazaire, a port city west of Nantes. Each car was marked, "forty men or eight horses." Captain Fish did not think much of our arrival port and was glad to have us move on. He told us that the French civil and military authorities were directed not to fraternize with soldiers of color from America. Only necessary communication to advance the war effort was desired. American interests, mostly in the South, wanted Negroes to return home unbridled with any libertarian notions. They wanted their social order to be maintained.

Otis Ellison and I were in the same car. He hailed from Harlem, on the East Side, near the Manhattan Casino. He entertained us with his harmonica while we meandered past quaint towns along the coast. I could see the walled coastal town of Vannes through a small window opening. Twilight obscured most of the details, but I was impressed with the sun setting just over the ancient city wall. Our battalion reached St. Nazaire the evening of January third. We marched to camp about two miles outside of the city of Montoir de Bretagne.

The camp was similar to Camp Wadsworth in its lack of hygienic hospitality. It was not waterproofed, and men filled the hospital tents with measles, mumps, and the flu. We spent almost six weeks clearing swamps, laying railroad track, and constructing supply dumps alongside men of the Service of Supply. The colonel helped distract our misery with inspection contests and a one-week pass. A few men from our company, including Otis and Howard Butler, headed for St. Nazaire. There were many Black men working the docks, women attired in their familiar black clothes, and military police. We were told that there was one street that was not off limits to American soldiers of color. A well-meaning "MP," or member of the military police, from Massachusetts directed us. After four weeks of slave labor, we were feeling our oats. Our sergeant, veteran Jefferson Marshall, reminded us about the colonel's mandate and the views of the High Command in France.

Once in town, Howard made a beeline for a millinery shop. He was keen on buying leather gloves. I bargained for a French nightgown for Bea. At midday we ate at a tavern established in 1784. We sat at a table in the basement, near a stone wall. A girl of about fifteen years of age waited on us. She did not speak English, so I did my best to translate. She had the most beautiful, peach like skin, and her deep blue eyes twinkled as she gave us a warm smile. Although slight of build, she carried half her weight in plates and mugs. Howard starred at her relentlessly while I asked her for grogs of wine and warm bread. She said, "Oui," and departed before Howard made her more uncomfortable. We downed mutton stew, bread, cheese, and wine until the sun set.

Howard was feeling light when he remarked, "I could live in France. No colored bathrooms, no segregation, nowhere. I might return one day if I don't 'go west.'"

Otis chimed in, "I'm used to 'Harlum', dat's my home, warts and all. France is a dark land now. The dev'l has his grip on de land. How's about you, Virg?"

I looked into my grog and responded, "Boys, I'm goin' home. Bea and I are goin' to make America a better place for the next generation. As Reverend Powell said, 'We will get to the promised land someday!'"

After our fifty-franc bill was paid, we drifted over to what Howard called a "comfort house." He and Otis availed themselves of the women of pleasure. I was honor bound to keep drinking at the ancient bar. A busty woman, scantily attired, approached me with a request to sit next to me. She introduced herself as Elouise. I obliged and bought her a drink. She had premature aging lines on her brow and eyes, but her body was that of a young woman. She told me that her father died at Verdun, and her brother was crippled by shrapnel the prior year. Elouise plied her trade, in the world's oldest profession, to help feed and care for her family. She asked me about America. An hour passed until my friends and I went to a boarding house for a well-deserved rest.

When we returned to camp, Sergeant Marshall told us that our commander had written to General Pershing for a combat assignment. In mid-February, the regimental band Lieutenant James Europe had built, was sent to Aix-Les-Bains to play for the wounded. Captain Arthur Little was designated to "CO" the assignment. He was a newspaperman, prior to the war. The band was glad to be out of the labor business, but some were apprehensive about seeing the gravely wounded, disfigured, French *poilu*. This translated as "hairy ones," referring to the facial hair adorning most of the foot soldiers.

Sergeant Marshall summoned me after morning drills. Marshall was a tough bastard, but by definition that is what a sergeant is supposed to be. His prominent jaw was his most distinguishing feature. He stood about six feet tall, and had broad shoulders on his imposing frame. Jefferson, by name, but no one called him by his Christian name, was a veteran with the Tenth Cavalry in the Philippines.

"Carpenter, the captain wants to see you, pronto," he barked.

I went straight away to Fish's command tent. He greeted me while looking at a map. "Private Carpenter, how are you getting along?"

While standing at attention, I snapped, "Very well, Sir."

The captain sat back in his chair, looked up at me and asked, "How would you like to be Corporal Carpenter? You are an educated man, and we need leaders when we go into combat. Stand at ease, Virgil, and speak frankly."

I was fixated on his officer's uniform with the Sam Browne belt. I responded, "Captain Fish, you are right that I am an educated man, but I can only guess about my leadership abilities."

He stood up as the chair rocked due to his abruptness. "Private, I am offering you a promotion — want it?"

Without hesitation, I declared, "Yes Captain. I will serve where and when needed."

"Good," he said as he sat back down. "You will get on-the-job training from Marshall. He will also give you an NCO field manual to read. Any questions?"

"No Sir, thank you, Sir." After an exchange of salutes, I headed over to the colored YMCA in the city.

By mid-March we boarded trains going east. I was in charge of about thirty-eight men in my car. I received my stripes the week prior. We passed Le Mans, Orleans, Troyes, and many small villages in between. As we got into the Champagne Region, west of the Argonne Forest, the ravages of almost four years of war seared into our minds. We passed hospital trains loaded with French wounded. Their groans could not be drowned out by the noises of our train. The ones I could see through the windows looked downtrodden, haggard, and unkempt. The front lines between the French and British zones were under heavy attack by fresh German troops who had arrived from the Russian front. Russia had collapsed politically and sued for peace with Imperial Germany.

In turn it, appeared that the German High Command's gamble was to drive a wedge between the two Allies, capture Paris, and win in the West before hordes of American "Sammies" could assist the beleaguered Allies. It seemed like their plan was making progress because Pershing agreed to turn over the four regiments of the Negro 93rd Infantry Division to the French Army. We were told that General Pershing was hell bent on creating his own American

Army, but he was pressured by the Brits and French to parcel out some units in this dire situation.

On the 21st, our battalion camped at Rémincourt. It was a village located just west of the regiment's HQ at Givy-en-Argonne. These villages all looked the same to me. That day we traded in all of our American equipment for French ones. The only items that we kept were our uniforms. We received the French Adrian helmets, Lebel rifles, ammo, and grenades. The Lebel was not as accurate or as reliable as our Springfield. We also kept our U.S. great coats. It had smaller and fewer pockets than the French coats, so we had to discard some rations. Our regiment was assigned to the French Fourth Army, commanded by the fearless, one-armed General Gouraud. Our regiment was now designated the 369th U.S. Infantry Regiment, replacing the New York Fifteenth name in France. We did continue to march with our New York regimental flag, nevertheless. We also carried the regimental symbol flag, "Don't Tread on Me," serpent and all.

Within the Fourth Army, we were assigned to the Sixteenth Division, commanded by General Le Gallais. We were given French instructors and liaison officers in order to amalgamate us into their ways of war. For the next three weeks, we were taught trench warfare, and use of the Chauchat, a French machine gun rifle with a semi-circular bullet chamber. It was notorious for misfiring in wet weather. Our instructors were very impressed with our ability to toss hand grenades at long distances. We told them that playing baseball as civilians was a benefit. We also got accustomed to their rations, especially a hearty soup. This consisted of beans, vegetables, and any meat available. Wine was their staple source of liquid nourishment. The French handled wine much better than our men. In fact, the colonel had to reduce our wine ration and mitigate it with more sugar.

We could hear the artillery trading blows just east of where we camped, on the other side of the Aisne River. By mid-April we settled into a camp at Maffrecourt, west of St. Menehould. The town lay just west of the Aisne River. K Company was on guard duty. The trenches were ready for us as elements of the regiment held a four-and-a-half-kilometer sector. Corporal Horace Pippin and I were responsible for guard duty assignments. The Boche, which was French slang for German soldiers, would lob artillery at us in order to intimidate the newly arrived Americans. We wore our gas masks a lot in order to become accustomed to these uncomfortable but lifesaving devises. It was difficult to soldier wearing it under normal circumstances, but when the gas shells came in, the panic and anxiety would befall us. The mask would fog up, and our eyes would tear up. Eventually most of us got used to it as a necessary evil. Even our horses and messenger dogs wore masks. It was an unworldly sight.

While warming up to coffee on a chilly, damp April morning, Horace and I were reminiscing. He was living in Paterson, New Jersey when he joined up with the New York Fifteenth. Horace was not much of a talker. He took out a piece of paper and a charcoal stick. I asked, "What are you going to do, my portrait?"

He moistened the charcoal with his tongue and said, "Very funny, Virgil. I'm gonna' make a pictur' of some soldiers with their masks on, in the trench. A pic is worth a thousand words. People back home don't know the shit that goes on here, and we's just started."

Horace started to draw. I stared at him. He had a wide smile, broad nose and a bold, prominent jaw. I could see the charcoal obey his artistic commands. He finished just before the rain began.

I remarked, "This sure beats my diary for getting your point across. Do you see any money in it for you after the war?"

A shell exploded near us as Horace was about to reply. We were covered by dirt and a slice of stone dented my helmet, knocking me on my back. He just said, "Let's get in our dugout."

That afternoon, the NCO's of the Third Battalion got a lesson on repairing defensive positions, including wire and lookouts. A French lieutenant and sergeant from the division were instructive and very respectful. It was a refreshing change. With the session concluding, Captain Fish and the battalion's French liaison officer, Captain Le Van, made some comments to the instructors in French. Le Van placed his hands behind his back and remarked, "*Bien, Bien.*" Looking at us he added, "How are you getting along? Are you accustomed to the sounds of the different types of ordinances being fired at you?"

Captain Fish interjected, "Speak up men."

Sergeant Marshall responded, "Sir, the Boche are like clockwork. Shelling with chlorine or phosgene gas, followed by high explosives at 5:30 a.m. and shrapnel bursts, or whiz-bangs at 5:00 p.m."

Le Van eyed me for some reason. He was a stout man of about thirtyish. He had a scar over his left eye, and he had a thin, long mustache that curled up at the ends: very French. Le Van had a noticeable limp as he approached both Pippin and me.

He asked, "Men, are you confident you can defend this sector? Can you engage the enemy?"

"We do not doubt our resolve nor our ability to support the French, Sir," I replied with some trepidation.

I was going to comment on the unreliability of the Lebel rifle, but I did not want to rile our captain. As I was semi-fluent in French, due to my education at Hampton, I took the liberty of asking Le Van what he did before the war.

He smiled and replied loudly, "*Alors, mon ami.* I was a police officer. But unlike civilian life, here murder is legal."

The captain continued, "Corporal, you have heard of the famous police inspector, Alphonse Bertillon, no?"

"No, I am sorry," I replied.

Now the captain spoke in an animated way, using his hands for enhanced description, "He was famous for the promotion and standardizing the use of fingerprints in order to identify, arrest, and convict criminals. I worked under him. Like most great men, he was petulant, self-absorbed, stubborn, and had a saturnine magnetism. My mentor died just before the war."

"*Et vous?*" he queried, as he stroked his mustache.

All I could muster was, "Sir, I taught English literature at the City College of New York."

He nodded, and then we parted, as we had to return to our duties. On the fourteenth of April, we were hit with a heavy barrage. We sent up a rocket signal and took cover as best we could in dugouts along the trench lines. The Machine Gun Company was ordered into action and counterbattery artillery responded with a "box" type barrage. When the enemy stopped, we fixed bayonets in anticipation of an attack, but none came. We had several men wounded from shrapnel and accidents. A week later, we were on our own. The

French instructors left, only Captain Le Van remained.

On May 1, we relieved the First Battalion at Melzicourt, near the Aisne River. The village was about ten kilometers from where we were, and closer to the main action. We paraded with the division in front of the Fourth Army General, Gouraud. He saluted the regiment and then told us that the tide was turning in favor of the Allies. During the next few days, we practiced using our Labels, Chauchats, rifle grenades and Hotchkiss machine guns. We were feeling pretty damn good.

On the 11th, I got a letter from Bea dated April 8, 1918. She stated that her father had the influenza, but he was being cared for at home. Bea sent a package of cookies and my favorite cigars that arrived two days later. I shared the cookies with my squad, but kept most of the cigars. Sergeant Marshall approached me while I was at rest smoking one of the cigars and daydreaming about Coney Island with Bea.

"Carpenter, I need to have a word. The CO wants you to head up a motorcycle unit. The unit will consist of six cyclists that will send and receive messages amongst the companies in the battalion. Three additional cyclists will do the same between battalions, and you will liaison with the Fourth Moroccan Division. Do you know anything about cycles?" he snapped.

I thought back to when I helped my father repair his lumber truck and replied, "I know something about engines but never rode on a two-wheeler."

With his hands on his hips, he proclaimed, "Virgil, a Frenchman will train you and your men. If you don't screw this up, you'll be put in for a promotion."

Twelve men from the regiment assembled at Maffrécourt for training. They figured that two or three would drop out or get injured during that time. The French lieutenant introduced me as the squad leader. Marcel Reynard was tall, in his mid-twenties, with a goatee, and a pronounced limp, like Captain Le Van. He showed us the Indian PowerPlus Big Train model. It could go up to sixty miles an hour, and it had a three-speed hand shift transmission. The suspension was state of the art. The headlight was magnificent. It had no sidecar but was equipped with mounted leather side bags.

We were given Model FN M1910 pistols. It was a semi-automatic with a seven round .32 caliber clip. A favorite with the Americans. I am told that it was this model that was used by the assassin Gavrillo Princip, from Serbia, to kill Archduke Ferdinand and his wife that touched off the war.

After a day of riding, falling, and learning about the "Indian," we lost two men, leaving a contingent of ten.

The battalions stayed about twelve days in the front-line trenches, and ten days in reserve drilling, training, and resting. The balance of the month, they were about six to eight kilometers at a rest area. We had a bastard of a time with rats and lice. We set cats and French "ratters," a combination of an English Bulldog and local ratters, on the rats. These rats could be as large as a cat. Still, it was a losing battle. We assisted in shooting and stabbing them. The lice were consistent like the shelling. We had to wait to go in reserve in order to strip down, then boil and delouse our clothing with a gasoline mixture.

At the end of May, we learned that our own Sergeant Henry Johnson, a former Red Cap porter from the New York Central in Albany, and his sidekick, Needham Roberts, had an altercation with more than twenty Boche on a trench raid. Roberts was severely wounded, but he managed to wound or kill several of the enemy, while Henry attacked with a Bolo knife and the butt of his broken rifle. Henry was wounded in several places as he attacked the Germans, who were attempting to carry off Roberts. He came from behind, stabbed one in the head, and clubbed another. In the end, it was determined that the famous heroic duo fought off at least a score of the enemy, according to Captain Little's investigation. The skirmish became known as the Battle of Henry Johnson, as told by *The New York World*. The French were enthusiastic to award medals to both, welcoming American participation.

In early June, our battalion was back at Maffrécourt. I got an order to send messages from our regimental commanders to the commanders of the Moroccan Division on our right flank. I had to leave at midnight in order to minimize detection. My assignment was to travel east, past St. Menehould, just west of Clermont-en-Argonne, a large village straddling the slow-moving

Aire River. I was passing mobile kitchen units and dodging enemy shells that would harass traffic, trying to support the front-line troops. Somewhere just east of the village of Las Islettes, I was distracted by some wild turkeys, hit a deep shell hole, and my bike spun off and hit a tree. I woke up two days later in a small bed with goose feather pillows. The room had family pictures on the wall and dresser. A youngster, about twelve, came in with new bandages and compresses. Still out of focus, I asked in broken French, "Where am I? Who are you?"

The young girl kept to her business and with a small giggle, answered, "I am Charlotte, Charlotte Toulouse. You are at our farm house. You had an accident. My mother and our helper moved you here. Your motorcycle is hidden under a mound of hay."

I rested my head back down looking to assess my injuries. Charlotte, wearing a beige, cotton dress and work boots left abruptly. Her mother and helper entered the sunlit room. One of them came closer and said, "I am Rosalie Toulouse, and this is Christina Peretti from Corsica. The two of us, and my two children, run this farm. The men have either died or are still at war. I did some nursing at the beginning of the war, near Reims. You have a concussion, a few broken ribs, three broken fingers, and bruises. You cannot be moved now."

I asked her to repeat her diagnosis since my comprehension of French was not fluent. She was slim, and very plain looking, with a head scarf that hid her ample raven hair. Her hands were rough and strong, typical of farm work. She added, "You are an American? New to the front, no?"

"Yes," I murmured. "I need to send orders to our Allies about four kilometers to the east — the Moroccans." She turned to Christina for a private conversation then addressed me again.

"You are bedridden; your orders may be obsolete now. I can have Christina take them to the Moroccans now, but you must give us your name, unit, and password, or we will not risk it."

Christina sat at the edge of my bed for the information. I trusted them. She was younger than Rosalie, dark skinned with black hair and green eyes. She leaned over showing her ample breasts underneath her low-cut work smock. My senses were alert enough to appreciate her attributes.

She said softly, "I have seen many Senegalese soldiers with their red turbans wrapped around their French helmets and Moroccans with their machetes, but you are my first dark American soldier. You are not much darker than me. I will deliver your orders on horse-back. I will tell them where you are. Now rest."

I lapsed back into a twilight state. Christina returned later in the day. She said the Moroccans were pigs, but the orders were delivered to one of the officers. They said that they would collect me in a day if it was safe. I dictated a letter to Christina for Bea. She wrote it in French. I knew that Bea would be able to get it translated.

The next day came a thundering rain. The exchange of artillery and machine gun fire subsided. My ribs were mending, and my head felt better. My three fingers were splinted by Rosalie. Christina nursed me with hearty soup, brandy and soft cheese. While I was resting, she lay next to me and sang French songs. She smelled like lavender and persimmon. Her hair was wet and tied in braids. Her warm, firm body was comforting. I felt guilty, but we just lay there without any carnal intentions. She did most of the talking, as I still felt somewhat "out of focus." Christina came to France at age sixteen just when the war broke out. She was related to Rosalie's brother. She helped work the farm in the absence of the men. Christina was unattached and what I would call a "hard scrabble" woman.

My rescue did not come that day. The following day, I was able to get up, eat, and use to the commode on my own. After her chores, Rosalie came in to see me. I asked her about my motorcycle. She said that it was banged up, and the light was broken, and she did not know if it could start. After lunch, we talked a lot about home, America, and hopes for the future. Rosalie wanted to marry and have her own farm. She kissed me on the cheek as I dozed off. Her feminine touch was greatly appreciated.

Two days later, the shelling picked up. A shell hit the barn, destroying most of it. Some of the livestock were killed. I had enough strength to get to my cycle. With a few tools and Rosalie's assistance, I was able to start it. I offered my affectionate thanks to the Madame and her two children. Christina embraced me as we said farewell. Then, simultaneously, we kissed. I held her close and stroked her hair with my eyes closed. It seemed like war made fair game of clandestine affections. Perhaps being in an exotic land made my defenses weak for her. As I sped down the dirt lane, I looked back at Christina. I wondered if I would ever see her again.

Chapter Seven

Trial by Fire

A
s I slowly made my way to Maffrécourt, I could not get my mind off Christina. However, I would keep those thoughts to myself. Sergeant Marshall and Corporal Pippin met me. I debriefed both. They told me that the battalion was moving to Melzicourt, again! The Fourth Army was preparing for a major German attack. After a visit to the field hospital, I was able to rest for another day. After only two days at Melzi, we assembled all battalions at Maffrécourt on July 3. On Independence Day, we celebrated with baseball games and a concert by the French Eighty-Fifth Division and our own, now famous, band at Chalons-en-Argonne, a town west of camp. After the celebration, our regiment moved out. Our Third Battalion marched up to Berzieux, several kilometers north. We were the lead battalion. The men were billeted in surrounding villages during daylight, and slept from dawn to about noon. An influenza breakout diminished our combat readiness. The sick were segregated at the hospital in order to reduce possible contagion. When I was there, I witnessed soldiers in desperate conditions. It did not appear to be a typical influenza.

I received letters from Bea and Millie. They were postmarked from early June. Bea was volunteering with a Harlem home front food drive for our regiment. Millie and her husband, Robert, had modernized the farm with a model 1915 Ford truck and a Ford Harvester. The war provided opportunities, even for so-called second-class citizens. Robert was not able to enlist due to having flat feet.

While I was recuperating at the Toulouse home, I had missed a few combat highlights. Our Lieutenant Europe was gassed in a trench raid. He was hospitalized. Corporal Pippin and a few men picked off some Boche and a tree sniper on a raid. On June 6, the Germans counterattacked with artillery and infantry causing the French to make a hurried retreat. Our colonel was indignant stating firmly, "My men never retire. They go forward, or they die." We held our ground that day. On the 12th, our Third Battalion held off a German raid at Montplaisir. Our machine gun leader, Lieutenant Lewis Shaw, was promoted to captain due to his heroism.

After the festivities on Independence Day, we were relieved by the French Ninth Cuirassiers, a dismounted cavalry regiment. We were then assigned to assist the French 161st Division facing Butte de Mesnil, near Minancourt. This was rolling, wooded farm country. All these villages seemed the same to me, some more damaged than others. There were buildings, only two or three stories in height, with rooms exposed to the elements, and debris of wood, stone, and brick were strewn about. Dead livestock, bloated, decaying bodies, both soldiers and civilians were left behind. It was the horrendous smell that seared into one's senses more than the sights. The display of carnage was numbing, but the putrefied odors of death and decay carried on from village to sordid village. We were exposed to heavy enemy artillery, so much so, that we preferred to advance rather than stay put. Our motto was, "God damn, let's go!"

I was reassigned as an NCO with K Company. My short time with the regiment's motorcycle unit was over. One evening I was sharing a foxhole with Private McKinley Anderson, or Mac, who was from somewhere on Long Island, when I crawled back about twenty yards to relieve myself, behind a tree. At that moment, a shrapnel shell exploded. My ears were ringing, and pieces of metal, rock, wood, and dirt were flying in all directions. The tree saved me. A smoking piece of shrapnel was sticking into the tree opposite me at head height! I crawled back to find the foxhole destroyed and Mac had "gone west." His head and right arm were missing. The sight forced me to throw up my rations.

Our regiment was seeing changes to our officer and NCO personnel. Some desired transfer to the tank corps like Lieutenant Castles:
some wanted to join the 370th Regiment, an all-Black unit, because
the "brass" had just limited the number of Black officers in our regiment. It was understandable for men to seek promotion.

After ten days at the Butte we relieved the Fourth Moroccan
Regiment of the 161st Division. Their machetes were used for killing and human souvenirs. The French could not celebrate Bastille
Day as the Germans had plans of their own. They hit us with what
seemed like every kind of artillery they had: trench mortars, "Jack
Johnsons," heavy high explosives, and the hated mustard gas. We
moved to a reverse slope at Camp Bravard, which offered some
respite from the onslaught. The memory of what happened to Mac
took hold of me. I became unhinged, starring at my shaking hands
for minutes at a time.

Suddenly, Sergeant Marshal, his uniform covered in mud and pine
needles, approached me, took his gas mask off for a few seconds,
and shouted, "Virgil, take this message to the HQ of the Moroccan
Regiment, on our right. Give it only to the CO or his Chief of Staff.
You can see Captain Le Van for the best route and details. Take a
private with you. We can't use carrier pigeons now, the shelling is too
intense, and our wire has been cut. There is still some time before
daylight, so make haste." While the sergeant was refitting his mask,
I nodded, keeping my shaking hands by my side.

I crawled to Le Van's dugout at about 2:00 a.m. His prominent
mustache was pressed against the lip of a tin cup filled with coffee
and brandy. He offered me a stool and pulled out a well-worn,
waxed map.

He sat back and examined me, "Corporal, your sergeant recommended you. I hope the rain, mud, and shelling have not spoiled
your enthusiasm."

I shook off some water like a dog and replied, "No, Sir. In fact,
mud is the enemy of the damn lice."

Le Van smiled and nodded. He went on, "The HQ of the Moroccans is across this stream, just north of Vargemoulin-Hurlus. This
is about one kilo due east of where we are. The message is in code.
Avoid star shells. Come back with their message to me by 6:00 a.m.

Is this clear?" he asked, while he finished his strong coffee.

"Yes, Sir. We have three pistols, five grenades, and two knives between us."

Le Van motioned to me as I retired. "Do not hasten so abruptly. I offer you some of my strong coffee. A toast to our comradeship and victory." After a few dry minutes, and draining the coffee, I was off.

A kilometer did not seem very far, but the shelling and the ungodly weather made the journey seem like a slow crawl. My hands were shaky, regardless of Le Van's coffee, and my mind was racing. The gas mask was resting on my chest. The mud made it impossible for me to see through it. Private Riley Barnes followed closely. I selected him because he was small and fast. I was taking a chance; maybe this time I would not be so lucky. With the assistance of light coming from the lightning-like shelling, we crossed a swampy area outside the decimated wooded front. We rested by the stream for a few lonely minutes. The mud was caked on our puttees and most of our trousers. The warm July night made the rain more tolerable. Memories of Bea, Christina, and Mac raced around my tortured mind. Forcing myself to focus on my assignment, we forded the stream that was waist high but slow moving. We crawled along the mud on the east side of the bank. Halted by two men pointing Lebel rifles at our faces, I knew we were at the right place. After some quick interrogation, they took us to their CO. To my surprise, the division commander was present, and he was none other than General Lebouc. He was discussing plans for a counterattack with his officers in the spacious dugout. The general's aide took my message, read it, and then whispered into Lebouc's ear.

The general looked up at me as his monocle dropped from his right eye, and said in broken English, "*Bon.* Please give my greetings to your colonel and Captain Le Van. My adjutant will give you my orders. Please warm yourselves with hot coffee."

We sat there for ten minutes, and then we began our return trip. After crossing the stream again, we were showered with flying dirt and rock from a Jack Johnson. We were knocked over. I was hit by a section of tree and twisted my ankle. I was lucky. We finally crawled and limped back to our trench lines. With the aid of Riley, I reached Le Van's dugout. It was 5:45 a.m., and a dreary daylight overtook the night. Le Van was in the company of Captain Fish and two other officers of my company. Fish was a commanding figure with his campaign hat on, even in a squalid, dimly lit dugout.

He approached me, "Corporal, good work! Let's see what we have from the general. You are relieved to go to the field hospital to rest your leg."

The doctor had an attendant wash me down, tape my swollen ankle and place me on bed rest for two days. My boot could not fit over my lame ankle. I could see many of our wounded men due to shelling. A few died, and many others had leg, arm, body, and head wounds that made the doctors and nurses scramble to save as many as fate allowed. I was placed on a bed next to a soldier unfamiliar to me. His head was bandaged. All I could see in the dim light, were his mouth and chin. Blood was seeping through some of his bandages. I did not think about my ankle now.

I was able to rejoin my unit on the 17th. We had recaptured Minaucourt and the Butte. The "Blue Devils," or French Alpine Chasseurs, were on our left, and the Moroccans were on our right flank. During our advance, we captured a large stash of German Mauser rifles and ammo. We preferred anything to the Lebel, so we made fast friends with the enemy rifles. During the last two weeks of July, the division was advancing and counterattacking along the edge of the Argonne Forest. Captain Fish was transferred to AEF for training, and Captain David L'Esperance took over Company K. We lost several men in the company to enemy artillery and machine gun fire. Also, a handful were gassed and out of action.

The regiment's famous band went to Paris in August to entertain the troops and war weary citizens. Our Battalion Commander, Major Spencer, told us that Marshall Foch, the overall Allied Commander, refused the return of the Ninety-Third Division back to the AEF. We were to stay with the French Army for the duration. Sinhalese *camion* drivers took most of the regiment to Somme-Bionne, several miles south of where we had been fighting, in order to retool and absorb new recruits. We received new gas masks, as the original ones did not accurately fit the wider noses of Negroes.

We set up camp in the villages all around this area. I had marched past these same war-torn places. Decimated farm houses and barns were all too familiar. The smell of sulphur and decaying flesh enveloped us like a Jersey fog. Our platoon set up shop in a barn, damaged only on a small section of its roof and rear corner.

One night, after consuming our soup and cheap Le Pinard wine, Horace Pippin, Otis Ellison, Emmet Parker, and I were cleaning our newly acquired Mausers. Otis was slim, but very muscular. Parker was our best marksman, although Pippin would argue this point. Emmet was a slippery sort, never to be trusted with women or gambling. The dimple on his chin and the space between his front teeth were distinguishing features of this cussin' son of the Bronx. We were running out of ammo, but the Germans knew how to make weapons. The only thing the Allies outfoxed them on was the tank. The Brits surprised the Boche a couple of years ago at the Somme. The Tommies and the French had more mobile tanks than the late arrival German monsters. It seemed to us that the tanks were useful when working but, all too often, they broke down.

Otis leaning against a bale of hay up against the barn wall, lit up a smoke and exclaimed, "Gents, they're playing us 'niggas' for fools. I don't see shit happenin' if and when we return."

Horace and I looked at each other, while Emmet continued cleaning his deadly friend. After a long smoke-filled silence, Horace replied, "Son, you may be right, but we are goin' to assist these French like the men we are. No son of a bitch will say that we cut and ran. In fact, we are goin' to kick so much German ass that even the most nigga' hatin' bastard will take notice."

Otis snuffed out his smoke and remarked, "Corporal, you done spoke the gospel. I'm a true beleva'." We all laughed and lit up another American smoke before we got some shuteye.

August melted away into September. Our company, and other elements of the regiment, moved south to St. Ouen-Domprot, then through the town of Vitry-le-Francois. This town was located on the banks of the Marne River, southeast of Chalons-en-Champagne. The area was relatively unharmed by war except for the occasional long-range artillery. Some of these huge cannons made twenty-five to fifty-foot craters, spraying shrapnel for hundreds of yards. By early September the regiment consolidated, and the band had returned from Paris. On the seventh, we marched nearly twenty miles toward the front, again. The trip north and east went slowly due to the Allied onslaught of men, machines, and animals. Our division was advancing with the French 157th and the Second Moroccan Divisions. The latter had a red hand insignia on their uniforms.

Late in the month, the battalion crossed the shallow Dormoise River, just east of Minaucourt and south of Ripont. These were villages we had secured the prior month. The next day, the great Meuse-Argonne offensive began. The sky lit up with grey and black puffs of artillery smoke. Airplanes on both sides played a deadly game of cat and mouse. One German Fokker was in a death spiral not more than two hundred yards from us. The sun was blotted out as we floundered in the hazy twilight to put on our gas masks. We were in a reverse slope of pine trees for some counterbattery protection, but the German mortars and gas shells found us. Trees were sliced down, and the branches rained down on us, wounding at random. Our soup wagon was destroyed along with two horses. The blast mixture of soup, soil, rock, and animals instilled more fear than usual. Out of the smoke-filled mist, a dog appeared. It was limping toward me. I was impressed by his will to survive. The smell of food must have tempted him to brave these man-made elements. He stopped about twenty paces from the wrecked wagon, with soup draining into the pine strewn mud. I approached him slowly, bending with my hand down in a patting motion. The wounded dog was brindle colored with white markings, and he looked like a mix of Boxer and German Shepard. I petted his unkempt, but short fur. He was starving.

I yelled to one of my men, "Get a tin and pour in some soup."

The dog hesitated, but his fear was overcome by hunger. In a minute, the soup was devoured. He followed me.

Someone yelled out, "What the hell are we goin' to do with your new friend?"

We moved on, carrying as many rations as we could, dog in tow. I named him Wilson.

Sergeant Marshall appeared from the foggy haze, lifted his mask and yelled out, "Virgil, we are advancing. Just got orders from the captain. The battalion is going to secure a tunnel about four hundred yards north. There is a gap between our division and the Moroccans that needs to be eliminated. I am leading elements of our company to knock out any machine gun nests west of the tunnel. Once the area is secure, we are advancing on to Ripont. You will be next to me in case I am out of action."

I nodded, and we moved out amidst the shelling and through the muddy woods. During our approach the tunnel, Marshall ordered us to advance with rifle grenades, Chauchats, and one Hotchkiss gun firing in concert. The enemy opened up with their heavy Maxim machine guns and stick grenades. I was next to the sergeant when a grenade exploded, killing a private and sending me on my ass with his blood and flesh covering me. Marshall was yelling something, but I could not hear him, nor could I get up. I remember being dragged into a shell hole. I must have passed out. I woke up with a dead German next to me, shot in the head. Reinforcements came to our aid. I was helped to the newly conquered trench where I found the intrepid Marshall. He was enjoying a smoke and commented, "Corporal, you missed the best part. Any broken bones?"

"No, Sergeant. I was just knocked out, still ringing in the ears," I shouted.

"Get cleaned up. We are moving on Ripont. You can join the company there. I am putting you in charge of the kitchen detail. It will give you time to recover," he stated. Then he inhaled another puff.

I was able to secure some hot coffee and hardtack. The Mauser ammo was exhausted, so I had to use the cursed Lebel again. The next morning, I entered Ripont. A lot of coffee dipped hardtack made the muddy journey almost bearable.

Marshall was in a destroyed church, sitting against the remnants of the altar. I knelt down and asked, "Sarg, want coffee?"

He just answered, "Get some shuteye. We move out soon."

Spying Pippin, I made my way over to him and a few other men lying across the few remaining pews. Only Pippin was awake. He lit up a new smoke, savored it, and said, "Hey Virgil, you look like shit. Welcome to the party."

I could barely hear him. My ears were still ringing. "Shit? No, more like dried blood and guts. Smells as bad. I can't hear for shit though, that happened near the tunnel. How are you, old man?"

"I'm alive, good enough for me. Get some rest, there's some room," he motioned to a spot nearby.

"I see you are using some charcoal to draw," I remarked.

"Yah, my type of diary," he murmured.

"Let me see," I exclaimed. Horace wiped away the smoke from his eyes and handed the paper to me. I tried not to smudge the work.

"It is a somber portrayal of soldiers braving hell on earth," I said.

"Get some sleep, man," he reminded me. I complied.

In a few hours, we departed the remains of the village for a place called Bellevue Signal. We passed a company of French Regulars moving to the east, to the Argonne. Their great coats were coated with dried mud and pine needles. Their faces were gaunt, bearded, with expressionless, hopeless eyes. I wondered if I would look like them after a year. The era of cavalry charges was gone, replaced with monster artillery, poison gases, machine guns, and airplanes dropping bombs.

Our battalion reached a swamp east of the Dormoise River. The distinct sound of Austrian "Eighty-Eights," almost four-inch-wide shells, firing at us made this adventure an unusual hell. The shells pounded the swamp. Sprays of mud flew in every direction. If the enemy used gas, we would have been blinded. My company found a bridge on the east end of the swamp. Marshall and Pippin found me in the weeds. The sergeant ordered Pippin and me to take twenty men and eliminate any snipers along the bridge prior to crossing. A score of us fanned out approaching the wooden structure. Machine gun fire and German "Seventy-Seven" field artillery rained down on the hapless. Pippin went off with a squad to my right as the rest of us advanced. Two of my men were hit, Private Pearson was felled by a head shot, and Private Barnes went down next to me. I leaned over and saw the light go out of his eyes, that were left lifeless and staring. I was frozen with fear. I was in shock. Two men dragged me across the secured bridge. Pippin had taken out a machine gun nest, making our survival possible. The company suffered significant losses.

My gas mask was on, but I don't remember putting it on. My right arm and both hands were shaking. I could not get a grip. Marshall approached me while I lay near a stone wall.

"What the fuck happened to you?" he demanded, as he rolled a smoke.

Holding my helmet in order to hide my shakes, I replied, "Sergeant, don't know. This was not my first rodeo. I just snapped, can't explain it."

He gazed at me through the smoke, wiping the mud from his forehead. "We are moving out to another village. I was going to ask the captain to promote you, but that won't happen. Get your shit together man, we need you. You're an intelligent sort. Don't fuck up again or I'll have your stripes. Pippin has been wounded in the neck and shoulder. Don't fuck up." He dashed off before I could respond. It was better that way.

I was told that we had about forty-eight men enter that swamp, and only eight or nine came out without being killed or wounded. The battalion captured about five hundred Boche and over a dozen Maxims in the last two days. Corporal Elmer Earl and I were the only two corporals active for duty in K Company now. Elmer had rescued several of the men in the swamp. I could not hold a candle to him.

We moved the night of September 29, past Fontaine-en-Dormois on the way to Séchault, a village with an important rail line to secure. At dawn, on the thirtieth, we reached the outskirts of the village. The company was able to get some rest in a field surrounding one huge, slightly damaged, stone barn. A lonely oak tree invited me, so I rested, my Adrian helmet covering my dirty face. I was thinking about home — home in bucolic Virginia. The smell and sounds of war melted away, melted away.

Chapter Eight

Les Femmes en Noir

I looked away, west to Paris, the blood orange sun beating down on me. I closed my eyes and inhaled the corrupted air, laid low by mustard gas, and imagined I was back home on the Rappahannock. It was four hundred and eighty-six paces from the back porch to my castle. Past the rows of ripening pumpkins in the late August sun; up the well-worn lane; past the white, mildly dented, mail box number 1670. I kicked some dust covered pebbles while I looked down to avoid the huge setting sun shining on the vast rows of sugar corn stalks. Instinctively, I turned right into the cornfield where a path was made. Only sixty paces more — hurry the sun is setting! There, I see, unmolested, four towering walls of corn that harbor room for my kingdom, my solitude. I look up, arms and legs apart, leaving the world behind. It is my castle, my Eden, and no intruders pass these walls. I can drift away anytime, anyplace, be anyone … drift away.

The blue-black sky suddenly opened up with a torrent of rain. Eyes closed, mouth open, I embraced the wetness, the constant, relentless ping, ping of water. Then, as quickly as the rain began, it ended. I tasted the sun again; I was immortal!

"Virgil, Corporal Carpenter!" The sergeant major's shrill voice punctured my reverie. "The war is in front of you! The only goddamn things behind you are the dead and the Second Battalion comin' up."

Sergeant Marshall pointed his finger at me to make sure he

had my full attention. "Corporal, I need you to pick the three fastest privates in the platoon. About a half a kilometer to the southwest is a patch of apple trees. Take a horse cart with you, all the draft animals here are either dead or they are needed somewhere else."

Marshall's eyes darted across the provincial wasteland, as he put his hands on his hips and continued "Put the cart in the middle of the field and see to it that you empty the field of apples working from the corners to the middle. No damn green ones either. We got enough men out with dysentery, influenza, and wounds. I want you all back here in ninety."

He moved closer to me, looked me up and down, then barked, "Can you handle that, corporal?"

"Yes, Sergeant, I can, I will." I focused on his helmet when I responded. I hoped I sounded convincing.

"Get goin', double quick, and watch out for snipers," he added, then moved to the front of the platoon and ordered a bread detail.

Marshall had it in for me ever since that bloody skirmish by the Dormoise River swamp. He had no tolerance for shell shock or the shakes. He killed my promotion. I protested, but inside I knew I froze, like a damn statue. Maybe too much education is not good for soldiering. But I couldn't think of that now; I must not let him down, again.

"Okay Henry, Otis, and Parker, come with me," I yelled over the controlled chaos around me. "Henry and Otis, look for a cart that ain't broken and follow Parker and me. We got to be back by that red brick building in ninety minutes," I shouted as we hurried down to the left.

Henry Beale was from the Bronx. He joined the Fifteenth while working as an elevator man at the Woolworth building in Manhattan. He was about twenty-two, tall and lean, with dark eyes like coal and a part down the center of his short kinky hair. Light skinned; he could pass for Italian to some. A damn good dice player and self-assured ladies' man, too. My friend Otis, from East Harlem, joined with the recruiting efforts of Lieutenant Europe and his jazz band. Otis did a lot of praying, and was a devout Baptist. He was hoping God would get him through the war. And Emmet

Parker, he was a peculiar sort. Trigger happy to kill Boche. He had a chip on his shoulder, was odd, so the guys said, but he was as swift as greased lightning. Emmet was the blackest, Black man in the company.

Parker and I were making haste down the rut-laden path, doin' "360's" and watching for snipers, while Otis and Henry hauled the empty cart like a rickshaw. Emmet stated the obvious, "Da Sarg is one tough son of a bitch."

"Yes," I snapped, "he's seen more shit with the Tenth Infantry in Cuba and the Philippines than this whole platoon has seen. He knows more than a handful of green lieutenants from West Point. Could have been an officer, if he wanted."

"Why didn't he then?" shrugged Parker while his eyes darted in all directions.

"Don't know, don't know," I replied as I looked to my right and saw we were at our destination.

We made it in good time. I stopped to survey a few targeted acres and cleared my throat.

"Emmet, take the northwest corner; Otis, start opposite of Emmet; Henry, you start near the path. I'll take what's left. Use your helmets to forage the apples, only the ripe ones. We got forty minutes, so let's move."

I tried to sound like Marshall, but I fooled no one. I got about a dozen apples, then ran to the cart and repeated this several times. Suddenly, I heard the crush of pebbles from behind me, like so many steps. I grabbed my pistol and turned. An ensemble of females stopped abruptly. An old woman spoke.

"This is our land," she uttered in French, hesitantly. Her silver hair fell around her aged shoulders. She looked like a woman of over sixty, but war can age anyone prematurely. She was dressed in black, a heavy fabric that could stand the trials of field labor. Her hands looked strong and rough. With her was a young woman, maybe her daughter, also dressed in black. Her hair was the color of corn stalks, and her eyes were a piercing blue. Next to her was a girl, maybe six or seven years old, dressed in taffeta, frilled at the hem. The girl had golden yellow hair with deep hazel-colored eyes. She was clutching a porcelain doll with raven colored hair and rosy cheeks, dressed in Victorian clothing.

I stammered in broken French, "We have orders, Madame, to pick apples for our men. Our food wagons are not up, and the soldiers have had no food for thirty hours. We just came from Ripont and Bellevue Signal. We have to advance soon."

I was hoping this explanation would relieve her anxiety. She said nothing. The old woman stretched out her arms, the younger females joined her, with the girl reaching out to me in order to complete a circle.

The girl murmured, "*Un soldat chocolat*, Mama."

Her mother gave her a menacing eye and told her to hush. The elderly woman closed her eyes, made the Sign of the Cross, and knelt down on the apple-strewn ground with the others. I'm Protestant, and not a very good one. Still, I felt compelled to get on my knees as if a great weight of gravity overcame me. I reached out to the girl's doll and her grandmother to complete the circle.

Eyes closed, finally the elderly woman softly said, "In the name of my martyred husband and my son, I prevail on you God, to grant victory and comfort to these liberators from America. We beg you, restore peace to our land, in the name of the Father, Son and Holy Ghost, Amen."

We rose together. She reached out and touched my face with a firm caress, looked into my eyes and whispered, "You will live, son, to see another war." Then she kissed me on both cheeks, as was the custom.

I stepped back, almost tripping over my helmet, then composed myself and asked, "How do you know, how do you know this?"

Suddenly, Parker was racing down to me, helmet in hand. I turned to him while he shouted, "Who are they? What did they say?"

"Nothing," I called out, "the old woman prayed for victory and peace." I picked up my helmet and added, "she said I would live to see another war. Do you believe that crap?"

Parker stopped and, slightly out of breath, asked, "Did she say anything about me?"

"No", I replied. I turned around, but they had vanished, like an apparition.

"Parker, round up the others. Our time here is up; we got to go."

I dare not disappoint Marshall. A strange feeling came over me as I led the men away. I was unafraid now. It was as if I was anointed by an angelic hand and had become … immortal.

Chapter Nine

Son of Fredericksburg

With our apple detail completed, we proceeded down the ruddy path to our encampment, just southwest of Séchault. The shelling became more intense now. I ran into Captain Fish and the sergeant.

The latter yelled out, "Get those apples to the men. We move out in two hours. The First Battalion and the Machine Gun Company have started to assault the village. French counter batteries are sighting the enemy's guns east of the village for support. Don't go beyond the reverse slope, mustard gas still lingers in the fields there."

He was loading his pistol and asked, "I see that mutt is still following you. Give him up. He's no messenger dog."

I knew he was right. I saluted the captain and moved out. Maybe I could find a villager in Séchault, or the next village, to take Wilson.

The boys were glad for the apples, but it did not make up for the loss of our soup kitchen. Wilson was very popular with the men. The sounds of artillery did not frighten him. I only hoped that a gas attack was not in the cards, as we had no mask for a dog, just the horses.

I ran into Otis as he was ducking for cover in the small, bullet ridden and partially destroyed church. Wilson was undeterred by the intrusion as he was treated to leftovers and an apple. We had a few dozen men in there just nodding off, reading mail, or cleaning weapons. All were waiting for orders.

Otis lit a smoke and whispered to me, "Virg, what do ya think of Parker?"

"What do you mean?" I asked. He was watching the ash grow as he took another drag and responded, "Well, guys are talking about him. He got into a fight when we were in Ripont with Ben, Ben Cleveland." "For what?" I asked.

Otis put out his butt and drew closer to me. "Da ruma is he's queer. Ben knocked him down for some unnatural advance. Ben could have spilled da beans, but dat would have been da end of 'Park.'"

"Otis, what the hell do you want me to do?" I exclaimed.

Wilson ran off to beg for more to eat. Otis lit up again nervously and replied, "Don't rightly know, but I hope he keeps to himself fo' his sake, ya know."

As I whistled for Wilson I responded, "All I know is that he is a good combat soldier, good with a rifle and grenade. Hopefully he is as good learning a lesson. Fuck, we don't need this shit."

In a few minutes, I had my helmet over my face blotting out the world. This reprieve did not last long. Otis interrupted my solace with an existential question.

"Does you think we can return alive? We done lost so many men. This is one fucked up war."

I put on my helmet, spotted Wilson next to me, and finally replied, "I'm surprised I lasted this long. Six months taking everything the German bastards could throw at us, not to mention the influenza, pneumonia. Half of the men have died, spitting up blood from pneumonia and poison gases. I figure if I made it out alive, I'm 'aces' man, aces. Keep your head down, don't do anything stupid and you may survive."

"Maybe I'll die from smoking and the bad wine first," Otis countered.

"Just remember, we are the Black Rattlers. The only thing that can kill us is a mongoose," I droned. We laughed, lit another smoke and downed what was left of our *vin rouge*.

Suddenly, all the men came to attention. Captain Fish entered our sanctuary with Sergeant Earl and Corporal Pippin. Fish just returned to the company.

Fish was a model looking officer, with his strapped leggings,

Sam Browne belt, polished boots, and campaign hat enhancing his reputation as a leader. He approached us and asked for us to kneel around him.

"Men, Major Little's battalion and other elements of the regiment have entered the village of Séchault. As you know this is an important crossroads and rail junction. They are being counterattacked from the woods east of the village. We need to flank the enemy first, south and east of the village. We have to hook up with Little's men. Once we reach the woods, enemy machine gun emplacements will be laying down enfilading fire. We are going to fan out into squads of twenty men. Several of our lieutenants are inactive or dead, and Sergeant Marshall is out with shrapnel to his leg and back. I have asked Earl and Pippin to gather their men; the rest will be going with Corporal Carpenter. All I can tell you men is this assault is our most important so far. We came here to fight, we came here for the French, we came here for our brothers in arms, and above all, we came here to make the Boche fear us." The men retired.

He then stood next to me and said, "It is just the two of us now. Corporal, you could have been promoted by now, but Marshall told me that you froze at Signal Ridge."

"Yes, Captain, for several minutes in the swamp. I became disoriented, numb to what was going on. I recovered once we got to Bussy Farm," I replied, looking him in the eye.

Ham pointed his finger at me and said, "You might get your new stripes once this is over today, or maybe death will find you or I, but we are going to drive those bastards back to Berlin. Are you clear?"

"Yes, Sir", I snapped.

"Okay then, I want you to take nine of the best grenade throwers and Chauchat men. I'm thinking Parker, Ellison, Beale, Cleveland, and McCowin.

You pick the rest. Your squad needs to take out a machine gun position to the left of Pippin's men. Artillery hasn't been able to take them out. The area is wooded, but there is some cover. Load up on grenades and ammo. Leave everything else behind except your masks. We move out in five. I am counting on you to prove Marshall wrong."

I composed myself as best I could, and remembered what the old French woman told me yesterday. Could she be right? Did she have divine knowledge of my fate? I prayed she did. The captain scurried off as the relentless sounds of artillery and machine gun fire increased.

Otis came over to me and inquired, "What did da capt'in say?"

I replied, "Give me a smoke please and round up eight men. I'll give you the names on a piece of paper. Have them here in two minutes, and keep Parker and Cleveland apart."

The men assembled, and I asked them to take a knee. Summoning a commanding tone, I took one last puff and said, "Captain Fish has assigned me the task of leading you all on an assault to destroy a machine gun nest outside of the village north of here. We have to get this done before dark, before they counterattack our men in the village. Parker, you will be on my extreme left with a rifle grenade and Cleveland, you do the same on my right. Everyone carry as many stick grenades as possible. We might have to lob these fifty yards or more. Otis, if I am out of action, you take over. Men, we need to take them out. Sergeant Earl's and Corporal Pippin's men will be doing the same dirty work to our right. God speed, move out."

The terrain was wet and muddy from the autumn rains. Leaves and pine needles covered the moist dirt. As we crossed the road outside of the village, Maxims opened up on us. The ping, ping of bullets flew around us like so many bees. We dove for cover in a ditch parallel to the road. One of my men cried out, then there was silence. We were about a hundred and fifty yards from the flash of fire in the woods. There was a stone wall about a hundred yards in front of us; from there we had a shot to take out the Maxims. I ordered Cleveland and Parker to lay down rifle grenade fire as a diversion. The rest of us could run to the safety of the wall. We ran in a zigzag manner while, for a brief moment, the rate of enemy fire had died down. The rifle grenades provided some cover, but Parker's rifle jammed after a few rounds. Otis was hit in the leg and started to crawl forward. As we reached the wall, Cleveland was hit several times. We had no *brancardiers* or stretcher bearers. We were alone in a world of soldiers. The incoming fire was brutal. I could not hear myself or anyone else. My right hand began to shake, and my ears were ringing as bullets ricocheted off the wall. We could not stay here for long. Only seven of us were alive, two assumed dead, and Otis bleeding out. I ordered the grenades to be tossed. Parker hurdled over the safety of the wall. I yelled at him, but he began flinging grenades as he ran to the woods. Parker was hit again and again as his last grenade blew up near the Maxims. Without any thought, I screamed, "BAYONETS, FIX BAYONETS", to my startled men, as I leaped forward grenades in hand. Instinctively, the others followed me. While I entered the woods, I lobed two grenades, then fired my pistol. I went down with a bullet to my left leg. I was spun around and shot two Boche as they ran from their destroyed death machines. I made it to a tree, leaned against it and kept on firing at the fleeing enemy. More enemy went down. A grenade came for me. I rolled over, but it exploded. That is all I remembered.

I woke up at the field hospital at St. Menehould. It was night and the smells of chloroform, sulphur, and rot permeated my nostrils. After noticing my leg bandaged, I felt my head. It was bandaged too. My right eye and part of my head was covered with gauze. I laid back, the dim light hiding what was around me, except for the beds next to me. The darkness did not hide the groans and cries. I saw the outline of a uniform and yelled out, "Nurse, nurse."

She approached me, knelt down, and whispered, "*Parlez-vous francais?*"

The young woman wore a white dress with a blue smock. The red cross on her uniform was stained with the blood of her charges. Her auburn hair was cut short and partly covered by her two-cornered cap.

Her blue eyes reflected the dim light. I replied, "*Je parle francois en petite peu.* I am American. *Parlez-vous anglais?*"

Her eyes had a hollowness, probably due to a lack of sleep. She answered, "Yes. How can I help you?"

"All I remember is an explosion. What happened to me? I need water, please," I groaned.

"The explosion damaged your right eye and cheek. The surgeon had to remove the eye. That is the worst of it. I am sorry, but as the daylight comes, you will see that you fared better than most others here. *Pardon*, I will get you water." I said nothing, but my mind raced with thoughts of self-pity.

The morning came, and the sun laid bare everything the nurse told me. Human carnage revealed itself in every way. I had never seen so many bandages, legless and armless men, men with grievous head wounds, and men with corrupted lungs. I still felt sorry for myself. A nurse came over, an older, more senior woman.

She said, "I am nurse supervisor Audette. I understand you are an American. We need to change your dressing before we feed you."

I sat up and let her do her job. I made an instinctive motion to touch my face but Audette stopped me.

"You must let it heal. Let me work," she implored.

I ate my oatmeal and drank my coffee half dazed. A voice from the bed next to me pierced my thoughts, "You American?" he asked in French.

I could tell from his accent that he was African. "Yes, I whispered. I am with the American 369th Regiment assigned to the French Fourth Army. I was injured at Séchault a few days ago."

"I am sorry, my friend. My name is Kadid Kolda, youngest son of Chief Kolda of Senegal. I was gassed outside of Juniville last summer. I am just beginning to feel normal."

Self-conscious of my wound, I replied, "Virgil Carpenter from New York. I am glad you are better. Are you going back to your unit?"

"No, no," he mused. He declared that he was too weak to assume combat duty for another few weeks.

In a few days, I was able to walk with the aid of crutches. It was the first time I was able to go outside. I sat on a bench making small talk with two other wounded men and, for a brief moment, I forgot about my injuries. On my return, I became disoriented and ended up in the influenza ward. The smell of strychnine, vomit, and blood told me that I was lost. More and more men were dead and dying from this insidious disease.

A Negro nurse appeared and asked, "Soldier, let me escort you to your ward. I am Amelia Benson, from Baltimore." She led me to my bed and gave me some coffee. We talked about home for a few minutes, then she departed.

The next day, Colonel Hayward, Major Little, and a couple of other officers visited the hospital. Captain Le Van, our liaison officer, also joined our leaders. The group surrounded my bed. The colonel asked about me and my injuries. He said that my squad took heavy losses, but we helped rid the woods of the enemy. The regiment was being assigned to the Vosges Region after suffering heavy losses, including the heroic death of Lieutenant Shaw, Commander of our Machine Gun Company.

The colonel then whispered, "Corporal, I approved your promotion to sergeant." He saluted and moved on.

Le Van leaned over and remarked, "We will fix you up. Our surgeons do wonderful work, be optimistic, son."

In mid-October, I was moved to the army hospital at Casernes de Vincennes, located on the east side of Paris. It was an old army complex built in the mid-nineteenth century. My leg was on the mend. I was able to walk with a limp. My concern was with my face. The bandages were less grotesque than a week ago. A surgeon came by with a nurse.

The French doctor told me in a very direct way, "Soldier, I am going to let you see your wound. Tomorrow, I will place an artificial eye in your socket. I will do what I can to reduce the scaring around the eye and cheek. Any questions?"

"No", was the only response I could muster.

The nurse removed the gauze and bandages. She dabbed my affected area with solution that stung, then she handed a mirror to me. All I could focus on was the hole where my eye had been. I dropped the mirror on the bed as the nurse surrounded us with privacy curtains.

She leaned over and told me, "I have seen the doctors do miracles with your type of wound. You will see." She held my hand briefly, then left me. I thought about how Bea would react, and if my students would accept me. I read letters from her and my family for several hours as the light from the October sun subsided into twilight.

Today became tomorrow. The surgeon and his assistant labored over me in the early light and sterility of the operating room. Bandages were reapplied, and I rested for a day. The next week, I wandered the grounds and hallways of this fortress outside of the City of Light. As October was ending, I received a letter from Captain Fish. He wrote about how proud he was of the company, especially Corporal Pippin and I. Most of all, he greeted me as Sergeant Carpenter. It was a costly promotion, but I could live out my life knowing that I was a credit to my unit, my race and, most of all, to myself.

On the 30th, a visitor came to see me. Kadid Kolda was in his Senegalese uniform, a sergeant like me. His machete hung ominously near his belt buckle.

He hugged me and said, "I inquired about where you were taken and in two days I am here, before you!"

I looked at him with some jealousy and replied. "My friend, they released you? You look every bit the warrior."

He laughed and replied, "We amused each other for half a month, but I am also here on business. I am assigned to a Senegalese delegation meeting with high government officials, maybe even Clemenceau! Being the son of a chief, even the youngest son, is a blessing."

We walked outside on the path leading to the main gate. I lit up a smoke and remarked, "Kadid, you were a big help to me at St. Menehould. I cannot thank you enough."

"You can thank me by going to Montparnasse with me. I know a Moroccan café on St. Germain Boulevard that has the strongest coffee and best *brochette* in Paris."

I inquired, "Can you wait three days? My bandages come off in two days, and I still have a week's pass in Paris. It's a reward for losing an eye."

Kadid smiled and agreed, "Yes, it is settled. I will pick you up on Thursday afternoon. I must return to the front by Sunday evening with my delegation. You will be my guest in Paris."

"I will send a message to my CO. If I feel up to it, I will return to my unit in a supply truck."

Kadid put his arm around me and told me that he would ask his colonel if I could return to the front with him. He wished me well and departed.

On Wednesday morning, the 6th of November, my bandages came off. By the late afternoon, I was in front of a mirror. The surgeon waited for a response. I just stared into the mirror hoping that if I held it at a different angle, my opinion would change.

He declared," Well, soldier, can you accept yourself?"

I placed the mirror on the bed and replied, "I can get along with the new eye, but the scars — can anything be done with the scars?"

He ran his hand through his greying hair and said, "Let it heal. Someday we may be able to graft skin to the affected area. Cosmetic surgery is making great advances."

"I need the biggest eye patch you have. That will be my cosmetic surgery for now," I pronounced.

At least an eye patch was in fashion, I told myself. Thursday came and so did Kadid. He came in a Renault touring car, thanks to his delegation. He gave me the "once over" and proclaimed, "My friend, you look more the soldier with that eye patch than most. The women will love it."

I settled into the sedan and replied, "As long as they do not pity me."

It was a cool, cloudy November afternoon as we drove along the Seine. Paris was everything I remembered. Even the somber dress and mood of the inhabitants did not dull the grandeur of this ancient city. We pulled up to the café on St. Germain. We were greeted with a pale of smoke and aromas of perfume and spicy cuisine.

Kadid and I settled at a table near the window. We gazed at the people and traffic. A bar maid approached us. She was about fifty — at least she looked fifty, with streaks of grey distributed in her dark blond hair. She was very thin, almost frail looking. She asked bluntly, "What is your pleasure?"

Kadid replied, "My friend and I will have *Le Soixante-Quinze*, or the '75'." He lit up a small cigar and said, "It is all the rage: gin, champagne, lemon juice and sugar."

We drank as twilight waned and darkness came to Paris. Two women approached us and asked if they could have a seat. Before we replied, they sat. One woman looked very young, maybe seventeen, and her companion appeared to be ten years and "miles" older. Each wore white and navy taffeta dresses, revealing ample cleavage. The younger girl had brown hair and hazel eyes with an abundance of rouge, while the older woman was blond with dark roots, and had blue eyes enhanced with a lot of mascara.

Kadid remarked, "We are both married. My friend takes his vows seriously. I do not, but we are here to drink and eat."

They laughed. The older woman was not fazed and replied, "If you are not going to fuck us, at least buy us a drink."

We returned the laughter and complied with the request. We ordered *brochette*, and Moroccan bread. Their company was worth the cost. I forgot about my wound. That, alone, was worth a thousand francs.

At about 2:00 a.m. they kissed us farewell. We drove to Kadid's hotel in Montparnasse. The room was small, but it was a palace compared to sleeping in the mud at the front. The next morning Kadid was off on business leaving me to be a sightseer. After a breakfast of eggs, sausage and cheese, I took the underground to the Louvre. Rumors of an armistice buzzed around Paris like leaves falling to the ground. I spent all day marveling at the artwork, still remaining despite the war. I ran into a White officer from our division at the Egyptian pavilion. We talked for ten minutes, and he informed me of the regiment's whereabouts in Alsace, near Belfort.

I had dinner at the Café de la Paix, near the Sorbonne. It was a treat, but pricey. The next day, the ninth, Kadid and I toured the Right Bank, then parked at *Sacré-Coeur* in the Montmartre District. We sat on a stone wall and surveyed much of Paris from this commanding height. After several small cigars, we ventured to Bouillon Chantrer on Rue de Faubourg for dinner. The restaurant enchanted us with its carved woodworking and beveled mirrors, mosaics and gold leaf lettering. We consumed 75's and oysters as the night descended and lights twinkled on inside the bistro. Kadid and I could never have done this in New York, no less Richmond. The French treated us like men, of any color. My eye patch even earned us a free drink. *Viva La France!*

On Sunday, the 10th, I was able to join Kadid's delegation back to the front. We reached Reims that evening. I went to the great Cathedral of Reims and gave thanks that I was alive. We departed again at six a.m., the morning of Monday, the eleventh of November.

We had just reached St. Menehould when soldiers and the inhabitants erupted in jubilation. The long-awaited armistice had come on the eleventh hour of this 11th day of November 1918.

Kadid and I melted into the throng. A growing number got down on their knees and prayed on the cobblestone streets and dirt paths. Church bells rang out joining the chorus of cheers and the singing of *La Marseillaise*. We bade each other farewell and promised to write. I visited the field hospital in town to find out where my battalion was located. A nurse directed me to a convalescing private from Company H. After some small talk, this comrade in arms from Harlem told me he learned that the "Third" was billeted at Schoenen-Steinback near the Rhine River.

The next morning, I headed northwest to Clermont-en-Argonne. My hope was to see Christina again. I found the farm at midday. It was on the east side of the Aire River, on the road to Clermont. The area was beat up from the long Meuse-Argonne Offensive. I searched the house and the out buildings. No one was there. The sun was setting on the grey horizon. I had to leave. I wrote a letter to Christina thanking her for nursing me. I folded the paper and wrote "For Christina" on the flap. They must have evacuated, but I knew they would return and rebuild.

I arrived at the hallowed and hollowed out city of Verdun by late evening. The city was a shell of its former grandeur. This hellhole was the site of the bloodiest battle in the history of mankind. It lasted almost all of 1916. Four out of every five French soldiers either died or were wounded during the slaughter. The Germans suffered beyond their calculations. The next morning, I hitched a ride on a *camion* to my destination. By early evening, I found my company. Captain Fish greeted me with an uncharacteristic grin.

"Sergeant, that patch suits you. Welcome back, Virgil."

I saluted and replied, "Thank you, Sir. I see we crossed the Rhine."

The captain took off his campaign hat and said, "Our regiment was the first American unit to cross into Germany. An honor only the French awarded to us. We are moving out to Fessenheimn on the French side of the Rhine on Monday. In the meantime, no fraternizing with the townspeople. See the sergeant major for an update."

I found Marshall in a small hotel lobby. I asked him about his health, and if he knew where Wilson was.

He was chewing on a fireplace match and replied, "Good to see you, Sergeant Carpenter. Sorry about your eye. We lost a lot of men over the last two months of the war. I'm on the mend. No one has seen your dog. He probably found a new home. Let me fill you in." After thirty minutes, I retired to my cot, exhausted.

On Sunday, after services, I got mail from Bea and Millie. They were postmarked in September. Millie told me that father was failing and Mr. Hitchcock, my benefactor, had passed on in late August. Bea relayed the thoughts and prayers of her family and my colleagues at the college. I missed her. My reply letter did not mention the injury. Forewarning her by letter would only have served to create a lot of anxiety. On Monday, the battalion moved out to Fessenheim as the captain stated. These towns, untouched by war, were a welcome relief to behold. What a difference a few miles made!

By mid-December, we arrived at Mulhouse, near the Swiss and German border. It was a lovely Alsatian town where two tributaries to the Rhine run through it. I am told that Alfred Dreyfus hailed from Mulhouse. He was the French Jewish artillery officer accused of treason and later exonerated in the famous Dreyfus Affair.

On the 13th, the regiment was decorated by General LeBouc. The proclamation came from General Gourard, the Fourth Army Commander. A French colonel and our battalion commander, Major L'Esperance, gave out decorations. I received my own *Croix-de-Guerre*, a medal the French awarded to individuals or units who displayed acts of heroism during the war. A week later, we marched through Belfort and billeted at Bavilliers. The band played on Christmas. Jazz was in the air. Lieutenant Europe was the only Negro officer left in the regiment. The others had been transferred out. On the last day of the year, we marched about five miles to Morvillars. We reached Le Mans on the 4th of January 1919.

We finally exchanged our French equipment for American at Le Mans. We did not miss our Lebels. After another cold week, we reached our port of departure, Brest. All illusions of our Black status disappeared at Brest. American MPs, our own, were told to take the "piss and vinegar" out of us. It appeared that the High

Command did not want our new-found ideas of freedom to be washed up on post war American shores. We found this to be true very quickly. One of our privates was beaten down by two MPs apparently for being bold enough to interrupt them while asking for directions. Our Major Little, upon hearing of this outrage, dressed down the MPs. We chanted, "Who won the war?" as we marched through Brest.

The regiment was punished. We were delayed in our long-awaited departure for three dismal weeks.

Before we embarked, I found a tidy little shop on a popular cobblestone street. The storekeeper was dressed in black. She did not seem moved nor impressed by the end of fighting. I suspect all emotion was drained from her years ago. She greeted me with deference and a slight smile. I picked out several gifts for Bea, Millie, and a few others. The gift for Bea was an embroidered French shawl made in Arles.

She thanked me for my patronage and said, "Did you sing and dance when the war ended?"

I reflected on this and replied, "I did at first, but I saw all the women in black and stopped."

The middle-aged woman gave me my parcels and responded, "In one generation the graves will go unattended, the young ones will forget. I pray your fight was not in vain."

The last letter I received in France was from Millie. Mother's sister, Florence, or Flo, had died in November, a victim of the influenza. She was only fifty-four, one of many tens of thousands of Americans on both sides of the Atlantic who had died from the worldwide epidemic. Flo was my aunt who never married. She treated Millie, Mary, and me like her own. Another piece of news was that father was now bedridden. His health had been declining for years. Surprisingly, the flu had not taken him.

On February 1, our battalion and the Machine Gun Company finally departed on the S.S. France to New York. I nervously awaited my homecoming. I exposed my wound to the sun and salty air on deck, hoping for improvement. I had second thoughts about not writing to Bea about my facial wound. I did not want to cause her distress, but this decision was now causing me a great deal of despair.

We arrived at the great port on the 12th. Immediately, we boarded trains for Camp Upton on Long Island, for physical exams and demobilization work. On the sixteenth, we returned to New York. A parade was in store for us the next day, a high honor not bestowed on us by the AEF in Paris. Bent but unbroken after one hundred and ninety days at the front, the great Harlem Hellfighters would march up Fifth Avenue and into immortality.

Chapter Ten

Return to Normality

O ur battalion headed to the armory in Harlem on the 16th of February. A banquet was held in our honor. Family and friends were invited to share food and drink. I composed myself near a darkly lit corner on the second floor. Waiting for Bea, I got into a conversation with Alvin McGowan and Sergeant Earl. All of us earned the *Croix de Guerre* and Distinguished Service Cross. Elmer brought back several wounded men at Bellevue Station, where I was sorely tested. Alvin also brought back a dozen wounded southeast of Séchault. We lit cigars and drank hard liquor.

I piped up, "We better enjoy our drinks, 'cause Prohibition may be upon us soon."

They laughed and said, "What, you say?"

I savored another puff and replied, "Let me fill you in, brothers. Congress is taking up the end of liquor sales in these United States. No shit, this could happen."

We changed the subject. Then I spotted my wife. She must have had her hair done by Madame Walker's famous salon. A red dress with white fringe adorned her slim figure. I remained in the shadows as she hurried over to me. My heart beat rapidly. She instinctively hugged and kissed me. Then my "war face" stopped her cold.

"Virgil, what happened to you? I never got a letter from you saying you was wounded," she exclaimed as tears rolled down her cheeks.

My friends had retreated. I came closer to the smoke filled, artificial light.

"I did not want to worry you. It happened when we attacked a village in late September. I feared giving you the details of my injuries."

Bea touched my scarred cheek and asked, "Your eye, when will it heal?"

"This patch hides a bigger scar. Behind it is an artificial eye the French doctors fitted for me. The scaring around it is partially hidden by the patch. I was afraid that you would be repulsed. Are you?" I asked.

She drew closer to me and said, "I like your sergeant's stripes." Then we kissed. We did not care who might be watching.

The next morning, we assembled at Thirty-Fifth Street and marched down near the Metropolitan Life building at Madison Park on Twenty-Third Street. We then marched up Fifth Avenue. Colonel Hayward led the regiment of over two thousand men. A few staff officers and the wounded joined the phalanx of men in touring convertibles. The most notable of our wounded was Henry Johnson. He and Needham Roberts killed or wounded nearly a score of Germans last May while on sentinel duty. Roberts was too wounded to return, but Henry enjoyed the limelight of being a New York hero and national symbol for our race.

Lieutenant Europe's famous band played many war and jazz tunes on our march such as, "Onward Christian Soldiers," "Battle Hymn of the Republic," "Over There," and "On Patrol in No Man's Land." The band marched with its tubas, trombones, French horns, clarinets, drums, and other pieces led by Europe, Assistant Conductor, Eugene Mikell, and drum major and vocalist, Noble Sissle. Europe was the only Negro officer marching with us today. The sea of humanity crowded into many rows deep along the route. New Yorkers hung from rooftops, windows, fire escapes, and shopfronts. American flags adorned the buildings in a sea of red, white, and blue flying in the sunny, brisk February breeze. I could see Gold Star armbands on some spectators in the immense crowd, and white badges and signs labeled Welcome, Fighting Fifteenth dotted the parade route. We marched with our U.S. Regimental and Black Rattler flags.

The review stand, located on Sixtieth Street and Fifth Avenue, included dignitaries like Governor Al Smith, former Governor Charles Whitman, Mayor John Hylan, William R. Hearst, John Wanamaker, Emmett Scott, the Negro Affairs Assistant to the Secretary of War, generals and admirals. Many Negro leaders attended like Eugene DuBois and Madame Walker, who drew much fanfare. The band struck up, *Marche du Regiment de Sambre et Meuse* as we passed the dignitaries. It was the most popular French parade theme since the time of Napoleon. We reached 110th Street and marched to Lenox Avenue, then continued into Harlem, our home. The band played "Here Comes My Daddy Now." The crowd went crazy. Muffled horns drew out the best jazz melody.

As I marched with my company, flashbacks invaded my consciousness: Christina, Séchault, Wilson, Kadid, Marshall, Fish, and Pippin formed a mosaic of people, places and things that memories are made from. We continued across 145th Street, the heart of Harlem, then down to Lexington Avenue to the Seventy-First Street Regimental Armory, where the famous Delmonico Restaurant catered a lunch in our honor. The colonel toasted us and gave remarks of commendation to our great regiment. We reached our termination point of Thirty-Third Street and Lexington via subway. By the 19th the month, we were mustered out of the service of Uncle Sam.

It did not take me long to unpack. I hung up my uniform, put my medals in a glass case, and I retrieved two diaries that was hidden in my great coat. The civilian clothes I put on made me more aware of my wound. The scars seemed more out of place without a uniform to validate them. Before Bea greeted me, the smell of her chicken cooking on the iron stove permeated into the hallway. She was wearing a white pinafore dress, a navy-blue blouse and white headband as I entered our humble apartment.

I took off my eye patch and asked. "Can you still love me?"

Wiping her hands in her apron, she said nothing. A long kiss was my answer. After dinner, she did cry in the bathroom. I let her alone as I drank Scotch and water.

A few nights later, my nightmares awakened my terrified wife. Sweat permeated my nightshirt, and my breathing was very rapid. Bea tried to calm me. She asked in a whisper, "What is it, Virgil?"

I laid back down as Bea went to get a cold, wet hand towel. I lit a cigarette and said, "What I saw, smelt, felt, knew — chokes me. I have dreams of soldiers drowning in a black sea. I am sitting high on a leafless tree not being able to save them."

I did not want to talk about it any longer. We lay in bed, in each other's arms, the cigarette smoke lingering up in the air above us, kissing the ceiling.

By early March, I went to see the Assistant Dean of English at CCNY. His office was a mess, with books and papers scattered all about. He was unfamiliar to me. My file was on his cluttered desk. A portly man of middle age, he wore a three-piece navy-blue suit with a pocket watch in prominent view on his vest, and sported a wedding ring on a chubby finger.

He was pleasant but made no eye contact while he asked, "Virgil, I see that your tenure here has been a credit to this institution and the students you served. Tell me, what are your plans?"

I looked at him, giving him full view of my abnormal profile and replied, "Dean, I would like to resume my duties here, to continue as I had before I left for war. That is what was understood when I left for France."

He fiddled with his pocket watch, then stood up and stated, "I am unaware of our pledge to you. We have had a few other veterans return, although none as injured as you. Can you tell me that these young men and women who have not been touched by war will see you in an undistracted light?"

I got up to meet him eye to eye and said, "I appreciate your bluntness. I cannot answer your concern with confidence, but these young men and women have seen wounded men on the streets and in their communities. Some have been to funerals of a brother, father, uncle, or teacher. They need to know 'Over There' is 'Over Here' now. They need to know why tens of thousands of American boys died or were wounded physically or mentally."

The dean walked around his desk, looked out his window, and demurred. "Mr. Carpenter, you made a good argument. Maybe you should have been a lawyer. Anyway, you can begin next semester. For now, you can fill in at English and literature lectures. The provost would also like you to write an article about French attitudes toward your regiment, you and the soldiers." I thanked him and left, pondering about his concerns.

During the spring, I caught up with old friends and family. I tried not to notice the stares, the way strangers turned their eyes from me on the streets, in the subway, and in public places. What hurt the most was the same thing occurred with some people I had known before the war. The pity, the inability to relate got under my skin. Bea could tell it affected my mood, my outlook. We had arguments and, worse, long periods of silence. The strain of peace was a hard adjustment for both of us. Filling in for professors turned out to be a less than rewarding experience. The students' first impression of me was, I believe, biased by my visible wound. They did not have a full semester to get accustomed to the "intellectual" me. Maybe the following term would be better, when I would have my own classes, and a return to some kind of normalcy.

Our President Wilson was in Paris negotiating with the Allied powers and other interested parties for a durable peace. He was pushing France, England, and Italy toward a League of Nations and reconciliation in order to prevent another debacle. It appeared that the Allied powers, who had suffered much more than America, wanted their "pound of flesh." For all his faults, Wilson wanted to make sure that the "boys did not die in vain". The appeal from Lincoln a half-century ago which was stipulated in his Gettysburg Address, still rang loudly to a new generation of Americans. I think Wilson had his work cut out for him, as the victorious Prime Ministers Clemenceau, Lloyd George, and Orlando were ganging up on the idealistic Wilson. Even at home, the Congress was given a Republican majority after the mid-term elections of 1918, making any peace treaty vulnerable to a hostile Senate.

The one local tragedy for our Hellfighters came in May. Our hero, the charismatic band leader, Lieutenant James R. Europe, was mortally wounded by one of his deranged band members at Boston's Mechanics Hall. His funeral was attended by many military and civic dignitaries. Without him, one could argue that the regiment would not have been fully formed. It was a very tough and difficult loss for the regiment's veterans, his followers, and to the world of music.

Spring turned to summer. Tensions were building across the country between the races. The industrialization of America and the war had turned the country into a world power. This fact and the sinister Jim Crow laws led to a migration of Negroes north. Lynchings were also on the rise as Whites feared the increased militancy of their dark-skinned neighbors. It caused friction in many northern cities like Chicago, St. Louis, and Omaha that were changing demographically. There was also resentment amongst some Whites as Negroes took their jobs for lower pay, a prospect many employers favored, however.

New York City had gone through its race bloodletting during the Conscription race riots of 1863. By and large, the newly arrived Irish-Americans rioted against the military draft laws during the Civil War. Authorities and Negroes bore the brunt of their anger. Many scores of Negroes in the city were killed. It took the Sixth Corps of the Army of the Potomac, about 15,000 soldiers, to quell the riots and establish order. The summer of 1919 became known as "Red Summer." Race riots broke out in more than a score of cities across America, and even in Washington, DC. President Wilson said very little about this calamity happening under his own nose, nor did he admonish the lynchings. Chicago was the worst. A riot started in late July when a Black man swam too close to the White section of a beach. He was murdered. Fists, knives, and guns were used all along the border of the Southside. The recently returning Negro veterans did not back down. Like in East St. Louis, over a decade ago, lives and property were destroyed. The National Guard was called in to support the overwhelmed local authorities. *The New York Times* was one of the many newspapers that displayed their establishment bias in print. Our Negro leaders decried the riots as a repudiation and insult to the sacrifices made by the Negro Americans during the Great War. Even Eugene DuBois lambasted the administration in Washington in his *Crisis* Magazine. A foul mood crept into the people of Harlem.

I was jolted back to a more personal reality when Millie sent me a telegram notifying me that our father died. It was not unexpected. Regardless of the public discord, Bea and I headed for Fredericksburg. The early August heat and humidity made the train ride more intolerable than usual. I had instructed Bea about the social differences south of the Mason-Dixon line. She was painfully aware of this, as we moved to the rear of the Richmond bound train in Baltimore. Bea was very supportive, and our bickering had subsided. The long journey was uneventful, with the exception of inquisitive stares by adults and open-mouthed gazes by children. This was mostly generated by my wound and eye patch.

We arrived at the family farm the following morning. The main house cried out for a new coat of paint. Other than that, my return was like a visit to an old friend. As my family poured out onto the porch to greet us, I was now glad that Bea wrote to Millie about my war injuries in some detail. Millie ran to me, unfazed by my change in appearance. She hugged me tenderly with her lips pressed against my cheek. The hugging, tears, and kissing continued. I saw Millie's daughter, seven-year-old Paulette, hesitate on the veranda. She ran back into the house. I could only think of one reason.

Millie and Bea, dressed in black, looked like sisters. The only differences were Millie's hair was longer and greyer, while Bea had brighter eyes, more make-up, and a wide brimmed black hat with a navy bow. We sat down to a late breakfast of flapjacks, eggs, bacon, and corn muffins. My family had only seen Bea once, at our marriage. We talked about topics ranging from Madame C.J. Walker, to the prospect of Prohibition, the Spanish Flu, to the recent riots. Changing women's fashion also crept into the conversation. No one brought up France. Paulette did ask if my face hurt. The smiles were muted as I said, "No, sometimes it hurts, inside."

Paulette, as children often do, pressed the issue, "What do you mean, Uncle Virgil?"

Her mother admonished her in a delicate way, but I responded, "Sometimes, Paulette, grownups fear people that do not look like them. They also fear what to say to someone like me, and some people just have hatred in their hearts."

She ran over to me, crying. As she hugged me, she whispered, "I ran from you. Am I evil?"

"No, no, you were just scared. Think of each scar as a child I saved." This seemed to calm her down. "This a perfect time to give you a surprise," I exclaimed.

I opened up my carpet bag and took out a doll. It was one of the gifts I bought in Brest. The doll was a French peasant girl. Paulette lit up and hugged me. I distributed the other gifts, with millinery for Millie and Mother.

Dad was laid out in the parlor the next two afternoons and evenings. Many friends, family, and customers from the Old Shiloh Church and much of Fredericksburg filed in. Even some Whites came, including Mrs. Hitchcock and Adeline. Adeline was a young woman now. She did not seem unhinged by my wound. She told me that she had volunteered at a local military hospital. Needless to say, Adeline saw men in worse shape than I.

It was raining the morning we made our way to church. Just before I gave my eulogy, the August sun made a grand entrance. I walked up to the parish podium and began to speak, "Those of us who knew Charles Carpenter, really knew him, knew he was a flawed man; a man drawn to temptation and sin. You might ask if this is a way for a son to begin a eulogy of his father. A eulogy usually embellishes on the good deeds and graces of the recently departed. We are urged to implore heaven to see the best in him or her. We are all sinners, those old enough to know right from wrong. Not the grandeur of a church, nor the inspiration of a choir, nor the clergy, can drive this reality from mortals. I believe it is my duty as a son to tell you all that my father, on balance, was a good man — better than most. By the grace and courage of his mother, Ruth, they escaped the wrath of slavery when the Grand Army of the Potomac crossed the Rappahannock in a futile attempt to defeat Lee's Army. Ruth and her son built a life. My father built a prosperous business. His struggles, and the untimely death of his daughter, Mary, led him to cope in ways we may call sinful. For those of you who claim perfection, you may cast a stone, but for the rest, we are better off to have known him. God grant him everlasting peace."

The sun hung high overhead. We buried him next to Mary, in the church yard cemetery, on the hill near Caroline Street, overlooking the river. We returned to the farm. Millie and Bea made lemonade and iced tea, as the family assembled on the back porch. It was a calm, hot afternoon. You could smell the corn and pumpkins, if you concentrated long enough. Robert, Millie's husband, asked me about France. I did not say much, other than I was glad about not fighting "cooties" in the mud any longer, having to endure the noise, and the "slumgullion," French beef stew.

The family slipped back into the house. I changed clothing, took a sickle from the barn, and walked to the cornfield. After about a hundred paces into the ripened corn, I cut down a space, large enough to lie down. As I had done many times before, I closed my eyes. All I could hear was the sound of crickets. I would fish on the Rappahannock with Millie on a day like today. We would catch white perch and catfish. We put them in a basket lined with sawdust. Mother cooked our catch for dinner. Apple or pumpkin pie would top off the feast. I lost track of time for a while, caught in my reverie. Then I heard Bea calling out for me from the porch. I gave Millie three dollars. She knew what it was for. We laughed.

September, and a new school year, came. President Wilson was barnstorming the country in his special train, in order to elicit support for the Paris Peace Treaty. Senator Lodge from Massachusetts, and many of his Republican colleagues, held sway on its approval. In fact, some senators were following the President, making speeches denouncing the treaty. I read that Wilson abruptly went back to Washington after his speech in Pueblo, Colorado.

One day in November, one of my freshman students was making fun of my eye patch while he thought I was not looking. I called him out. We got into a shoving match. I knocked him down. The next day, I was called for by the provost. His office was intimidating. I sat in front of him, separated by his immense desk. He rightfully admonished me, and warned me of not repeating that kind of behavior. My insecurity grew with every passing stare. My patience was frayed.

Just before Christmas, I happened to be in the Hell's Kitchen section of Manhattan with Bea. We decided, on a whim, to have our fortunes told. We walked up to the second floor of a five-story brownstone on the corner of Ninth Avenue. A cigar store was on the first floor. The smell permeated the upper levels. We were greeted by a young woman with a pronounced accent. I asked, "Are you from Central Europe?"

She held my hand for inspection and, replied, "I came here from Hungary, after the war broke out. I was lucky. I have family here. I see you did not escape the war unharmed. Please sit. I am Marta."

The raven-haired woman, with brown eyes and large, dangling earrings, closed the drapes as Bea sat in the outer room. This refugee from Hungary examined my hands, then she dealt two tarot cards. She sat back and lit a corn pipe. The smoke lingered around a stained-glass lamp.

She said with certainty, "You will live for a long time. Your life will be complex and filled with both joy and tragedy. The war you have been part of will not be your last." She turned up another card and continued, "You will journey to distant lands."

I begged her for more details, but she told me all she was prepared to tell me. I departed. All I could think of was the old woman, back in France, who predicted that I would live through the war and see another one. A shiver went through me like an icy wind. Bea was next. She came out after ten minutes. She humored me, but I could tell that the fortuneteller had disturbed my wife. I let it go.

The following summer of 1920, Bea informed me that she was in a "family way." She was due in early spring. We were very happy. We decided to move into a larger apartment. It was located further from my work, but it had the extra bedroom. Bea and her mother made nursery plans. I was still having nightmares, even though my doctor had given me sedatives to take. Bea found it increasingly difficult to manage or comfort me.

The summer wore on. Women won the right to vote. Women's suffrage had won out through their sacrifices during the war, and their relentless marches in support of their cause. The Republicans won the White House in 1920. Warren G. Harding was elected our twenty-ninth President. The Wilsonian Era had ended. He was a broken man, as broken as a man with shell shock, like another victim of the war. The treaty he urged the Senate to ratify did not materialize. He had to wonder if his boys died in vain.

A few days after Harding was sworn in, Bea went into labor. I was lecturing when I got a phone call urging me to go to Presbyterian Hospital uptown. Bea was taken there in an ambulance. It was not a good sign; the labor came five weeks early. I ask myself now if it matters how she died. To the coroner it did. Internal bleeding and kidney failure were the official causes. All I can recall is a flurry of nurses and young doctors trying to stop the hemorrhaging. For a while, Bea appeared to be on the mend. I went to get a coffee for thirty minutes, but when I returned, a doctor, stained with her blood, pronounced her gone. I was escorted out. It took three order-lies to pry me from her bed. No final words or goodbyes. An orderly and an aide came. The bed would have clean white sheets, and the walls and floor would be sanitized. And the light had gone out in my life.

My son, our son, died a day later. The umbilical cord was wrapped around his tiny neck, so said the doctor. He could not recover. I named him Charles Frederick Carpenter. Bea's family took care of the funeral details. I was in a stupor and not very helpful.

The eyes of the dead appear different than sleeping eyes. They are transfixed on another world. My anger clouded any judgment. Millie had come up from Virginia to console me. The funeral was presid-ed over by the Reverend Adam Clayton Powell of the Abyssinian Baptist Church, the one we were married in four years ago. The pews were filled with family, friends, colleagues, neighbors, and Hellfighter veterans.

President Harding coined the phrase, a "return to normalcy," indicating that after the Great War, America was ready to move on. I did not embrace this. My personal anger and sorrow were magni-fied by the events around me. My race had not enjoyed the fruits of wartime sacrifice as we had been led to believe. Lynching was on the rise. The Ku Klux Klan, or KKK, was spreading north and west. Negroes turned inward in New York City, where the era of hot jazz, fast dance, and illegal booze substituted for social and political progress. I found myself frequenting a speakeasy on Lenox Avenue. I became friends with cheap whiskey so much so, that my conduct at the school became intolerable. The provost dismissed me but gave me a good recommendation. He pitied me. He advised me to seek help, spiritual help.

I did not want to be driven to drink like my father. So, on the advice of the Hungarian fortuneteller, whom I visited on several occasions, I went to see an acupuncturist in Chinatown. Mott Street was a world away from Harlem. Ducks and pigs hung from shop windows, and street vendors with exotic, tourist type notions hawked their wares in broken English. The street was very crowded. After attending several sessions, and taking herbal concoctions every day, I returned to some semblance of normalcy.

That fall I landed a teaching job at Hunter College, several subway stops south from my apartment. One of my colleagues, an officer with the 370th Regiment during the war, suggested that I attend a séance. I asked why. Clarence Peyton, Professor Peyton, a Cornell graduate, rolled a cigarette and replied, "Brother, you can talk to the spirits, even if they don't return the favor. Your inner scars may fade. Give it a go. I know a woman who holds them at her apartment on Houston Street near the bridge. She lost a son in the Argonne and a daughter to the Spanish Flu. She is the best. Here is her card."

A week later, I took the underground to her place. I had a smoke first, then went inside the three-story walkup. I was greeted by a child of maybe eight, who said, "Welcome. Please take off your hat, coat and shoes."

She led me into another room. It was lit only with a small beveled glass lamp and many candles. The smell of incense enveloped the small room. Five souls sat around a large mahogany table. The woman facing me with an ornamental blue headband said, "Welcome, we will start now."

At the center of the table were articles of clothing or mementos of lost loved ones. I brought the scarf from France that I had given Bea. Shortly after midnight, my turn came. The medium wore the scarf as we held hands. After several incantations, two candles blew out. The medium told me that two spirits had entered, two female spirits. I asked if they were my wife and sister.

With her eyes remaining closed, the grey-haired woman said, "They rest together in time, not place. They are with you, like the wind."

The ordeal consoled me. Was it real? Maybe, maybe not, but a peace came over me like a warm rain in the middle of a cornfield in August.

Chapter Eleven

Going Home

The late spring morning started off unseasonably cool and dreary as the iron horse lumbered out of Pennsylvania Station. The New York Central train proceeded south toward Central Jersey. The sun made its appearance in a bold way, piercing my shade less window, causing me to use my copy of the *New York World* as a shield. I sat in the last car, toward the rear. We were headed south of the Mason-Dixon line. I was traveling to Fredericksburg to see my kin. It had been three years since I made the trip in the summer of 1919. We had laid my father to rest at the age of sixty-three, buried at the Old Shiloh Baptist Church for coloreds, just north of Caroline Street, near the Rappahannock River. He had spent many hours there, fishin' and reminiscing with his buddies. He kept company there with his beloved daughter, Mary.

It had been a year now since my wife and child died. My grieving was tempered by teaching at Hunter College in New York City. Now that the school year was over, I had no reason to delay my trip. Mother was in poor health due, in part, to her battle with typhoid soon after father passed. Emily, her younger sister, died in 1918 from the Spanish Flu epidemic, adding to her grief. She had been like a mother to Emily. At least for now, my sister, Millie, and her husband were taking care of her as best they could. Paulette, their rambunctious daughter, gave Mom cause to live.

The "Central" pulled into DC's Union Station at about 1:00 p.m., nearly on time. I took a reprieve to answer nature's call and get some refreshment. It was a beautiful afternoon; dogwoods and Japanese Cherry trees in full bloom; their fragrant smell penetrated the Pullman car. While returning to my seat, I came upon two new passengers. A Negro girl, about six or seven years of age, dressed in a cream-colored taffeta dress with pony tails down to her waist, gave me a nervous stare. She was accompanied by her mother or guardian, a light skinned Negro and, about thirtyish. She was well dressed with a flower adorning her straw hat.

The lady settled in. She turned to me and said, "I am sorry, but it is very crowded in our section. I hope you do not mind."

"No, no, this is quite fine with me. I could use your company," I responded politely.

I began to feel self-conscious about my war wound and eye patch, hoping the girl would not ask her escort or me about it.

"Where are you off to?" I inquired, without making eye contact.

"We are going to Richmond to see family. Pardon me, I am Rachel and this is Alice, my daughter."

"Virgil Carpenter, ma'am. I'm traveling from New York to Fredericksburg to see my kin. It has been three long years since I have seen them," I stated, feeling more confident now.

She tried not to stare, but I could tell she was struggling not to look. Rachel responded, "Alice and I live in Washington. My husband works for the Treasury Department. He was not able to join us."

Some silence passed between us. With some reluctance, I admitted that I was a widower and teach at Hunter College.

"I am sorry for your loss," she replied sympathetically. "There is nothing like a caring family."

The countryside passed us by as we gazed out the window. We talked about the future and tenderly left the past unspoken. I talked to Alice about school, her friends and her aspirations, young as she was. Rachel asked if I was in the war as we approached my station.

"Yes, I was with the 369th Infantry Regiment, commonly known as the Harlem Hellfighters," I said with pride.

"I've heard of them and their band. The best in the whole army, I hear," she held her head high and smiled. "You must have seen some terrible things in France." Then she added, "Sorry, I should not pry."

I looked out the window for a few nervous seconds then replied, "Well, we fought without retreating for about six solid months straight; the longest of any American regiment. I am damn proud of that, but we fought for us, our unit, and each other. That is how we survived. The sights were numbing, but the mud, lice, rats, the decay of flesh and the shelling, one never grew accustomed to it. If you were not there, words cannot describe the hell. No fiction of hell or horror stories can equal what we went through. If I go to hell in the afterlife, it will not be my first time. Sorry to burden you with my answer, Rachel. We wanted to show the racists in the army and those at home, that the Negro race is not a second-class race. All we wanted was a fair chance to prove ourselves. I hope our combat legacy will make your daughter's life brighter in this land of democracy."

We made our way toward Fredericksburg. I stared out my window with a nostalgic fondness at the fields rich with stalks of corn and other local produce. The shanties dotting the rural landscape were sporting more and more tin lizzies. Autos and their flesh and blood rivals seemed to be coexisting for now. But the future favors the mechanical.

We entered the station as I gathered my gifts. Rachel, Alice, and I bade each other a good journey and much happiness in the future. Rachel took my hand and told me in a peaceful tone, "We honor your sacrifice and courage, but your dream may not come in our lifetimes. Alice, I pray, may be the beneficiary of your sacrifice."

I was not inhibited by my deformity now and replied, "Doing good is not easy. It is a difficult thing, but we have no choice."

The trip would have been worthwhile if only to have met them. I turned and walked to the bus station for a short ride to my destination.

After about a thirty-minute walk from my stop, I came upon my childhood refuge. The farm house was in the progress of being painted eggshell white. The smell of the new coat lingered in the sultry afternoon breeze. Pumpkins, corn, tomatoes, and cucumbers were growing in the same places I remembered as a boy. Paulette, anticipating my arrival, was sitting on the front porch rocker. As I swung open the yet to be painted gate, she jumped up and ran over to me.

"Uncle Virgil, Uncle Virgil," she hollered as she sprang into my gift laden arms.

"My sweet Paulette, look at you, how you've grown! You have become a young lady," I said admiringly. "You are in the fifth grade," I declared.

"Uncle, I will be in the sixth grade come August," she stated with great emphasis on "sixth."

"You must tell me all about your studies and classmates," I added. "I can hardly wait, but let us find Mama and Granny."

"What is in those packages?" she asked, as she led me to the house.

"Most are gifts for the family and most of all, for YOU!" I said with a grin.

We came upon Thomas, the farm's caretaker. He had been with us for nearly ten years. He was in his fifties now, but as sturdy as steel, with balding grey hair. Thomas was outfitted with his trademark blue overalls and white undershirt. He was slow of mind, but a kind and hard-working soul. He was on the ladder, painting the side porch ceiling, when we approached.

Paulette blurted out, "Thomas look, look, my Uncle Virgil has just arrived from New York."

"Well bless my eyes, you look as young and snappy as you did last I seen ya'," Thomas cried out as he descended the ladder like a school boy. I held out my hand, but he instantly hugged me and looked up and down with admiration.

"I will take you all to Millie and Mom. Robert is gone to town to pick up some goods. He'll be back rightfully soon," stated Thomas, as we headed to the rear of the house.

Robert, Millie's husband, loved to take the work horses and wagon to town. He found them more reliable than the Ford trucks that were gaining in popularity. Paulette held on to her wrapped gift in one hand and held my arm with the other as we made our way to the back porch. Millie and Mom were rocking in their chairs, nursing some homemade lemonade.

Paulette ran ahead and proclaimed, "Uncle Virgil is here, Uncle Virgil is here!"

We hugged and kissed for a while as the lemonade grew warmer and warmer. As I brushed away my teary cheeks, Millie said, "Virgil, you must be weary. Let me fetch you some cold lemonade and tea cakes. Sit down in the shade, between us."

Millie's premature greying hair, newly bobbed as was the current trend, did not take away from her placid loveliness. She was tall and slim, wearing an off-white cotton dress with half-length sleeves. Thomas bade me goodbye for the moment as he rushed off to finish painting before dark.

Millie returned with refreshments, including her famous peach pie. Anyone could tell that she was proud of her domestic abilities.

"Momma, can I open the gift Uncle Virgil gave me, please?", asked Paulette.

"Well, if your uncle doesn't mind and that you'll keep hushed while we talk, then commence to open it up," proclaimed Millie.

Paulette ravaged the wrapping paper and string as quickly as I took a sip of my lemonade. Her eyes lit up as she exclaimed. "Look, look, a grown-up doll! Is she a city doll, from New York? I have never seen such fancy clothes!"

"I hope you will get many years of happiness with her," I said with pride. "What will you name her?"

"I think I will call her Mary, after your sister, yes, Mary will be her name," she whispered as she stroked her auburn hair.

My mother's eyes welled up as she heard her name. Mary had been only sixteen when she passed from consumption, and the memory seemed always to be fresh. Mary's kind personality had always broken through the ill will and ignorance of our times. Mother never got over her loss, while Dad was more stoic, as he immersed himself in the commerce of the farm and corn whiskey.

Now that Paulette was preoccupied with her doll, I told Millie and Mom that I would present their gifts when Robert returned. We talked about the good times growing up, embarrassing moments and events we were none too proud of, but we were young and fool-ish then. We reminisced about our beloved Bella, a mixed breed dog, who looked after us. She lived for nearly fifteen years. We planted an apple tree over her grave to commemorate her life. We amused each other with exaggerations of our fishing prowess on the river, and stories we brought up about our horse rides from town to Tappah-annock to get the best ice cream in all Virginia! I loved strawberry while Millie craved chocolate and Mary relished peach. We talked until three glasses of lemonade were consumed. Momma labored, even in the evening shade, so we helped her into bed for a nap. Little did I know, I would never see her again after that visit.

Millie was in the kitchen now, chopping veggies and, without any hesitation, she asked, "How are you getting along? You have been in my prayers more than ever since Beatrice's passing."

I looked down and replied, "She was my rock, especially when I returned from France; scars and all. It is not easy being a disfigured Negro in New York. Their brand of racism is subtler than down South, but it's there."

Millie was looking out to the corn fields as dusk's orange light kissed the tall, maturing stalks.

After a long pause, she turned to me and said, "We have it better than most coloreds. We get along, but at times it hurts to know that you are just as good as most and better than some White folk. How can you prove that here?"

"Someday things will change, but that will take decades and much sacrifice," I explained in a not too resolute tone.

"Do you plan on more children?" I blurted out.

"Virgil, aren't you to the point!" replied Millie as she savored her last drops of lemonade. "We tried, but no luck so far. I would like a brother or sister for Paulette; she is growing like a weed. For now, her family, friends, both real and imaginary, keep her engaged." She shot me a smile, then said, "Virgil, you get refreshed and rest a spell while I continue to fix dinner. That's an order! Paulette will help me. Robert will be home shortly. We're fixin' to have quite a spread!"

I retired as ordered and proceeded to take a well-deserved bath. After a long and relaxing soak, I sat upon the narrow, but comfortable bed. I daydreamed about my life with Bea and what, if anything, I could have done to save her life. I reflected on fond memories and the smell of sunflowers and apple trees dotting the farm until I heard a knock on the door.

"Dinner is ready. I hope you are hungry," remarked Paulette in a playful voice.

"I'll be along in a jiffy," I said with a yawn; then I reached for a comb and my shoes. I brought the gifts for Mom and Millie with me.

Momma, at the head of the table, declared, "Son, sit by me. We can talk about your big city or whatever suits your fancy."

Robert spoke up, "Virgil, why don't you say grace. It would please us."

I was surprised and not prepared, but I did not want to disappoint. As I bowed my head, I paused to conjure up what our chaplain would say during the war, "Lord bless this bounty of food and the company privileged to enjoy it.

It nourishes both body and soul. Bless us and our dearly departed whom are not forgotten. May they share in your heavenly kingdom forever, Amen."

Paulette quickly added an "Amen" followed by the others.

We savored the biscuits and chicken that were as good as I had ever remembered, along with mashed potatoes with gravy, and garden vegetables.

After an hour or so of reminiscing and eating, I said to Millie, "You and Paulette deserve much praise. I am overtaken by this fabulous meal. Now I know better than to surrender, 'cause I believe your famous apple pie is close behind. Before we partake in dessert, let me offer a short reprieve and give you, Robert, and Mom, my gifts."

While Millie reached to take the box, she remarked that my presence was gift enough. She gently unwrapped the gift and discovered a music box that played her favorite waltz.

"Oh, Virgil, this must have cost you a pretty penny! You're so kind. I will treasure it. Robert, isn't it just beautiful?" she inquired with joy.

He leaned over to her and whispered, "If you love it, so do I."

While Millie was still admiring the music box, I gave Mom her gift. She kissed me and said, "Son, you do me proud."

She opened the box to find a hat, a "Sunday" hat imported from Paris. "Try it on," I prompted.

The others joined in, chanting "Wear the hat!"

"You win, son. If it fits as beautifully as it looks, I will be the talk of the congregation." She adorned her head without the aid of a mirror. Everyone applauded their approval. Mom started to cry. Low and behold, the apple pie made its appearance just in time. The next few days were filled up being Paulette's playmate, helping

Thomas with chores, and talking to Millie and Mom. I admit that I returned often to the exact location I used to go to find refuge as a child, the cornfield. I preferred going at dusk. I cut down enough stalks so I could lay down and daydream while the red-orange sun and lofty clouds passed over me. This was my "castle." My reverie was that of a boy, before the world, my world, went mad. When I returned to the farmhouse, I gave Millie five dollars. She knew what it was for.

After dinner, I stood on the back porch, smoking a corn pipe and nursing more cold lemonade. I turned around. Mom approached, walking with the aid of her mahogany cane.

"Son, tell me you are goin' to be okay. I pray every day for you. You have had a very rough time the last few years," she lamented, then she put her arm on my shoulder.

I put the pipe down on the porch rail then said, "I think of my burden every time I look in the mirror or see a mother strolling her child. When I pass a cemetery and see the flag and fresh flowers adorning the grave stones of the dearly departed, I feel guilty being alive," I remarked. I took a long drag on the pipe.

The smoke lingered on this calm night. Mother stood up straight, looked at me in the eye and replied, "Great things are ahead for you. You will see. Light will shine through the darkness. You are meant to make your mark on this world, son."

I held her hand with both of my own and whispered, "You have faith for both of us. Let's see what is in store for me. I am optimistic because hell cannot be any worse that what I experienced in war."

On Sunday, we went to church in the wagon. Some autos and some horses occupied the church lot. It seemed like a strange but peaceful coexistence. As I entered, I scanned familiar faces and many new ones. All seemed to stare at me as I made my way to the pew. Were they looking at the returning son, the stranger, or a wounded vet?

As the choir finished Psalm 123, Pastor Easterly lifted his arms and exclaimed, "Congregation, we are blessed and honored to have with us today a war hero and respected professor from New York, Virgil Carpenter."

Men, women, and children stood up, clapped, and nodded their approval. I stood motionless for a few long moments then said, "Thank you. You are too kind. I looked forward to being here with you all."

The pastor's sermon spoke to the community's duty to further their education, commerce and brotherhood in order to make gains for our race. The fruits of the Civil War were very slow to ripen.

The next day, it was finally time for me to depart. I felt the burden of guilt leaving as my mother looked so frail. We embraced for a long time while I promised to return the following year. After a short walk to the main road, I waited for the station bus to arrive. I waited twenty minutes after it was due; then I decided to hitch a ride to the station, or close to it. I did not get any takers or fifteen minutes, then a small truck pulled over.

"Hey Mac, where are you goin'?" asked the young, White female driver. She was accompanied by a canine passenger in the front seat, a mutt from what I could see.

"I'm headed to the Fredericksburg train depot; a 2:10 p.m. train to catch," I stated, as I hurried up to the truck with my valise.

I approached her. I could tell that she was dressed conservatively for work, but her outfit did not disguise her feminine appeal. She had wavy blond hair, an alabaster complexion, and a slim figure. I got in. Her dog started to lick me.

"Oh, don't you mind Pastor, he friends up to every soul, every human that is. I'm Maggie," she stated as she engaged the clutch and got underway.

"I am obliged to you, miss. I take it that you are fixin' to go my way?" I asked hopefully.

"Richmond is my destination, got some harvester parts to pick up, but I am going past your station," responded Maggie. She engaged the second gear while starting up a conversation.

"I hope you don't mind me asking, but why is your dog named Pastor?"

She giggled and replied, "Well, I named him Pastor so people could think I'm always seeing the pastor. Where are you from? You don't have a local voice."

"Pardon me, I'm Virgil. I grew up in these parts but migrated to New York before the war. I came here to visit family." While she shifted gears again, she asked, "Did you go to France? You got wounded there, right? I'd love to visit France someday."

I looked out the open window and responded, "Yes, I volunteered in 1917 with the 369th Infantry Regiment from New York. We were known as the Harlem Hellfighters. We served with the French Army because the High Command would not let us fight alongside of the White American soldiers. We were honored by the French to be the first unit to cross the Rhine River into Germany. Do you think I saw action because of my scars?"

Maggie unloaded a Lucky Strike from a new pack on the dashboard, lit it and blew out a nice smoke ring. She cleared her throat and said, "Yes, I admit as much. Do you want a smoke?"

"Don't mind if I do," I declared. I took a drag. It relaxed me.

Suddenly, the truck blew a tire and veered to the right. Maggie was able to stop off the roadside without further damage, although Pastor was barking up a storm. She asked if I wanted to hitch another ride, but I said that I would help her with the fixin'. As I pulled the damaged tire off the truck, another vehicle approached. It was a coupe, a Chevrolet, with two men — White men. I was a bit uneasy about this. Both men exited their auto. The driver and his pal looked about my age, casually dressed, with straw hats.

The driver approached Maggie, took off his hat, fanned himself and asked, "Miss, need some help, I see. We have time."

Maggie fixed her blond locks with a few pins and retorted, "No thanks gents, we have it under control."

The driver wiped his brow, looked in my direction and said, "Hey boy, I think we can take over. Four hands are better than two, especially nigga' hands."

He was trying to impress Maggie, but she scolded him saying, "Don't you talk that way, you backwater trash talker. He fought in the war; got himself wounded too."

"Well pardon me, but, a war nigga' is still a nigga' down here. Don't you know they feel they are as good as you and me, now?" he said.

I was still holding the tire iron as I straightened up as both men moved closer to me.

"I'm no nigger. I am one educated son of a bitch who fought for

OUR country in France. I faced tougher bastards than you will ever become," I shouted, gripping the iron tighter.

I did not give a god-damn now. I had not much to lose, but I was not going to lose my dignity. Both thugs charged at me and, without hesitation or thought, I boxed the passenger 'till he was bloody, and then I hit the driver with the tire iron. He fell back and hit the truck. Maggie ran over, but it was too late for her to stop the fray. She kneeled over the driver, checked his pulse, then turned to me and said, "He's dead!"

I checked the passenger; he was alive, but unconscious.

"What do we do now?" asked Maggie, as she looked for oncoming vehicles.

"I do not want to get you involved. I am a Black man who just killed a White man in the South. I am not staying to find out my fate."

"This was self-defense, damn it. If you want out, I will get you to the station. You can tie up the driver and disable his Chevy. I will say you forced me to drive you," she blurted out in an unnaturally calm tone, as she lit up another Lucky Strike.

"I have killed men before, but all with the sanction of the army. I will do what you think best, but I will not surrender myself. I will not be lynched."

She tossed the butt aside and said, "Well, let's not waste time!"

Maggie engaged the clutch with abandon. She went through all four gears in seconds. We were cruising doing sixty down a dusty, dirt road. My heart was racing much, much faster. I reached for another cigarette. I realized that I was in the middle of a shit storm.

Chapter Twelve

Alias

I decided to not stretch my luck and hid in the back of her truck. It took forty-five daunting minutes to get to the Main Street Station. I tied Maggie up in the cargo area as she requested. She wistfully bade me farewell and good luck. An unusual woman she was, a free spirit. Her dog barked at me repeatedly. I proceeded to the ornate, turn of the century style station.

I bought a ticket on the FFV, Fast Flying Virginian, to the nation's capital. My eye patch profile was pressed against the window as I nervously read the Richmond paper. I was hoping for a two-to three-hour head start. I took off my eye patch once the train arrived at Union Station in D.C. My esthetics were a minor concern to the prospect of a noose. On a hunch, I boarded a train to Philly, hoping to throw the police off my trail. I did not dare stop, having slept enroute. Near a bridge crossing the Delaware River, I paid for a ride on a truck delivering flour to Brooklyn. I was able to telephone my friend and war chum, Howard Butler. He slept late into the morning because his gigs with the Clef Club band lasted until the wee hours of the morning. He sounded annoyed when I called. I heard female company in the background.

"Howard, Howard, listen … listen carefully. I am in Brooklyn. I was visiting my family in Virginia. On my way back home, trouble found me. I got into a scrabble with two rednecks, killed one and wounded another in self-defense. They are goin' to hang me unless I can get the hell out of the country," I snapped. I lit up a smoke out of habit.

Howard must have dropped the phone. He finally replied, "Man, you fuckin' wid me? Tell me you be fuckin' wid me."

"No, "I shouted. "I have to be quick. Go to my apartment house and let me know if you see cops or anyone looking like one. Stay there till I call you, okay?"

Howard then said," Professor, fuckin', killa. I'll be your peep, sergeant."

It was raining, so I bought an umbrella and walked across the Brooklyn Bridge to the Lower East Side. I paid to ride in a fish truck on its way to Midtown. Deciding against using the subway, I walked the side streets mostly, until I got to Central Park. I was running out of money and daylight — not a good combination. I had enough for a cab to my street. I spotted Howard. He was having a smoke with a young *femme* at the corner. Howard and I engaged in some small talk, then he led me away from his companion. I gave him my key and asked him to scope out my place. After fifteen minutes, he reported the place was clean. I loaded what I could into one suitcase and loaded another with valuables. Howard offered a room at his place where I could stay while he was away working.

Once we got to his bohemian looking apartment, I gave him the suitcase of valuables and asked him to sell what he could. I told him that I would send a message when I got to my destination. My eclectic friend gave me a fair payday for a man on the run. In addition, I gave Howard all my diaries. I asked him to hide them and, then ultimately, store them in a safe deposit box.

That night was the first rest I had in two days. I would call or write to Millie when I thought it was safe. Howard had some good cigars and Scotch at his place. I hung out the escape ladder platform and started to diminish his supply. The sounds and smells of Harlem were a far cry from the bucolic farm in Fredericksburg. I could hear the rhythmic comforts of Jazz and Blues meander down Lenox Avenue into the dimly lit street.

I asked Howard to accompany me to the Irving National Bank in the morning, earlier than he normally rose. He spotted no police, only an old Pinkerton guard. Banks often hired private police for protection. Howard would distract him while I made my withdrawal. I approached Becky, the unengaging teller, and looked her in the eyes. Asserting myself, I handed her the bank slip.

She remarked, "Virgil, I have not seen you forever. You want to withdraw two hundred dollars of the two hundred-twenty you have?"

I looked over at Howard who was distracting the guard, and responded, "Becky, I am moving and need the money for deposit and rent. I have to meet the landlord by eleven, thanks."

With the money in hand, I walked briskly out. Howard handed me my suitcase. We shook hands, and I promised to write or send word.

I made my way to the harbor by midday after a diversion to Chinatown for fish and noodles. Spotting a man who looked in charge, supervising the freighter's loading, I approached him. Sporting a full beard and a white scarf around his neck, he made the first move. With an odd English accent, he broke the silence, "What the hell do you bloody want?"

I inquired, "Where is she destined for, please?"

He noticed my deformity at the same time I realized part of his left ear was missing. Unfazed, he took out a Madura wrapped cigar and replied, "See that flag? Malta. She flies the Maltese colors, man. She is bound for Liverpool, why?"

I lit up his cigar and one I kept from Howard's supply and replied, "Sir, I need to leave in a hurry. I killed a man in self-defense, but there are two strikes against a man of my color."

He gave me a look over as he barked out orders and said, "You are not the first desperate soul asking to disappear. It's against the law." He laughed.

"I will pay you fifty dollars and work on the voyage," I proposed.

"Fuck," he replied, "even if I agreed, I'd have to pay off a few mates to keep their tongues tied."

"A hundred American dollars," I quickly responded.

He nodded and said, "My name is Jock. I don't want to know yours. Tell me, mate, in the bloody war?"

"Yes, these scars are the compliments of combat near the Argonne. I traded my looks for sergeant stripes."

Jock took another puff and laughed. "I have to get on board. I was with the ANZACs, the Australian and New Zealand Army Corps, under General Monash, near Albert. It was a fuckin' shit show. Get on board before I change my mind. Report to seaman Fisher in the morning."

The last few days seemed like a surreal event. My once docile life had turned into a murder mystery. I was a fugitive. My life's education, training, and service to my country was for what? Part of me wanted to go back to Virginia and stand trial. The prospect of hanging or jail time repelled me. But there was something else compelling me to go back to France. The freedom, it was the freedom I experienced there.

I bunked with a mix of Commonwealth men from Canada, Australia, New Zealand, and Bermuda. Barton Taylor, a merchant marine hailed from Houston, made a point of saying he didn't give a shit about a man's skin color, just his ability to do his share. We drank to that. The next day, I helped the cook prepare meals and scrubbed the aft deck. The sea was rough. I got tossed around so violently that morning, that my breakfast found home overboard. For two days I stocked coal in the boilers. It was back breaking work. I was covered in soot but, oddly, it covered my scars, so I did not mind. After my shift, I'd go on deck for a pint and a cigar.

After one particular shift had finished, Jock approached me with his own lit cigar and a bottle of Jamaican rum. His back was against the quarterdeck rail. He said, "Lad, the soot suits you. No 'coppers' here, but you might get pinched in Liverpool. We will let you disembark at night with a few chums who know safe places."

I thanked him for his hospitality. He replied, "The Crown lost many blokes in the war. I'm sure you can get work in Liverpool or Birmingham."

I took in the sea mist and inquired, "Won't I need papers?"

He laughed loudly. "Just show money and you'll get anything you need. I was gassed at St. Quentin and Soissons. I must have gotten immune, except for the mustard gas. It lingered on every godforsaken blade of grass or piece of bloody mud. That's why I prefer the ocean. Few assholes out here." We continued to drink, smoke and look out into the void.

We passed the Isle of Man and slowly made our way to Liverpool Harbor. The ship entered the River Mersey. We docked on the starboard side, south of Seaforth. The freighter was boarded by the port authorities. I was hidden below deck. Jock informed me that it was a routine inventory and manifest inspection. As planned, I departed with Alfie and Percy at one in the morning under a waning moon. We walked past Stanley Dock and up into Vauxhall, a working class and migrant neighborhood of the city. We crashed at a boarding house on Scotland Road. Alfie was a bloke from the neighborhood. He and his pals fought at Ypres in Belgium, a real hellhole. The whole city was destroyed, including the famous Cloth Hall. The mud and shelling were relentless. Soldiers drowned in the sea of grey-black mud if they found themselves off the duckboards. Alfie had a handlebar mustache, a schoolboy personality, but was deadly with a knife and razor. Percy was the oldest. He fought in the Boer War as a lad, and was a sergeant major with the Brit Fifth Army under several generals. The Fifth was smashed during the German Offensive of early 1918. Percy, a balding gent from Wales, did not talk of the war. We called him "monk."

The next morning, Alfie took me to a basement under a Burgess Chemist store. Percy was at the local pub. I had made a living on the English language and literature, but for the life of me, I could not understand the Cockney accent nor English spoken by the different nationalities here. A bearded man wearing a yarmulke, sat behind an old compartment desk looking through a magnifying glass. He looked up and said in Cockney tinged with a Yiddish accent, "Alfie tells me you need papers."

"Yes, I hitched a ride on his freighter. I don't plan to stay long. My destination is France."

The old man continued to look through his glass and replied, "Don't be in such a bloody hurry. You need papers anyway. You don't want to be picked up as a communist or worse."

He began talking to himself in Yiddish, wrote down some numbers, and continued, "Passport and work papers will be ten pounds up front. I only take currency of the Crown."

We left. Alfie took me to a bank where longshoremen did their banking, near Albert Dock. For five pounds he exchanged my dollars for coin of the realm. In two days, I became a legal visitor from Canada, Hamilton Ottawa, to be specific.

I landed a job at a tobacco warehouse at Stanley Dock. After work, two blokes and I went to Ye Hole in Ye Wall Pub on Hackins Hey, near Albert Dock. It was dimly lit with a huge bar and a lot of stained glass. I was less self-conscious about my war wound there. Some of the men were scarred as well: most were Great War vets. A picture of King George the Fifth hung as a reminder to "King and Country." We found God or peace in the pints. I usually found Percy there losing money at darts. One night a rough challenged me to darts. He gave me three to one odds on account of my eye. I told him to "piss off." We banged around until calmer heads broke it up. Little did I know, race riots plagued Liverpool like Chicago in 1919; different reasons, same effect.

I got a room at a boarding house on Scotland Road. I just wanted to mix in. My nightmares about France, Bea, and the altercation near Richmond led me to drink and take to night walking. I was tempting fate on the heartless, black streets of Vauxhall. One evening, wanting company from the fairer sex, I approached a tart on Prince Edwin Street. She was with a bloke talking under a street light.

She asked me for a light and said, "Looking for company, mate?"

I could tell that she was already experienced at a young age. A long pin was prominently displayed in her hat in the smoky light. I also assumed she was armed with a small pistol in her black purse or a knife in her black boot. Regardless, I replied, "I could oblige. Your place will do. My place is strict on women guests."

She demurred, "Okay then, love. What happened to you? War, I guess. Poor lad. Not from here, ay?"

"Canada," I said. "The war took my eye. Let's go." She tossed her chestnut hair, her most angelic feature, as she stepped aside from the light.

"Five pounds," she said as we entered her abode. "I need to support my mum and brother. He ain't right; got shell shock at Ypres. Can't do a lick of work," she exclaimed as she disrobed. I took in her erotic form. I thought of nothing but my lust for her

I gave her a "fiver" and told her an extra guinea was in store if she treated me right.

"What's your name?" I inquired.

"Mary. Just call me Mary. I won't ask yours," she responded, lowering her green, racoon painted, eyes. She was boyishly thin, but "Mary" had all the right curves. After a couple of hours of carnal indulgence, we talked about everything on our minds from socialist rallies, kidney pie, the Royals and Paris. I got dressed as the light invaded her only window. I gave her the guinea and asked if she ever used that ten-inch pin or knife. She whispered, "Like me, no virgin, love." I went to work with a cigar and her lipstick on my lips.

After three months, I saved enough money to go to London. From there, I planned to travel to Paris. I wanted to find Captain Le Van and Christina. Paris became the home of a large number of Negroes from America, veterans, artists, and others seeking liberty and freedom. I stayed over in London for a few days.

My destination was Whitechapel, at the east end of the city. I had a feeling that I was being tailed. When you're on the run, you envision eyes all about you. I was a stranger in a strange land surrounded by strangers. And I felt totally alone.

In many ways, Whitechapel was similar to the Lower East Side of Manhattan. Neighborhoods of Jews, Orientals, Indians, Russians, East Europeans, and native Londoners went about their business on the crooked streets and dark passageways of this transitional section of Great London.

I stayed at a boardinghouse run by a semi-toothless middle-aged woman who I could barely understand. All we could clearly agree on was the rent at five shillings a day. The three-story lodging was on Commercial Street, near Leman Street. Tall tales, myths and, most of all, paraphernalia for sale about serial killer Jack the Ripper and his loathsome deeds, some thirty years ago, still attracted tourists. I stayed there long enough to read up on Canada and especially, Hamilton, the "steel town" of Ontario Provence. I wanted to authenticate my new identity as much as possible. Hamilton was a small city on the west bank of Lake Ontario, much like Richmond, with water to its east and many smoke stacks that gave a dingy character to its streets. I also read up on the Thirty-Eighth Battalion, the Cameron Highlanders of Ottawa, in the library. Questions about my service would come up. I knew the Negroes in Canada and from the States served with Canadian units. They were treated better than my bronze-colored brothers in the AEF. This battalion served with great distinction in France and Flanders. Captain Le Van did mention that he was a liaison officer with the Canadian Corps before he was assigned to the Hellfighters.

From London, I boarded a ferry to Calais. My passport was inspected without incident. From the port, I took a train to Paris. We passed ground fought over by Tommies, Poilu, and the Boche. Farmers and laborers, from the colonies, were busy reclaiming the tortured land. I resolved to never try to find the unhappy killing grounds of four years past. The acrid smell of gas lingered near the blasted earth, and I felt it would never smell the same. Where a lowly, frightened, but brave soldier would breathe his last lonely breath would never look the same to anyone who fought here. The battlefields are now for the tourists, the grieving mothers, and the cemetery builders. It was September of 1922, almost four years since my near-death incident at Séchault, and my return to this land gave me pause for deep reflection.

The train trip terminated at the St.-Lazare Station. I found a small cafe close to the train station. I eventually flagged a taxi driver, a cigarette dangling from his lips, driving recklessly with his one hand, took pity on me. He did not rip me off. Often, this was the case with many English and foreign tourists. This one-armed bandit took me to an economy hotel because the owner was his sister, Louise. She had a girl, about Paulette's age, hanging on her pinafore. Louise hugged her one-armed brother. I was able to understand some of the conversation. Her husband left her and the children shortly after the war. She believed he lived in Marseilles, but it was only a guess. She asked me if I understood French. I replied, *Un petite peu.*"

Louise gave me and my belongings the once over and began with a rundown of the costs. "The room is twelve francs a day, breakfast is two francs, and wine is sixty centimes."

She escorted me to room number eleven after a short walk up a dark, narrow staircase to the second floor. I gave her ten francs for her kindness. Without expression, she retired with her daughter still clinging to her. The room was plastered with cracks running in a series of meaningless diagonal patterns. It had a wood fireplace, a narrow bed, and a table for two. The running water and toilet facilities were located in a common room at the end of the dimly lit corridor.

The next morning, I sought out Louise for her guidance. I had been in Paris during the war, but things change quickly. I handed my black-haired, green-eyed "concierge" twenty francs for her expertise. We sat and had *café au lait* and a *baguette* with fresh butter. She had facial hair covering her upper lip. She could have shaved or bleached it, but I think leaving it like that told the world, "I do not give a fuck." Her thin lips were covered with foam as she lit up a cigarette.

"What is on your mind?" she asked.

I reached for a *Voltigeur* cigar, the name is a reference to some French military units created by Emperor Napoleon, I had purchased the night prior and replied, "Please Madame, tell me what to avoid in this neighborhood. I also need to find my friend, Captain Henri Le Van. He served with the Sixteenth Division late in the war. Where can I go to search his whereabouts?"

She drank more coffee and replied with a question, "You speak French with an American accent, no? Tell me my dark, one-eyed friend, what is your purpose here?"

"Canadian, I corrected her. "I am from Hamilton, Canada. I plan to relocate here, and the only one I know is the captain. We knew one another when we served near Arras," I explained. I fixated on her translucent green eyes.

"The war has scarred all of us: soldiers, wives, and children are all punished by man's cruelty and ignorance." She spoke slowly so I could understand clearly.

She told me to patronize the Closerie, Café du Parnasse and La Rotonde as the cafés of choice in the Latin Quarter. She cautioned me to keep away from the streets and alleys of Montmartre south of Rue de Clichy, as it was dotted with brothels and boys with lead pipes seeking victims. In short, Louise educated me about the risks of dark places, Russian cafés on Boulevard Montparnasse, Moroccan fur merchants, watered down liquor, and *mousseux*, or fake champagne.

She leaned against the low-back wicker chair and continued her lecture on life in Montparnasse, until she was interrupted by her daughter, Madeline. So, we parted. I asked for a continuance of our conversation in the evening. She replied, *"Oui, vingt francs, s'il vous plait."*

On her recommendation, I made my way to the Négre de Toulouse restaurant on Montparnasse Boulevard for lunch. The establishment had its famous red and white checkered napkins and crowded tables. I could pick up on English spoken amongst some of the patrons. Louise told me that Americans and Brits were flocking to the Latin Quarter. Some were literary types, artists, and jazz players, all wanting to be discovered in this bohemian enclave that exuded eroticism, eccentricity, and equality. I ordered *cervelas*, a wide sausage with mustard sauce, and Corsican wine. It reminded me of Christina and war. I did not look out of place. Black, White, all mixed in uninhibited harmony. There were men with Legion of Honor ribbons and other war medals, and the lame and disfigured all trying to move forward to better days. It was as if the world was in a hurry to forget the recent horrors of the war.

The "age of deference" and Victorian mores had ended, giving way to self-indulgence after years of deprivation and destruction. Upon finishing my five-franc meal, tip included, I strolled over to a kiosk for some reading. Pictures of the famous and the infamous dotted its facades. The most noticeable picture was that of the renowned Moulin Rouge. I picked up a copy of *Le Petit Journal*, the Paris edition of *The New York Herald*, and *The Chicago Tribune* in order to enhance my French reading skills.

As the crisp autumn day wore on, I walked up Montparnasse Boulevard, past a church, until I reached La Rotonde Café. As Louise had described it to me, it was crammed with little tables, a large dance floor, and high vaulted ceilings. Paintings adorned most of the ivory-colored walls. The variety of art was impressive, from Impressionist to the most obscure modern works by the locals. I was awed by the café's capacity. I ordered a bottle of champagne. It only cost forty francs. It had to last for at least an hour or two. Three men sitting next to me were American. Their conversation centered around their employer, *The Chicago Tribune*, and their accommodations at Hotel de Lisbonne. The most impressive information, spilled in my direction, was the central heating and the cost, only ten dollars a month!

That evening, I had dinner with Louise. We walked the cobblestone streets past the Cluny Museum, and past the two ancient churches separated by Rue St. Jacques. We walked the *quai* toward the Pont de La Tournelle. I held the door open for her as we entered the Tour D'Argent, a very old and equally expensive restaurant. Louise was going to make me pay for her information. She preferred *amaretto*, a popular sweet Italian liquor, while I indulged in a "75" cocktail.

While eating paté and escargot, the famous French dish of snails in butter sauce, she continued my education of a beginner's guide to Paris. This time, I wrote down items that I could not afford to forget, like the way one can sniff out fake champagne, taxi price gouging, *poivrottes*, or female drunkards, and prostitutes who frequented cafés and clubs.

After an entrée of duck, potatoes, and Brussel sprouts, Louise told me to go to the Army Archives at Vincennes which was located at the southeastern edge of Paris. "You will never pass French," she exclaimed. "Just tell the authorities what you told me, stick to it. Look them in the eye, and do not forget to compliment them, again and again."

We finished dinner with *eau-de-vie*, a colorless brandy. The bill was costly for me, but I needed an ally in my new home. Louise and I strolled back to the hotel. I could actually feel the emancipation in the air. I did not have to walk on one side of the street or be wary of establishments that I could not patronize. Regardless of the feeling of liberation, I carried a knife in my boot and my service revolver, my constant companion in the trenches.

That next Monday, I took the Metro to Vincennes. It was already early in October, almost four years since the war ended. Leaves from the poplar and elm trees fell precipitously on the cobblestones while a light rain prompted the cosmopolitan pedestrians to walk with purpose. The Chateau de Vincennes appeared as a formidable fortress. A dry moat surrounded the front with an intimidating drawbridge at the entrance. I summoned the courage to present myself and state my intentions.

The guard inspected my forged Liverpool documents, looked at me several times, then pointed to the building at the end of a long, crushed stone pathway. I entered the anteroom. An officer checked my credentials. His moustache was slim and well groomed. You could tell that he was proud of the way it complimented his narrow face and blue eyes. He asked for my agenda. I explained. The officer asked me questions about my visit to France. I think he wanted to make sure I was not a communist or an agitator. France had enough of them to export. I approached the counter. There were stacks and stacks of boxes behind the impatient, bespeckled, and bald employee who served me. He told me to return in a week. They needed to research my request. Dejected, I returned to my familiar La Rotonde.

After I sat down, a one-legged beggar approached me. The white aproned waiter demanded that he make haste, but I gave the poor soul three francs for his trouble. The poor man muttered, *"Mort, mort pour La France,"* as he limped away. I sat there sipping on *vin rouge* as I wondered how I would be able to write Millie without being uncovered. A post from France could be a risk I dare not take. My only hope was to give my letter to an American or Brit I could trust. The letter had to wait.

It was getting chilly as I returned to my hotel. I lit a fire and put *boulets*, egg-shaped lumps of coal dust, on the wood for extra effect. My savings, dwindling after a fortnight in Paris, was hidden in the hollowed-out soles of two old boots. I was restless. Images and flashbacks of my unfortunate incident outside Fredericksburg, and the untimely death of Bea and our child, invaded my soul like a slow, but unrelenting cancer. I left my room for drink and noise. I found The Closerie, a clean, well-lit café on the corner of Boulevards Montparnasse and St. Michel. It was hopping with the eccentricity and excitement of the Latin Quarter. I was asked to join a table of fellow dark-skinned men from the States. The man across from me introduced himself as Sidney Bechet from New Orleans. He was in his twenties and wore a white and black trimmed fedora. He was altogether handsomely attired, possessing a boyish face. A clarinetist by trade, he emigrated to Paris after the war and was playing with the "Jazz Kings" at the Casino de Paris. The other gent was also a musician, a drummer with the Kings. We drank Rum St. James and talked of the City of Light till the doors closed. I pitched my story about being a Canadian and living abroad. Sidney invited me to his club. I made a new friend.

I returned to the Chateau de Vincennes. Now familiar with their protocol, I handed my signed request at the counter. I was given a folder marked, "Liaison officers — Sixteenth Division, Fourth Army." Armed with a notepad and the folder, I sat at a long table filled with students and people seeking loved ones. It did not take long to locate the identity of Le Van. He was discharged on February 12, 1919. It listed his address as number Six Avenue Eugenie, Le Vésinet. Maybe he relocated or maybe I was in luck. I approached a young lady at the counter and asked where to find Le Vésinet. She was kind enough to point to a map, placed her index finger on a particular spot and remarked,

"Monsieur, c'est le Vésinet, oust de Paris."

My research told me that the village was predominately residential, with all the necessary shops and eateries located on or near Boulevard Carnot. Some of the town was hilly, and the cobblestone roads would wind around and up the hills that overlooked western Paris and the Seine River. I decided to take a taxi on Sunday afternoon to find my friend. The ride took me past the Arc de Triomphe on the tree lined Avenue of Les Champs Elysées, over the Seine and into Le Vésinet. Shortly after entering the town, the driver continued on a street with a synagogue on the right; then we came to Le Van's address. A woman answered the door. She looked more German than French to me. She had curly brown hair that was cropped short around her neck and wore a light blue, calf length skirt and ivory laced blouse with elbow length sleeves. Her most distinguishing feature was a strip of grey hair over her right eye. She asked, "Whom do you seek, Sir?" apparently unfazed by my eye.

"I am looking for Henri Le Van. I knew him during the war," I replied.

"I am his wife," she replied. "Henri is in the garden. Let me take you to him."

Henri heard us approach. He was holding pruning shears as he walked toward us with a noticeable limp. He was wounded at the battle of Chemin des Dames in 1917. Putting on his pince-nez, he remarked, "I know you. Please help me."

He was balding now, his remaining hair was peppered with grey, but he looked no worse for wear. "Virgil Carpenter, Sergeant Carpenter of the 369th U.S. Infantry," I exclaimed.

He dropped his shears and proceeded to kiss me on both cheeks in the French manner, "*Ah, mon Dieu*, tell me, what brings you here?" He led me inside to his study. "Claire, please bring us some cognac," he shouted back to his wife.

We made small talk and spoke of the trials and tribulations of the challenging times of the war that seemed like a hundred years ago. I told him that when I look in the mirror, I see the war. We toasted to comrades gone but not forgotten. I told the captain my sorry story from the death of my wife, homicide in self- defense to my voyage to Liverpool and eventually to Paris. Henri took a long sip of cognac, swirled the remaining liquid around gently and said, "Sergeant, I am a Chief Detective of homicide with the Metropolitan Police. Let me see your forged papers. You will never pass as French."

I must have "stepped in shit" that day. On the run and I seek out the police! As soon as Le Van told me that he was with the police, I was reminded that he told me that when I first met him during the war. As I was about to respond, Henri put up his empty hand and added, "I see you are now a Canadian, very good. Joshua Clément, a decent name, but I take it that your fictitious father was from Quebec, no?"

I nervously changed the subject. "Mr. Le Van, I did not realize you are a police authority. I wanted to seek you out for friendship and guidance. You must not get involved with me, Sir."

Le Van got up slowly and pointed to his *Croix de Guerre* medal that was showcased on his library wall. "I am a Jew. I know what persecution feels like. I will not give up a brother who fought and bled for France. Now be quiet and let me think."

He walked to the decanter and asked, "Why are you here, in France?" A long pause ensued. "No hesitation, you will be found out for your silence," he demanded as he offered me more cognac.

"I came to learn from the great writers in Paris," I replied nervously.

"Well, have you written anything?" Henri quipped.

"Only opinions and letters to the editor," I remarked, as I took out and played with my partially used Partagas cigar.

Henri looked into his cognac and added, "You need to make your story and the little details convincing. The "devil" is in the details, man. Let the major help you, ask you questions, and the details." Le Van placed the long ash from his own cigar in the ashtray and went on. "Yes, yes, you must see my friend from Toronto. He lives at the Hotel LaValliere on Avenue d'Orléans. Major Paul Drummond. Ask for him. I worked with his division after the battle for Vimy Ridge in 1917."

"Monsieur Le Van, do you not think that too many people will 'spoil the soup'?" I asked.

Le Van finished his drink and replied, "You will like him. He had American Negroes under his command. Most of them from New York and Detroit. Give him my card. Tell me, what are you doing for work or are you a wealthy man?"

I laughed. "I am spending my money and washing dishes for smokes and wine."

Henri topped off our glasses and asked me, "Virgil, how would you like to work for me? I need someone who can fix things and maintain my automobile. I need a driver, a fast driver, like you. You can live in Paris. It is dead out here. We can figure out the details later. Well, do you have a better offer?"

Claire came in and asked if we wanted something to eat. Henri implored her to bring in her duck paté and baguettes.

I blew cigar smoke out the open window, then I replied, "This is a very generous offer, but I would like to teach English literature as a tutor."

"I can accommodate you. See my friend at the École Normale Supérieure, near where you mentioned you are staying. Ask for Professor Denfert. Give him my card. Do not see him until you talk to the major though, and memorize everything he tells you. I will meet with you in Paris in two weeks to give you new papers. Two weeks — at Café Voltaire at noon. I work on Sundays to help my Christian brothers."

"I cannot thank you enough, Sir," I demurred.

"No, no, you have been through too much sergeant. You stay in France. She is flawed, but she will be a land you can call home."

On Tuesday, I phoned the hotel and asked for the major. We met at the café under his hotel the next day at one p.m. The major greeted me while I was at an outside table. It was not difficult for him to seek out a Black man with an eye patch. He introduced himself and lit a Turkish cigarette. Drummond wore a navy, pinstriped suit with cordovan, English shoes. He had greying hair, parted in the middle, with no distinguishing features other than a tattoo of a "Cross of Remembrance" on his right hand. We talked of Paris during and after the war. He was working for a Toronto importer and had been in Paris for three years. I ordered ham and cheese on a baguette with butter. I washed it down with *vin rouge*. Paul ordered oysters and wine from Bordeaux. He looked at my papers, then he quietly asked me to take notes about "all things Hamilton and Ottawa," my Catholic steel plant foreman father and a Baptist, half Black mother originally from Cincinnati. The major told me that he would get my updated background information to Le Van. I paid for lunch and took his card.

I met Detective Le Van at Café Voltaire on the third Sunday of October at noon, as directed. The café was old, located north of the Luxembourg Gardens, at One Place de L'Odéon. It was too chilly to sit outdoors. We sat near the bar and lit up some smokes. He ordered a *demi-blonde* and beef stew, while I settled for a Rum St. James and a cheese plate. He gave me my new work papers, a license to drive, and returned my old passport.

"Did you memorize everything?" he asked. He dipped a piece of warm baguette into his stew while waiting for my reply.

"Yes, I am Joshua Clément from Hamilton, Ontario, Canada, residing in Paris."

"Good!" he exclaimed. "You can visit with Professor Denfert. He is aware you will be calling. Contact me after you meet."

We parted. I walked down the pedestrian street of rue de la Bûcherie and looked into the window of Shakespeare and Company, a bookstore on the same street. A slightly built woman opened the door, "Please come in," she urged.

I took off my English cap and said, "Josh Clément, from Canada."

"Sylvia Beach from New Jersey," she stated smartly. She was a wisp of a female, with brown hair and eyes, with a cigarette dangling on her red lips. "Do you want me to converse in English?" she asked.

"No, please. I need to practice," I replied.

"So far, so good," she said. "Please look around. Ask me if you need any help. Most everything is in English. If you are looking for French texts, my friend, Adrienne, owns La Maison des Amis des Livres, across the street."

I looked around in the back of the crammed store and found two men having a heated debate. The gent with a tweed suit and bowtie looked up at me in a curious way. He noted, "Between my good right eye and your left eye, we can see like one." The man with a small eye patch on his left eye introduced himself as James Joyce.

The other chap had on a three-piece suit and a plain tie. He had a strong jaw and piercing almond eyes. "Hemingway, Ernest Hemingway," he barked. *"Parlez vous anglaise?"*

I gave my "name, rank and serial number." Hemingway responded that he was in Paris as a reporter for *The Toronto Star*. He asked me about Hamilton and my time with the Thirty-Eighth Battalion. This was my first in depth recitation of my fictional past. I was keen on changing the subject when Ernest asked, "Do you know any homosexuals? Who is your favorite author?"

He was trying to get a rise out of me. I returned the "volley" with, "Yes, I even dated a lesbian. Tolstoy, Roosevelt, Dickens, Twain, and DuBois are authors I admire, to name a few."

"Roosevelt?" Hemingway exclaimed. "He's no author."

"That's where we disagree. I like his *Strenuous Life* for one," I replied.

Joyce and Hemingway continued to argue as I went about my business. Ernest yelled out, "Clément, I like you. Look me up. Seventy-four Rue de Cardinal Lemoine, behind the Panthéon."

I picked out two magazines, *Collier's* and *The Saturday Evening Post*. Sylvia approached me, burdened with a stack of hardcover books and said, "We have memberships. You can rent books. We can also exchange currency. The annual membership is only fifty francs, about four American dollars. I will give you a copy of *Ulysses*, to rent, if you have the stomach for literary surrealism. I am the publisher!" It is Joyce's tour de force, she told me. I realized I had just met some very interesting and eclectic powerhouses.

On a late October day, I visited Professor Denfert at the École. It was a short walk down several poster-filled passageways and boulevards lined with chestnut trees. I had to wait for an hour to see him. He sat behind a desk obscured by papers and books. The bookcases were impressive despite the cracking plaster wall behind them. Maybe the shelling during the war caused the damage. The professor wore a black cloak draped over his well-worn, three-piece suit. His goatee was closely trimmed, while his light brown hair seemed to defy gravity, what many of us called "anarchist" hair. We exchanged pleasantries for about ten minutes, then he pronounced, "I owe Inspector Le Van a favor or two. Let us talk in English. We can discuss Twain and Dickens. If you pass, you can tutor to start. Lecturing, well, we can discuss lecturing at another time." We talked longer than I believe Denfert had planned, but I passed his test.

Between my panic attacks and the nightmares, I thought of Christina. I had hoped of being happy once more, but I felt guilty. Many of my colleagues in arms died so young. Maybe she was married with children, or maybe she died in the war. It was too early to visit. I feared my past and its effect on others. Maybe I would have the courage to seek her out in the spring.

With the fourth anniversary of the Armistice approaching, I decided to move to another hotel. I had heard about the Hotel de Lisbonne. It was located off Boulevard St. Michel. The rent was cheaper, only ten dollars a month. A desk clerk, who hailed from Martinique, led me down a long corridor to my room. It had central heating, wash bowls, and hot water on Sundays. A bathhouse was located across the street, inconvenient, but on balance, a trade up for me. Yvonne, the clerk, told me that some reporters from *The Tribune* lived here. It struck me as a good omen.

After reviewing a parade on the 11th and listening to a few soap box rants from socialists and those from other political persuasions, I took up Hemingway's invitation to meet him at the home of Gertrude Stein at Twenty-seven Rue de Fleurus. The building was relatively new, built during "La Belle Epoch." The ornate iron gates also served as a secure entrance. I was let in.

The black and white parquet floors in the hallway coordinated with the white-on-white plaster walls. A middle-aged woman greeted me, "I am Alice, Alice Toklas. We are expecting you. Gertrude and Hem are in her study. Your coat, please."

I intruded on a four-way discussion. Hemingway was standing against a picture laden wall, next to the only woman, Gertrude Stein, reclining like Cleopatra on an ottoman. Middle-aged, with a cherubic, German-like face, she was in a word, stocky.

"Don't be shy, Hemingway loves all Canadians, except *Canadiens*. Let me introduce you to Ford Maddox Ford." We shook hands. She added, "James Joyce. Ernest mentioned you already met Joyce and his *Ulysses* at Sylvia's place. She and James are very chummy since she opted to publish his scandalous book."

Joyce was seated with his legs crossed as he added a meek, "Hello."

Ford was a rotund man, bald and dressed very conservatively British. He stood and greeted me, "I hear you are from Hamilton. What brings you to Paris, mate?"

"Literature and literary types like you," I responded.

Before Ford could continue, Gertrude chimed in, "Mr. Clément, what have you contributed to the world of literature?"

"Nothing as yet. I am a teacher," I stated.

Alice joined us. Gertrude remarked, "Those who cannot do, teach."

They had a chuckle at my expense, but my blood was up. I begged off a glass of champagne Alice offered, and I went on, "I was a soldier of the Crown. I spilled my blood several times for France and democracy. I will write. It will not be the tortured writing of Dada, not as surrealistic as *Ulysses*, but it will be god-damn honest and a good read."

I felt as if I unloaded verbal shrapnel on the now intensely quiet, smoke-filled room. Hemingway lit up another cigarette and said, "That's why I like this Canadian."

Gertrude halted Alice's rebuff and added, "I had that coming. You cannot always take the 'Baltimore' out of me. Now, let's get down to serious drinking and gossip."

We spent the next several hours talking about parts of Joyce's work, Picasso's love affairs, Germany's financial woes and, of course,

Gertrude. She promised to review anything, I wrote. Hemingway was going to Switzerland with his wife, and I was getting used to being an "alias." Ford was kind enough to post a parcel from me to Millie from London in December. I wanted her and the family to know that I was safe. I took up my time tutoring and working for Le Van, repairing his auto and home.

As the new year began, the assassination of Marius Plateau was on the lips of many in Paris. He was the Secretary of the League of Action Francaise and the Head of Camelots du Roi, a right wing, anti-Semitic, militant group. Inspector Le Van and I raced to the scene. A woman named Germaine Berton shot Marius. She tried to commit suicide, but the *gendarmes* stopped her. The inspector interrogated her. I took copious notes. Miss Berton was very young, with short black hair, thin lipped with drawn cheeks and resolute eyes of coal. She admitted to Le Van that she killed Plateau, because he and his group wanted France to occupy the German Ruhr, and for revenge of the assassination of the Socialist leader, Jean Jaurès, at the beginning of the war. She became an anarchist, self-styled Joan of Arc, without an army. Le Van was contemptuous of her, but I could tell he had no love for Plateau, nor his kind.

I lasted out the sullen winter in Paris. My writing attempts languished over vin rouge and "75" cocktails at various cafés in Montparnasse. I could not write of the war without giving myself away, so I started to write about a village near Arras, once described to me by Major Drummond. The focus would be on a French girl and a large oak tree, made infamous by the war. But more on that later. I often became distracted now, gazing at the colorful buds opening on the tree-lined streets. Many beautiful types of flowers appeared in pots around the city. Spring had come to Paris.

Chapter Thirteen

Assassination

It was the first Sunday in April, an ordinary, cool and cloudy day. I was pruning a row of chestnut trees lining the pebbled pathway leading from the Inspector's stucco and stone, mid-nineteenth century villa. The opposite end of the path led to his neighbor's stone wall. I ignored the telephone ringing, as I was in a precarious position on the ladder, and I knew that Henri was home, reading the newspaper *Le Monde*, after breakfast. Suddenly, the screen door snapped opened with such authority, it hit Henri from behind as he was making his way in my direction.

He dusted off his breakfast cloak and shouted, "Joshua, come down, we need to make haste to Paris, the Pavillion de la Reine. I have a new assignment, a very grave one."

He got into the habit of calling me by my alias. I threw down the pruning shears while I hurried down the ladder. Before landing, I called out, "A murder, no doubt?"

The Inspector turned away and snapped back as he entered the door, "A murder, yes, an assassination, is more accurate. We must hurry!"

I did not bother to store the ladder or tools; by the tone of his voice, time was precious. With a piece of buttered baguette lodged in my mouth, I backed up the black 1921 Renault sedan out of the garage. Petrol and oil were topped off as Henri was entering the passenger seat. He looked out the window, lighting his Meerschaum pipe. He simply stated, "Place des Vosges, please."

We motored with abandon, at times, speeding 120 kilometers per hour while blasting the horn because of our urgent mission. Shortly after we passed the Place de la Bastille, we made our way to Le Marais, in a few hurried minutes, we arrived at the hotel. It was an upscale building. The exterior had the typical blocked archway and ivy growing on the white façade. The Inspector exited the sedan, not waiting for me to open his door. He approached the *gendarme* at the entrance and commenced with business, "When did you arrive?"

The middle-aged officer, perfectly outfitted, but slightly over-weight retorted, "We arrived at about nine forty-five. A man is stationed at the rear of the hotel and a third in the lobby. No one has been permitted to go in or leave."

"Very well," commented Henri.

He pointed with his ornately carved walking stick, as we made our way through the portico and into the reception lobby. A man adorned with an unkempt goatee and an even more disheveled spring suit, rushed to the inspector. It seemed that he could not wait to rid himself of what he knew.

"Inspector, Monsieur Inspector, I am glad, I mean relieved to see you," he blurted out.

Henri leaned on his walking stick. He focused a critical eye on the man and with a very slow, but authoritative voice stated, "I am Henri Le Van, Chief Inspector, and this is my man, Joshua Clément. Whom, besides you, are aware of the situation? What is your name and position?"

"My name is Guy Devereux, the Day Manager."

"Please speak up and tell me all you know; do not leave anything out," the Inspector stated flatly. Impatiently, he looked up the stairway.

Devereux was looking down at first. He was uneasy, possibly he was making a point not to stare at my wound. Now he peered directly into Henri's eyes and said nervously, "Well, I am actually the Assistant Day Manager. The Day Manager is Monsieur Dupont. He is off today. Should I call him?"

"That is not important now. Tell me, who else knows about this?"

Guy was trying to maintain his composure. He combed his sparse, brown hair with his fingers and replied, "Only the chambermaid and Paul, the bellman. She, I mean Louise, found Minister Lamoreaux on the bed at about 9:00 a.m. He was very pale, very dead. His papers are on the bureau."

"Please show me to the room. Bring Louise and Paul with you, and also ask the reception clerk if anyone departed or checked out of the hotel since he has been on duty. I will talk to him and the other employees soon," remarked the Inspector.

We made our way up the spiral staircase, Le Van trailing, to room number 204. It was locked. The bellman fumbled with the keys as he picked out the correct one and slowly turned the lock. Paul, a young man of about twenty with a neat, thin mustache, explained that he locked the room until the police arrived. We entered with caution, as Paul led the way. The chamber was in neat order, but in need of fresh paint and a better area rug. A view of the street, lined with budding poplar trees, stood in contrast to the death scene. I guessed this was one of the best rooms. The smell of cigar smoke was still evident, even with a partially opened window. Louise appeared to be in her thirties, but looks can be deceiving. She was still fetching with an athletic build. Her chestnut brown hair was coiled in a bun, and she regarded us with large grey-blue eyes. The minister's body lay diagonally, face up on the bed. Henri asked Louise if this was how she found the body. She nodded affirmatively without hesitation. With a strong sense of purpose, she told Le Van that when no one responded to her knocking, she entered and found the deceased, naked on the bed.

"I saw that he was very pale, and he had no pulse. I was a nurse's aide during the war," she added. "He looked like the dead men I had seen. I also found his identification papers on the bureau, near the cigar. I ran out of the chamber to get assistance and ran into Paul. He proceeded to lock the door. We told Monsieur Devereux what we had seen," explained Louise.

My boss was now fixated on Louise. He responded, "You have a distinct accent. I assume that you are NOT from the Paris area."

She looked down and explained, "I am from Alsace, the town of Mulhouse. After the start of the war, I made my way to Paris."

The inspector changed the subject, "It is very important that both of you tell no one about this. You know who he is," commanded Henri, as he gazed around the room. "Devereux, please bring back all your help who were on duty yesterday and at night. I will start interviewing them here, beginning with the desk clerk. Remember, no one is to leave until I have interviewed everyone," exhorted Le Van.

"Mr. Clément, please open all the windows. The smell of a stale cigar distracts me," noted Henri. "What do you think?", asked the Inspector, as he took out his magnifying glass to look closely at the bed.

I was staring at the opened bottle of champagne on the night stand and spoke hesitantly, "I think he was poisoned by a woman, not his wife, of course. It could have been a casual affair with someone he did not need to impress. It appears that the murderer wanted the authorities to know it was not from natural causes. I cannot guess as to the motive though definitely not theft."

"You are very perceptive. Do you think we are seeing an assassination, a 'Plateau' type of assassination?" queried Henri, then he continued before I could reply saying, "Obviously, we need to analyze the contents and glasses for poison."

The Inspector finished talking. He leaned over to the pillows, then he looked at me with his familiar smirk. "There is a faint odor of perfume on one of the pillows; the one furthest from the night stand. The cigar smell could not fully overpower the scent. Maybe you are correct, yes, a woman might be our customer. Please ring Dr. Adrian. The body must be examined for any foul play. The district police need to transport the body to him quickly then, and I need to tell his wife."

Henri turned to me and remarked, "I am glad that I had the privilege to work with Alfonse Bertillon before the war. He was ahead of his time. Bertillon was instrumental in the development of fingerprinting and profiling. It is much more difficult now to be a murderer." He added, "Also, contact one of my fingerprint experts. We need him to dust for prints, especially on the glass. Tell the manager that this room must be sealed. No one is allowed entry until we are finished with whatever forensic evidence we can find."

Le Van looked out the window to get a bit of fresh spring air and said, "I shall continue the search of the chamber and question the guests. Please call the district for two additional inspectors. This will not be an easy case to solve. Important people will be on edge and the newspapers will have more papers to sell. Joshua, do you think this is the work of the communists?"

I felt the cool breeze hit my face and replied, "Maybe, but I will take odds you will get to the bottom of it."

Henri excused himself after a more thorough investigation of the bed chamber in order to question the guests and employees. I made my way to the cobblestone path leading to the hotel, lit a cigarette, and took in the brisk April air. A *gendarme* who was guarding the entrance approached me and inquired, "I am told you are with Inspector Le Van. What do you believe happened?"

He appeared to be about my age, but with premature streaks of grey in his thick hair. He studied me with deep set blue eyes.

As I inhaled another drag, I responded, "Well, I cannot say on two accounts. First, I do not know who the killer is and, second, I cannot divulge the status of an ongoing investigation."

"Yes, of course," he agreed, regarding me closely for a moment. I am Jacques Molière. "You seem to have an American accent, correct?"

Putting out my cigarette butt with the heel of my shoe, I replied, "I'm Joshua Clément. Glad to meet you. I'm Canadian, from Hamilton, close to the American border."

"What is your business with the Inspector, if I may be so bold as to ask?" he looked at me quizzically.

I lit another smoke and turned toward to the lazy Sunday traffic before replying, "I came to Paris to learn, learn from the new literary personalities. I knew Le Van during the war. He was my only good contact here."

We talked about our units and posts as well as the shortcomings of our gear, the food and, especially, the Chauchat machine gun. I was keen on changing the subject or ending this conversation with him, when Jacques said, "Well, I better get back to my post before my commander reprimands me."

"Yes, I need to check in with Le Van. I hope the future is kind to you. God rest our brave comrades," I lamented as I made my way back to the scene of the crime.

The Inspector intercepted me as I reached the front desk. "We have just interviewed all the guests. If I am to believe them, no one saw anything, no one heard anything. Come with me to interrogate the employees."

"You seem parched. Do you want some wine, water?" I asked. As he eyed the bellman approaching, he commented, "Yes, now is a good time for a glass of house wine." He turned to the man behind the front desk and, in his deep baritone voice, asked, "Please have someone bring my associate and I a glass of your red house wine. What is your name, please?"

"My name is Paul LeGrand." He then pointed to the bellman and stated, "Please bring the Inspector and his associate our best Bordeaux; I think the 1909 or 1913 will do." Paul had a neatly groomed goatee but tobacco-stained teeth.

"Well, Paul, did you see the deceased and any guest that accompanied him last evening?" probed the Inspector.

"No," responded the clerk. "But a female I did not recognize exited the hotel at about 5:00 a.m."

"Give me a description; her face, features, clothing, everything you can recall," demanded Henri.

"Let me try," stated Paul in a nervous tone. "She was young, maybe twenty-five to thirty, it was hard to tell. She wore a cape with a hood up around her head. She did have reddish hair, probably shoulder length; the hood made it difficult to see. She also wore a white chemise. The cape was blue. It must have been her with the deputy. Who else would be leaving at such an hour?" stated Paul, then he spotted the bellman approaching with our wine.

The few employees that were on duty that evening made themselves available for interviews. No good information was obtained, other than from the desk clerk. We quickly finished our Bordeaux. Henri looked at his watch and commented, "It is nearly 3:00 o'clock, and I need to speak to Lamoreaux's wife. Let's go. I will tell her as little as I can get away with for now. Sunday in Paris is never good for me."

• Chapter Fourteen •

Christina

The moon's profile was disappearing behind its starry curtain at the dawn of another simmering July day at the front. The evening's bombardment impregnated the raw earth not more than five hundred meters to the east. My nostrils were filled with the pungent odor of sulphur, phosgene, and decay, as I motored down a pockmarked lane on my trusty Indian motorcycle.

The haze and fog gradually lifted. I noticed a wounded black walnut tree standing witness to this holocaust of nature. I had seen a black walnut before, at Camp Upton on Long Island. The roots emanate like a python over and under the earth. It is a grand tree, a sage witness to the foils and follies of mankind. I approached with reverence. I disengaged the clutch and stopped my Indian about forty paces from a large branch parallel to, and twenty feet above, the muddy earth. When the haze evaporated, I could see the unholy fruit now ripening under the ascending yellow orb.

Suspended by ropes were three soldiers, French soldiers. Two were, as the peasants called them, *poilu*, or the "hairy ones," and a third looked Russian, blond and clean shaven. I moved my motorcycle next to one of the dangling men, and I jumped on him, hoisting myself far enough to cut him loose. I repeated this twice more. It was a bitter harvest.

Orders be damned, I dug a wide grave with my entrenching spade. I laid the men side by side, cut off their insignias, took their identification, pictures of loved ones, and letters for safe keeping. I made a cross and used motor oil to write: *"Mort Pour La France, Trois Hommes."* I knelt down opposite the cross, but no words came out. I just thought of better times. Slowly, I opened my eyes. I saw death, not an apparition in black, but a boy emaciated with no eyes, pointing to me and shouting with a man's voice, "You are the fourth Horseman. The sword or the the pen, you decide." Trembling, I declared that the world would know they died honorably. I swore to give their personal effects to Captain Le Van.

The sweat was pouring down my neck and chest, as I awakened from another nightmare. I rushed to open the window to my hotel room. A welcomed gush of brisk air began to cool my body and slow my racing mind. It was only 5:00 a.m. on a May morning. While I leaned out, I saw the street cleaners and a produce truck make their pondering way down the cobblestone street below my hotel. I lit a cigar and grabbed a bottle of Alsatian wine for company. My sleep medication went down better with wine and a cigar, even at dawn — especially at dawn. Another day in Paris, in springtime. My own heaven and hell. I made up my mind in that moment; I needed to go to the bathhouse across the street, and I must see Christina.

I drove to Le Van's home in his Renault. With the top down at 8:00 a.m. and my scarf trailing in the breeze, I felt like I was flying. When I entered the gravel car path, Henri was already waiting, not a good sign. He emptied his fancy pipe of ash and barked, "Mr. Clément, you are tardy, and I need to be early!"

I wished I had a hardtop, as his barking could not be drowned out by the crush of stone. I returned the volley, "Sorry, Inspector. I had a bad night."

We made haste to the district police headquarters. I asked Le Van about his meeting with the minister's wife. Le Van paused briefly, holding on to his lionhead cane knob with both hands, and commented, "She was not surprised about his carnal affairs, but she was devastated by his murder and the public manner of his demise. She could not hide her concern regarding the future of her social standing. Mrs. Lamoreaux could not recall any enemies other than the politically lethal ones at the General Assembly. She could not, or would not, remember any of his lovers, but she did remark that he frequented Zelli's in Montmartre and the Hole in the Wall, both nightclubs, near the Rue des Italiens. Zelli's is well run and classy, but the 'Hole" is seedy, a dope peddling, watered down liquor den."

He pointed his cane toward me and said, "We will start at these places."

Passing the Arc de Triomphe, I blurted out, "Henri, I am going to find Christina."

"Well, are you asking or telling me, Joshua?"

"I need to go, Sir."

Le Van looked out on to the Louvre as the sun reflected its morning light like a thousand prisms. He demurred, "We are in the middle of an important investigation. I need you with me. You are very insightful, a natural talent." After blowing the horn at a slow driver, I responded, "Very well, I will delay my journey for one week but no more."

Le Van said, *"D'accord, d'accord, mon ami."*

We arrived at the post war headquarters by 8:45 a.m. We reviewed the minister's confidential file, security clearance and war documents. He served as Chief of Staff in the Army Group in Champagne under Commander Franchet d'Esperey. He was also connected to Premier Poincaré. A formidable pedigree. By mid-morning, we arrived at the Hole. Its rear exit was precariously close to the sewers of Paris, a convenient site to dump anything. Although Le Van had been here before on business and was familiar with the place, I was surprised by the red painted façade and its long narrow bar.

Le Van showed his credentials to the day manager. A rotund, bald man with questionable personal hygiene, he asked us to sit down and offered us a demi-blonde, or an espresso. We settled for sparkling water.

Le Van proceeded. "We need to know if you have seen this man. I have enough photos for you to hand out to your employees and patrons, including the prostitutes. We need your cooperation to solve this case. I do not need to remind you that I can have the gendarmes here every day and night unless you help us."

The manager's cherubic face turned red as he remarked, "Inspector, please, give me two days. If anyone knows anything, you will have it."

"*D'accord*, we will return at noon in forty-eight hours," stated Le Van.

We proceeded to La Pêche Miraculeuse on the Left Bank of the Seine, at Bas Meudon for lunch. We took a table outside. It was a bit frosty, but the ambiance could not be beat. I had *du boeuf, frites et carottes*, while Le Van had duck paté and escargot. We shared a bottle of burgundy wine. I could not help thinking that this was a world away from Fredericksburg.

We ventured to Zelli's in Montmartre. I enjoyed a Cuban cigar, making damn sure no ashes made its way into the treasured Renault. We arrived at the famous club at three p.m. The club was open all night and served breakfast to its nocturnal patrons. It had wall to wall mirrors with pictures of celebrities in prideful view. The bandstand and dance floor were strategically located in the rear and center. The tables were crowded with white linen tablecloths neatly placed for maximum revenue. Royal type boxes, with private telephones, were located on the balcony for its "A" list patrons. We sat at the American style bar waiting for Joe Zelli, the charismatic owner. He had us wait for fifteen minutes before approaching us in his formal attire, tuxedo and all. Black hair slicked back, slightly balding, and with a jocular smile, he greeted us, "Gentlemen, let me apologize for the delay by offering you some champagne."

Le Van responded, "No, just sparkling water, please."

We got down to business. Henri began, "Monsieur Zelli, we need your help. This matter needs your immediate attention. The Deputy Defense Minister was murdered two days ago. His wife told me the minister frequented your establishment."

Mr. Zelli sat back sipping Kentucky Bourbon and replied, "Inspector, I have seen Lamoreaux. I have talked to the man. He had both male and female companions. I will ask around. I know two of his associates, both men. You will have their names and contact information. I do not know them well, just acquaintances. How is the water?"

Henri responded, "Thank you, we will be back in two days, say 4:00 p.m., to get all the intel you have. Your cooperation is greatly appreciated in advance."

We repeated our visits. At the Hole, the day manager, now

accompanied by his thin lipped, bespeckled attorney, told us that the Deputy was seen with a blond, smartly attired in a Chanel suit, drinking with him the evening of the murder. We expunged all the details about her we could manage, but it was not much.

Confronting a heavy rain, two days later, we arrived at Zelli's at the appointed hour. Joe greeted us accompanied by two of his lovely girls and a Black man by the name of Eugene Bullard. I had heard of him. He had a legendary military career. He escaped the discrimination of his American homeland, but not in the unforeseen manner I suffered. Eugene became the first Black fighter pilot of the war, fighting for France. He also fought as an infantry man at Verdun. He earned several war medals, including the Croix de Guerre. He now worked at Zelli's as a drummer, a business manager and a booking agent for other Black musicians.

While the Inspector interviewed the trio, I had a drink with Eugene. A man's man, he carried the conversation. "What do you do for fun?" he mused.

"I like to drive, especially motorcycles, and I 'hunt down' new literary types in Paris," I replied as I lit a smoke.

He nursed his brandy and added, "I used to box … professionally, before the war, mostly light heavyweights. That is history. I like to be around musicians and sportsmen. I take it you fought in the war?"

"Yes, with the Canadian Corps. I knew the Inspector when he served as our liaison officer," I blurted out from memory.

We talked about the Deputy as our drinks disappeared. We discussed no profound information, other than learning that Lamoreaux occasionally patronized the club, but not for the past two weeks. We exchanged personal info. I made a new friend, north of the Seine.

"So, we have a blond wearing Chanel," pointed out Henri in a sarcastic tone. "I am sure of the Chanel, but not that she is blond; blond wig perhaps, no?" continued Le Van as he puffed on his favorite pipe.

"I do not doubt you, Inspector. Always be skeptical, and never underestimate your adversary," I commented as we drove back to the scene of the crime with a police sketch artist in tow.

The hotel looked more becoming in its nocturnal state. We arrived at 9:00 p.m., after dinner. Le Van assembled the reception clerk, night manager, bellhop, and the chambermaid on duty the evening of the crime. Louise was annoyed at coming in especially for this interview. The police artist elicited responses to his questions from each employee who saw the perpetrator in Chanel. Although there was disagreement, our artist came up with a composite sketch that the assembled could agree upon. Le Van had copies made, and the sketch was distributed at cafés, clubs, and brothels all over Paris.

The week passed with no resolution. I bade farewell to Henri, Professor Denfert, and Sylvia Beach. My ten-day excursion began with a trek to the Champagne Region, south of Reims. I had the luxury of using Le Van's touring car. I stopped first at Belleau Wood and Château Thierry, west of Reims. Five years prior it was the scene of horrendous fighting and hand to hand combat. The Marines showed up to fight. They suffered great losses, but saved Paris in the Second Battle of the Marne. I was able to retrieve some battle souvenirs, like a rifle stock, canteen, broken bayonet, and an empty "seventy-five" shell. All I had to do was walk behind a farmer plowing the reclaimed fields and war debris would be harvested. It is surreal how four years of hell can be covered over, like a blanket over a mutilated body.

My next stop was at Épernay, the center of Champagne country. I stayed at a small inn. The room was on the second floor. One could hardly stand up straight as the multi-angled ceiling was pitched low. I ate beef stew, washed down with a baguette and, of course, affordable champagne. I motored south until I found a field of sunflowers. They were magnificent, standing six to eight feet tall, with the flowers as large as one's head. I approached the aged, stocky owner and asked him the cost to cut down a six by eight-foot section. He was hesitant at first, but finally demanded a hundred francs. I accepted, and he handed me a sickle as he watched with intense curiosity. I carefully cut down the allotted amount and rested on my back. My solitude lasted about two hours. My mind raced upon images of my family, Bea, Pippin, Fish, and Christina. I also flashbacked to fishing with Millie and father on the Rappahannock, cat fish in tow, as we declared victory at day's end. It wasn't my "castle of corn," but it was a good substitute.

The sun hung directly overhead. I was fixin' to depart when a young girl, who lived at the farm, asked me about my eye patch and scars. I spared her the gory details. We sat at the edge of the sunflower field. I just told this girl with short, golden hair, that I had a bad accident during the war. I retreated to the auto with a few sunflowers for some of my favorite women.

The next day I motored past the route our regiment had taken, but I did not stop to reminisce as it was too painful. I passed the army hospital at St. Menehould, and then crossed over to Clermont-en-Argonne. By midday, I reached Aubréville, north of Clermont, where I had crashed my motorcycle. With sunflowers and a bottle of champagne in hand, I walked to the farmhouse with trepidation. A young man answered the door. He introduced himself as André, son of Rosalie. Her son survived. André summoned Rosalie from the kitchen. She barely recognized me. After some small talk, she told me about leaving the farm during the Argonne offensive. They returned by Christmas of 1918. André survived, but Rosalie's husband died from gas poisoning about three months before the war ended. Rosalie and her three children managed the farm. Christina had left for Corsica in 1919, but she returned the next year. Rosalie said that France was in her blood. She went on to say that Christina was the governess for three children of a widow living in Reims in a chateau by the Marne River.

Rosalie implored me to stay the night and have dinner with the family. She knew that I was the Black American who recovered from my accident, so no bullshit story from me would do. I only told them that I missed France and the liberty the country had to offer. I wanted to learn from the rich literary bastion in Montparnasse. Knowing that Christina was not married made me feel hopeful and somewhat guilty. I showed off the Renault, neglecting to mention it wasn't my own, and we went for a joy ride. We bumped along, top down, all around the bucolic town. We drank local wine and sang local songs, while André and I smoked my cigars to the despair of the ladies of the house. Next morning, I left my generous hostess and headed for Reims on the District 931 road. This was a road that gave you time to think, breathe, and reminisce — a road that made a good cigar even better.

I finally reached Reims, the City of Kings, by noon. I needed courage, so I entered the great Cathedral of Reims there. To me, it was as impressive as Notre-Dame in Paris. The reliefs, the gargoyles, and patron saints seemed to speak to me. The exterior was blackened and damaged by the war. I found a pew in the rear and prayed for my dearly departed ones. I prayed to have the guts and luck to make a good impression on Christina.

The chateau was on Rue de Henrot, overlooking the Marne from the east. It was relatively small by chateau standards, but tidy, and the landscaping was impeccable. I parked the Renault in a noticeable place, and then "manned up" at the door. Christina answered. She dropped the Lady Edith style hat she was holding as she set her green eyes scanning me. Without much hesitation, she hugged me and kissed me on each cheek. She was alone. The lady of the house and her children had gone to visit relatives nearby.

I said, "Christina, you look as lovely now as you did when we met. I needed to find you. I hope you are not offended by my forwardness, nor appearance. I was wounded about two months after my accident."

She invited me into the parlor and gave me an iced peach tea she had just prepared. "I have wondered what happened to you. I thought you were married and living in America," she declared as she sat on the sofa, near me.

I responded after downing an ample amount of her tea, "Christina, my wife and child died in childbirth in 1921. I had to leave the country; the pain was too great. I love France. I love most things French."

We struck up a long conversation about the past and the present that lasted for several hours. She agreed to meet me for dinner the next day, if her employer agreed. I gave her my contact number at the local hotel to confirm our rendezvous.

We met at a restaurant on Rue Gambetta at 7:30. Christina was wearing a Chanel number with her Edith hat and a lizard lapel pin. She was fetching, as her dark complexion gleamed next to the neon lights. I wore a tweed suit and my black eye patch. My self-image rose as the minutes passed. Time slowed to a crawl as her perfume took my mind off the *poisson* and *fromage*. I gathered confidence from the Pouilly-Fuissé that went down so easily. We talked about life, love, love lost, and the future. I told Christina about my official and not so official work with the Inspector, as well as my tutoring. She was captivated and captivating. I had to leave for Paris the next day. Given the time constraint, I confessed my feelings for her over an espresso. Her long pause deflated me.

Then she replied, "Virgil, I was smitten with you at the farm."

My heart raced over the "speed limit!" We agreed that she would travel to Paris in June.

The next day, I made my way back to Paris. My students and Le Van were eager to get me back in the saddle. The last Saturday in May, I accepted Bullard's invite to Zelli's. He played the drums with the Jazz Kings. The "Memphis Blues" were in the air. I drank several 75's that night with the company of a few musicians, an English heiress, Bullard, and his friend and co-worker, Langston Hughes. Hughes was a Black poet from America, another ex-pat seeking fame, freedom, fortune, and fraternity. Langston looked imperious. With his wavy black hair and impulsive, deeply set eyes, I felt he was someone to know, even though he worked as a cook. I stayed till dawn. We had a breakfast of sausage, eggs, and cheese at Zelli's before I departed. During my walk down Boulevard Clichy toward Rue d'Amsterdam, I heard footsteps following me, an uncommon sound for 6:00 a.m. on a Sunday. I turned abruptly. I saw two juveniles with lead pipes that were up to no good. Louise, the innkeeper, had warned me of this when I first came to Paris. I took out my bolo knife and my M1910 pistol. They ran like the devil. Besides Le Van, these companions were my best "friends."

The assassination of Deputy Lamoreaux had gone cold, but the political heat was as warm as an August day in southern France. Christina was arriving on the 17th of June. I met her at the Gare D'Austerlitz. She planned to stay at a women's hostel near the Sorbonne, close to me. We immediately went to Café Voltaire. I wanted to impress her. She loved the interior and was fascinated by the multi-lingual babel spoken there.

I took her to Shakespeare and Company to meet Sylvia. We went arm in arm down the narrow streets. Sylvia greeted us, but she was in a foul mood. Apparently, Joyce's *Ulysses* was being banned in London and in several American cities. As I was showing Christina around, Ford M. Ford, the British author, and Hemingway were discussing the sexual preferences of several luminaries, including Gertrude. They made sure to speak softly enough not to attract the attention of Sylvia. I introduced Christina. Hemingway commented that my *amour* and I could both pass as Corsican. He was half correct. We participated in their *tête-a-tête* for a score of minutes. I bought a *Colliers* magazine and left for the hotel. I could tell that Christina was confused when Sylvia and Hemingway called me Joshua, not Virgil. The silence was deafening as we walked alone together toward the Sorbonne.

Finally, I could not hold back anymore, "I told you the truth, but not the whole truth," I began, breaking the silence between us. "I was afraid. I panicked as to what you would think. I had to escape America because I killed a man in self-defense when I was visiting family in Virginia. Do you know what they do to a Negro from the North who kills a native White man in the South? Do you?"

Christina looked away and said, "You must trust me, or we have no future."

I begged her forgiveness and promised to honor her demand, regardless. I walked her to the door and kissed her endlessly. After several outings, she returned to Reims. We did not make love. I held out hopes for her next visit, in August.

While July's heat bore down on the slate roofs of Montparnasse, I was preparing myself for the wedding of my friend, Eugene Bullard. He was marrying Marcelle E. Henriette, a White, wealthy woman from an élite Parisian family. On the 17th, the ceremony took place at City Hall in the Tenth District, just south of Montmartre. The affair began at Brasiererie Universelle in the afternoon, located at the Avenue de L'Opéra and Rue Daunou. Ah, scallops with bacon and truffles went well with Don Perignon! We took taxis to Montmartre and celebrated all night, until we practically dropped from drink and exhaustion.

I went to the rooftop of my hotel, still very much awake from all the espresso I consumed, and copied a love poem for my Christina:

"To the Beloved Woman"

By Renée Vivien

When you came, with lingering steps in the mist,
The heavens mingled crystal and bronze with gold.
Your body could be glimpsed dimly weaving,
Suppler than the wave, fresher than the foam.
The summer evening seemed an oriental dream of rose and
sandalwood.
I was trembling. Tall white lilies sacred
Were perishing in your hands, like chill tapers.
Their scents were drifting from your fingers
In the exhausted breath of supreme anguish.
Agony and love.
Shivering on my mute lips I felt
The sweetness and the fright of your first kiss.
Under your steps, I heard lyres breaking
Crying to the skies a poet's proud boredom
Among the floods of sound languishingly ebbed
Raven, you appeared to me.

I was tutoring a student in English literature, specifically Kipling and Doyle, on a Saturday morning in August, August 4th, to be exact, when I received a message from Le Van. It read, I will meet you at the Montrmartre Cemetery, across from Rue de Maistre at eleven, sharp. I took the Metro straight away and met Henri and two gendarmes at the appointed hour.

Le Van was sporting a full beard now. He pointed with his cane and remarked, "It is the munitions minister. He was stabbed with an ice pick. The assailant left the weapon next to the body. I believe the murders of Lamoreaux and this minister are related. Do you know what day it is today, Joshua?"

I looked puzzled and could only reply, "Something to do with the war, a significant date, no?"

Le Van replied impatiently, "Obviously. It is the day Germany invaded Belgium, nine years ago. The person, female, is sending us a message. These are revenge assassinations."

Henri instructed the two uniformed police and I to seek out every brothel, club, café, and hotel within a ten-block radius, including the Moulin Rouge. At the end of the long day, we all met at Zelli's for a debriefing.

The minister was at the Moulin Rouge until approximately two a.m. He was with a redheaded *femme* with a red and black flapper hat and tailored suit. Her hemline was noticeably short according to two eye witnesses. The minister was recently separated from his wife. He also served as a staff officer under General Pétain, Commander of the French Army during the last two years of the war. The Minister also had financial ties to Citroën, an auto and munitions manufacturer, during the war. These murders created a panic amongst the political class. Security was increased for the government hierarchy. Police presence increased at all the large and popular hangouts and hotels. We were sure that our suspect was female, in her thirties, well dressed, with a skill to concealing her true identity. The papers had a field day with the political distress and turmoil. Tremendous pressure was placed on Le Van and the Prefect of Police to solve the case.

By the end of August, Christina came back to Paris and to me. We spent the first two days as sightseers. On the third day, I took her boating at the Bois de Boulogne. I kissed more than rowed. We picnicked on the banks of the pond. All I saw was Christina, my Corsican goddess. After a dinner at the L'Oriental restaurant, under the Hotel Lavalliere, we made love in my tiny room. She made me feel whole, and the rush of life came upon me again. We were naked, smoking petite cigars, and drinking Scotch whiskey as the sun broke the darkness all too soon.

The next evening, I took Christina to Zelli's at a time the action was beginning. The joint was jumping with hot jazz. Bullard came over to our table after his set. He was settling into married life and hobnobbing with the well to do. Eugene was becoming the "Man of Montmartre." I was glad that I knew him. Langston joined us at midnight. We drank Bordeaux wine until dawn. We stayed to have breakfast and watch the sun rise over Sacré-Coeur. Christina had to return to Reims. I planned to visit her in October. My thoughts centered around seeing her.

Le Van's frustration increased every week that passed. The tension amongst the politicians diminished with increased police protection and a growing awareness by the elected and appointed elite not to be careless.

By the time the leaves were falling in early October, I went on an auto tour with Stein, Toklas, Beach, and Hemingway in Gertrude's Ford convertible. Gertrude rode as a passenger "goddess" in the front as Alice, her life partner, drove. Sylvia was flanked by Hemingway and me. We drove west along the Quai, toward the direction of Versailles. Stein, Beach, and Ernest did a lot of bantering about Joyce, poet Ezra Pound, and Picasso. Ernest interjected about his experience at the Italian front and bullfighting whenever he found the conversation boring, which was frequently for him. We had lunch at a local bistro. Gertrude paid, entitling her to verbal dominance, which was par for the course. Alice and I had our own conversation about California, London, and cheese from France verses Italy.

By late October, I motored back to Reims. A flat tire notwithstanding, I made good time. Christina introduced me to her employer and lady of the house, Madame Labatt, originally from Lyon. In her late forties, she favored outfits of the late Edwardian period, with wide hats and ankle length dresses, as if the war never happened. She was handsome, not pretty, and well spoken.

The Madame invited me for dinner. Her children giggled at my eye patch, but she scolded them in a sophisticated tone. I spent some time sightseeing the Champagne country as Christina had her duties. She had Wednesday off, so I took her on a ride through the vineyards. We had lunch at a café twenty kilometers south of Épernay. I proposed to my love. The engagement ring was dessert! My Corsican said that she, too, had been hiding something from me. My heart sank. She told me that she was in love with a childhood sweetheart during the war. He died late in the war, killed in action by artillery fire. His name was Jon Domain. When I heard the name, I felt that I was living in a twisted reality. He was one of the three men I cut down from the black walnut tree, not far from her farm. I told Christina that I had been the one who found him and two others lying dead from wounds. I had given his effects to Le Van. She began to cry and excused herself.

We strolled outside upon her return. She told me that the pain of losing a lover again was too high a price for her. Nevertheless, we made love in a field at dusk. I must give her time, I thought, more time to win her over.

Chapter Fifteen

All That Jazz

O f all the crazy, moribund and surreal dreams I have had, this one disturbed me even more than the nightmare images at the Western Front. I am a boy living in a modest home with a stone foundation built before the Civil War. Visions can be so specific. I do not know why. In the basement, deep in the back, is the body of a young girl, hidden behind the mortar and stone. Only I know her whereabouts. Did I kill her? The secret is hidden for years until I move away. The new owners do not find my secret, but I feel I am on borrowed time. Now, as an old man, the remains are located. I am questioned under a bright light by the authorities. They are unconvinced by my responses. They keep looking for evidence. I keep looking over my shoulder, like a man on the run. I hope to die as an innocent man ... then I wake up. I take a sedative, light a smoke, and drink whiskey or wine.

I wrote and phoned my Corsican on a regular basis, hoping my predictability would woo her over. I was not happy with my progress. Just after the sixth anniversary of the Armistice, I stopped by Sylvia's store. Hemingway told me to stop writing her for a fortnight. Well, it worked; Christina called me. She confessed that she missed me, then she scolded me tenderly. We decided we would meet for Christmas in Reims.

To celebrate Thanksgiving Day, Le Van had me over for dinner. We did not let on that the dinner had any cultural meaning for me, as an American. Goose was served with several legumes and a potato, along with some mushroom soup. Champagne and Amaretto were served during and after the meal. Le Van brought me in to his study for a smoke and some Port. He had his reason for a *tête-a-tête*.

"Joshua," Henri interjected, as he lit up his pipe, "I believe our perpetrator is a young woman driven by collective revenge. I do not believe she is an organized radical. The political murders of Marius Plateau and Léon Daudet, of L'Action Française, were too business-like. These murders by our suspect were too personal, with a flair for the dramatic. I am rounding up any woman looking like our police sketch who had a close family war death, what say you?"

I puffed on my Partagas cigar and replied, "Henri, I agree with your assessment. Do it quickly, so your suspect does not have a good chance to leave Paris."

"*Bon,*" remarked Le Van, without further comment. We talked about Christina and the luminaries of the Summer Olympics, especially Suzanne Lenglen. She was the gold medal winner for tennis. A French native, she was given the name "La Divine." She wore Poiret designed sportswear dedicated to the modern, non-corseted woman.

In early December, I visited Eugene and Marcelle Bullard at their Rue Franklin home. Their daughter, Josephine, was only five months old. Marcelle, dressed in a wool French serge dress and a navy-blue hair ribbon, served us black tea and puff pastries that were magnificent! We talked about the recent assassinations. I could not divulge any police details, but I did convey my thoughts about the motive. I confided in Eugene that I planned to marry Christina next year, God willing. We stepped outside in the cold but calm air for a cigar to remanence.

At the time Le Van was rounding up suspects, the police were raiding clubs and cabarets to shake down Black musicians. Political and civilian pressure made this a high priority, because White, French musicians were losing jobs to Black American expats. Also, certain elements were concerned about the mix of cultures and the dilution of French mores. This bully intrusion did not last long, as the public demanded hot jazz, and lots of it as only Black musicians could play it. They had originated it after all, and came from a history of soul and suffering.

By December 15, Le Van, with the help of the Prefect of Police, rounded up one hundred twenty-eight female suspects. They were interrogated based on looks, build, occupation, family, political background, and strength and confirmation of their alibis. Of this number, only six were designated as prime suspects. They were all fingerprinted and checked against the database. Two had criminal records, one for theft and one for prostitution, but none for assault nor murder. They were all tailed by plain clothes detectives reporting to Henri. The noose had been tightened.

I was hoping that Christmas 1924 would be a special time. My letters, as few as they were, had gotten to my sister. I had received several from her in kind. The police had visited my family on two occasions inquiring about my whereabouts. Honestly, Millie could not tell them. She did not know where I resided, only that I was alive and living in Europe, parts unknown. Sylvia Beach had a very clandestine manner of posting letters. I considered her a dear friend and fellow American. I found the courage to buy an engagement ring with the assistance of Mrs. Bullard. I also purchased gifts for the children and the lady of the house. "Brown Santa" was coming to Reims! As I was entering the Gard L'Est train Station, a small group of girls were selling lilies. I bought some for the chateau. Later, I was told that I had patronized the communists.

After a festive dinner at the chateau, I was desperate to get Christina alone. We drove the short distance to Épernay. We had espresso and cakes at an inn on Champagne Avenue. Christina wore an all-wool Jersey blouse in turquoise and a lavender colored dress. Faux pearls adorned her lovely, long neck.

I was trembling inside as I spoke, "My love, life is fragile and uncertain, but love is a constant. Without love there is no hope. Venture with me on a journey of life and love, dearest." I gave her the ring and waited.

She did not respond. Tears rolled down her olive hued cheeks as her eyes began to twinkle and she fondled the eternal gift. We kissed and she whispered, "Yes, in sickness and in health till death do us part."

I was a happy man, as happy as when Bea told me that she was with child. We set the date of June 20, 1925. We were to be married at the Cathedral in Reims. I agreed to convert to Catholicism. It was a concern she had that I put to rest. Christina compromised by agreeing to live with me in Paris after the wedding.

I spent New Year's Eve at Zelli's. Eugene was kind enough to reserve a table for me. I hosted several musicians while they took a break from their sets. Eugene also paid for the champagne. At the table behind me was a set of couples from the States. At about 11:30, after an abundance of drink, the two men taunted me.

"Hey, nigger, how did you rate being up front? In Georgia, you'd be on the street or worse," they rattled on.

I fired back, "Shut your pie holes."

Fists flew, I was knocked down. Eugene saw this from his drummer's vantage point. He came to my aid. We fought back-to-back. It was no match, as Eugene could have beaten both to a pulp all by himself. They exited with their women. Zelli posted two guards with pistols in case they wanted to reclaim their lost pride. Despite this unpleasant incident, I looked forward to enjoying the New Year with Christina.

Later in January, I received a telegram from Kadid Kolda, my Senegalese warrior. He planned to visit Paris at the end of the month. I responded that, this time, I would be showing him around. Kadid showed up in a pinstripe suit and a leopard skin sash. He stood out like the French Tricolor! Between my tutoring and obligations to Le Van, I took my friend to Zelli's and the *quinguettes* or cabarets in Pigalle. In Montmartre, we visited an art gallery that showed Picasso, cubism, and other surrealist works. Dali was my favorite. There is meaning in every drooping clock, every stretched arm, and every "Madonna."

We strolled down Boulevard St. Germain the next day to visit Sylvia and Adrienne. Joyce happened to be there, talking to both about the publishing of his *Ulysses* into French. He and I had a kinship as "one eyed" Parisian transplants. Nevertheless, Kadid was the center of attention. How many times do you get to explore Paris with a Senegalese prince? After this experience, I took the prince to the Dingo Bar. Kadid loved it because most of the patrons were females of various wants and needs. We struck up a conversation with the chief barman, Jimmie Charters, the "mayor" of this establishment. We talked about his boxing days, as well as his respect for Bullard's boxing prowess. Jimmie was good enough to treat us to a couple of champagne cocktails. A Negress waitress cozied up to Kadid and his leopard sash. He finally excused himself for the night and paid for the tab. I was left with Jimmie.

On Kadid's last day, we went to Luna Amusement Park, near the city's frontier. We rode the Ferris wheel that looked out over the Seine. At night, we spent time at a club on Rue St. Charles. We were able to get a table that looked out upon the Eiffel Tower lit up in art deco style, and spelling out the word "Citroën." It was great advertising for the auto giant. We drank Rum St. James and ate *crêpes au boeuf* until 2:00 a.m. I saw him off at the Gare D'Austerlitz. We had a great time!

February did not begin as happily as the month prior. I received another impromptu call from Henri. A third assassination had occurred. This time a senator, with fascist inclinations, was electrocuted at the Hotel Crillon, an upper crust bastion for tourists and those having discreet affairs of the heart. I met Henri and two policemen at the hotel, located near the Jardin des Tuileries on the Right Bank. The night manager was still on duty. It was about nine a.m. The significance of this date was the ninth anniversary of the beginning of the deadliest battle of the Great War, Verdun. We went immediately to room 616. The chamber had black and white parquet floors. It was a large and well-appointed suite with a bar. This was certainly a step up from the murder scene of the Deputy Defense Minister. Le Van, followed by the four of us, saw the corpse in the bath tub, electrocuted by an electric iron. This time the coroner showed up to estimate the time of death at about 4:00 a.m. The authorities dusted for clues, evidence, and anything they might find. They found a few blond hairs and a calling card that read, *"Mort pour La France."* This motto was inscribed on grave stones of unknown soldiers. Le Van was as irritated as I had ever seen him. The interviewing of the help uncovered nothing. It was as if the staff was trained to be "blind." Le Van had all six suspects sent to police headquarters for questioning. Henri fingerprinted all six, but none matched these suspects. In the end, he had to release them. They were still tailed, daily.

The heat was very much on Le Van to solve this political murder spree. He was told that if another assassination occurred, he would be taken off the case. These suspects were either innocent, or the guilty one knew she was being tracked. All the ministers had twen-ty-four-hour police protection. Senior members of the government also had the same protection. Whoever she was, she was very good at what she did.

Henri was grasping at straws. He kept mumbling to himself, "What would Bertillon do, what would Bertillon do?" He had the six suspects checked for nurse or midwife experience. Of the six, three were nurses or nurse aids during the war. Le Van had the phone of two women wiretapped per court order. The third woman had no phone. By the end of February, all six had their homes inspect-ed. They were looking for an ice pick, gun, knife, wigs, or corre-spondence that would link one to the murders. One had a revolver and two wigs. Her name was Michelle LeGrand. She lived off of Boulevard St. Germain, near the Pont Neuf. She fit the descrip-tion. Le Van grilled this petite brunette at the station for nearly ten hours. Exhausted, she confessed. We expressed hope that the case was solved. My suspicions dampened any overt reaction of joy. The evidence against Miss LeGrand was weak. Henri was not one hundred percent sure either. He figured if she was not the murder-ess, the real one would kill again to exonerate her. A sigh of relief fell over the government.

I had some time off and, after a lunch at Sylvia's, I proceeded to the Dingo. I ran into Hemingway at a table near the long, polished brass bar. He was with a young and spirited couple. Hemingway hailed me, "Josh sit and meet two new friends from the States."

The gent introduced himself as F. Scott Fitzgerald and his wife Zelda from Alabama. Scott and Zelda were drinking champagne cocktails while Ernest drank dark beer. Scott seemed shy, but became more and more verbose as he nursed more alcohol. He was very good looking, tall, and his brown hair was parted like a two-lane road. Zelda was harder to read. She was attractive with short, dark blond hair and seemed to have a gift for the non sequitur. She wore a revealing French ratiné dress. Both smoked profusely, but I could not complain. Hemingway bragged about boxing and bullfighting, while Scott professed his suffering over writing masterpieces for the ages. I did not shed light on myself, instead I concentrated on Zelda. It was my experience that people loved to talk about themselves. I got more out of listening than talking a lot. She appreciated being appreciated. I could tell that she was a fragile being. We promised to meet again at one of the new clubs in March or April.

The trial of Miss LeGrand began at the end of March. The courtroom was packed with standing room only. The evidence against her was not strong, nor was her defense attorney. Michelle denied the validity of her confession. The eye witnesses at the hotels pointed her out. The verdict was guilty on all counts. LeGrand was subsequently sentenced to death come June if an appeal did not overrule the sentence.

Meanwhile, Christina and I planned for our wedding. It would be a small affair of about fifty or sixty guests, with some friends, her employer, and a few relatives from Corsica. By the beginning of April, I was baptized a Roman Catholic. Her mother was pleased. Religion was more important than my color or my wound. After the reception, we would travel to the South of France and to Monte Carlo for two weeks.

Christina visited me in April. Chestnut trees were in bloom, and poplars and oaks opened their limbs to the dewy sky. We hardly went outside. We made love, drank Burgundy wine and, when we did venture outside, we frequented La Rotonde. Zelda invited us to the Chat Noir Cabaret in Montmartre. We had a table for eight that consisted of Scott and Zelda, Ernest and his wife, Hadley, Eugene and Marcelle, and the two of us. We were greeted by Ada Louise Smith, the Negro owner. She was best known as "Bricktop" due to her flaming red hair. She looked very mature in her cloche hat and tissue gingham outfit. With swinging feet and arms flailing, we all danced the "Black Bottom" to the tune of "Jazz Baby"*...

My daddy was a rag-time trombone player,
My Mommy was a rag-time cabaret-er.
They met one day at a tango tea,
There was a syncopated wedding.
And then came me!
Folks think the way I walk is a Fad,
But it's a birthday present from my mommy and dad-dy.
I'm a jazz baby, little jazz baby, that's me.

*Originally recorded by Marion Harris just after the war.

I must admit, Christina allowed for my lack of depth perception. Her feet were swift and adept. The jazz was exceptional, as was the saxophone and clarinet playing of Sidney Becket, the best in all Paris, if not the entire uncivilized world.

I received a letter from Millie by way of Maddox Ford. It was dated the previous March. Mother had died from heart failure, or just a broken heart. My big sister stated that she had a large turnout. Mother had called out to Mary and me just before she died. Being over three thousand miles away can seem like another kind of death. Millie had reassured her that I was alive and doing well. She was the last of my family to be born a slave.

Michelle Joan LeGrand was due for a date with the guillotine on June fifteenth, only ten days away. No appeal had been forthcoming. My wedding was set for the twentieth. I was working on the Renault at Henri's home when he received one of those calls. I could tell, as he began to rant like a madman. She struck again! This was either a copycat murder or Miss LeGrand was innocent.

Henri shouted to me while I had the motor running, "The Deputy Colonial Minister for African Affairs was killed with a pistol today, in broad daylight and with a silencer, no less. One shot to the back of the head at close range. The woman ran and caught a taxi. The driver and witnesses got a good look at her. We need to go."

The Deputy Minister was shot near Place de la Concorde on Avenue Gabriel. He was taken to the American Ambassador's residence nearby. When Henri and I arrived, two *gendarmes*, and a police coroner was attending to the still warm body. The police had charge of the taxi driver, three witnesses, and most importantly, the murder weapon! They were brought to the police headquarters in the First District. After exhaustive interviewing, a more detailed and accurate portrait of the murderess was crafted by the police sketch artist.

The taxi driver now appeared before Henri. He seemed to be a middle-aged local. The inspector got down to business, "Please tell me all about your passenger. I need to know her physical description and what she told you."

André, the taxi driver, described a woman in her thirties with blond hair, but he was not helpful with what she was wearing except for her hat and handbag. He did tell Henri that she asked him to drive her to the Louvre. But that information was not nearly as enlightening as what followed, "The woman was not a local. She had a familiar accent. I think she was from Alsace," André declared with confidence.

"She left the pistol in the rear seat floor. It probably dropped out of her handbag. She ran out throwing my fare money at me as she left," he added.

Le Van had an epiphany. He leaped up from his chair, his cane thumped to the floor, and yelled at me, "The accent, the accent! I just recalled that the chambermaid who worked at the Pavillon de la Reine came from Alsace. If Bertillon was alive, I would kiss him. Our next interview is with Louise, the chambermaid."

Luckily, she was on duty. Louise was summoned. She was interrogated in the anteroom. The hotel manager, a police officer and I were witness. After a few long hours, Louise Pardou confessed to aiding her sister with the first murder. She was offered a reduced sentence if she told us everything she knew.

Claire Dupris. She lived near the Gare de Lyon on Rue Chaligny, a working-class neighborhood. She had been a Red Cross nurse at Verdun. Her husband and younger brother were killed in the war. She was bringing up three children, ages ten to fifteen. According to Louise, Claire just snapped and sought revenge. We worked up a profile. The fingerprints in the taxi matched only one suspect, Claire Dupris!

Claire Dupris's likeness was distributed all over Paris and at all major towns in France. It seemed like all of France was looking for her. Michelle Joan LeGrand was set free. I believed that Claire would murder again, not only because she wanted to, but because she wanted to save the life of an innocent woman. Henri agreed.

One afternoon, I had a conversation with Henri while I was repairing a fence at his home. He said that he believed that the assassin would strike again on August 1 or 4. Both dates were significant to the beginning of the war. Extra police and undercover agents were posted at key logistical areas all around Paris.

August 1 came and went, with nothing of assassination in the air. Le Van and I were at the police headquarters early on the 4th. At about 12:30 p.m., a deputy from Lyon was leaving his office near City Hall when Claire Dupuis struck. She walked up to him with a parasol in hand. A knife was fixed to the handle. She stabbed him, but the blade hit his pocket watch. A struggle with the deputy ensued. She freed herself and ran from her failed assassination, but an alert detective disabled her and forced her to the ground. She had done great damage and had caused tremendous angst to the country.

At court she confessed that her losses filled her with anger over those who supported and profited from the war. Although in some quarters there was sympathy for her, she was sentenced to the guillotine. Mr. Deible, the famed executioner, cut her head from her body in this public affair. To many, she was *"Mort Pour La France."*

Shortly thereafter, I had to journey to Reims for my vows with Christina. As I was packing, a call came in to me from Miss Stein. She declared, "Mr. Clément, Ford wired me. He received a letter that read, *the catfish is arriving in Paris on the twelfth. Meet me at the Gare de L'Ouest at noon.* The note was dated on the 17th of May.

Who is catfish?" wondered Miss Stein.

I swallowed a lump in my throat and replied, "My sister, Millie. She married and moved to Virginia long ago. Catfish is my pet name for her."

I called Christina to tell her that I would arrive a day later on account of Millie.

The rain came down in buckets, but the eighty-degree temperature made the trip to the station tolerable. Millie only had two suitcases, not counting a third for shoes. Her face had not changed noticeably in the two years since I last laid eyes on her. But her appearance changed greatly with her cloche hat, bobbed hair, and a tissue gingham dress cut just below the knees. She looked like an advertisement out of *The Saturday Evening Post*. The Roaring Twenties arrived for Millie with great panache. We hugged under the station's great clock. Driving to Reims would be the cure for catching up on lost time. She had come solo. There was not enough money for more, besides her marriage to Robert was becoming a strained relationship. Maybe it was a good thing that they spend time apart. God, had I missed her, Paulette, and Mom.

As we passed the cities of Meaux, Château-Thierry, and points east, we talked about things great and small. We talked about catfish, ice cream at Tappahannock, Bea, and the growing Ku Klux Klan. Millie was very interested in my new-found friends like Stein, Hemingway, Joyce, Beach, and Bullard to name a few.

"Who are you most impressed with?" she inquired.

I answered in a diplomatic way, replying, "Each one brings a unique talent to civilization, but Eugene Bullard is my hero." I went on and on about his distinguished military and civilian careers, noting that he was still only thirty! My sister gushed about Paulette going to high school the following year, a young woman waiting for a cloche hat and bobbed hair.

We arrived at the château as the sun made its appearance through the low clouds. Christina greeted us warmly. Her mother, sister, aunt, and uncle had arrived yesterday from Bastia, Corsica with the wedding dress. Bastia is an old port city on the northeast corner of the Mediterranean island. A walled bastion built by Genoese rulers, the French claimed the island in 1769 after the Battle of Ponte Novo, allowing for a mix of the two cultures.

Christina and Madame Labatt took charge of Millie's hospitality, while I was left with my fiancé's relatives. All eight leering eyes were on me, an unfair advantage. I parsed my words carefully, making sure that no offense was perceived. We did have some things in common, being all Catholic, all dark skinned, and all speaking some sort of French. The similarities ended there, however. The family and guests had a large meal that evening. I could not get Christina alone, so I sat back, lit a Partagas cigar, and gazed at the Meuse River while everyone mingled.

Time and space do not allow for me to expound upon the roster of guests. In short, the notables included Eugene and Mrs. Bullard, F. Scott and Mrs. Fitzgerald, Miss Stein and Miss Toklas, Sylvia Beach and Adrienne Monnier, Langston Hughes, Henri and Mrs. Le Van, and Kadid and Mrs. Kolda. Neither the Hemingways nor the Joyces could attend. We actually had sixty-six guests. Due to Madame Labatt's influence, the ceremony took place at the great Cathedral of Reims, where all the kings of France were coronated, with a handful of exceptions. It was hard to believe that this edifice to God was started in 1211 and withstood, to a large extent, the shelling during the Great War.

Christina's uncle walked her down the long, imposing aisle. She was as radiant as a sun goddess. The Bishop of Reims performed the marriage vows. On an occasion like this, time becomes warped, and it was all a blur to me. Henri gave me the ring, and Christina and I exchanged vows before witnesses and God. The reception took place at the château. The sunny, cloudless day, prompted the guests to mingle or enjoy the grounds and the grand view largely in solitude. Champagne and Corsican and French wines were abundantly consumed along with a large variety of cheese, lamb, fish, and pastries. Bullard was helpful in controlling the outbursts of F. Scott, often a result of excessive imbibing. Henri had a police photographer take pictures. I paid him for his services.

We celebrated for two days and two nights to all types of music. Jazz was the most popular, thanks to Eugene's connections. About thirty odd remaining guests bade us farewell. Millie stayed as the Madame's guest for another three days. Christina and I departed on our honeymoon journey to Épernay and the Champagne Region in the decorated Renault. We spent two days trolling around the dirt roads in and out of the hectares of vines, carefully pruned and nursed for the best crops possible. We were invited to several private tastings, and purchased a bottle of champagne at each stop. At ten miles per hour, it was fairly safe to drink and drive along the hilly dirt roads. We made love at dusk near a town called Sézanne along the Grand Morin. The sun set softly on our sweaty bronze bodies.

We ventured to Beaune the next day. It was cloudy, but warm. The town was a bucolic gem in the center of Burgundy country. The town center had a mechanical pony ride for the children. Christina shopped for local millinery, while I was partial to tasting local wines. The next day, we patronized the farmers' market. Scores of vendors from cheese and fish mongers to sausage and bread vendors, and clothing retailers, lined the road outside the town. We bought food for our picnic. We stopped at a village called Sully, west of Beaune and near the Central Canal, for our gastronomical indulgence.

The next day, we traveled to the walled city of Avignon. This ancient city on the Rhône River was the home of the Popes in the fourteenth century. It was the largest city near the estate of *Châteauneuf-du-Pape*, the "wine of the Popes." No doubt, I purchased several bottles with 1913 and 1919 vintages. We spent the day strolling along the steep, hilly, walled streets shopping and eating. We walked the long stone pier on the Rhône and stayed there until a shower forced us inside the walls. We stayed at a small hotel in the center of the city. The innkeeper greeted us with a six-inch mustache and bushy eyebrows. He was kind enough to give us honeymooners a bottle of "Pape" on the house. Although we were on holiday, our Renault was working overtime. At Avignon, I had her tuned up and purring for the second half of our honeymoon.

Arles was our next stop. This is where many of the French colonial troops rested for the winter during the war. Sub-Saharan troops could not withstand the harsh Northern European winters. Arles also had an ancient Roman Coliseum that had been converted into a bull fighting arena. My wife spent most of her time eye shopping at the open-air vendors. She patronized a few, picking out locally made shawls and tableware.

We drove to Aix-en-Provence and Marseilles, driving leisurely and taking our time. Our final destination was Monte Carlo. Christina was a better Black Jack player than I. She won a few hundred francs, while I lost almost the same. In the end, it was a lot of entertainment for little money. We returned to Reims exhausted, but well rested. My love for Christina was as great as my love for Bea, just in a slightly different way. Those who have been in love twice will understand this.

We returned to the house, and Christina collected her belongings and gifts from our wedding before we headed back to Paris. We arrived at Belleau Wood via a poplar lined rural route. After a bit of lunch, we drove slowly to the new American Cemetery where this great battle had taken place. I walked past a few remaining artifacts of war, and then knelt down in front of hundreds of crosses, hundreds of lost Marines, White Marines, and I wept for them all.

The first thing we did in Paris was to look for a larger apartment. We found a modest two-bedroom apartment, one with a private bath and kitchenette in the Greneville section of the Fifteenth District. Our new place was located on Rue Charles, just two blocks from the Seine. We only had to walk up three flights. Our new place was closer to where Le Van lived, but further from where I tutored. Christina took care of the furnishings, deciding on an Art Deco motif. She obtained a job at the end of July as a governess to a vice-president at Citroën. The family lived in the Trocadero District, on the other side of the Seine.

Shortly thereafter, Christina and I attended a ceremony for inspector Le Van. He was to be given the Ordre national de la Légion d'honneur! None other than the president of the senate bestowed this honor to Henri. He told us that it was the honor of a lifetime. We drank champagne and more champagne to our friend.

By September, Christina informed me that she was pregnant. I was thrilled, but fearful. I pleaded with her to stop work after the fifth month and she agreed.

In early November, Bullard invited Christina and I to the Théâtre des Champs-Elysées to see La Revue Nègre. The star was Josephine Baker, another expat from St. Louis and New York. Nudity was not a novelty in post-war Parisian clubs, but Josephine brought an exotic and unique flair to dancing. The audience was mesmerized by her erotic gyrations. She could also belt out a siren song, but her pelvic movements stole the show.

During her break, she came over to see Eugene. She sat down with the authority of a written invitation. Josephine said that her friends called her "Tumpy," a nickname from childhood because she had been such a chubby baby. She was slightly darker than my light brown exterior. She was not, by strict definition, beautiful. I'd say Baker was exotically cute, with slicked-back black hair, audacious eye make-up and thin, long lips that pouted as if on command. Her flower-patterned blue silk robe covered her feather skirt, which was nothing more than a loin cloth. After the performance, she invited us backstage for a few private songs and champagne. She was truly happy to see fellow American Negroes in her new homeland.

Early in 1926, I had saved enough money to get a procedure called plastic surgery. I was desperate to improve my esthetic appearance, and minimize the odds of getting arrested as a fugitive from justice. World War One certainly proved the cliché, "Necessity is the mother of invention." This was true for bombs falling from five thousand feet, artillery shells flying fifty miles, the invention of the tank, but also for medical advancements. I did some research with the help of Henri. Doctor Marcel Mâcon, from Neuilly, was the man to see. Christina, Henri, and I went to meet him. The doctor and his nurse examined me for over an hour. They took bodily fluids, x-rays, and photos. I had to return at the end of the. At the next appointment, Christina stayed behind. She was ready to go into labor soon.

Dr. Mâcon gave me the news, "Mr. Clément, there is hope for you. We can graft skin from your thigh and place it on the most affected areas. The bad news is that the graft might not take. You will be given anesthesia. Not everyone copes well with going 'under.' Please talk it over with your wife and call me."

I left with a mix of joy and apprehension. After a long conversation with my wife over two espressos, we decided to do it saying, *"Toujours l'audace!"* We allowed our courage to lead us.

On a dreary February day, Henri accompanied me for the potentially life-changing trip to Neuilly. I was told that the procedure took three plus hours. The anesthesia caused post-surgical problems. My pulse was low, and my blood pressure was weak. The doctor had to use two different injections to induce me from my temporary coma. Most of my head was bandaged. I was at the mini-hospital or clinic he ran for a week. Henri and several friends were kind enough to look after my wife. The bandages were reapplied several times. At the appointed time, the famed physician and his assistant unwrapped me. I was too anxious to wait. I begged for a mirror. Henri was with me at this point. He said, *"Bon*, the coloring is slightly different at the affected area, but you look much, much better, like Douglas Fairbanks, no?"

I looked. The area was still puffy and red, but my scarring was decidedly less noticeable. They rebandaged the affected area after an application of ointment was applied. I had to apply this cream twice each day for a week, then I needed to see Mâcon again. But the surgery took. My love, my wife, kissed my cheek and cried for joy. I was told that in six months or more, I would need another surgery to improve the area around my eye socket. No eye patch was necessary unless I wanted to use it as a fashion statement.

On March 17, Christina gave birth at the American Hospital

in Paris. The institution had over a hundred beds. Although it was dedicated to victims of the Great War, by 1926, the hospital took in maternity cases. After only three hours of labor, my love gave birth to our daughter, Alexa Blanche Annette Clément, at 11:30 in the morning. I was gleeful that both were thriving. Alexa was too small to discern her features in detail, other than to say she was a miracle of nature.

Christina was in a sweaty glow. They came home on the 20th, just in time for spring, for new life in Paris.

Chapter Sixteen

The Halcyon Years

I didn't know how I would measure up as a father. My parents seemed so much smarter now. But I was determined to be a good husband and father.

Christina was home with Alexa, while I doubled down on my tutoring. I also taught an English literature class thanks to Professor Denfert's confidence in me. Christina also looked after two other children from local families for some extra francs. Inspector Le Van bought a new Renault, a 1925 Model 45 Tourer convertible. It was magnificent. It was white with a green "ragtop," a sort of folding canvas roof. The spare tire was in front of the driver's door. It was a stealthy beast. I was proud to drive her. With a 9.2 liter, six-cylinder engine, she could fly at up to a hundred miles per hour.

Despite the pressures of work and family responsibilities, I took some time alone at the Ile de la Cité, one of the two islands on the Seine in Paris. I took out my tackle box and baited my line for carp, black crappie, or possibly eel. By June, I could spend an entire Saturday morning there with a good cigar and a flask of spiked espresso. I would have flashbacks of father, Millie, and I fishing the Rappahannock. My life with Bea became a "what if" reverie. France was my home now. I needed to focus on the future, and the future of my new family.

Alexa was waking up at around 5:00 a.m., often interrupting my ongoing nightmares about the dead girl in the basement, and I not being able to get out of a shell hole during the war. Christina would make me ginger tea with rosemary to calm me. Still, I struggled to move away from those images.

When we had the time, we would stroll along the *quai* with Alexa in her perambulator up to the Pont de L'Alma and back past the Eiffel Tower. Paris was wonderful for walking and taking in all sorts of sights. If you visited Paris in 1926 you would have seen the Black Rage. This referred to women wearing black stockings, little black dresses, bobbed hair, and dark, mysterious make-up. The negress influence was changing the culture. Luminaries like Josephine Baker, Florence Embry Jones, and Ada Bricktop Smith caused designers and cosmetic giants like Chanel and Rubenstein to take notice.

The "joints" were jumpin' with dances like the Black Bottom and The Charleston. The war years were long in the rear-view mirror, except for bitter remnants of the war, broken men with broken bodies, broken faces, and broken minds. Such reminders were found on street corners, in Metro stations, cafés, and parks. It was reminiscent of a line by the great poet and war hero, Siegfried Sassoon; "Look up and swear by the green of the spring, you will never forget."

By late summer, Eugene Bullard invited Christina and I to his new club, Le Grand Duc, in Montmartre. We encountered Langston Hughes there. The main attraction was Florence Embry Jones, the great jazz singer. She was not the exotic type, nor an exhibitionist like Miss Baker, but she could belt out a tune better than any jazz song stylist in Paris. She captivated an audience with her range and sophisticated style. We danced The Charleston like teenagers.

One Sunday at the shank end of August, Christina and I went to La Rotonde for a short break. I had gotten time off from my work with Henri. We secured a table outside in order to eye intriguing pedestrians wearing their "Sunday best" outfits. We watched women in pleated Chanel skirts or Poiret one-piece crêpe dresses and cloche hats, men in pinstripe suits and the finest haberdashery strutted Montparnasse for the likes of us. That was why the bohemian attraction of Montparnasse was on the wane. The same artists who came here for its non-conformist lifestyle were leaving due to tourism, conformity, and commercialism. Like Hemingway's marriage, Montparnasse was falling out of favor. Hemingway was restless for his private life to change, and Montparnasse had outlived its uniqueness.

The café was like a tower of Babel. Russian, Flemish, Swedish, Spanish, Italian, all forms of English and, of course, French were heard scattered about as freely as the espresso. I heard people talking about Poincaré's return to power, Mussolini, the recent wine vintages, and Josephine Baker.

On one particular evening, tourists from Canada were sitting at a nearby table. One tall, blond chap attempted to ask me directions in broken French. I made the mistake of replying in English. We struck up a conversation and, before long, I got into my character as an expat from Hamilton, Ontario. Edwaurd, the tourist, hailed from West Ottawa. He and his long-legged wife were on holiday celebrating five years of marriage. The telltale signs of my wound brought up the war. I told my new-found friend that I served with the Thirty-Eighth Battalion, the Cameron Highlanders from Ottawa. Edwaurd was also with the Highlanders, as it turned out. What a bit of shitty luck. I was able to remember the minute details like the battalion's insignia, its motto of "Advance," and my company commander's name. Fortunately, for me, he was with another company. He asked why I did not join the Hamilton Battalion. I paused to take a sip of espresso. I replied that my best friend was in Ottawa, so we joined as pals. Apparently, my performance passed muster. He gave me his calling card in the event I returned to Canada. But it was a stark reminder of living life as an "alias," and the troubles that still haunted me.

On the first Wednesday in September, I was at the district police station with Henri when he received a call. A girl, maybe nine or ten, but not having reached puberty as yet, was found in a dumpster behind a meat market in the Marais. We made quick use of the Renault. A small crowd surrounded the poor child. Henri bellowed out, "Make room, make room, go about your affairs. If anyone knows or has seen anything suspicious, please remain."

Only the meat monger remained. He insisted that he discovered the girl as he was depositing refuse in the bin. He knew nothing more. The girl was examined at the coroner's office. He determined that she was about nine years old.

The autopsy revealed that the girl had deadly traces of arsenic in her body which was evidenced by a yellow tinge to her skin. No one claimed her. Le Van ordered a search of all orphanages in Paris. Police went out with her photograph in hand. No leads were turned up after two weeks. Her picture was displayed in every daily newspaper, but nothing was forthcoming. The case went cold.

Le Van invited my family to a Yom Kippur dinner. The Jewish holy day affair was new to us. It was an honor for our family to join my friend's family. But Henri's thoughts were on the case of the young child. He was confounded by this child's death, as he admitted to me, while we walked his grounds after dinner.

It did not take too long for another child to turn up dead. This child was a boy of about ten years old. He was found in the Père Lachaise Cemetery in the Twentieth District. The autopsy showed that death was caused by arsenic, yet again. This time, pictures of the girl and boy were shown to all residents and employees over the age of five at every orphanage. A detective found witnesses at the Little Angels Orphanage near the Hôpital St. Louis in the Tenth District, not far from Le Marais.

Le Van and I arrived at the orphanage early in the evening of October twenty-second. He interviewed several employees and wards of the state. A police doctor was present to examine all the children between the ages of five and twelve. Of the fourteen charges, three had evidence of arsenic poisoning. Henri was focused on the owner, Madame Jouvet. Traces of arsenic were discovered in her office and in the closet, next to the meal hall. She finally confessed under the pressure of glaring lights and many hours at the police station. In the end, Madame Jouvet's motive was to profit by receiving state money for wards no longer there to care for or feed. Although Henri had his murderess, he had another hunch. Jouvet had run the orphanage since 1915. Why did these killings just occur? The Inspector had an area behind their little cemetery dug up on a tip he received from one of the cooking staff. The morbid scene was laid bare, with over a dozen skeletons of preadolescent boys and girls. A former employee, a Serbian national, had dug the graves for the Madame. He had vanished about six months ago. We surmised that he returned to his native country. Madame Jouvet was found guilty of these heinous murders over the past ten plus years. Our Mr. Deible applied his grim trade on behalf of the state. She was executed, at dawn, about a month after her trial.

On a chilly, Saturday evening in late November, Christina, Eugene, and Mrs. Bullard, and I attended the Folies Bergères. The reputation of this edifice of theatrical spectacles was well known since 1869. It had the most elegant lobby in the Moorish tradition, a Turkish bath, and a promenade replete with lady escorts. It was not an establishment for the faint of heart. Josephine Baker starred in "La Folie du Jour." She performed the "Danse Sauvage" wearing a costume made famous by a string of artificial bananas on a short loin cloth type of skirt. A series of necklaces adorned her breasts that protruded as her hips moved in provocative, rhythmic motions. Our ladies were not fazed by it all, but the men were titillated as much by Baker's exotic gyrations and crossed eyes as by her nudity.

Our quartet was invited to Baker's home after the show. To our surprise, a monkey and two negresses were already there. The women were semi-conscious and semi-clad. Baker, undaunted by the scene, asked us for our drink order. One of the bare breasted *femmes* woke up and nonchalantly wrapped around a bright red robe over her athletic body. She disappeared into the bedroom. The remaining woman was sprawled out mumbling incoherently.

Josephine talked unabashedly about her loves, relationships and life. It was as if she were still on stage. She seemed to become a caricature of herself, playing the part of her theatrical persona. After a while, Christina and I had to depart and return home to Alexa and her impatient caretaker. Mrs. Bullard was expecting a child anytime, and she was taking a risk by staying out any longer. In fact, a week later, Marcelle gave birth to Eugene Junior.

Just before Christmas, Alexa came down with a bad cold. She was not as yet in a year old. Christina was in a panic. A local doctor came to our apartment and prescribed two medications and a petroleum-based plaster. After two more anxious days, her fever jumped up to a hundred and four degrees. We brought Alexa to the Hôpital des Enfants Malades on Rue de Sèyres. Her fever was due to pneumonia. I remembered this disease all too well from the war. Lungs filled up with a bloody mucus that caused death. I prayed to God at the hospital chapel. I prayed for mercy. I swore that I would teach English at one of the orphanages if Alexa was allowed to live. My prayers were answered the next evening when Alexa's fever broke. Christina was glad that I pledged a good deed to God.

A light snow was covering the bare trees along the quai on the first Saturday in February of 1927. Christina and I went to see the L'Hôtel Claridge. Hot jazz was rocking the place. Women dressed in sleeveless, form fitting dresses, strings of pearls or beads, and short, cropped or bobbed hair, stomped the dance floor with their four-inch heels, while others went barefoot. The world had turned upside down compared to a dour decade ago. I wondered when this party would come to an end.

The trumpeter was familiar to me, but I could not place his name or where I met him. At the end of the set, he came over to my table. He said, "Virgil, Virgil Carpenter from Company K, I'm is Arthur Briggs. What the hell are you doin' here, man? Who's your lady?"

I could not reply immediately. Christina chimed in, "I am Christina, his wife and mother of his daughter, please join us."

I decided to spill the beans, as much as I did not want to increase my odds of getting caught. "Arty, before I answer you, you must swear to God, and on your mother's life, that you will not tell anyone, I mean anyone."

He leaned over, intrigued by my response, "Virgil, I swear, swear to God your secret is my secret. Give me the low down."

I told Arty that I'd meet him in the lobby after the show. I wanted privacy. The show was great, but this web of lies spoiled my mood. Christina and I went through the motions, though, dancing the "One Step."

I met Briggs at 2:00 a.m. in the elegant hotel lobby. Arty's best feature, other than the way he played his muffled trumpet, was his prominent jaw. I offered him a cigar as we sat in one of the hotel's unused anterooms. The whole story took about twenty minutes. Christina was kind enough to wait in the lobby with one last drink. Arty was impressed. He had had his run-ins with the law as well. He figured we had a kinship of sorts. Somehow, I believed his promise. I reminded him to call me Joshua Clément.

Our family enjoyed many outings and events during this time.

I was not at Bourget Field, outside of Paris, when the aviator from Detroit, a guy named Charles Lindbergh, landed on May 21 at 10:21 p.m. But thousands of others were there to celebrate the first solo transatlantic flight. I was there on the 26th for his parade, as were a hundred thousand other Parisians. He rode in an open touring car like a conquering hero. I had Alexa on my shoulders, as Christina and I waved both French and American flags.

To Christina's consternation, I frequented Josephine Baker's new club, Chez Joséphine, on a fairly regular basis. Located in Montmartre, not far from Zelli's, Josephine danced her "savage dances" from midnight until dawn, mingling with the customers between sets. She fed her pet goat, Touttoute, between acts. My wife had nothing against her except for Josephine's voracious sexual variety. I came for her songs like "I Found a New Baby" and "Blue Skies," her dancing, and her *joie de vivre*. Not bad for a twenty-one-year-old negress from St. Louis!

As autumn came to Paris, Christina informed me she was pregnant again. This time there was less drama and more gleeful anticipation. We celebrated at the new La Coupole restaurant. It opened late in the year on Boulevard du Montparnasse. It was a shrine to Art Deco. The main floor was both a café and eclectic restaurant. The top floor was an open-air restaurant in a more formal atmosphere. It soon became *the* place to be seen in Montparnasse and all of Paris. We loved the chaos.

Hemingway came solo as his marriage to Hadley had disintegrated. We toasted to our long-lost comrades at the American style bar while Ernest declared he was leaving Paris. In his wake, he left his one true, loyal friend, Sylvia Beach, but a trail of bad blood with many others. Hemingway was well known for agitating friends that could have been his advocates, like Gertrude Stein and James Joyce, to name a few.

The Roaring Twenties roared no louder than in 1928. Bobbed hair, flapper hats and dresses, drinking, drugs, and dancing were at the forefront, much like a party on a continuous loop. The Great War taught us that life was fleeting.

In June, our son was born. We named him Paul Jean Clément. Alexa brooded over him like a second mother. My friends, Baker and Hemingway, had left Paris. Josephine was on tour in Berlin, and Ernest was on honeymoon with his new wife, Pauline. She was more elegant, sophisticated and unpredictable than Hadley. It would prove to be a challenge for Hemingway.

The excitement of Paris also took on the pallor of darker undercurrents. My work with Le Van showed me that. Murders were fairly commonplace, fueled by jealous rages, revenge, and greed. We dealt with a numbing procession of clues and, in most cases, eventual capture and justice. But one murderer stood out this particular year. A hospital groundskeeper had found a young man dead on the lawn of Hôpital Beaujon on June 8 at about 6:00 a.m. This victim had his two femur bones taken out. Le Van, the police photographer, and I arrived just after the *gendarmes* cordoned off the crime scene. There were no clues except for a medal of St. Jude, patron saint for hopeless causes, left on the victim. As usual, we dusted for fingerprints. In addition, the man's wallet and his money were intact.

Henri commented, "What we do know is the murderer is skilled with a knife, like a surgeon."

On Le Van's hunch, we started to look for a malcontent with some surgical knowledge. We had all the medical schools checked out for dropouts within the past three years. There were eighty-seven names, and eighty were men. The police rounded up everyone who did not have an airtight alibi or was too distant from Paris. In all, sixteen men were photographed and fingerprinted. Nothing at the crime scene implicated these detainees. Despite this, four of the suspects were tailed on the Le Van's orders. The murderer struck again on August 10. This time the victim was a middle-aged man. He was dumped off at Hôpital Laënnec in the Seventh District. The man had his spleen and liver taken out and placed neatly on his chest. A medal of St. Jude was placed on his forehead. Like the first murder, robbery was ruled out.

Le Van and his detectives found a connection. Both victims had frequented homosexual clubs in Montmartre and Montparnasse. Pictures of the sixteen suspects were distributed to the barmen and regular patrons, but no leads were forthcoming. The next victim did not come until a few days before Christmas. Again, a man, about twentyish, sprawled out naked on the grounds of the École de

Médicine, near Sylvia Beach's bookstore. This time the man's large intestines were excised, and again a St. Jude medal was placed on the body. Again, robbery was not the motive. The police could not make a connection between the victim and any of the known homosexual clubs. We came into a bit of luck due to the heightened awareness at the hospitals in Paris. A security guard had spotted a taxi at the scene just before the body was found.

The inspector began an in-depth examination of the security guard. After almost two hours of intense and repetitive questioning, Le Van got enough details to narrow the investigation 's scope. The vehicle in question had white-wheel tires, a tool box on the runner, two-tone coloring, four doors, incorporated a fold-down roof in the rear and most significantly, it had an advertisement on the driver's door.

Le Van, the coroner, and I discussed our options. The coroner stated that the murderer definitely had medical training, was big enough to carry the victims, and could be a taxi driver. Of the sixteen suspects, none drove a taxi, a dead-end for now. The Inspector had his unit investigate all taxi establishments, carrying a drawing of the taxi as described by our witness. After two long weeks, there were four taxi establishments that had such cabs.

Le Van personally interviewed the employees and drivers. After about ten days, he ascertained that two had medical training based upon incriminating statements. One was originally from the Amiens area, a surgeon's assistant with the French Ninth Corps. He was not on duty during the first and third murders. The other dropped out of medical school four years prior after his fiancé died at the hospital in Grenelle, the Fifteenth District, where I lived now! The police searched the homes of both men. The apartment of the man in Grenelle had newspaper clippings of the murders along with a "memorial" of sorts to his fiancé. His name was Claude Ravelle, a twenty-nine-year-old taxi driver who had attended the École de Médicine until 1925.

After further investigation, it was uncovered that an elderly doctor by the name of Eugene Duchene operated on Ravelle's fiancé in 1925. She had an intestinal growth and did not survive the surgery. Ravelle blamed the surgeon. Before he could take out his revenge,

Duchene died from a heart attack. This surgeon had a sordid past. He was a well-known customer of a homosexual club in the Pigalle area

Our suspect was spotted at the Gare de L'Ouest on February third, 1929. Instead of surrendering, he committed suicide by leaping in front of an oncoming train. Thus, ended another murder spree and mystery in Paris. I had seen so much death I was numb to it, except for the murder of children. My detective work with Le Van was, in a word, satisfying.

On the lighter side of life, Christina and I were invited to Josephine Baker's new home, "Le Beau Chene," a chateau in Le Vésinet on the Ile de France It was a lovely residential area with much greenery, lakes, and parks. Christina could not come as our son had the colic. The party began on a dreary, cold day in March. Miss Baker had taken off from work. I came on time, which was an hour early according to Josephine's maid. The chateau was a three-story masterpiece of eighteenth-century French architecture. The carriage house was large enough to live in. The ample grounds had a partially covered path with a fountain. I could only dream of such a life, but she had acquired this at the tender age of twenty-three.

Josephine greeted me with a pet snake around her neck as if it were a necklace. I was not intimidated; after all, this was Josephine. She showed me up the winding staircase to her bedroom. Her pet cheetah was roaming around with a studded collar. I was intimidated by that!

Without any hesitation, she blurted out, "Joshua, my dear, Berlin was such a bore. The patrons were fabulous, but those brown shirted bullies were a disgrace to the German Republic. It was like having the Klan in Germany. I was glad I was not lynched!"

I kept my eyes on the four-legged carnivore and responded, "I had no idea, Jo. I'm glad you are back in Paris."

The doorbell rang. The famous and infamous came calling; Count Pepito, Eugene Bullard, Mildred Hudgins, Bricktop Smith, Sidney Bechet, Cole Porter, Caroline Reagan, and Colette. Some were lovers, some were lesbian lovers, and some were just friends.

Cole played the piano while Bricktop and Josephine sang between drinks. Cole and Baker sang, *"Let's do it, Let's Fall in Love,"* one of his biggest hits, to the inebriated who gathered on her parquet floors. I eventually departed with Eugene at midnight. The party carried on.

When one is in the middle of history, it does not feel like it. It's most often in retrospect, that one realizes the impact of events, even though one is living through them. I read that the New York Stock Exchange crashed in late October.

I understood intellectually the meaning of a huge drop in stock values, but it did not hit me or many others the way it impacted those who had money in the market. It wasn't just the financial repercussions that were so devastating but the emotional fallout. I did not realize that the plunge was caused by several interrelated factors. The stock market was like the wild west, unbridled capitalism at work. It caused huge upheavals in American life and ushered in the terrible consequence of The Great Depression.

That same month, Christina and I went to the Joyces' silver wedding anniversary celebration. Sylvia Beach planned the event. Ernest and Pauline Hemingway attended along with many other literati and luminaries on both sides of the Seine. Sylvia was upset because she turned down publishing *"Lady Chatterley's Lover"* by Mr. D.H. Lawrence. His attendance chilled her mood. Adrienne tried to console her, while Miss Stein was gleeful at Sylvia's melancholia. Gertrude was ever the one to latch onto the emotional tremors of a situation.

In November, Georges Clemenceau, or "The Tiger" as he was known, died. He and Marshall Foch had put the backbone in France's survival late in the war while the country was barely hanging on. After the Versailles Treaty, Clemenceau and Foch had disagreed on the terms laid out for Germany. Clemenceau's view was for harsh reparations, while Foch wanted a more liberal approach to a starving Germany. The Tiger had won out. His funeral procession was attended by many tens of thousands of men, many with war medals and some who had lost limbs.

With the Roaring Twenties fading into history, I did more tutoring and teaching. One day in early March, while I was teaching a course on "Great British Authors of the Eighteenth Century," a young man, born just before the war began asked, "Professor Clément, how terrible was the war?"

It struck me as such a simple but direct question. I did not answer in the typical way. I asked each student to say his or her name and street address out loud quickly. It took a few seconds shy of three minutes for the thirty students to do this. I told the young, impressionable youth that if one of them read out the names and addresses of all the soldiers who perished during the war for eight hours a day, five days a week, much like a full-time job, it would take a full eight years to read all the names. This tally excludes all the civilians who died. My eighteen-year-old student would be twenty-six by the time this exercise ended. This analogy was understood intellectually and emotionally by my inquisitive young man.

Eventually the economic decline in the States began to affect France as 1931 began. Trade suffered and jobs were being lost. As a result, the political fringes grew in popularity. The communists, supported by the Soviet Union, staged demonstrations all over France, especially in Marseilles, Lyon, and Paris. The Fascist Party, under the patriotic banner of nationalism, promised cultural purity, jobs, and a strong military. The two fanatical ends clashed and left many wounded, dead, and disillusioned. The financial depression in America had helped cause similar financial doldrums in Europe. This and political unrest had planted seeds of disharmony in France and beyond.

I became a French citizen in 1933, ten years after my unscheduled entrance to my new home. Christina, seven-year-old Alexa, five-year-old Paul and the Le Vans witnessed the ceremony. We celebrated at La Rotonde. I was so pleased that my adopted country was proud of me. Henri and I had our usual *Soixante-Quinze* cocktails and saluted France.

As the children and political extremism grew, Christina and I talked about leaving Paris for the country. It was fanciful talk, but there was genuine impetus behind this banter. Christina usually won our debates. Political assassinations were increasing with the unemployment rate. Even the clubs and cafés were losing their clientele.

Millie, via Adeline Hitchcock and Ford M. Ford, wrote to me that Pauline graduated high school with honors. She was going to attend Hampton Institute in the fall. It was quite a legacy! Robert got into an auto accident with his 1929 Ford truck. Luckily for him, the truck took the brunt of the crash. He only broke two ribs and his ankle. The other driver received a harsher outcome. Robert was fined $50 for his share of responsibility. Other than this news, everything at home seemed relatively stable.

The calendar spilled over into 1934. I was a sad witness to the bankruptcy of the once great and powerful Citroën manufacturing company. Its demise was largely due to André Citroën's gambling, his myopic ill-founded focus on the automatic transmission, and the unfortunate timing of the Great Depression. It was another example of the extremes of the era, and the often-fatal reaction of human beings who responded to destabilizing times in still more destructive behaviors.

In this same year, Adolph Hitler became Chancellor of Germany. His claim to fame was his ability to mesmerize a crowd, use Communists and Jews as scapegoats, and to promise near full employment for the masses. The German Republic was already flaunting the Versailles Treaty by conducting rearmament activities. Ceremonies of book burnings across Germany added to the consolidation of Nazi power and propaganda. Books such as Joyce's *Ulysses* were banned and destroyed.

Morbidly interested in the political direction of Germany, I rented Adolf Hitler's autobiography, *Mein Kampf* or "My Struggle," from Sylvia Beach's book store. The book was vicious, repetitive, and showed the writer's neurotic and narcissistic tendencies. He wrote the Jews must be eliminated from all of Europe, Germany must expand, and communism was a scourge on mankind. The book was a best seller. It was clear that a pall was growing over Europe, and the lights were dimming.

France's response was reactionary. Poincaré's government, through his Defense Minister André Maginot, began a massive project to build a static defense system from Switzerland to the Ardennes. A line of impregnable fortresses would repel any attack by Germany. There was disagreement, though. Some military leaders felt that the fortresses could not repel an airborne attack. In any event, France and Great Britain pledged peace at any cost, leaving Italy and Germany to flex their muscles and ignore the League of Nations.

Even in the midst of these chilling times, Christina and I attended to our growing family as normally as possible. We fished in the Seine and boated at the Bois de Boulogne. By 1936, Alexa had turned ten and Paul turned eight years old just as the Front Populaire, an alliance of left-wing movements, rose to power in France. The Socialist party's leader, Léon Blum, was attacked by the Camelots du Roi. This militant youth faction of the Action Française, the Nationalist Party sympathetic to the Fascists, was responsible for the attack. Strikes and marches dotted the landscape of Paris the entire year. It was a good time to be in the making of banners.

If this unrest was not enough, the Spanish Civil War broke out between the Royalists and the Franco Fascists. Human collateral damage was rife, much as it had been in Russia during the Great War. The Fascist German government tested its new armaments on behalf of Franco's forces in Spain.

Based on these dark and ominous events, as well as the needs of our growing children, we decided to move to Épernay, hoping for employment in the Champagne Region. Christina had connections there. My friend, Henri Le Van, sold me his old Renault at a very reasonable price. Off we went, future unknown.

Chapter Seventeen

Champagne and War

We left a less than gay Paris in the quiet of August with a spirited, but overloaded Renault sedan. Barely had we left behind the ancient walled gates of Paris, when my inquisitive Paul asked, "Father, where are we going?"

Christina responded for me, "We are going to the land where the champagne is made. It is beautiful, and you and Alexa will love it there."

My stoic Alexa, dressed in a white pinafore, but mature beyond her decade on this earth, said nothing. She looked out the window imagining life without her friends and the familiar places she knew as home. Paul tried his best to annoy her, but Alexa was not interested in playing along.

While we passed the industrial city of Meaux, about forty kilometers east of Paris, Paul asked, "Father, can we visit where you fought in the war?"

Again, Christina replied, "Paul, your father does not want to revisit the war. It was too painful, honey."

I decided to chime in, "Christina, it is fine. I'll take us to Belleau Wood, where a great battle was fought, just outside of Château-Thierry. It is on the way. Only a thirty-minute drive."

We lunched at the river town of Château-Thierry. After eighteen years, it looked untouched by the war, with the exception of bullet holes in the church and a few new buildings that replaced those destroyed by German artillery. After a stroll along the Marne River, we motored to Belleau Wood. On our short journey, we passed the Château-Thierry monument under construction. Even the reluctant Alexa was impressed with the beautiful, classic marble columned structure. Christina took pictures with our second-hand Leica camera. One of the laborers took a family picture of us in front of the massive steps.

We parked at the battlefield site. Time, Mother Nature, and man's intervention make any battlefield a caricature of its once horrific glory. I proceeded to be the family tour guide, pointing out the location of the Germans entrenched in the woods, and the direction of the Fifth and Sixth U.S. Marine Regiments attacking with elements of the U.S. Second Infantry Division. In this manner, the battle became alive to the children. I explained how the Maxim machine guns caused devesting casualties amongst the Marines, cut down in the open fields. Paul's and Alexa's eyes were fixated on every motion and word I uttered. We stood on the road going towards Torcy, which cut a path between the farmland that separated the Germans in the wood to the east and the Marines in the west.

I guided my family into the once held German Belleau Wood. I took my Bolo knife and dug near one of the sunken ditches. I dug up several 7.5-millimeter bullet casings, a partial bayonet, and what remained of an ammo belt. The girls and Paul were very impressed, and now each had a souvenir from hell. I explained that the Marines finally took over the wood using bayonets in one of the most brutal hand to hand encounters of the whole war.

By midday, we arrived at the Aisne-Marne American Cemetery. The paradox of war versus peace is no more evident than at a battlefield cemetery. During a battle, all sense of uniformity, order, and symmetry are gone. Only organized chaos and madness prevail. The mud and steel of a bayonet or artillery shell defile God's creations. At the cemetery, all is quiet, peaceful, and order reigns. The rows of marble crosses are perfectly aligned. The great tower watches over its immobile charges. American flags are raised and lowered with great reverence. All is quiet on the Western Front! We left after placing flowers and a flag on the grave of an unknown soldier.

We ventured to Reims for the remainder of the long August day. As dusk settled over the Marne Valley, we arrived in Reims with the children fast asleep.

They awoke as we entered the château on Rue de Henrot, the home of Madame LaBatt. Her eldest daughter, Jeanette, greeted us with kisses and hugs. She was only about twenty, but she ran the house for her frail mother and younger sister, Annette. Only an elderly caretaker and groundskeeper provided the fatherless family with support after Christina had departed. Jeanette was a lanky, sun kissed beauty. Her dark blond hair just touched her neckline.

After settling in, we dined at 9:00 o'clock. Madame LaBatt , now in her late fifties, looked elegant, but frail and gaunt. Christina had told me that she suffered from diabetes. She was not without wit, however, as she greeted me, "Virgil, how dapper you look! I see that Errol Flynn is copying you."

After a fine dinner of duck, legumes, and salad, Christina and I drank an aperitif with the lady of the house. We explained to her that we wanted a more provincial life for our children and feared for the future of France. We wanted to work for one of the champagne houses although we had virtually no field experience. Madame LaBatt poured another drink and remarked, "Change is not easy. The work of wine is hard work. I will reach out to a few of my friends. We will talk of this soon."

A few days passed while I worked on the estate's Citroën touring car. It needed new brakes and a clutch. As I was under the auto, partially covered with grease, Madame LaBatt leaned over and said, "Mr. Clément, can you and Christina drive us to see my friend at Mesnil-sur-Oger tomorrow morning?"

While I was positioning the flywheel, I replied. "Yes, the Citroën will be ready. I will test drive it before dinner."

She nodded and said, *"D'accord."*

We motored early the next morning, driving through the National Road Fifty-One south to Épernay, heart of Champagne country. Upon reaching this iconic town, we drove southeast on the district road lined with chestnut trees to our destination, the House of Delamotte. A lady greeted Madame LaBatt warmly. She appeared to be about forty, with thick wavy hair and a prominent nose. Her lips turned up as if to be constantly smiling, like the Mona Lisa. She introduced herself as Marie-Louise Lanson de Nonancourt.

She invited us into the drawing room of her château. Her youngest son, Charles, a lad of about twelve to fourteen years, joined us for espresso and croissants. Madame LaBatt explained to Marie our backgrounds and desire to live and work in the region, although we had no experience in wine making. I elaborated further on my history with fixing machinery and engines.

As morning waned, Madame de Nonancourt did the talking. "This house I inherited almost ten years ago was about the least respected wine maker in the Côte des Blancs. I have built it up, offering superior chardonnay that obtain Grand Cru ratings. I can afford two hard workers. Mr. Clément, you can repair the machinery and estate vehicles as well as assist with the plantings, pruning, and the harvest. Charles will teach you wine making. Mrs. Clément, you can also assist with the product, and I need some domestic help. Are we settled on this?"

Christina and I looked at each other and nodded, *"Oui! D'accord."*

Marie Louise replied, "I will make arrangements for your family to stay at Avize for now. There is a local school there, and a church."

We stayed for lunch that included some of the house champagne, and then I took a tour of the vineyard and its assets, led by Charles. The two ladies entertained themselves at the house. On the way home, we thanked Madame LaBatt profusely and took her to dinner in Épernay as the August sun began to set over the Marne River Valley.

We moved to the small village of Avize as September began. The apartment was above the only decent restaurant in the village. Mrs. Nonancourt made this possible. After two weeks at her new school, Alexa began to enjoy her surroundings. The noise of animals replaced those of traffic in Paris. Christina and I assisted with the production of the "must", a grape juice before it ferments into wine. Also, I maintained the Renault 1929 and 1932 trucks. Early on, I met their barrel maker, Richard. He had been with the House since 1928. He could make anything from wood. This stocky and balding man carved wooden horses and birds in his spare time. He explained that a riddling rack is a rack that holds several dozen bottles of wine during the fermentation process. The bottles are turned a quarter rotation twice each day in order for the sediment to drain toward the necks of the tilted bottles. A good riddler could turn twenty to thirty thousand bottles a day!

Several days before Christmas, Christina and I headed back to Paris. She had received a letter stating that her brother, Pierre, and cousin, Thomas, of the same surname, had opened up a café on Boulevard Raspail. They had arrived from Corsica and received financial assistance from Thomas's family, who owned Café Lizeaux. It was rumored that they were part of the Corsican Mafia, a rumor I believed from my experience in Paris.

We met them at their Restaurant Le Roxy. The outside was classy with inviting, oversized awnings. The inside offered large mirrors, art deco lighting and an American style bar with plenty of brass. We sat in the back, where music could be played in the evening. Pierre and Thomas looked like brothers, were olive skinned with black hair, and were about six feet tall. Thomas had a prominent nose, while Pierre wore a long mustache. Thomas was the flashier and more gregarious of the two. We spent several hours reminiscing, talking of Corsica, the Peretti family, and the turmoil in France. Current events like the Spanish Civil War, the Italian invasion of Ethiopia, the German takeover of the Ruhr Valley, and the Maginot Defense Line dotted the conversation between wine, cigars, and cheese. Both Pierre and Thomas showed contempt for both the Italians and Germans. Pierre did not serve in the Great War due to his limp, the result of a farm accident. Thomas served with the French Ninth Corps for more than three years. He was with the artillery brigade. He was lucky to have survived with only a shrapnel wound to his right thigh. He said the wound had earned him three weeks of rest.

Christina and I returned to Reims early on Christmas Eve day. Alexa and Paul were already at the LaBatt Château playing games with the LaBatt girls. We spent the holidays at the house counting our blessings and wondering what 1937 would bring to our family and to France.

Early in the new year, Marie-Louise Nonancourt directed Richard and I to build a guest house. Marie Louise wanted our family to move in and be closer to the work. We would be charged only half of the rent we were currently paying. Also, the walk to the school was only two and a half miles from the house. I also kept my promise to teach English at the church after services, most every Sunday.

The year unfolded with my wife and I learning new skills of plant-ing, pruning, cultivating, pest control, and harvesting the chardon-nay grapes. I also became the backup riddler for the house. It took a lot of discipline and concentration to turn thousands of bottles each day. We moved into the guest house in June, after school recessed for the summer. Alexa helped her mother in the kitchen, while Paul assisted me in the fields.

Richard made a wooden horse for Alexa, an eagle for Paul, and a French bull dog for Christina. He asked me what I would like. For some odd reason, I asked Richard for a three-quarter size crossbow with folding arms. I wanted to teach Paul a manly sport. Richard was enthusiastic about this challenge. By September, Richard handed me a beautiful crossbow made of oak that was finely polished. The wing span was about twenty inches when firing, and only five inches wide when folded, truly a work of art. Christina prepared a glorious meal for Richard, and I presented him with a model of the Cathe-dral of Reims as a token of my appreciation.

Paul and I made arrows out of metal, wood, and pheasant feath-ers. We spent many evening hours practicing our skill until the dark-ness overcame us. Occasionally, we would hunt for rabbit, quail, and turkey for our food. By November, Alexa joined us. She took to the crossbow with a rabid enthusiasm and skill that rivaled her brother's.

Other than the increasing saber rattling across Europe, 1937 was a good year for the House of Delamotte and our family. We were hoping for the same in 1938. But before winter's veil disappeared, Hitler invaded the Sudetenland in Czechoslovakia, where many Germans lived, and our Socialist Premier, León Blum, was succeed-ed by Edouard Daladier, a social liberal. Hitler's passive invasion was a bloodless coup. He was greeted as a liberator and hero for German Manifest Destiny. The world was on edge, as the bloodletting of the Great War had not subsided from the minds of the Europeans, especially for France. The country pinned its hopes on the Maginot Line, which ran from the Swiss border to the Ardenne Forest. The great military project was almost completed as spring brought an ill wind over the continent. It was advanced by our military and polit-ical leaders that our infantry and tanks would hold off any German invasion from the Ardennes to the English Channel. These national and global matters were of no concern for the vines that needed tending to as the spring weather began to heat the slopes of Chardonnay country.

Our lady of Delamotte purchased the Veuve Laurent-Perrier& Cie establishment located in Tours-Sur-Marne. The village is at the Marne River, about fifteen kilometers east, and the same distance north of the House of Delamotte. The House of Laurent-Perrier was founded in 1812. It produced champagne from the three main varietals, Chardonnay, Pinot noir, and Pinot Meunier. From what I was told by Maurice and Bernard, Marie's oldest sons, the Delamotte brand name was to be under the Laurent-Perrier stewardship. Both sons managed the new acquisition while Charles, the youngest son, helped managed Delamotte. All reported to Marie-Louise.

I worked in the facilities at both vineyards and managed the machinery. The only other free time I had was to teach English after Sunday Mass, when possible. Christina stayed at Le Mesnil, spending most of her time cooking and tending to the gardens. Alexa loved to help her mother cook while Paul "supervised" my machine maintenance.

Letters came from Inspector Le Van on a regular basis. I would also get letters and an occasional magazine from Sylvia Beach. I was glad to hear that Sylvia was awarded the French Legion of Honor in June. She was one of the most notable women in all of France — not bad for an American! In early September, I received a telegram from one of Millie's trusted friends that Robert, Millie's husband, died of a heart attack while driving his truck. The truck hit a tree. He was dead at the scene. Robert was only fifty, but the stress of keeping up the farm during the Depression, and his drinking, contributed to his early demise. Millie could only count on a small amount of life insurance, as Robert used a lot of the cash value to keep the farm going. Pauline was married now and living at the farm. Millie decided to take in a few boarders to defray costs. It pained both of us that I could not return home.

A few weeks later, Heir Hitler and the British Prime Minister, Neville Chamberlain, declared that war was now averted. It appears that the Sudetenland was sacrificed for a tenuous peace.

Peace or not, our 1938 harvest was good, not exceptional. Mrs. Nonancourt was busy finalizing the Laurent-Perrier deal. While our Laurent-Perrier family was processing the harvest, Germany went crazy on November ninth. The papers called it, "Kristallnacht" or the night of broken glass. Nazis, and those sympathetic to their cause, destroyed many Jewish businesses and houses of worship. It was a clear signal that Jews in Germany were outcasts and had no place in the "new Germany." Jews began to emigrate to America, England, and France. France began to move troops to the frontier and to the now completed Maginot Defense Line. Chamberlain's piece of paper and policy of appeasement began to lose their value. So ended 1938 with a crash of glass and the bated breath of a collective Europe in an uneasy peace.

The melancholy of world affairs did little to impact our provincial world during the bleak months of winter. Talk of black rot and doryphores, potato bugs, had the *vignerons*, or winegrowers, working hard in preparation for this unpredictable onslaught. These pests could be disastrous to crops. For some diversion and change of pace, we motored to Paris in March to see Christina's brother and cousin at their café. We had the great fortune to be invited to stay at the Le Van's. The Inspector and I passed idle time and bonded over cigars and cognac, reminiscing about the war, politics, and solving infamous homicides in which we had been involved together. Henri was now in his mid-fifties. He was hoping to retire by age sixty and move to the south of France, near Nice or St. Paul. Christina divided her time between her kin and assisting Mrs. Le Van with preparing the garden for spring.

Henri did not hesitate to tell me his anxiety about being a Jew in an increasingly Fascist Europe. He flicked cigar ash out the small opening of his study window and remarked, "I cannot believe our leaders. I cannot believe France. For all that a generation sacrificed, we cower at the sight of German aggression. In order to avoid another war, we actually invite a war. The Maginot Line is a false hope. Our military leaders are always fighting the last war while the Germans are inventing new means. It is an art for them, like a Monet or a Rodin. We should have crushed them in 1936 as they crossed into the Rhineland."

"You are correct, Inspector. Do you intend to emigrate to England or America?" I added.

"Not likely. I will do what France needs me to do. I am to set in my ways," he exclaimed. He drank more cognac and stared out the partially open window.

In addition to our visits to family and the Le Van's, we made time for Sylvia Beach and her partner, Adrienne. Both were nervous about the future of France and literary liberty. Sylvia was now as French as Chardonnay. She was a fighter and would stay regardless of an invasion. She was eternally thankful for the financial support she was receiving from some authors and patrons. Many of her clients went to England or America. Christina and I went to see Eugene Bullard at his L'Escadrille Club on Five Rue Fontaine. He was very engaging, but I could tell his divorce and the events in Europe left him melancholy and anxious about the future. This worried me. Eugene was a lion of life. Was I just naïve about what was happening?

With the arrival of the summer winds, the *vignerons* of the region had used the copper sulphate remedy sparingly to fight the fungal disease of the dreaded beetle infestation. It could have been a lot worse. Th dry weather was more of a challenge for a crop that could produce a low sugar content. I was fixing an old Renault truck when Richard came running into the barn ranting, "It is over, we are at war, again!"

The oil from the old filter spilled on my face, causing me to hit my head on the oil pan. I blurted out, "What the hell are you talking about?" I reached for a rag.

As Richard helped me recover, he said, "Germany just invaded Poland. France and England have declared war on Germany."

I wiped the oil from my face and said nothing. I thought about my friends who died in France twenty odd years ago. I thought of our future. I was glad to be a long way from Paris. I was sick of war. Fuck war.

Marie-Louise called a meeting of all her employees and family. She said that regardless of what happened, Europe and the world needed wine. She stated, "If there is life in the human heart, wine will be there to quench man's thirst for liberty."

Christina and I feared for our children. By the time September ended, Poland had fallen, the French government outlawed the Communist Party, and advocated the deportation of illegal immigrants. Gas masks were distributed as mandatory for both military, police, and civilians. This brought back bad memories and more nightmares than I had had since Alexa was born.

All France braced for an invasion. France and its allies were on high alert on The Maginot Line and from the frontier all the way into Belgium. The French leaders believed that the Germans would follow the same strategy they used in 1914. But the Germans were too smart to be predictable.

We overcame our nervous predisposition by the necessity of our harvest. Our crop was not vintage, nor was it terrible, just mediocre. To our surprise, there was no invasion. People started to call our declaration of war the, "Phony War." Nevertheless, Marie-Louise shipped several hundred cases of her best years to America for safe-keeping. She was not complacent about her well-earned business.

We endured a somber Christmas season buoyed by collective prayer and goodwill. Father Blanchard held a special holiday event for all the children in the Avize parish area. The children relished the celebration and gifts. Alexa held on tightly to her mother's hand. I had read in the newspaper that Josephine Baker was performing at the American Hospital in Paris for the holidays. She, like Sylvia Beach, loved liberty and defied subjugation and defeatism. I felt privileged to know them. 1940, a nice round number, would prove to be no mediocre year.

With spring breathing life into the land, the invasion finally came. I remember hearing of it as I was pruning vines. I stopped and dreamed of fishing on the Rappahannock with Millie and father after church on a still August day. Even as I instinctively felt the fear of another war, my thoughts brought me back to home, the fields, and my quiet moments in my "castle of corn" that seemed so far away from me now. I took the liberty of spending a short time lying on the pathway between the rows of vines. My mind drifted away to earlier, less complicated times. Rose, one of the field workers, woke me from my reverie. Clouds had covered the sun's warmth. A chill wind blew over the slope as I continued my work.

The Allied strategy to Germany's aggression was predictable

and uninspired. It was predicated on the assumption that Germany would advance the bulk of its armies through Belgium, as they did in the last war. The invasion forces would have none of it. They attacked with a large concentration of armor through the "impassable" Ardenne Forest. From there, they squeezed the Anglo-French forces like a vise. As with some chess matches, the first move sealed the fate of France.

As the invasion progressed, the Daldier government failed, leaving Paul Reynaud the leader of a doomed state. A change of military leaders could not curtail the swift enemy advance. Refugees from Belgium and Northern France, including Paris, clogged all the roads leading south, hindering whatever military counterattacks the Allies could muster. The only serious counterattack was from some French and British armored units near Arras. Their attack caused a temporary slowdown in the invasion. Our General De Gaulle helped lead the attack, but our forces were outnumbered and outgunned by the superior German tanks. Soon, Belgium sued for peace. The French government fled to Marseilles in early June. The entire British Expeditionary Force was surrounded at Dunkirk for a week until a large, mostly private, flotilla of small ships rescued almost three hundred thousand soldiers from certain annihilation in early June.

By mid-June, German military units entered Paris for the second time in seventy years. This time Hitler would demand much, much more from a defeated France than Chancellor Otto von Bismarck. The surrender documents were signed at the same place the World War One Armistice documents were signed at Compiègne. France was completely humiliated. Over two million soldiers were captured by German forces and held hostage in Germany. The Great War hero, General Pétain, and his lieutenant, Paul Laval, formed a new government located at Vichy. The coast and all of Northern France were now under occupied forces, the Alsace and Lorraine provinces officially returned to Germany, and Italy took control of southeastern France, up to the Rhône River. This Vichy government was now a puppet state of the Reich.

Before the Germans reached our corner of France, Mrs. Nonancourt had a few of us build a wall where the champagne was housed in order to hide over a thousand precious bottles. A statue of our patron saint, Vincent of Saragossa, was placed on the wall to help deceive the *tête carrées*, or square heads. The entire Champagne Region was within the Occupied Zone. We had to go on German clock time. Our constitution was abolished by the end of July. Also, elements of the Fourteenth Panzer Corps of Army Group B controlled the area surrounding Epérnay, the capital of Champagne country. Eventually, the Germans devalued the franc to one-third of what it was in order for the occupiers to buy French goods, including wine, cheaply at the expense of its subjugated people.

The 1940 crop proved to be as distasteful as the year for France. The only good thing was we did not need to carry around our gas masks. I received a letter from Sylvia. She and Adrienne did not flee Paris. They stayed to defend their books. Sylvia's father passed away as well as James Joyce. She mentioned the *passeurs*, or guides, were helping Jews cross over to Vichy or Spain for money. The first anti-Semitic laws were passed by the Vichy Government in August in order to comply with their masters in Berlin. Sylvia wrote that a large number of Metro stations were closed by the Germans, and that the last car on each train was designated for Jews and Blacks only. All city buildings had the swastika flag flown as a daily reminder of humiliation.

At the end of August, the Gestapo came to the House of Laurent-Perrier. The head of this delegation was Otto Klaebisch, a *weinführer*, or German importer of wine. All of the employees were interrogated. We had to show our nationality and work papers to men in black uniforms. We also had to describe our work duties. I was singled out for special interrogation since I was a naturalized French citizen. Marie-Louise intervened on my behalf after three hours of questioning. She stated that I was indispensable to the functioning of the vineyard due to my mechanical abilities. I was released for the time being.

Marie-Louise begged this uniformed *weinführer* for sugar in order to process the current crop. Shortages of sugar and other items needed to process the harvest hindered its quantity and quality. The pompous wine importer told Marie-Louise that he would satisfy her request only if she turned over enough late 1930-decade bottles for sale to him. It was an offer she could not refuse.

Harvesting the crop was also hampered by the 8:00 o'clock curfew. We had to use blue bicycle lights and blackout curtains as the sun set. Patrols checked our ID cards and searched us for weapons and contraband. I kept the crossbow, pistol, and Bolo knife hidden in one of the trucks.

Christina received a letter from her cousin, Thomas, in Paris. Her brother, Pierre, refused to serve a German officer at the café. He was arrested and sent to Gestapo headquarters at Avenue Foch. From there, he was sent to Mont Valérian prison in Paris. I tried to console her, but she sank into a depression like I had never seen since Alexa was very ill as an infant. We feared for our children; there was no escape and almost no hope.

On a frosty, windblown night in November, I had another reoccurring nightmare about the girl walled up in the basement of my childhood home. I was interrogated under bright, hot lights by three old men in black robes. I was dragged away to a solitary confinement cell. Soon, I woke up in a sweat. Christina offered me some wine. I drank the *piquette* for consolation. 1940 ended with a terrible harvest, German occupation of most of Europe, and little hope for liberty. With the lights fading into the night, we wondered if 1941 could be worse.

On an unusually warm Saturday in late January, Paul and I went to the woods near Avize and practiced with our crossbows all morning. We unloaded several clips from my Browning army pistol. We made haste for Le Mesnil before we attracted unwanted attention from either the Germans or their *collabos*, as their collaborators were known. Given the food and supply shortages, a black market developed for commodities and information. One had to hoard trust like vintage champagne.

Christina was growing more disconcerted and anxious about the fate of her brother. I told her that Thomas would keep her informed. Going to Paris and confronting the police or the German authorities might only get her in trouble. She could not be consoled. She was hellbent on going by March if Pierre was not released.

I needed to go to Reims for machine parts. I dreaded the journey as there was a Gestapo headquarters there. I was stopped by German guards as I motored up to the Marne River Bridge from the south. I handed over my ID and work papers. I could tell that these guards were not combat quality. They were almost my age, along with matching waistlines. I was interrogated about my business in Reims. Regardless of my sincerity, they decided that I needed to go to see the Gestapo. I was placed in a waiting cell for three hours, then I was taken to a stone cellar. It was cold and damp, good for wine, but not for people.

A Gestapo officer sat down across from me and offered me a cigarette. I took it. He was surprisingly young, spoke fluent French, and had the best polished black boots I had ever seen. Although I explained my background duties at Laurent-Perrier, he seemed unconvinced by my faux Canadian heritage. This adroit officer had me taken to a holding cell with other detainees. Maybe he thought that my North American ties could help him and his cause. My war experiences helped me cope with the intended sensory deprivations. After three days and a loss of some weight, I was released into the custody of Mrs. Nonancourt. She frantically called upon her nemesis, Otto Klaebisch, for his assistance. He did help, but it cost her some of her best 1927 and 1928 champagnes. Also, her allotment to the Germans was increased by ten percent for this year. She admonished me for not taking someone else with me. I got my machine parts at a heavy cost.

Later that month, I received a letter from Sylvia dated the prior month. She lamented about Hemingway and Bullard leaving for America. She also stated that Gertrude and Alice had left Paris, but would not divulge their whereabouts. Blacks and Jews were not wanted in occupied Europe. Jewish liberties were being squeezed with every decree and proclamation.

When the Ides of March came, Christina took a train to Paris. I could not chance the trip. She went with Thomas to the Mont Valérian prison. No answers were forthcoming for the first two days. I had urged her to visit the Le Vans. I had not heard from Henri by letter nor phone for three months. My wife came back by the end of March. Her reddened eyes and numb expression told a sorry story. Her brother was executed as a reprisal for one of the German officers who was assassinated by a resistance fighter. She and Thomas were able to retrieve his body and bury him outside of Paris. His remains could not be shipped to the Peretti family plot in Corsica. The Le Vans were under house surveillance. Only his war experience and police work saved him from eviction, for the present time.

One night, early in May, a family of four invaded the calm of our home. We let the parents and two children inside. After serving tea and cakes, we discovered that the family left Reims in haste fearing deportation. They were foreign Jews, originally from Frankfort. We introduced them to Marie-Louise in the morning. She was sympathetic, but she could not afford to risk the security of her family or employees. Also, she could not trust every employee not to collaborate. The family rested for two days. I took them to Father Blanchard. He had a plan. The children would go to a local family for care while the war lasted. The parents could be hidden in the rectory. The frightened parents agreed to the audacious plan. The family's intuition proved correct as the first round up of Jews began in Paris by mid-May. Most were interred at a camp east of Paris named Drancy.

Christina and I made a decision to send our children to a local summer camp. They were not happy about this, but these were turbulent times. This was a French attempt to emulate the youth camps program introduced in Germany with the Third Reich. We could not stand to see Alexa and Paul go. They pledged their love and allegiance to us and everything French. A sense of psychological malaise shrouded the populace. I kept myself busy with my machines and trucks. I dreamed of a field of corn, but there was none.

By the time our children came back from leadership camp, a second, larger round up of Jews occurred in Paris. I wondered about the Le Vans. Alexa did not appear to have changed from the experience, but Paul came back with a sense of cultural confidence and superiority. Also, we found out that he got into several altercations with other boys. My wife and I feared for their values. Christina was adamant about not sending them next year.

The year's harvest was just as bad as the prior year. A lack of sugar and other needed supplies hindered the fermentation processes. Mrs. Nonancourt had to use cases from pre-1940 years in order to meet her German quota.

By the end of the year, Jews were issued special ID cards. This was just a means of getting the Jewish population inventoried.

As the German invasion of Russia stalled on the frozen steppes outside Stalingrad, Moscow, and Leningrad, the French Resistance movement began to flex its growing talent for misinformation and disruption. They were getting bolder and more violent. Now, with America in the fight, hope got a shot in the arm. 1942 would be an interesting year, if we could survive it.

For Christina and me, the loss of control over our lives was becoming intolerable. We were willing to put up with a lot as a sacrifice for our children, but the murder of her brother and the indoctrination of our children changed my wife into a freedom fighter. I was more reluctant. I feared that collaborators would rat on us. War and human survival call on even the most well-intentioned to turn against each other, and the Germans were counting on that.

At first, Christina would pass coded messages from Father Blanchard to a woman named "Georgette." Early in March, a factory making precision aircraft parts was demolished with explosives. The next month, a rail line was destroyed leading to Reims from the east. The Germans and their French military puppets rounded up more hostages. A dozen resisters, so they claimed, were shot. In some cases, French collaborators were responsible for turning in their own countrymen. I was fearful for Christina, but she was a determined and stubborn Corsican. The violence and repression increased as each month passed. In May, two bridges were blown up that crossed the Marne outside of Reims. The Germans took control of the French police in Paris under the command of SS General Carl Oberg.

Also, a fascist art exhibit began in Paris, highlighting their anti-Semitic world views. By June, all Jews had to wear a yellow Star of David on their outer clothing in the Occupied Zone. I heard that some non-Jews also wore the Star in solidarity. Our wine *führer*, Otto Klaebisch, commandeered the chateau owned by Bertrand de Vogüé, head of Veuve Clicquot-Ponsardin. Our only hope was to occasionally listen to wireless radio broadcasts from the BBC indicating the setbacks of the Germans in Russia. Anyone caught listening to the BBC could be executed. The cell Georgette belonged to had one imbedded in a truck that defied enemy detection. We had heard conflicting stories as to who was leading the Resistance in our

region. Leaders were often susceptible to being turned in by agents
or double agents. Christina became more militant with the temporary loss of our freedoms and the growing success of the resistance
movement.

During the summer, the BBC informed us that a huge round up
of Jews in Paris had taken place. Men, women and even children
were taken to the Vélodrome d'Hiver, as a holding area, then they
were taken to the dreaded Drancy internment center. Deportations
in the Occupied Zone and Vichy France increased. Their final destination was to the slave labor camps in Germany and other occupied
countries. I called Henri, but a German woman answered the phone.
She stated than an SS colonel had taken over the Le Van's home.
She said that she did not know the whereabouts of the couple. I
surmised that they were taken to Drancy. This hit me harder than
the news of the thousands of Jews being deported. Henri treated
me like family. I was despondent. The following week, Adrienne
Monnier sent me a letter. Her longtime partner, Sylvia, was taken to
an internment camp for women at Vittel. The letter dropped from
my hand in an involuntary reflex. The world had truly gone mad.

Christina and I were working at the Tours-Sur-Marne facility
when a military *camion* arrived. The truck had human cargo. The
driver and two SS guards were in the front. They came for a foreign-
born Jewish couple who were employees of the company for several
years. Christina began to sob uncontrollably for her friend. I suddenly remembered what the old woman told me in 1918 at Séchault:
"You will survive yet another war." I ran for the truck and took out
my Browning pistol. When the *camion* headed north toward Reims,
I shot off my pistol and shouted, "Who is with me?"

Richard, and a worker by the name of Maurice, joined me. All
we had was my pistol, a Bolo knife, the crossbow, and an axe. We
made haste, following the District Nine Road north to Reims in
one of our trucks. With the sun beginning to set, we approached our
target near the village of Fontaine-Sur-Ay. We accelerated quickly
and came along the side of the German vehicle. I did not hesitate.
I shot the driver, then I fired away at the other two guards. The
truck drifted, slowed, then hit a ditch and turned sideways. I got out
and killed the last moving German bastard through the neck with

my crossbow, yelling "Die you motherfuckers." I removed my arrow and shot him in the head, for good measure, all my stored-up anger getting more than the best of me.

We opened the back of the truck. To my surprise, there was a bloodied German soldier amongst the frantic hostages. Before he could reach his rifle, I shot him at close range. I continued my rant and screamed, "Eat shit and die." My blood was up, and all the hostages knew it. We counted eighteen souls on board. A young woman was dead at the scene, and a few others were wounded. The men righted the truck. Maurice drove it to the woods near Verzy. The dead Germans were hidden near Mont Sinaï as darkness blanketed the wooded ravine. Richard and I crammed the civilians, including the dead woman, into our truck and took them to the church at Avize. Father Blanchard, I hoped, would know what to do. I had just killed four of the enemy in a few seconds. It felt good, but I was in deep. I wasn't sure what I was going to do next. All I knew was that I must stay alive.

Chapter Eighteen

Total War

Within a day of our assault on the German truck, most of the rescued prisoners were on their way to the French Alps, Nice, or Spain with the assistance of trusted *passeurs*. The woman was buried at the church, and two of the injured were allowed to recover at the rectory. The German and French authorities rounded up suspected Resistance members in Reims and at several other rural locations. Our good deed was swiftly punished with fresh hostages, deportations, and executions. It was total war, and there were no civilians.

Christina was adamant about taking her two Jewish co-workers to Georgette's Resistance cell. On the second night after the incident, she kissed me goodbye and told me not to worry. "Love you, 'VC'," were her last words to me.

I replied, "*Bon chance*, my Corsican beauty."

She left with a lantern and her two charges. They were to meet with Georgette's cell in a trunk about a half kilometer east of Avize. She did not return. Apparently, the Germans located the wireless BBC signal, or they were tipped off by collaborators. The truck was still in a field with a few weapons and Christina's lantern, but no wireless and no bodies. I was frantic. Marie-Louise went to Gestapo headquarters the next day. Her clout with Otto Blaebisch did not help. All she was told was that subversives were either shot or deported to Germany.

Although Marie-Louise had a bad cold and would have been

better off in bed, she did not hesitate to venture to the women's detention center at Vittel. I begged to be her driver. Petrol was a very scarce commodity, but we were able to gather enough for the journey. We brought along a large baguette filled with ham and Alsatian cheese, a bottle of Burgundy, and two cases of champagne hidden away in the trunk for bribes. Marie-Louise had a travel pass directly from Otto Blaebisch. It came in handy as we were stopped twice and questioned by French authorities. She did all the talking. She knew how to handle these bullies with a mixture of patrician charm and bluntness.

We arrived at the military style detention center by early morning. The camp was a large fenced-in area where most of Vittel's hotels were grouped around a manicured park. Only barbed wire in the storm-fences, and Nazi flags, portrayed the surreal place as a prison rather than a resort. A driving rain came down as we approached the main gate. Mrs. Nonancourt did not take *"Non"* from the much younger French gatekeeper. After ten long minutes, the impetuous guard let us through after he received the go-ahead on the guard phone. We were taken to the camp headquarters without the courtesy of an umbrella. The muddy chalk dirt covered our shoes after only a few steps from the Citroën to the building.

Marie-Louise was not impressed with the lack of courtesy. She asked for the person in charge. She expected to see the German Commandant, but an SS captain greeted us and invited Marie and I into his office. He had balding blond hair when he took off his skull and crossbones military cap. He placed a cigarette in his lips, lit up, and offered us the same. He had the thinnest lips I had ever recalled, barely lips at all. We made small talk about the weather and champagne. It was uncomfortable. Then he matter-of-factly asked me, "Is that a war injury?"

Without hesitation, I replied, "Yes, near Arras, beating back Bavarians too drunk with wine they stole while advancing."

The imperious captain laughed and lit another cigarette. Marie-Louise interjected, "Captain, you have been very hospitable. We beg your indulgence to locate a person by the name of Christina Clément, one of my employees. The Captain, Heinz Freitag, called for a sergeant to check the records. Nazis kept meticulous records.

The sergeant came back after several minutes and spoke German to his superior.

Captain Freitag was blunt, but respectful, "She is an enemy of the Reich. Her Resistance cell was caught with contraband, weapons, and deportees. She was taken to a work camp in Germany. Two of her group were executed. You are lucky she did not suffer the same fate. There is nothing I can do for you."

Marie begged and bribed him, but he only became more petulant. His only hopeful response was that he would ask to which camp she had been sent.

Before we adjourned, I asked if I could see Sylvia Beach, an American. I told the captain that I had known her when I lived near her in Paris. Marie-Louise was becoming worried and impatient with my obtuse request. She diverted Captain Freitag's attention by asking him to accept a case of champagne for his hospitality. He signaled his sergeant to secure Sylvia for a short meeting with me. While the captain was being entertained by Marie-Louise and her champagne, a guard brought in Sylvia.

Besides her drawn, placid expression, she was the same wisp of a woman I had always remembered. We hugged and held hands from across a large, oak table. She began, "I have met many British and Canadian women here. Some are bitter and territorial, but most are accepting and helpful to one another. I am thrilled to see you, but why are you here?"

"Christina, my wife, was captured by the Germans. She was trying to help a Jewish couple escape. They sent her to Germany, to a labor camp," my voice quivered as I tried to explain.

She leaned over and whispered, "Be strong for her and your children. She will return when the war is over."

All I could muster was, "I will try."

I could not tell Sylvia that I was the hunted one for killing four Germans recently. I risked execution every day I remained. We talked of Hemingway, Joyce, Stein, Adrienne and our former days in Paris for the remaining time we shared. Finally, we hugged and said, "After the war."

Marie-Louise and I left absent one case of champagne but with a little hope. I was sick with anxiety about Christina and my own possible capture. I obsessed about what I was going to tell Alexa and Paul when they returned from camp.

Two nights later, I was startled by a knock on my door at 2:00 a.m. Maurice's son, Albert, had bicycled from the Nonancourt Château to tell me that the Gestapo was looking for me. Marie-Louise's son, Charles, had turned on a light in the corner window as a warning. The phone lines had been cut. I had no time to think. It was run or die. I took a few items of clothing and some sundries and ran to my Renault. I took my pistol, knife, and crossbow. I wrapped a large piece of cheese and a bottle of wine in a sack to hold me over for two or three days. I asked Albert to promise to tell Father Blanchard to look after my children if I did not return soon. I gave him my medallion of St. Vincent to give to Alexa for safekeeping.

Albert, still out of breath, said, "Mr. Clément, do not worry. Our Marie-Louise will protect your children. God speed."

I drove the Renault in the dark down a dirt road to a hill that overlooked the vineyard. I could see the Gestapo sedan approach my home. They spent time searching it, then they set it on fire. It felt like I was abandoning my family. While the fire lit up the moonless night, I felt the greatest horror and fear for those left behind — especially my children. Still, I knew that I had to stay alive.

With a head start and the night as protection, I motored through the forest roads south of Épernay toward Montmort-Lucy. I was able to syphon some fuel from a parked truck. From this village that bordered the forest, I traveled to the Village of Condé-en-Brie, about ten kilometers southeast of Château-Thierry, just before the sun rose. I abandoned my Renault by a church. I drank my wine and ate cheese in the woods west of the village. Night fell. Oddly, I welcomed the darkness. I walked west towards Château-Thierry. I arrived at the marketplace by 3:00 a.m. undetected and very tired. I bribed a truck driver with fifty francs to hide me under his cargo of produce on his way to Paris.

Before noon, I made it to the Latin Quarter. I needed to get to Thomas's café. It would not be difficult to recognize a dark-skinned man with facial scars. After a brisk walk, I made it to the rear entrance of the café. A knock on the door brought the cook. He could see that I was in need of a bath and a shave.

I said, "I need to see Thomas, Thomas Peretti. It is very important, please."

After wiping his hands on his already soiled apron, he let me in, but he cautioned me to stay in the entranceway, near the bar. I could see the cook whisper to Thomas as he walked in my direction. He sported a few streaks of grey hair and thin black rimmed eyeglasses. Thomas looked at me, then we hugged. He knew that I was in trouble. In his office, with a cup of espresso, I told him the whole sad story. He flew into a rage. His two closest cousins, one dead and one in a labor camp in Germany, made him curse up a storm. I could see that he wanted to kill someone.

Thomas led me to his apartment over the café. I lingered in the tub for over an hour, closed my eyes and dreamed of Christina and I strolling down the *quai* on a warm, star lit evening. With a knock on the door, I came to reality. It was a waiter. He asked me to be ready to see Thomas in fifteen minutes. After a well needed shave, I pressed some new clothes and headed to the office. Thomas was seated behind his small desk. There was another man standing near the coatrack. He was younger than both of us, but his grey and black trimmed fedora gave him an air of maturity. Thomas introduced him as "Charlemagne." He began speaking with authority. I forgot about his youth.

The small office began to fill with cigarette smoke, but the door and window remained closed. The young, secretive man fanned away the smoke with his fedora while still puffing away and continued with his monologue.

"Very few are to be trusted. We often change plans and give out misinformation in order to catch those who would betray us. We are always being infiltrated by spies and collaborators. Trust no one and talk to no one unless they have been vetted by us. We are fighting an underground war literally and figuratively. Innocents will die. It cannot be helped. The closer the Allies get to victory, the harsher the Germans will become. They will take drastic measures to suppress us. We have no choice but to fight back. The enemy is losing in Russia, and the Americans will soon be fighting the Germans in North Africa."

He reminded me of Captain Fish, without the uniform. Other

than his height, he was not physically similar to "Ham," but he showed the same deftness, maturity, and resolve.

Charlemagne interrupted his train of thought and asked Thomas, "What shall we call your fugitive in-law? What *nom de guerre?*"

Thomas crushed his cigarette butt against the ashtray and quipped, "Renault."

"What do you think?" asked the amused Charlemagne.

I gave it some thought, took a drag and replied, "It is as good a name as any."

The young Resistance leader told me that I would receive coded messages. I was to carry out my assignment alone or with a specific person as designated in the message. The code needed to be memorized. I had three days to do it. Someone would test me, and we would both destroy the code given to me. Thomas, code name "Rasputin," stated that his café was not considered a safehouse due to the questionable patronage. The Gestapo and its spies had a distrust for Corsicans, probably for good reason. He gave me an address on Boulevard Arago, not far from the café. I was to ask for "Woodrow" after dark.

All I could say to Thomas was, "This is fuckin' unbelievable! I leave Paris in order to live a peaceful life, and now I am fighting Nazis as a guerilla fighter."

Thomas put his arm around me and remarked, "We are all casualties of this goddamn war. We must choose to be victims, or we must fight." He kissed me on both cheeks and said, "Now go get something to eat and start to learn the code. You will meet Woodrow tonight."

Due to the 8:00 p.m. curfew, it was dangerous to be out. Thomas believed that the short walk would be worth the risk. Shortly after midnight, we crossed the Montparnasse Cemetery close to Boulevard Raspail. Fortunately, the waning moon did not provide much light. We crossed the grounds between the Children's and Cochin Hospitals and made it to my destination by 1:00 a.m. Thomas knocked softly once. A woman was already waiting at the door. After an exchange of passwords, she welcomed us. In the dark, she led us up three flights to her apartment at the top of the old building. She lit one small used candle.

"I am Woodrow," she stated.

I replied, "Renault, Madame."

Names can be deceiving. The woman wore a tattered frock over her navy-blue blouse and beige slacks. She had light brown hair wrapped neatly in a bun. The candle threw off a harsh shadow on her cherubic face. It was difficult to guess her age.

Woodrow broke the silence, "I don't have much. Every damn thing is rationed or too expensive on the black market. I have tea for hot or water and wine for cool. I do not smoke, but you can."

"Wine, please," I replied.

Thomas interjected, "Renault is kin. He is here because he is on the run. That is all I can say."

While she handed me the wine, I could see that even without make-up, she looked more appealing in a friendlier light.

"We are all here for different reasons, but we do what we believe we must do," Woodrow demurred. She added, "You will not be here for long, it is too dangerous to stay in one place. I will look after you."

We talked of better times as the three of us finished her bottle. Thomas wished me well as he faded into the dark hallway.

For seventeen long days, I felt like a prisoner in this small, dimly lit apartment. At times I believed I would have been better off hiding out in the Vosges Mountains with the other fugitives. I spent my time thinking about the "what ifs" of my life, what fate awaited my family, and immersing myself in newspapers. Woodrow made sure I knew the code. She said it changed from month to month. I did make two letter drop offs at a location on Rue de Biévre, near the river of the same name. I always made the drop off at 7:00 a.m. It only took me four minutes to bike there from my location.

By October, I was moved to another location; ironically it was on Rue de Biévre. My new home was in an attic of another three-story walkup. A tailor shop was on the street floor. My contact was the tailor. His code name was "Bercy." He walked with a pronounced limp caused by a wound from the last war. Bercy shaved his head and had a goatee. He definitely had a special, unique look.

He gave me sunglasses and a pair of tinted reading glasses in order to help hide my scars. Bercy knew how to camouflage me. On a cloudless, sunny day in late October, Bercy and I bicycled to Le Jockey Club, near Boulevard de Montparnasse, on Rue Campagne Première. It was located close to the cemetery. I felt almost invisible peddling along the mostly pedestrian traffic with my *chapeau* and sunglasses. The club was not patronized by German military, but one had to be wary of collaborators and spies. We sat at a dark corner under a dingy Moët poster. We drank cheap Bordeaux and ate cheese, cold beets, and bread. The mission was simple: to get me the confidence to go out during the day. My social life had been strictly nocturnal for the last two months.

November of 1942 turned out to be a turning point in the war for France. On the eleventh, Armistice Day, the German military occupied Vichy France, and its ally, Italy, invaded Corsica. After Vichy was taken over by the Germans, the authorities interred Americans living there. This turn of events was largely due to the increasing viability and impact of the Resistance. In addition, the German Army had suffered major setbacks in Stalingrad and other areas of Russia.

I received a coded message from Thomas. He was livid about his homeland, Corsica, being occupied by "inferior" Italians. He asked me to do an assignment with his cell. We met in Bercy's basement. He brought a bottle of Corsican wine. After listening to his tirade about the Italian occupation of his homeland, he got down to business and said, "Our mission is to take out two collaborators. They were responsible for sabotaging an entire cell of the Comet Resistance Network."

His request startled me. I responded incredulously, "Are you shitting me? I'll kill Gestapo and SS, but not French citizens."

Thomas leaned into me and continued, "Look, these traitors are worse than the "Jerries." They turned against their own. We can expect trouble from the enemy, but we will take swift revenge on traitors."

I took more wine and asked, "How do you know they are traitors?"

He replied, "We know. They delivered a phony order to the wrong people. Are you in?"

"Yes," I whispered and then lit up a cigarette while I was thinking of my family. There was a lot of time to think.

Woodrow and I carried out the mission. The two targets left Le Dôme Café and walked down an alleyway. We bicycled from behind. I used my Bolo knife, and Woodrow killed her female target with an ice pick. She drew the letter "C" on the woman's forehead with lipstick. We raced off separately. I eventually reached Bercy's before curfew.

I trained to be an English Literature professor; now I am just a killer with a cause. I wondered what would have happened to me if I had stood trial back in Virginia. Maybe this was my punishment. I spent Christmas in Bercy's attic. He served me sausage, cheese, turnips, and a lot of bread. I washed it all down with cheap wine. I was just glad this fuckin' year was over. We drank to that.

1943 started off as dismally as 1942 ended. The Milice paramilitary force was formed by the Vichy government in order to counteract the Resistance. The members were mostly French street thugs. They stood out with their uniform of blue jacket and trousers, brown shirt, and wide blue beret. They were usually armed with a Spanish copy of the Smith and Wesson Model Ten revolver. In February, the STO, or Service du Travail Obligatore, was formed. It required young men over the age of twenty and, to a lesser extent, single women, to be sent to Germany to work for the war effort. This new conscription law caused large numbers of young men to flee. It was a powerful recruiting tool for the Resistance Movement. Also, an increasing number of Jews, including children, were being deported as an unusually cold and grey winter laid claim to Paris.

I was very cold in Bercy's attic. There were times that I could see my breath as the frost clung to the window panes like a work of art. Coal was in short supply. One day in early March, Thomas and Woodrow dropped by. He had another mission. He, Woodrow, and I were to kill two Gestapo agents as they left their headquarters in the Jewish Quarter, located on Rue des Rosiers, in the Third District. Agents would arrive at about 6:00 p.m. driving in the usual black Citroën "Traction-Avant." These Gestapo would interrogate new hostages during the evening shift. Thomas laid out the details. The building was guarded by two regular German soldiers with submachine guns. When the targets got out, we would come from opposite directions using grenades and British Sten submachine guns.

Woodrow would be walking with a stroller; a Browning automatic pistol was to substitute for a baby.

The Gestapo car was late. Woodrow stopped into a smoke shop in order to slow her trip. The car finally arrived fifteen minutes late, uncommon for Germans. In addition, an SS officer lit up a cigarette near one of the guards. Thomas and I were coming from opposite directions. At the same time, we kneeled and blasted the guards and the SS officer while Woodrow shot at the Gestapo. Bullets were flying in all directions. Thomas was hit by shrapnel from the side-walk and Woodrow was shot in the stomach by one of the Gestapo who was on the ground. I finished him off. Woodrow was bleeding out, dying. Thomas and I threw grenades at the entrance of the building and the Citroën. I helped him escape; his shoulder was bleeding through his jacket. We were able to make it to a safehouse located on Rue Santerre, close to the Rothschild Hospital, in the old Marais District. Thomas was patched up, but it was too dangerous to stay in this location.

The next morning, a meat truck took me to the rear of Bercy's store. My bald friend told me that it was not safe to stay. I had to hide out in the Bièvre River Sewer Gallery beneath Boulevard Arago until he could figure things out. Bercy led me to my new home. The accommodations included blankets, some clothing, and a few toiletries. He or someone using the password "suplice" would bring food and drink to me every other day. Needless to say, I had a new-found respect for his attic. I stayed in this godforsaken hellhole for close to two weeks. I cursed my decision to go to Paris almost as much as I cursed Thomas. I needed a shave and a shower quickly or the Germans would smell me out.

Bercy came with a sewer guide. He worked for the city sewer department and went by the code name "Baton Rouge." I called him "BR." He was a slight man with a bushy mustache and bushy black eyebrows to match. We departed with his portable headlight as our guide. We advanced through quarry tunnels and then made our way up the Médicis Aqueduct complex, all the way to a shelter beneath the city water department. This area was located just west of the Catacombs' public entrance. BR departed within minutes of our arrival. I was greeted by six members of a Resistance Group. The leader, by the name of "Picasso," introduced me to the nameless men and women. I was self-conscious about my hygiene.

Although I was in a lot of water in the past few weeks, I needed a good bath or shower. Picasso heard about my raid against the Gestapo interrogation center. He was impressed and gave me his condolences regarding Woodrow.

After one long day that I slept through, I was taken by subway tunnel to a safehouse on Avenue de Ségur in the Seventh District. I was led to a basement by a preadolescent girl dressed in a dark frock covering a beige blouse. She gave me soup and bread. She left without saying a word. The next morning, the same girl showed me the bathroom. She handed me a bar of soap and a towel. I asked her for her name, but she just smiled and retired. The tub was old, made of porcelain, and cracked in several places. I was familiar with this type from the last war. I soaked for several hours until my skin looked like a prune. I lathered up and took a long, hot shave. I finally was able to recognize myself. With a clean set of clothing, I felt like a human again.

A woman knocked and entered. She was probably the girl's mother. Before I began to speak, she said, "No names please. You can stay in the basement until you receive your next message, then you must leave. It won't be long, maybe seven to ten days."

She looked like a tall Sylvia Beach. The woman must have saved most of the food for her daughter. She looked gaunt, but strong of will.

I asked her, "What is the date today?"

She responded, "April, April 5. I have some bread and preserves for you, yes?"

I continued, "Any news? I have been hiding out for almost a month."

While serving me the little food she had, she replied, "Yes, American bombers attacked the Renault factory. I am surprised you did not hear it."

"I must have slept like a log," I demurred.

We only talked of times and places before the war, when we did talk, for the eleven days of my stay.

I received a message from Thomas that he was picking me up for an assignment later in the day. He hugged me as he entered the basement. I could feel his revolver and at least two grenades under his sportscoat. Thomas explained that our mission was to kill all the passengers arriving in a black Citroën sedan, probably Gestapo or SS men. We were to bicycle to the Eighth District at Eleven Rue des Saussaies. Thomas told me the building was famous for gang rapes, beatings, torture, and mutilations of Resistance members. I brought my Bolo knife and two automatic pistols. He told me that if we were separated, I must go to the L'Ètoile de Kléber, a brothel near Avenue Foch, owned by Madame "Billy."

We cycled on the shady side of the street as we made our way up Avenue Gabriel. At an intersection, I was stopped by two Milice thugs. They asked for my papers and my business. Before I tried to answer, one of the toughs in a blue béret searched me. In a few seconds, I was on the ground with a pistol pointed at the back of my head. My life flashed before me, then I heard two shots. The shots were not for me. I got up before I was trampled by frantic civilians. Thomas grabbed me by my arm and yelled, "Run!" My bicycle was disabled in the melee. As we crossed over to a side street, more shots rang out. Thomas staggered, then fell. I ran back to him. He was shot in the back and the neck. All he could say was, "Live."

As I stood up, I was hit by a bullet to my left shoulder. I ran in a zig zag pattern until I found an unattended bicycle. I stole it. I cycled up to the Arc de Triomphe, and I finally arrived at the renowned brothel. I felt lightheaded due to the loss of blood. Staggering to the back door, I knocked until I passed out.

When I came to, I was in a bed in a window lit attic bandaged and dehydrated. A slightly overweight, middle-aged woman handed me a glass of milk. The scent of her perfume reminded me of Madame Walker's Salon in New York. She bent over and whispered, "Take it, you lost a lot of blood. One of my doctor clients patched you up. My name is Aline Soccodato, but everyone calls me "Madame Billy."

I mustered a weak "Thank You," and asked how long I'd been here. Billy straightened up and replied, "You have been my guest for over two days. I have many guests; most pay and some do not. You are safe here. You are in the eye of the storm."

I was too weak to continue the conversation. The next day, I began to run a high fever. Billy sent for her doctor friend. I began to hallucinate. Images of soldiers hanging from a tree, talking to me, brought back a flood of bad memories. Apparently, I was being treated for pneumonia and an infection from my wound. I could not be moved. I would recover or die.

Billy had two of her staff look after me: a Jewish cook she was hiding, and one of her working girls who had seen duty as a nurse during the German invasion. The cook, Gilbert, came bearing a gift of chicken soup and vegetable stew. He had been separated from his family during the July 1942 round up of Jews in Paris. A Parisian lawyer and friend of his family told Gilbert about Billy. The young woman who tended to me, Rochelle, gave me the doctor's medicine and redressed my wound regularly. She looked like Madame LaBatt's older daughter, Jeanette, except for her pronounced make-up and short, red hair.

For all of three weeks, Gilbert and Rochelle cared for me in the "eye of the storm." By June, I was recovering nicely. I was walking up and down the establishment's floors to gain my strength when I ran into Madame Billy. The sun broke the night's grip on Paris, all the guests had gone, and the girls were sleeping.

Billy asked, "I see you are getting better. Was it the chicken soup or the touch of Rochelle?"

I reflected on her question and replied, "Both. Is it too early for a smoke?"

Billy looked more matronly without her "game face" make-up and softly responded, "Let's go to the kitchen for some strong coffee and a cigarette. Gilbert will fix us some ham and cheese on brioche."

As we relaxed at a long wooden table, she remarked, "My German clients, even the SS, come here to satisfy their fantasies. They do not think or do not want to think about what could be taking place in this labyrinth. You are safer here than in the sewers. So, tell me, what is your *nom de guerre?*"

My appetite had taken hold over me as I enjoyed my brioche. I finally looked up and replied, "Renault. I kill. My brother-in-law died in prison. My wife's cousin was killed on our last mission. My wife is somewhere in Germany. I need to get in contact with Madame Marie-Louise de Nonancourt. She employed my wife and

I at her vineyards. I need to get word to my children. Can you help me?"

"The German bastards intercept all types of communiques," she stated with agitation as she lit up another cigarette. "Who do you know that can go to your employer face to face? Both must be beyond reproach."

I instantly thought of Madame LaBatt. She was in ill health, but Jeanette could take her to see Marie-Louise. Billy stated that she had a good, reliable friend in Château-Thierry. She would drive to see her confidant and give her instructions. She did not trust telephones. Billy had the luxury of owning and using an automobile, thanks to the German authorities. Her friend would take a train to Reims to see Madame LaBatt. I handed a list of coded words to use to ensure that any letter from her friend would be safe if confiscated.

By mid-June, I received my response from Marie-Louise. The whereabouts of my wife were still a mystery. All Captain Freitag could tell her was that Christina was somewhere in Southeastern Germany. Alexa was working full time for the winery while she completed high school. Paul was assisting with the maintenance of the estate's machinery. Marie-Louise told my children that I was safe in Paris.

By July, I was fully recovered, physically. I read a lot of newspapers about current events outside my myopic world. The Gestapo took over the running of the Drancy Internment camp from the French. This meant more and quicker deportations to Germany or elsewhere. Jean Moulin, a Resistance Leader and strong disciple of General De Gaulle, was tortured and died on July eighth in Metz at the hands of the Gestapo. I felt better about killing those bastards after reading the news.

On Bastille Day, Billy told me that I needed to leave. I could not stay indefinitely. Others needed her assistance. I begged her. I wanted no more of the kill or be killed movement. Billy relented, a little. She told me that I could stay until September. I could work from dawn to mid-afternoon, repairing things in the house. I accepted her offer without hesitation.

I milked my stay as long as I could, until the end of September. Billy inquired if I would like Rochelle to keep me company before

I departed. I declined, but I did desire a kiss. I wanted to pretend I was with Christina, if just for a minute. Rochelle made it feel real, but I dare not ask for more.

I was offered a safehouse in Neuilly, a village just west of Paris, but I refused. About six weeks prior, Communist Resistance fighters fought German Regulars at the town hall. The Resistance was overwhelmed and retreated with heavy casualties. I thought it best not to try my luck there. I did stay at three safehouses in the Fifteenth District as the autumn sun cast its long shadow on the city late in 1943. I had to endure an attic with a partially false floor.

At another house, I was holed up in a sub-basement area near the coal bin as camouflage. The last house had me in an eight by ten-foot room behind a false wall. The entrance was behind a solid oak dresser. I always felt spied upon. My anxiety about collaborators increased with every move, and every hostile measure our oppressors promulgated on an increasingly belligerent populace.

By January 1944, I followed my gut and made it to a French Resistance Command post located near the Catacombs' public entrance. Picasso was still there. I only recognized a few faces from my previous stay. I saw at least a dozen members talking, smoking, eating, or sleeping. I confided in Picasso about my failed mission with Thomas, my stay with Madame Saccodato, and the forgettable safehouses. The youthful leader, with piercing blue eyes and straight, unruly jet-black hair, gave me a crash update on German retreats in Italy and Russia. Picasso enlightened me about the Allied liberation of Corsica in October. About thirty thousand German troops evacuated the island via Bastia, the Peretti family home. I lit up a cigarette with Picasso. I had only hoped Pierre and Thomas would have been alive to see it happen. I prayed that Christina heard the news before me.

Although this ragtag leader was half my age, I respected his tenacity and audacity. We drank some *pinard* and talked of better days. We did not talk about family lest we be caught and tortured. We did reminisce about our favorite clubs, cafés, and restaurants. I did bring up my frequent visits to Shakespeare and Company. Picasso knew of Sylvia Beach, but had never met her. We were both surprised and happy to hear that the Germans released her last spring. I admittedly bragged about my acquaintances with Hemingway, Stein, Joyce, Bullard, and other luminaries now deceased, hiding, or back in their home countries.

Picasso introduced me to his second in command," Monica." She starred at my ancient scars which must have had a sinister look under the glare of the table candles.

After a long, uncomfortable moment, she said, "I met you, yes, when I was very young, at Zelli's in Montmartre. Hum, maybe 1927 or 28. I remember the scar, I am sorry, but even the eye patch did not hide it all."

Reflexively, I turned away from the garish light. It could be true; she looked about thirty-five or older. I would not make a bet on a woman's age.

She continued, "You were with a woman, a real head turner, with a dark complexion for a white woman. I was with my lover, a woman in her late twenties. My first lover. Men or women, I do not discriminate. Shocked?"

"No, I dated a lesbian a long time ago, before you could talk. She let me in on her secret. I was naïve then. I was a student of literature. Now, I am a reluctant soldier, a killer, a survivor. Who you sleep with is no concern for me."

We drank to fatalism, and hope, and to liberation. My bi-sexual comrade looked like a French tango dancer, with her tight skirt and striped blouse. She had severely cropped black hair, not much longer than Picasso's. Her steely grey eyes looked through me as if she had lost her thought. She raised one leg on the table showing her much sought-after black stockings.

The next morning, we got down to business. We could feel the momentum was on our side. Like a wounded animal, we sensed the fear in the mood of our oppressors. We met in a concrete, dank room with poor ventilation. Picasso, Monica, an unkempt young man with horned rim spectacles named Beju, and I sat around a small square table that took up almost half the room. A guard was posted outside.

Picasso began, "A *camion* of replacement guards is arriving at the Hôtel Meurice in four days. It is the headquarters of a German garrison. We were lucky to get this bit of intel from a loose lipped German officer in the company of a bar maid. Our mission is to kill all inside the troop truck. There should be between twenty and twenty-five."

I interrupted, "I have killed Germans before the two of you were born. I've killed or helped kill ten or more over the past year. I have no stomach for more blood. I'll help blow up rails or buildings, but this is more than I bargained for. The only bastard I want to kill is the SS colonel who confiscated the home of my good friend, Inspector Le Van."

Monica got up and said, "Picasso, you are wasting your time with him."

There was a long silence as we began to fog the small room with the smoke of our newly lit cigarettes. Picasso ran his finger through his unruly hair, looked into the murky smoke, and replied, "We are not here for revenge or personal agendas. If you help us on this mission, we will help you with your revenge."

Monica and Beju disagreed, but I accepted his deal.

I proposed that we attack from the air. We needed to infiltrate the hotel posing as delivery men. Two of the attack group would go to the roof with grenades, M1 carbines, and pistols. Monica and Beju would be at a café. She would carry a Sten gun and grenades. I would have two pistols and my Bolo knife. I would bicycle toward the truck after the attack began, to clean up. The men on the roof would use a rope to repel down from the rear of the hotel. We went over the plan and contingencies for two days. Weapons were checked and rechecked.

We got into our positions and waited and waited. The *camion* finally arrived at dusk on a bitter, clear day, late in January. Before the truck came to a full stop outside the hotel, Picasso and his comrade opened fire with their M1 rifles. Making a hole in the truck canopy, they lobbed grenades from several floors above. It was sheer mayhem. Monica and Beju took positions behind a car from across the street. Machine gun fire and grenades exploded in the concentrated area at the hotel. We only had a few more seconds before Germans would pour out of their headquarters with machine guns. Some of the Germans were on fire, making easy targets. I bicycled until I got to within twenty yards of the scorched scene. I popped off two guards coming out of the hotel and three more in the street. Fire started to come from the German survivors. I released my grenades in their direction and rode my bicycle a few blocks until I reached a designated safehouse.

The next day, I reached my Resistance enclave. Everyone made it back except Beju. He was mortally wounded. Monica finished him off. Without much of a choice, and to limit the suffering, these were considered mercy killings. However, the mission was considered a great success. We estimated fifteen to twenty dead or wounded. There would be hell to pay. The group decided to hide out in the Catacombs in the Port Mahon Quarry, east of the Montparnasse Cemetery. We had enough provisions to last two to three weeks. We found a large stash of weapons there. Our outside contact was able to bring us some additional food and some cosmetic items. We all smelled, so no one noticed. We were told that the Germans had captured and executed several Resistance cells, including members of the Manouchian group. This cell was dominated by Jewish Communists, led by Missak Manouchian. We blamed collaborators. By the end of February, most of us returned to our cozy headquarters.

It was not until the end of March that Picasso began to plan the assassination of my SS colonel. His name was Heinz von Richter. He used Le Van's Renault. In early April, we missed our attempt on Richter as he was driven along a different route from Le Vésinet to Gestapo Headquarters. We tried three days later. This time we had a truck stall on one of the Seine River bridges, slowing traffic enough for me to shoot Richter and his driver from my bicycle while horns were blaring, drowning out my shots.

I rode to a safehouse on Avenue Victor Hugo in the Sixteenth District near the Seine. The house was in an alleyway behind the avenue. I was fortunate enough to be housed with a goat in a shed. I was given a daily ration of bread, watered down milk, and cheese. On Sundays, I also received sausage. The goat and I kept company for six weeks; then my current guardian, an elderly widow with green eyes and a still agile figure, told me that the Allies landed in Northern France. All Paris was ablaze with chatter and hope, except the collaborators. Their fervor could not be suppressed. The Allies were here, coming from Normandy and from the South of France like an anvil. A few days later in the midst of our excitement, I learned that German troops massacred an entire town, Oradou-sur-Glane. Men, women, and children were gunned down or burnt alive in their church by those SS bastards. Hundreds of civilians were wiped out. An entire town gone! I decided to leave my friend, Rosette the goat, and make my way to my headquarters.

Picasso was there, but he was not in charge now. The size of the organization had grown much larger since April. Picasso's leader went by the name of Argonne. I could relate to that name. A large forest, near the Meuse River, is named Argonne. It was the place where the American Army fought their biggest and costliest battle during World War One. He looked nothing like Picasso. Argonne was short, thin, and balding. His left arm was partially paralyzed, and he walked with a limp. He was a chain smoker, not unusual. We were more open about our attacks. We lost men and women, but we all knew each lost life meant dignity for France. Monica was killed just before Bastille Day. She had killed as many Germans as anyone I had known. She was an emblem of The Resistance.

On July 14, Bastille Day, a rally sprung up at the Place Maubert near Boulevard St. Germain. French flags were flying everywhere. Hitler was burned in effigy. The table was set for the German evacuation as the Allied Forces broke out of Normandy into Central France. By mid-August, the railroad workers and police stopped working. On August fifteenth, the Resistance forces set up barricades in the streets to retard the retreat of our enemy. The Metro also closed down. We were firing at them from windows, roofs, and buildings as elements of the Free French Army, under General LeClerc, began to enter Paris from the north and west. We also attacked the paramilitary, Milice, with a vengeance. In that case, it was French against French. We inflicted a lot of casualties on the Germans and the Milice by the time Paris was liberated. Many of the Resistance members joined after the Allies landed. I did not have that luxury.

I did not wait around for all the celebrations, the round ups of collaborators, and political executions and retributions. All I wanted to do was see Sylvia Beach before I headed east with the Allies to find my way back home.

On August 22, I found Sylvia at her store with Adrienne at her side. We hugged and kissed while bullets could still be heard from the rooftops. I asked if she had any *Collier's* magazines. She laughed and said that she had the latest one from June 1940 hidden away. We only had iced lemon water to celebrate. She phoned the Ritz Hotel and asked for Hemingway. He was coming over with a few comrades and some champagne. I asked if he could find a bottle of Laurent-Perrier. The next call was to Marie-Louise, but we could not get through. We tried Madame LaBatt's home but had no luck there either. We sat in the back of her store and talked of the gay times with Joyce, Ford, Hemingway and others. It seemed like a century ago.

While the August sun began to set, Hemingway pulled up in a jeep with three associates. Apparently, he and some Free French he appropriated had "liberated" the Hôtel Ritz. He was working as a war correspondent traveling with American and Free French forces for the last two months. He was wearing an army waist jacket. He was bubbling with enthusiasm and pride. We opened three bottles of champagne in the street and drank from the bottles disregarding cyclists and other traffic while occasional shots rang out. We all had a very spartan dinner at Le Dôme. The only thing that was in abundance was cheap wine.

I went to see the Victory Parade at the end of August. Troops of all the Allied Nations marched down the Champs-Élysées to a jubilant crowd, many, many rows deep. French, American, British and other flags hung from lamp posts. For me, the one great missing feature was Black American troops. As in the First World War, this war had the same thing in common: the color of the soldiers in the parade was all white.

By early September, I traveled with refugees following the Twentieth Corps of Patton's Third Army to Reims. I arrived at Madame LaBatt's estate late on the sixth. Jeanette greeted me. Her mother was in bed, suffering from cancer. I was treated like family. Jeanette told me that German officers had occupied her home for more than a year. The next morning, Jeanette was kind enough to lend me her bicycle. It took me all morning to get to my hometown. I finally found Alexa at the home of Marie-Louise. I ran into the kitchen and found my Alexa. I fell to my knees. We cried and kissed for a long time. I composed myself and asked her about Paul.

She said, "Papa, they took him to Germany in June, to a factory. I do not know where. He is only sixteen! Mama has been gone for so long." She started to cry again.

We held each other tightly as the morning light flooded into the room. I whispered, "We have each other for now."

Chapter Nineteen

Long Road Home

I was long overdue writing to my family in Fredericksburg. Now that I was relatively safe, I sent a long letter to Millie via Adeline Hitchcock. Two weeks later I received her reply. Paulette and her husband had another child, a boy named Everett, in 1943. Vera, Millie's youngest, just turned sweet sixteen. I had never seen her. She sent pictures of both. Vera was light skinned, like me, with big hazel eyes. She appeared tall and thin with ponytails down to her lower back. Millie stated that there was always a space in the cornfield for me. She anguished about my wife and son. I did not tell her half of what I had endured so far.

Alexa often asked me about what I did in Paris and how I survived. She was a woman now, eighteen, thin as a pipe and tall with long, auburn hair. Her hazel eyes pierced my lonely heart. I let her talk about her ordeal. She was happy to release what she had held in for so long. It was cathartic for her. She had grown very close to Marie-Louise, who acted like a second mother to her. Alexa described how Paul was more influenced by the French authorities and German occupiers than she. His ideologically indoctrinated peers became his new family.

On an October evening, after the harvest, Alexa cornered me with rum cake and brandy. As she lit a cigarette for me, she inquired, "Papa, please tell me the truth about Paris. I am old enough. It will be good for you to get it out. You can confide in me."

I did not let the rum cake go to waste. I paused long enough to say,

"Darling Alexa, some wounds are too deep to reopen. All I can say is that I met many courageous patriots, men and women, who risked their lives for me and for the liberty of France. Thomas, your mother's cousin, helped me when I made it to Paris. He introduced me to the French Resistance. Thomas died fighting the enemy. I participated in the killing of our oppressors. I was protected by patriots in their basements, attics, and even in a barn. Sewers became my home. I do not want to get 'into the weeds' of how I did what and when. Can you understand?"

Alexa looked away from the candle on the long wooden table and sighed, "Momma, I fear for her. How long will this hideous war last?"

I let my cigarette burn out and replied, "The war will soon be over. The Allies are tightening the vise on Germany. The Russians are near the German border, and the Western Allies are close to the Rhine River. I hope it will be all over by the spring."

She cried, and I held her tightly and stroked her hair as the candle flickered with the breeze from the partially opened window.

Just before Christmas, we were shocked to learn that the German armored forces punched a hole in the American lines in the Ardennes Forest. It was a desperate plan to divide American and British forces and disrupt their supply lines through Belgium, all the way to the Port of Antwerp. The American First Army was caught off guard, as were the French over four years ago. Bad weather prevented Allied air power from attacking the German tank divisions. Finally, after two long weeks, elements of Patton's Third Army counterattacked, bringing relief to the beleaguered, half-frozen soldiers. The battle lasted an entire month amidst the snow and bitter cold. We all felt that Germany was near exhaustion. Killing now, seemed needless now, but Germany must agree to unconditional surrender, not just an armistice.

On May 7, Germany surrendered to Allied forces at Reims. Madame LaBatt did not live to see this. Her funeral was three months prior. I was glad to see her family and her girls, although not under such sad circumstances. The ground had been frozen. They were not able to bury her until the spring. Upon news of this surrender, Marie-Louise held a party for the entire Laurent-Perrier corporate family. It was a muted celebration. We all knew someone who was killed, deported, wounded, or missing due to the sixty months of war. We drank champagne from 1928. Marie-Louise and her remaining sons gave speeches.

Maurice, the eldest, was in a German concentration camp. Both he and Bernard had joined the French Resistance. Bernard fascinated us with his story of retrieving hundreds of cases of 1928 Champagne Salon. Sergeant de Nonancourt and his men reached Hitler's private wine cellar located at Kehlsteinhaus in Bavaria. He blew off the steel doors leading to the cellar. There was estimated to be about forty thousand cases hidden there, stolen by the Germans during the 1940 invasion. Bernard was awarded the Croix de Guerre. Regardless of our own personal losses, we clung together like one big family providing stability and emotional support. The seventeen-year-old champagne soothed the roughness of my harsh moods.

The jubilation of victory and peace subsided as May made way for June. We were all anxious to be reunited with our loved ones. I was repairing one of the old trucks at Le Mesnil when Paul arrived. He had been in Germany for a year. He was only seventeen, but he grew the height of two fists since I saw him last. We said nothing, just hugged and kissed as Alexa joined our embrace. After a long rest, we celebrated outside our unfinished, rebuilt cabin. Paul did not let Alexa nor I into his private world. He seemed normal, but I could tell he had fresh emotional scars. He was intensely private. His emotions were deep like a vein of gold hidden away in a dark place. Paul did explain that he was taken to the Krupp Arms factories in Essen, Germany. He spent twelve hours a day making munitions with other boys and women taken from occupied countries. My Paul lost weight. He weighed about a hundred twenty pounds on his five-foot ten-inch frame. We could make up the weight. I was more concerned about his emotional health.

Summer arrived. There was no Christina. We asked all the returning forced labor refugees about her, but to no avail. We were saddened to hear that Maurice de Nonancourt died in one of the concentration camps. I traveled to Reims in July to the missing persons center for the region. I was told that most of the women from this region were taken to Siemens, Bosch, Thyssen, or IG Farben factories, unless they were sent directly to concentration camps. I was given a list of women who had returned from these places.

I returned home to get Alexa and Paul to assist me. It felt like I was back with Henri Le Van solving a murder case. This time it was very personal. We wasted no time in tracking down women from the Reims-Épernay metropolitan area. We had Christina's pictures to show. We interviewed scores of women during the July heat, with no results.

On a sweltering day in early August, Alexa found a young woman who had worked at the IG Farben chemical factory, the Buna Werke facility, at the dreaded Auschwitz Concentration Camp. I met with this woman that evening at her apartment in Northern Reims. She invited Paul, Alexa, and I into her bare, but neat dwelling. She introduced herself as Claudia Launay. There were only two stick chairs at her small round table. Alexa sat in a rocker while Paul stood. Claudia was about Alexa's age. Her eyes appeared hollow and dark below the lower lids. Her blond hair was cut short, accentuating her long neck. Her loose, red blouse and long skirt did not do justice to her thin but still shapely figure. She offered us lemon water and rice crackers during the silence.

I said to Claudia, "My daughter informs me that you knew my wife at Auschwitz."

She took a sip of water and starred out the sole stark window. "I knew her, Christina, your Christina from Corsica. We worked at the chemical factory near the camp. We never got too close to anyone. We lost many workers. One day you are talking to them, then they are gone. The cots are never empty for long. There are always new bodies, more workers."

I continued impatiently," Do you know what happened to her? Please let us know all you can."

Claudia looked at me with those hollow eyes laid bare without make-up and replied, "Monsieur, I was freed by the Russians. I had not seen your wife for at least a month before our liberation. Maybe she was moved to a different barracks. I do not know. The Germans kept meticulous records. They know. Those bastards know. Your wife, she was a strong woman. I liked her. She helped me live through that hell. I was raped several times, lost count.

Maybe that is why I survived so long there — thirty months. I hope you find your Christina."

My heart sank. Alexa ran out of the apartment. I asked Paul to console her while I continued with Claudia. She remarked, "You have beautiful children."

I refused her offer for more water and said, "And you? Any family?"

Claudia rubbed her eyes and answered, "A brother in Marseilles. He is older, married with two children. Our parents are deceased. I hope that I did not offend your daughter. The war has blunted my conversation skills."

I thanked her for everything. We hugged, and I whispered that I wished her a happier future. I gave her a bottle of 1928 Champagne Salon and parted with, "Open it on a happy occasion."

Paul, Alexa, and I returned to Le Mesnil in a somber mood. The next day, I went to see Father Levesque at Avize. Father Blanchard had been murdered by the Gestapo for his resistance activities. The new priest was half of his predecessor's age. He had pepper colored hair and wore black rimmed glasses. Father Levesque invited me into his study. He offered me a glass of Pinot Noir. As he sat back in his large oak chair, he took off his biretta and exposed his receding hairline.

I began, "Father, I plan on going to Frankfort, to the chemical factory Christina worked at, to find out what happened to her. She has not returned. Please bless my journey, please pray for her. Here is her picture."

He leaned forward and spoke, "Although we live in a land of villages, your exploits are becoming legend here. I will pray for you and your wife. Here, take my rosary and a picture of Saint Christopher, our patron saint of travelers." I departed with some hope.

With the blessing of Mrs. De Nonancourt, I took her Citroën to Strasbourg. Once I reached this medieval, bucolic Alsatian city, I headed for the French Second Armored Division Headquarters. I asked for a travel permit to Frankfort. I was told to fill out forms, show my I.D., and return the next day. The queue line was very long, even at opening time. Finally, by mid-morning, a sergeant from Amiens listened to my request. I got my pass for seven days in the French Occupied Zone of Western Germany.

I drove across the Rhine River. The villages reminded me of the destroyed French villages and towns during my service in 1918. Remains of burnt-out tanks, vehicles, and artillery were strewn along the roads and in the fields. Driving up the east side of the Rhine also reminded me of my regiment's occupation duties after the Armistice, twenty-seven years prior. Towns like Ettingen and cities like Mannheim appeared eerily similar with the exception of current occupation forces and their assets of war. I stopped at a café across from the largely undamaged Baroque Palace in the center of Mannheim for a bite to eat. The colors of the season transcended the ugly starkness of human conflict.

I arrived at Frankfort too late to visit the Farben Headquarters. I stayed at a boarding house near the Opera House upon the advice of a French Occupation NCO. Frankfort, due to its industrial proclivity, did not escape the relative safety enjoyed by Mannheim. Much of Frankfort was bombed out. The area around the IG Farben complex was devastated. The building itself, however, was left largely intact. I was surprised to find that the Supreme Allied Commander, General Eisenhower, made his post war headquarters in the building. Also, many homeless city dwellers were accommodated in sections of the complex. Security was extremely tight. I had to go through a series of inspections and interviews before being allowed to enter the section of the complex that housed some Farben administrative personnel. After three hours of red tape, I found myself in the anteroom of a bureaucrat, by the name of Ruprecht Kassel, in charge of women labor personnel. I was not alone. In about one hour, I had an interview with an assistant. She was given Christina's photo and details as she typed away. I was told to return in two days, giving them time to do their research.

This reprieve gave me a chance to tour the city's ruins. It was very odd to see residents all dressed up walking nonchalantly past heaps of bricks and bombed out buildings on their way to work. French and American military tanks and trucks dotted the surreal landscape. I came across two Negro MPs. I offered them a smoke, and we talked about the war. The corporal, Frank Dozier from Detroit, told me of his exploits with the *femmes* of the seedier side of Paris. He gushed as he detailed how he was sexually bribed by madams needing to maintain their working relationships in the lower part of Montmartre. His ranking NCO interjected with a smoke dangling from his lips, "Doz, man, you ain't seen half the action you been gabbin' about. But I do tell, you got stories to spin back home. Jus' make sure no one goes gunnin' for you."

The sergeant hailed from Flint, Michigan. He just went by the name of "Hammer." I asked if things had changed for Negroes in America over the last twenty years. Hammer replied, "Shit, not really. Less lynching down South, but all the same bullshit. We is separate, not equal. Check back wid me in another twenty."

I returned to the bleak office of Heir Kassel as requested. After a two-hour wait, his secretary led me into his inner office. A desk, a coat rack, two chairs, and file cabinets, lots of file cabinets, lined the sparse office that had no pictures and needed a coat of paint. My heart was racing. I had gone over this scene in my mind for days. Heir Kassel sat in his wooden high-back chair behind his well-worn mahogany desk. He stood up and shook my hand. I sat down and looked at him directly, making him uneasy. He spoke fluent French. The Germans were meticulous recordkeepers, even with death, so I believed he had information for me. My fate was in the hands of this man, not much older than myself. He still wore a stiff collar, fashionable a generation ago. He had an abundance of grey hair and an even greyer complexion. He inhaled deeply before addressing me.

"I am so sorry Mr. Clément. Your wife died of typhus late last year. She was buried in a mass grave outside of the factory location near Auschwitz. This is all I know. I am deeply sorry for you and your family."

I was prepared for this intellectually, but not emotionally. I stared out the single window at the ruins below. Heir Kassel interrupted my silence, but it was just noise to me. I got up to leave, then I reached down and grabbed my Bolo knife from my ankle holster. With a quick thrust, I secured the knife against Kassel's throbbing white neck.

I said, "Feel the cold steel. You are a half inch from death."

My voice grew louder and louder. His secretary rushed in. She begged me to release her boss. I did, but not before I hauled off and punched him with a force that leveled the shocked German.

She ran out and came back with two soldiers. I surrendered peace-fully, numbly. Heir Kassel finally came to. His nose appeared to be broken. Wiping the blood from his face, he waved off the guards. He composed himself and addressed everyone in the office.

"I will not press any charges. I have been attacked before, and I will be attacked for as long as I have to tell civilians that their loved ones died at the hands of Germany. Your wife is buried in Mass Grave number A3. It will not profit you to visit now. Soviet domina-tion of Poland is not a guarantee of your safety; maybe in the future. Go, Mr. Clément, and take care of your children."

I left without my wife and Bolo knife. The journey home was like a morbid trip down memory lane. I seethed with anger and helplessness. I wondered why God would let this happen to a woman who only wanted to help those who needed help. Before I crossed over to Strasbourg, I came across a fallow, unplanted field. I decided to exit the Citroën and rest myself in it. Looking up at the cloudless sky, I closed my eyes and traveled back in time to Fredericksburg. I thought of Millie, Mary, and I together at the Civil War Cemetery, and alone fishing the Rappahannock River. The monuments and the garden of stones did not care of our pres-ence nor our skin color. I laid there until the sun finally set on this long, sad day. I made it home before the sun rose again, dreading what to say to my children.

Upon my return, they bolted into my bedroom as the sun's light pierced the room. Now I felt like Heir Kassel. They could read my face. There was not much to say. Alexa and I hugged. Paul stormed out cursing the gods. It was a difficult time. We buried ourselves in our work at Laurent-Perrier. Regardless, the strain of the surround-ings and recent memories prompted Paul and Alexa to want a new, fresh start in Paris.

By September of 1945, we bade farewell to the Nonancourt family and our colleagues. We settled in an obscure, nineteenth century walk-up in the Fifteenth District, near where Christina and I had lived when we first married. The apartment only had two bedrooms. Paul and I occupied the larger bedroom with a view of the fire escape. Neither of us was happy with this arrangement.

Paul entered college at Sciences Po in Paris. It's former name, École

Libre des Sciences Politiques was changed that year after France was liberated. My son wanted to become an economics major. He moved out in January to a shared apartment near the St.-Germain-des-Prés neighborhood, hugging the Seine River. Paul made the move to diffuse the tension between us. He partly blamed me for the death of his mother. Between his studies, he worked as a barman at a new Corsican club close to the college.

Alexa appreciated her relative privacy, but she still felt fettered by my paternal presence. She interviewed at several hotels as a waitress. Her real ambition was to become a sous chef. Alexa landed a job at the famous Hôtel Ritz, near the Louvre. My experience with this establishment for over ten years helped my daughter secure the job. She used her spare time learning from the sous chef there. Alexa joined with two other young women to share an apartment near the hotel. One roommate worked as an assistant to a Parliament Deputy, and the other worked as a tour guide in the Louvre by day and a café singer by night. I was fortunate enough to land a job as an auxiliary teacher at the same École Normale Supérieure that I taught at before I left Paris. I also worked at a motorcycle repair shop near my apartment. My drinking became as reflexive as breathing, and there was no one to stop me. I was barely able to maintain my jobs and some sobriety. I believed that I failed my wives, and that Paul was adrift, alone in a crowded world.

By the spring, we all traveled back to Laurent-Perrier. A dedication ceremony was planned for a headstone for Christina. Marie-Louise assisted. She was a saint. I broke down and cried like a child.

Her headstone read:

CHRISTINA MARIE CLÉMENT
Nee 25 Mai, 1898
Mort 14 Decembre, 1944
L'épouse de Joshua
La mère d'Alexa et Paul
Mort Pour La France
Toujours L'audace

We returned to Paris amid labor strikes due to lower wages and food shortages. Long lines at merchants frayed people's already unhinged nerves. One of the other memorable events in 1946 was that prostitution was officially outlawed. It is doubtful that the world's oldest profession would disappear, as different rules and different players filled any vacuum for opportunity. Also, General de Gaulle resigned his Presidency to write his memoirs. We all looked forward to reading how he single-handedly saved France.

Alexa was enjoying her bohemian life, on her own, in gay Paris. Sometime in 1947, she met an Italian who was visiting the city on business. They met at the hotel. She was secretive about the courtship until she asked me to meet him. We met on neutral grounds at the Luxembourg Gardens. We had espresso and sat near the fountain. His name was Phillipe Tommaso Pietra, and he was the son of an Italian father and an Alsatian mother. He was born in 1920 in Milan. Phillipe worked as an importer of meat products from Western European countries. He was good looking, but he was shorter than average. His trimmed mustache added depth to his boyish face. It was difficult to understand his accent that was a combination of French and Italian, and I had to listen intently. I could tell from their body language that they were in love. The way they looked and touched reminded me of Bea and Christina. Their romancing continued through 1947. Paul had just graduated with an economics degree and took a job with Citroën. He enjoyed women, though not any single one. Alexa became an assistant sous chef at the Ritz. She loved the culinary world. I worked with a lack of enthusiasm.

Later in the year, I visited Josephine Baker at Le Vésinet. Her home had been confiscated by the Germans and Allies during the war. She greeted me in lingerie and a turban. Josephine was only forty-one, still sexy, but the war had mellowed her vixen personality. We had not seen each other for many years. Her Black butler attended to our needs, mostly replenishing our glasses with liquor. We sat in her piano room while her friend, Colette, played melancholy notes as we consumed an abundance of champagne. We talked of the void of time in our relationship, avoiding the most traumatic events. She sang for me in French and in English. She sang and danced as in a trance, holding a bottle of champagne in her right hand and a cigarette in the other.

I was too drunk to leave. Ms. Baker put me up in a guest room above the spiral staircase on the second floor. The next morning, the house was empty except for the butler. Josephine had left a note on my table. It read:

> *Dear Joshua, we are survivors. There is a reason we are meant to carry on. Don't lose hope. Remember, 'The Sun Also Rises,' Love, your Josey."*

Throughout this period, I visited Sylvia Beach and confided in her like a drunk confides in a bartender. She could tell that I needed help. She helped the best she could with herbal teas and homeopathic remedies, but my depression and mood swings persisted. I attempted to bond with Paul by fishing with him at the Ile de Paris. He appeased me, and I felt better for the effort.

By the end of 1947, Alexa and Phillipe were engaged. The wedding was set at the Nonancourt château for June the next year. It was a beautiful affair. I walked the bride down the church aisle in Avize. Father Levesque officiated at this joyous occasion. We had about a hundred guests including the LaBatt sisters, and Sylvia Beach and her partner, Adrienne. Former associates of Laurent-Perrier and the Nonancourt family attended. Even Kadid Kolda and one of his wives from Senegal attended! We reminisced about our reckless times in Paris. The 1928 champagne flowed like water. It was a beautiful event; my daughter was so happy.

The new couple made their home in Montmartre. By the Christmas holidays, Alexa told me that they were moving to Milan, her husband's home base. I was devastated. I could not change the inevitable. Their move was decided. I was inconsolable. It seemed like I had turned into my father, children leaving me, and the bottle had become my best friend. I was a bit older than he when he passed away. How much longer could I last?

With Alexa in Milan, I attempted to get closer to Paul again. The war and the death of his mother had a deep, scaring effect on him. He coped, by working long hours and drinking like his father. We had dinner at my apartment on Rue de l'Église on a late July Sunday evening when the hot stale air was tempered only by the sunset. I was excited to discuss the new proclamation by President Truman to integrate the Armed Forces. It took two World Wars and political activism to do the right thing. There is no greater equalizer for respect than being together in a fire fight or foxhole. Paul was in a reticent mood; maybe the wine brought out his caustic disposition. I do not think my crêpes had anything to do with the tension in my small kitchen. Suddenly, he turned to me with fury in his eyes.

"Why did you not stop mother? You knew the danger," Paul demanded to know. His emotions poured out like a once dormant volcano.

I let him cool down, then I responded, "You knew your mother. She was determined to help her friends. I tried. I could not stop her. Do you think I wanted to risk my wife? Losing one wife is terrible, losing two is beyond comprehension."

There was a long, dead silence. I continued, "Paul, your mother could not live in a world that took away her freedom, her control over her life, regardless of the cost."

He left dissatisfied with my explanation. I finished off another bottle of Corsican wine, while I gazed out the open parlor window thinking about happier times, distant memories, and people I loved and lost.

The weeks and months passed. Paul and I had a civil, if not a close relationship. Alexa and her husband visited every August for three weeks, while I visited them in Milan during the Christmas holiday season. On February 10th of 1952, I became a grandfather. Alexa gave birth to a son and named him Christopher Pierre Albion Pietra. I was able to take time off from work to visit them. I wasn't sure who my grandson looked like, but I was just happy that he was a healthy baby boy. Alexa and I strolled Chris along the upscale Brera neighborhood, and in Sempione Park on an unusually warm day in late February. Her joy was tempered by the fact that her child, named after her mother, had no maternal grandmother. She really liked Milan. Alexa had no plans to return to France. Our time together passed quickly, filled with memories of Christina and the good times before the war. It was the happiest and most serene time I had spent since the invasion, a dozen years ago.

It was July 21, when tragedy struck my life again. The phone rang at 3:15 a.m. In the ten seconds it took me to answer the phone, my mind raced with melancholy thoughts. Did anything happen to Christopher, Alexa, or Paul? I feared the worst; I had a sense for the dark realities of life. Paul had died. He was driving from St. Denis just north of the Paris city limits and crashed into a large tree. He died alone and at the age of twenty-four. My second son had died. I lost two wives and two sons. Then I wondered if it was an accident or suicide?

He was buried at Montparnasse Cemetery. Alexa took care of the details. I was too frozen with guilt and mourning. The toll of personal loss left me numb. My daughter was worried for me. She forced me to see the priest at St.-Séverin Church. This clerical intervention only made me a stronger disciple of drink and drugs. Words of comfort and redemption were lost on me. It was easy for me to lose my job and my apartment. As an expert of living in subhuman places during the war, I did not find it a challenge living on the streets and parks during the warm weather. In the winter of 1953, I lived at several different boarding houses along the outer edges of Paris' Left Bank.

On a snowy day in February, I sought refuge at the shelter for the homeless at St.-Séverin Church. While I was consuming potato soup and bread, a Negro came up to me and sat down. He introduced himself as Lester Miller. He recognized me.

"Are you Sergeant Carpenter, Virgil Carpenter of the Hellfighters?" he inquired, as I continued to slurp down the remains of my soup.

My immediate inclination was to respond that my name was Joshua Clément, but I was tired of the bullshit. I turned to this bald Black man with a cropped white beard and said, "Yes, you are right. I am your man. Were you also with the 369th?"

Lester put his arm around me and replied, "Headquarters Company. I was a corporal with HQ. I recognized you during our training days in the States when I was with the Third Battalion."

"I'm surprised you noticed me after all this time, especially with my eye patch," I replied with some amazement.

Lester continued, "I returned to France in 1921, after the riots. I knew Henry Johnston from Arkansas. He was severely wounded in the Argonne only to be shot to pieces with his three brothers when he returned home. I worked at many jobs in Paris. During the last war, I laid low in the Pyrenees. Now I am the Director of Services for the Homeless in the Fifth and Sixth Districts. You are not the first Hellfighter I've come across over the years in Paris. Tell me about yourself."

I hesitated, then replied as I lit a cigarette, "I am like Job. That is why you found me here and not at The Ritz. I returned to Paris shortly after you."

Lester stroked his beard and asked, "Let me take you out for a good meal. I insist. You pick the joint. I won't take no for an answer."

I got up and said, "La Tour d'Argent, on the Quai de la Tournelle. Next Friday at eight, good for you?"

Lester shook my hand and replied, "Yes, at eight."

"Good, I'll shower and shave at a boarding house first," I mused. I left with another cigarette in hand.

I had the best meal in years. Lester could tell I was a heavy drinker, as I was unaffected by a full bottle of wine and two champagne cocktails. He was well aware that I needed help. He invited me to a game of checkers every Wednesday-checkers and cheese. Over the next several months, I opened up to my new confessor. Lester's history was not a lot different than mine, except I killed more men over the years. I trusted him. He focused on the positives of life. I drank less, smoked less, and prayed more.

With Paul gone and Alexa in Milan, I decided to file for a work visa application to America late in 1953. My niece, Vera Jenkins, lived with her husband, Charles, in Queens, New York. I planned to return to Harlem and teach French and English literature, if possible. I had been able to work as a tutor and supplement my income working with Lester. His mission to help the homeless and downtrodden soldiers from both wars helped me more than any expensive psychotherapy.

By the spring of 1955, I received approval from the State Department for my visa. I thanked my friend and soul saver, Lester, for all he had done to help me recover. We hugged goodbye, as only combat soldiers can.

Before sailing back to the States, I received approval to travel to Poland, to visit Auschwitz. I was able to travel with a group of

French petitioners and surviving French Jews. The train ride, once we left France, was peppered with frequent stops to inspect our paperwork. On June 5, we were able to enter the Auschwitz complex. A small group of Catholic nuns were our tour guides. I was able to go to the area where the Farben factory operated. Finally, I came to Mass Grave A3. I knelt down and collected a bottle of dirt. I asked the elderly nun who accompanied me to help me say a prayer for Christina. She gave me her rosary. I planted it in the grave. We prayed again, then I placed a French flag there. While still on my knees, I kissed the old nun's hand and thanked her. She responded, *"Vous vous reverrez dans la royaume eternal,"* meaning "You will meet again in the eternal kingdom."

I took a detour to Milan. I spent two weeks with Alexa, Phillipe, and young Christopher. He was almost four now. He had Christina's complexion and nose. We played games children play until either Chris or I fell asleep, exhausted. I doted on him to the exasperation of his mother. She and I walked the beautifully flowered parks and talked of our memories walking along the quai, many years ago. Alexa asked why I needed to go back to America. Why I would risk getting caught and standing trial in the South. I explained that I had to go with my gut.

I had no family left in France, and I did not want to live out the balance of my life in Italy. We said we would visit each other on a regular basis.

I arrived in Paris just in time to attend Adrienne Monnier's funeral in late June. I was one of hundreds who attended. As I stopped to give my condolences to Sylvia, her longtime life partner, I bid her farewell. I was returning to America with a *Collier's* magazine in tow. The next day, I bade farewell to Josey Baker. We drank champagne. We toasted to our friendship, our freedom, and to a changing America. She kissed me, bit my ear playfully and whispered, "Don't be foolish, the past still has a grip on the Ole South."

I boarded the SS United States in a second-class berth. She was a magnificent, new ship with two huge midship stacks. It was a very modern liner with bright colors, patriotic murals, and sleek modern furnishings. It contained none of the muddy colors or ornate features of the pre-war liners. Josephine was kind enough to send my letter to Millie before I left. If I was lucky, she would take a train to New York to meet me and her daughter, Vera.

We docked in New York Harbor at the end of July. Millie, her daughter, Vera, and Paulette greeted me. I had never seen Vera. She looked more like Millie than Paulette. Darling Paulette was a woman of thirty-two now. Her two children were back on the farm in Fredericksburg. She and her husband had taken over the operations of the farm a few years ago, while Millie began to enjoy a well-deserved semi-retirement. We took a taxi to Vera's place in Queens. Her apartment was on Jamaica Avenue in the Woodhaven neighborhood, just south of Forest Park. Vera and Charles had a two-bedroom apartment with an open kitchen and living room area. Vera's son, Phillip, was now ten years old. He was staying with Charles's mother that day.

Vera cooked like a Jewish grandmother. We talked and ate all day until I fell asleep on them at midnight. The next day, Millie, Paulette, and I strolled through Forest Park while Vera and Charles worked. The following day, we took the subway into Manhattan. Paulette led the way, as the unofficial tour guide, to the Empire State Building, Rockefeller Center, and the Statue of Liberty. We ate in Chinatown. Memories of Beatrice flooded back, as I retraced my steps with her from thirty-five years ago. New York was changing, America was changing. Change was the only constant, like time.

I landed a room in a boarding house in Harlem until I was able to find a job. By September, I secured work as a French instructor at the Cathedral High School at Sutton Place, in Manhattan. It was an all-girls private secondary school with a great reputation. I celebrated Christmas with my niece and her family. She told me that she was pregnant with her second child. Millie and Paulette called on Christmas Day. Alexa and her family called on New Year's Day. Life seemed to paint a brighter picture for me.

Mason Jenkins was born to Vera and Charles in the spring of 1956, my grand-nephew. I found an apartment near my old haunt at 131st Street and Amsterdam Avenue. I was sixty-five now and working for every meal.

By May, my employer had a new principal, Mrs. Alice Ettinger. She seemed very professional, well-educated and wanted to take the institution to a higher level of academic achievement. Just before the school year ended, Principal Ettinger called me into her office. As I entered, two men were standing on each side of her. I had a bad feeling about this immediately.

She began, "Mr. Clément, I had everyone's credentials audited. The university you listed in Ottawa never heard of you. Also, you had no legitimate address in Hamilton either. Your résumé does not check out."

I replied, "How did you find my real identity?"

The New York detective, while spinning his fedora, responded, "Your mistake was listing Vera Mason, your niece, as your local emergency contact on your employment application. After the principal contacted me, I went to see your niece. She was not home, but her son gave me enough to go on. I finally caught up with both Vera and her husband. There was enough information to piece together to trace you back to Fredericksburg, Virginia. Also, time could not totally erase the facial scars from the photos we obtained. Pictures don't lie."

The stoic man with the grey and black fedora interjected. "Is your real name Virgil Lincoln Carpenter? Did you grow up in Fredericksburg?"

I resigned to tell the bloody truth. "I think you already know the answers. My take is that you are a detective from the city, and your associate is from Fredericksburg."

The hatless man replied, "Virgil, you are correct on both counts. You are charged with second degree murder of Clyde McAdoo and assault and battery on Harrison Tyler. You are being extradited back to Fredericksburg to be arraigned. I don't think you have the energy to run away or give a fight, so I won't cuff you, but I need to check to see if you have any weapons."

After being frisked, I asked, "I have one phone call, don't I?"

The expressionless public servant spoke up, "Make your call and make it quick."

I called Millie from the Principal's phone. Without any small talk I began, "Millie, I've been arrested for killing a man while visiting you all back in '22. They are taking me back to Fredericksburg to stand trial. Please contact my family. Don't worry; I was aware this might happen. Give my love."

I reflected out loud to my three accusers, "You know, I've killed many men in two wars. For that, I am deemed a hero. I did not murder this man. I acted in self-defense."

The hatless man commented, "A jury will decide that, let's go."

Chapter Twenty

Requiem

I returned home to Fredericksburg after thirty-four long years, but not the way I had envisioned. Locked up in a jail next to the Old Court House on Princess Anne Street, my lone window offered no view that would have given me any solace. The court house was only two streets from the Rappahannock River, where I spent some of my youth fishing and day dreaming on its tranquil shores. I thought of my peaceful reveries enjoyed in my "castle of corn" in the fields long ago.

I'd been told that this edifice of justice was built over a century ago, housed runaway slaves, and was occupied by federal troops after the battle that bears the city's name. After two idle days in solitary confinement, I had a visitor, my court appointed attorney.

He introduced himself with a handkerchief in his left hand, "Hello, I'm Clifford Raymond, your court appointed attorney." He paused to blow his nose, "Sorry I have a bad case of hay fever. I'm fixin' to represent you, Mr. Carpenter. Can I call you Virgil?"

After we shook hands, he sat down on the undersized, wooden chair. All I could think of was that my life was in the hands of a man who looks like he just finished law school. His thick, black rimmed glasses and slicked backed black hair made Clifford appear to be ill-suited to convince a Southern jury of my innocence. His delicate white hands opened his leather-worn briefcase. I began to pepper him with questions.

"Mr. Raymond, where and when did you go to law school? Also, how many murder cases have you tried?" He put his pen down, looked at me directly, and replied, "I graduated from the University of Maryland School of Law in 1952.

My experience has been largely with felonies and rape. I have been involved in two murder trials."

I pounced on the last comment, "How did the trials end, and what color were the defendants?"

He sat back and said, "You are a smart one. Both were second degree charges. One was found guilty of manslaughter and the other was found guilty of the charge. Both were White. Can we continue about your case?"

"Sure, I just wanted to know who I am dealing with. Do you mind if I have a smoke?" I asked. I lit up before he nodded.

Attorney Raymond continued, "Mr. Carpenter, Virgil, are you guilty of second-degree murder?"

"No, and I will plead 'not guilty' when I am arraigned," I responded.

My young defender took a long look at me and continued. "Good, tell me your story. Include any small details and take your time."

I closed my eyes to collect my thoughts and began, "I remember waiting for the city bus to take me to the train station. I had just concluded my visit to my family. I was making my way back to New York City. After waiting a half hour after the bus was due, I began to hitchhike. A Ford truck picked me up. A young blond woman by the name of Maggie with a dog companion was kind enough to offer me a ride. After several minutes, the truck had to pull over due to a flat tire. Maggie and I began to change the tire when a coupe, I think a Chevy, pulled up beside us. The two young men were immediately hostile to me and provoked a fight. Both came at me, so I used the tire iron to fend them off. After hitting one with the iron, he hit the truck's bumper. I fought the other with my hands until he was knocked out. Maggie told me that the man I hit with the iron was dead. We completed our repair and raced to the train station. She suggested that I tie her up. I boarded the train and made my way back to New York in an indirect manner, to avoid capture. I feared that if I surrendered, I would be found guilty. Remember, the race riots had recently ended at that time. I was a northern Negro in the South. I was not partial to being hanged."

My attorney listened intently while taking notes. He blew his nose again and asked, "Why did this Maggie want you to tie her up?"

My response came quickly, "She did not want to be involved in a trial, nor did she want to be seen as aiding with my escape."

Attorney Raymond interjected, "Your case hangs on the testimony of your only witness, assuming we can find her after all these many years. Without her, it will be your word against that of Harrison Tyler. He owns a service station in town, has been a resident for about fifty-six years, and is well known."

After I finished my cigarette, all I could say is, "Find her."

The next day I was arraigned on the second floor of the court house. I pleaded "not guilty." The judge held me without bail. Two days later I received my first family visitors. Millie and Paulette came with cupcakes and cigarettes. Millie's silvery grey hair almost matched her linen dress. Paulette, now in her forties, was dressed in a light blue dress and white gloves. A white hat with blue trim completed her stylish attire. Paulette commanded the conversation. She asked about my lawyer and my defense. My niece was not satisfied with my defense attorney. She promised to intervene with more help. I begged her to back off, but she had the determination of my old Colonel William Hayward. We talked about the farm and our times together before the Great War. I joked about my jail accommodations and the great view. Afterwards, I relished the corn and blueberry cupcakes, a small consolation in my stark and desperate condition.

I received letters from Vera and Charles and from friends up north. About a month after my incarceration, I received a letter from New York. Its sender was none other than the Honorable Hamilton Fish III. Apparently, Paulette had written to him stating my case and pleading for his assistance. His lengthy letter made references to our interaction with Company K in France. He had promoted me on two occasions. He was very proud of the unit and the men of the Hellfighters Regiment. He finished by promising to help me.

Two weeks after I received Fish's letter, I was visited by my attorney and another counselor, Attorney Foster Reynolds from Washington, D.C. He introduced himself as a friend of the former Congressman Fish, and as a partner of that prestigious law firm.

He specialized in civil rights litigation. He had defended people of color for over twenty years. My new counselor looked like the editor of the "Daily Planet" on the Superman television program. He spoke in the same deep voice, and his perfectly groomed white hair was a match for that of Clark Kent's boss, Perry White.

My new lead counselor got down to business. "On the plus side it's 1956, not 1922. On the minus side, we do not have your witness, and you left the scene and the country. The key will be to have as many sympathetic jurors as possible. Selection will be critical. We need to find your Maggie."

"How do we do it?" I probed.

Reynolds offered me a cigarette and continued. "We need to flood the tri-state area with ads and notifications in all major and local newspapers. I have also hired a private detective to find her. We need to find Maggie."

I took another puff and replied, "I should have died at least ten times. I don't mind dyin'. I do mind losing to a racist son of a bitch."

We had a laugh and talked about the Yankees and Dodgers. I'd been in jail for two plus months now, and the jury was finally being selected. The selection process became a battle of wills between the prosecution and the defense. Dozens of potential jurors were eliminated for various prejudicial biases. The judge finally had to put a lid on this knock down struggle for juror advantage. After ten days, a jury was finalized. Of the twelve jurors, seven were White men, four were White women and one was Black, a Black dentist. My lawyer was pleased.

I had two lawyers, two paralegals, and a private detective working on my defense. I was lucky to have all this firepower. Now all I needed was Maggie to show up and testify. The first person the prosecutor called was the captain of the Fredericksburg Police Department. He testified that the police records showed that a Maggie P. Lawler was found bound in her 1920 Ford truck outside the train station. He added that she made a statement to the police about the incident. Miss Lawler told the police that there was an altercation, but she was not clear as to who began the fight. All she could recall was that the defendant was in a brawl with the two White men in a Chevy coupe. After she determined that Clyde McAdoo was dead and Harrison Tyler was out cold, the defendant was adamant about her driving him to the train station. He tied her up in order to gain time for his getaway.

I leaned back in my chair as I listened to the testimony. I whispered into Reynolds ear, "Not exactly a ringing endorsement for me."

Reynolds cross-examined the captain. He elicited from him that Maggie stated that the defendant did not assault nor make any sexual advances toward her. The prosecution called Harrison Tyler to take the witness stand. He approached the stand, now bald and fat but still defiantly arrogant. One could hardly believe that he promoted an attack on me years ago. He told his distorted and misguided story to the prosecutor and jury. I was tempted to leap up and say, "Liar, liar," but I got a grip on my emotions. Attorney Reynolds was prepared to chip away at this false testimony. He wore a subdued, light colored suit and spoke pleasantly to the jury.

Before he approached the witness stand, Reynolds passed the jury looking each juror in the eye. Then my counselor began, "Mr. Tyler, on the day of the incident you stated that the defendant started an altercation with you and the deceased. Why would a Black man in the South pick a fight with two White men while in the middle of changing a tire?"

Tyler looked awkwardly at the jury and said, "He was cross, because we wanted to help."

Reynolds shot back, "How did you know? I find that hard to believe."

The prosecutor objected. My attorney continued without any hesitation, "Isn't it the truth that you and Mr. McAdoo confronted the defendant and berated him, then attacked him for being a passenger in a White woman's vehicle?"

Tyler looked down and replied, "No."

Reynolds pressed the sweaty witness while the prosecution objected several times. The judge went back and forth overruling or sustaining, but Reynolds made sure that the jury had a lot to think about regarding Tyler's testimony.

My attorney continued with a new line of questioning. "Mr. Tyler, you understand the consequences of committing perjury in a capital murder trial?"

Before the witness could respond, the prosecutor objected. The judge overruled the motion but told my counselor to make his point quickly. Mr. Tyler stated that he was aware of the consequences for perjury.

Reynolds continued while leaning into the nervous Tyler. "Sir, have you ever been a member of the Ku Klux Klan?"

The prosecution objected again, but the impatient judge asked the witness to respond.

"Yes, I joined in 1924."

A follow up question was asked, "Mr. Tyler, are you still a Klan member?"

Tyler looked at the prosecutor for clairvoyant assistance before responding. "I am no longer a member. I resigned back in 1954, getting too old for all the fuss."

"Did you ever kill, beat up, cause any physical or property violence as a Klan member?" asked Reynolds.

The prosecutor objected on the grounds of "relevancy." The judge asked Reynolds as to where he was going with this line of questioning. The counselor stated that he wanted to establish a pattern or history of racial violence.

The witness replied while taking a handkerchief to his brow, "I was involved in cross burnings and ceremonies. We made sure our customs were honored, but I was not involved in any killings. I got into a few scuffles, nothing serious."

"I'm to believe that after thirty years in the Ku Klux Klan that was all you did?" shot back an irritated Reynolds.

The judge sustained another objection. Reynolds asked Tyler if Clyde McAdoo was ever a Klan member.

"I do not believe so. I am not sure," was his response.

My attorney pressed on, "Mr. Tyler, Clyde was a good friend. Was he a Klan member or not?"

Tyler remarked, "No, he died very young."

Reynolds continued, "Mr. Tyler, what was your view about Negroes in 1922?"

Another objection was voiced, but it was overruled. Tyler looked around the court and answered, "I believed, like most White folk in these parts, that the Negro had his place and Whites had their own place, you know — separate."

"You mean 'separate but equal' like the Supreme Court decided about sixty years ago?"

Tyler responded after the judge had overruled another objection, "Not sure about equal. Equal in talent and ability? I didn't think so at the time, but I can tell you that Jackie Robinson can hit as good as anybody."

Reynolds pressed on, "Weren't you and Clyde upset to see a Negro with a White woman, alone in a truck? I declare that your motive was to intimidate and possibly harm the defendant while trying to impress the woman. Isn't that the real truth?"

The sweat was dripping down Tyler's cherubic face as he began to answer, "Clyde and I was just looking to horse around. We meant no harm."

Reynolds closed by stating that he did not believe a fair-minded, intelligent jury would believe his story. The prosecutor took time to try to repair the damage to Tyler's reputation, focusing on his family and business.

Attorney Reynolds called in an expert medical witness, a recently retired coroner from Fredericksburg, Doctor Clayton Whitcher. He had an abundance of white hair and thick, horn-rimmed glasses. Walking to the stand with a silver tipped cane, he nodded a greeting to the judge and the bailiff. Dr. Whitcher took his place on the stand as he looked over to the jury. The former coroner testified that the 1922 autopsy report claimed that the cause of death was due to blunt force trauma.

Reynolds pinned him down asking, "Doctor, can you say with a hundred percent certainty that a tire iron caused Mr. McAdoo's death?"

The doctor replied that he believed that the deceased fell back on the truck bumper with such force and that caused the head trauma. He added that it would have been improbable for the deceased to have hit the back of his head if the defendant had hit him from behind. There were no contusions to the front of his head or body. The opposition did its best to cast doubt on the coroner's testimony. He asked if it was possible for the deceased to have turned half way while falling back. The doctor agreed.

The trial was nearing an end. As admirably as my D.C. lawyer was advocating on my behalf, I had little confidence in being set free. I had been in jail for about four months, and I was beginning to feel that the sewers of Paris had prepared me for my new home. Visits from Millie and Paulette buoyed my mood only slightly.

On the following Sunday morning, I got an unexpected visit from my two counselors. I began, "Gents, you all are working overtime. What's the word?"

Attorney Reynolds sat down and explained, "Virgil, we found your key witness, Maggie. Well, to be blunt, she found us. She was attending the trial for the last week, sitting in the back of the courtroom. She married, got divorced, then remarried. Her new name is Maggie Stephans. She saw the posting of the trial in her local Tidewater newspaper. I will notify the prosecution tomorrow. Hopefully, she will take the stand early next week.

I was excited and nervous at the same time. "Did she corroborate my story?" I asked.

"Yes, but we need to find out why her story was different in 1922," exclaimed Reynolds.

Maggie was grilled by my attorneys for two full days while the opposition made use of the time dissecting her background and her associates. The whole case would ride on her testimony, and everyone knew it. She took the stand on Thursday morning, a wet, chilly day in late September.

Mr. Reynolds began slowly, "Mrs. Stephans, you were just sworn in. Tell the jury the truth, the whole truth and nothing but the truth about the day in question."

Maggie had grey hair but was still lithe and athletic for a woman in her fifties. She told a story identical to mine, as she spoke directly to the jury.

Reynolds countered, "Why did your story change from the statement you gave in 1922? Which are we to believe?"

Maggie was prepared and responded. "The accounts of what occurred, as I have just told the court, are accurate, not dulled by the passing of time. In 1922 it was a taboo for a White woman to be alone with a Negro man. I just wanted to help the defendant get to the train station. I also did not want the police to think that I was helping him escape. That is why I suggested the defendant tie me up. I also told the police that Mr. Carpenter was headed for Chicago, a ploy to throw them off his trail. I am sorry, but I do not believe he would have received a fair trial even if I testified on his behalf in 1922. My testimony would have been tainted because of my association with the defendant."

The prosecutor approached the stand with a note card. He began, "Mrs. Stephans, have you ever dated or kissed a Negro?"

Reynolds stood up and objected, but the judge allowed the prosecutor to continue.

"Yes, only once, when World War One was over. He was a dry goods delivery boy who stopped by our home when the Armistice was declared."

The prosecutor pressed on, "Did you know the two young men who stopped to assist you?"

She declared, "No, I did not."

"Mrs. Stephans, did you see yourself as a bit of a rebel back then, assisting Negroes, kissing one, and helping them beyond your proper calling?"

Maggie looked him straight in the eyes and proceeded, "I was the Alice Roosevelt Longworth type, smoking and driving a truck, more of a tomboy than a white-laced type of girl. My fault was that I was color blind. I did not hold a prejudiced point of view toward Negroes. Mr. Carpenter was attacked by two White men that day. That is the God's honest truth."

The prosecutor and Maggie went at each other a bit longer. She seemed to have the longer claws. Both sides made their closing arguments. I believed that my team had the best hand and had played it well.

The jury deliberated for a day, then two days, then the verdict was reached. The courtroom came back in session. I rose to hear my fate.

The foreman read the verdict, "Not guilty of second-degree murder. Guilty of justifiable homicide. Guilty of leaving the scene and escaping."

I was confused and speechless. My lawyers hugged me, while I cried and thanked them. The judge demanded order. He decreed that my punishment on the third count was time served, and I was free to go. I had dodged another bullet in life.

After thanking Maggie and the jurors, Paulette, Millie, and I hugged for what seemed like an eternity. I rested back at their farm. Many family and friends were helping with the large dinner celebration. After the Indian summer sun set, I strolled back to the cornfield and found an empty, carved out spot for me, in the same place I had gone for decades. At sixty-five, I still relished looking up at the azure sky, as if it was my own. Daydreaming about people and places resonating in the forefront and recesses of my mind occupied my time. When the stars began to come out, I went back to reality. I thanked Millie for her hospitality and for my time in the cornfield. She said that she saved that spot since I left over thirty years ago. She admitted to "borrowing" it a number of times over the years.

The next morning, I visited the Old Shiloh Church Cemetery. Spending time at the graves of Mary, Mom, and Father was thera-peutic for me. I took a few days making nostalgic trips to my high school, Darbytown, and even the Hampton Institute. It's never the same as you remember it; time does not stand still for memories. I said my good-byes to my family and friends and headed north after almost six months. I was able to get my old job back with a lot of persuasion, but I could not begin until the January semester. I spent much of the Christmas holidays with Vera and her family in Queens.

In early December, I decided to pay a visit to former Congress-man Hamilton Fish III's office in Manhattan. If it wasn't for him, I may have been found guilty. I was fortunate that he was in. After waiting in his reception room for forty-five minutes, I was escorted to his office. It was smaller than I had expected, and full of pictures, plaques, and piles of papers.

He greeted me with a hearty handshake and said, "Virgil, you old dog, you dodged many bullets in your life, what's one more? Take a seat. Want a drink?" He motioned to his cabinet, "Got some bour-bon, Jim Beam. Let's celebrate, old man."

I could not refuse, and I thanked him, accepting a glass. He continued, "You know, Pearl Harbor happened on my birthday, that's a kick. Like Teddy Roosevelt, they thought I was too old to fight in the last war. I even got booted out five months before the war ended. Well, it was a good run of twenty-four years. I got an hour, tell me about your adventures in France."

We went through a lot of "Beam" in an hour. He looked greyer and paler than he did in his prime, but his bearing and posture were equal to the man I knew almost forty years ago. In short, he aged well, better than most. I explained in vivid detail my adventures with Captain Le Van, Christina, my children and the hair-raising trials of being a Resistance fighter for over two years. The time flew by.

Ham was astounded. He could hardly believe so much could happen to one person in only one lifetime. I gave him a Nazi dagger as a gift. It was a memento I took off one of the Germans I killed in the truck that was transporting many civilian hostages. I left with a strong smell of bourbon on my breath.

A few days before Christmas, I was visiting Rockefeller Center with Vera when I was stopped in my tracks with my jaw dropped. I ran into none other than Eugene Bullard. He was working as an elevator operator and seemed somewhat embarrassed to see me. We could not talk at length until he came off duty at 3:00 o'clock in the afternoon. Vera continued to shop while Eugene and I headed uptown to a neighborhood bar on Amsterdam Avenue. Pictures of Sugar Ray Robinson, Rocky Marciano, Archie Moore, Joe Lewis, and others covered the otherwise murky and dingy walls.

Eugene was wearing thick black framed eyeglasses. His build had not changed from his Montmartre days, but his face was tired and puffy.

He said, "Hell of a thing, I was a champion boxer, a war hero, an influential man in Paris with influential friends, ran a popular club, all in France. In America, I'm jus' an elevator operator, an ole fool."

I leaned over and said, "Eugene, history will remember you as the great man you are. America is not ready yet to celebrate Negro heroes. It's only been a few years since Jackie Robinson proved that he belongs in the Majors. Appreciation for him, you, Lewis, Owens, and others will come when the floodgates open for the Negro. It will be up to the next one or two generations to build on what we started."

We laughed and ordered our '75' cocktails. We saluted our dead comrades until the barkeep cut us off. We staggered to Eugene's apartment at 116th Street and passed out listening to music by Ella Fitzgerald and Billie Holiday.

We kept in touch. I even had the good fortune to see him on the "Today Show" with Dave Garroway, late in 1959. He was dressed in his elevator operator's uniform while Garroway displayed his more than two dozen medals. Finally, he was getting some recognition before he died. I visited Eugene as he was admitted to Metropolitan Hospital in August of 1961. He never made it out. He died of stomach cancer on October 12. Members of the Federation of French War Veterans, France Forever, the Verdun Society, and American Legion Paris Post Number One attended his Mass at Saint Vincent de Paul Church on the 17th.

He was buried in a cemetery in Flushing, Queens, grave number Seven, Section C, Plot number Fifty-Three. Simply, his headstone bore his name and years of his birth and death. Rest in Peace, soldier.

I celebrated Thanksgiving at the New York Presbyterian Hospital. I had had a heart attack. I was lucky it was not fatal. The surgeon opened up a closed artery and put me on blood thinners. I lost twenty pounds, a damn tough way to lose weight. Vera and Charles visited me, as well as a few remaining Hellfighters. The veterans talked a lot of bull about events long forgotten by most. I lived for those talks in Riverside Park. Occasionally one would pass away. We were only a handful that kept the torch burning.

I met Maria Ramos while taking a stroll in Riverside Park, near Grant's Tomb. She was walking her Boston Terrier. We struck up a conversation about dogs in general. I droned on about the dog Wilson I "adopted" while I was in France during the First War. This particular Saturday was a pleasant day with a mild breeze, good for one with a heart condition to be out for a stroll. Maria had an infectious smile and an optimistic personality. She was several years my junior, with black hair, brown eyes, and a dark, smooth complexion. She was heavier than Christina, but not by much, and short, coming only up to my nose. We strolled all the way up to where the Henry Hudson Parkway began. I found out that Maria had come to the states in 1954 after her husband died from cancer. She had a daughter in the Bronx and her son still lived in Puerto Rico, managing a hotel in San Juan. I managed to say little about myself. We agreed to follow up with a formal date at an Italian restaurant on the Grand Concourse.

Shortly afterwards, I received a letter from Alexa. She was planning to visit for a month with her children. Phillipe would join them after two weeks. Even a month did not seem long enough for me. Maria and I continued our relationship going on trips to Yankee Games, dinners, walks in the parks, and seeing an occasional movie like "Lawrence of Arabia" and "To Kill a Mockingbird." I could relate to that movie with an eerie reality.

Spending the month of June with Alexa and her boys was fantastic. They stayed at The Roosevelt Hotel in Midtown. They were very good to me. We traveled like typical tourists from Harlem to Battery Park. We even made a trip to Coney Island. I stayed away from the more aggressive rides. Alexa treated me to everything. At age seventy-one, I found it difficult to keep up, so we took rest stops for my benefit. Toward the end of their trip, I invited Maria to join us. Alexa was understanding. It had been eighteen years since her mother had died. Alexa and Phillipe promised to return the following year.

Maria and I wanted to retire, but the only feasible, economic solution were for us to live together. I was adamant about not getting married again. I felt like a "bad luck" husband. As a practicing Catholic, Maria did not want to live in sin. We settled on a very small Catholic ceremony with no celebration party. Our relationship was more companionship than carnal. We both retired in September of 1962. Maria moved into my humble apartment. We cobbled up enough money to enjoy a modest retirement.

A few weeks after we moved in Maria found the "box." All my original diaries, and ones I had to reconstruct were in the box. Over fifty years of journals, written during peace and war, were in that one wooden box. It fell from a shelf while Maria was unpacking. A page in one of the diaries that was spilled out onto the floor had been opened to the time that I was recuperating at Madame Billy's brothel. Maria admitted to reading the two open pages, no more.

She was quick to engage with me when I came home. "In the five years I have known you, you have never told me about the dark details of your complicated life," she exclaimed.

I was startled, then I replied, "A man cannot easily relive his emotional wounds, especially the horrors of war. I think a woman is better suited to express her feelings."

Maria pondered my statement as she sat down, then responded, "Maybe you are right. I can see your physical scars, but the ones inside must be very deep. All I ask is that you can confide in me, your wife. You can talk to me, and I will help heal your wounds."

She caressed by face, then we hugged. Over the next several years, I confided in her. Admittedly, there were a few deep, dark secrets that I kept to myself.

As time passed, I found myself in a routine of playing chess and checkers often with friends and Hellfighter vets. Maria and I had our own routines of walks together, and watching favorite television programs like "The Twilight Zone," "The Lucille Ball Show," Walt Disney programs, and "The Ed Sullivan Hour." We visited Vera's family in Queens and Maria's daughter, Rosa, in Yonkers. In 1966, we went to Puerto Rico to see Paulo, Maria's son. I had the great misfortune of having another heart attack there. I felt that I was on borrowed time now.

In early 1967, while I had been recovering in Harlem, we discovered that Maria had been diagnosed with colon cancer. She began radiation treatments shortly thereafter. She suffered with stoic Catholicism. We both felt that our stamina for life was ebbing.

Health issues stole the quality from our golden years together. Maria and I comforted each other; holding hands like school kids, as we slowly strolled on the pedestrian paths next to the Hudson River. Joggers and bicyclists passed us with regularity. We did not care. Maria was up to the task; she did help heal my emotional wounds.

I succumbed to using a cane when I turned seventy-eight, the same year that Vera moved to Hempstead, Long Island. Their eldest son, Paul, was fastidious and an achiever while Mason was a rebel with new, mischievous friends. Vera confided in me that neither Charles nor she could control Mason. His school counselors were also concerned about his future. He was smart, but he was wasting his talent on foolishness. After Mason and his cohorts were caught partying in an abandoned mansion and joy riding, Vera sent him to my hospital room for advice and some straight talk, while I was recuperating from another heart attack. He was only fourteen, but he had the potential for a life of criminality. He appeared at the partially open door very sheepishly. He had a large afro hairdo, fashionable at the time, and wore black jeans and a white tee shirt. Mason had grown a few inches since the last time I saw him.

I said, "Look me in the eye and shake my hand, like a man, Mason. Don't come a-slouching."

He conceded. I continued, "Good to see you. I here tell your Mama demanded your presence here. Take a seat."

Mason demurred and said, "Thanks."

"So, what's up?" I asked.

My young relative took a long sip of water offered from my nightstand, and responded, "Well Uncle Virgil, they don't care for my friends and some of my activities."

"Don't you get hot with that afro?" I commented, attempting something lighthearted to break the tension.

He looked incredulous and replied, "No, no, I don't." Then we both smiled.

Fighting to stay awake, I got to the point. "I am not going to compare you to your brother. You are your own man. Mason, I think your parents are concerned about your future. They are working hard for your future, to have a better life then they have and a more dignified one than I had. Don't be a follower, be a leader. Be your own man." I told my great nephew that a storm was coming.

He rushed to the window to verify my prediction. He corrected me.

I replied, "No son, a storm is coming for you, our race, and the country. Be prepared. Be part of the solution. You have the makings of a leader. Don't waste your time with discontented fools." I did not remember much after that, as the recently administered medication caused me to fall asleep.

Mason's next visit was at my apartment. Maria was well enough to journey to Yonkers to see her daughter, Rosa. Mason appeared at my door wearing blue jeans and another white tee shirt. Angela Davis, a civil rights activist from UCLA, would have been proud of his growing afro.

I welcomed him. "Good to see you again. What's new? Want some lemonade?"

Mason demurred, "Okay."

After some small talk, I got to the point. "Mason, have you taken to heart our conversation at the hospital?"

He ran his fingers through his voluminous hair and replied, "Yes. I moved on. I am more of a loner now. I'm lifting weights and studying more often. I am still bitter about how we are being treated in America and the racism that has persisted for many decades." He continued with passion in his voice, "We have been pushed around for too long. We need to fight in order to be treated as equals. Words on a document mean little if society, White society, pays no heed to the words like equality, liberty, justice, and opportunity. The only equal opportunity is fighting in Vietnam."

I thought before I replied. The silence lasted a minute, then I began, "Young man, I admire your passion. I do not disagree with the point you've made. I would like to have you consider this: your anger and hatred against Whites will not speed up equality in America. It will only hurt your part in shaping the destiny of our race. Yes, there is a long way to go for a colorless society, but we have traveled light years from my time. You don't know shit about inequality until your life is in constant danger every day. I could tell you stories that would make your afro turn white. You need to do the best and be the best you can be, force Whites to take notice and not deny you. Don't go around blaming them. That's the 'loser's limp,' son. This welfare bullshit is just making second class citizens and wards of the state for many Negroes."

Mason took another long sip of lemonade and said, "Can I hear some of your stories?"

I replied, "Yes, wait a minute."

I went to my closet and pulled out a diary dated September 1918. I started with a war story in order to captivate my young listener. I wanted him to be a constant visitor. Also, I wanted to be relevant again. Leaning on my cane, I began to paint a picture of war in France over a half century ago.

I said, "I found myself in a muddy, godforsaken shell hole somewhere near a destroyed village by the Aisne River. I was about a hundred miles east of Paris. I did not recall if it was a French or German hole, all the same. It smelled like a combination of sulphur and iron. It also smelled like death and decay. A chilly mist added to my misery. I fumbled around. Trying to reach the lip of my temporary liquid shelter, I stepped on a partially submerged, dead German soldier. I barfed up what little I had eaten many hours ago. Now machine gun bullets, and the rain, pinged at the grey, muddy water that filled up much of the shell hole."

I could see that Mason was listening intently, so I continued. "Pieces of mud flew into the cauldron as a result of more shelling on both sides. I could hear the savage cries of friendly soldiers advancing to support the men of my battalion."

Mason was sitting on the edge of his chair as he interrupted me.

"Uncle Virgil, were you shot?"

"No, just scared out of my wits," I replied. Then I continued, "I turned towards the fanatical onslaught as two Moroccan soldiers dove for cover in 'my' hole. One was shot in the shoulder, and the other red turbaned soldier from the Second Moroccan Division followed. Both had large Berber daggers and machetes, standard fare for these fearless warriors. They were infamous for not taking any prisoners. We communicated in French, as best we could. I aided in patching up the wounded Moroccan. At dusk, what was left of the Germans, counterattacked, hoping to improve their desperate situation. Our beat-up battalion and Moroccan allies were prepared for the attack. Hotchkiss and Chau-chat machine guns opened up on anything that moved across the twisted iron and mud spate landscape."

I had to sit down, as my energy began to fade. I took a drink of lemonade and continued. "Two Germans attempted to seek relief from the hail of bullets by invading our muddy sanctuary. My newly acquired Moroccan comrade killed one of them with his machete before his adversary could use his bayonet. I was chest high in mud wrestling for my life with the remaining German. The teenaged looking foe was getting the better of me when a dagger plunged through his back. My bloodthirsty Moroccan ally had put an end to this death struggle. I would rather have had the German taken prisoner, but that was not part of the 'code of conduct' for my red turbaned friend."

Mason sat mesmerized. He had a new appreciation for the meaning of hell. He became a frequent visitor over the next two years. He listened to me as I expounded on the writings of my many diaries dating back to the turn of the century. He learned about our family history and virtually every detail of my life covering marriages, my children, my experiences in the Great War, my time helping solve murders in Paris, making champagne, and my trying time as a Resistance Fighter in the last war. As the months progressed, I could see a change in Mason's attitude. He became focused on his success and his future. His grades got better. He made new friends, and we became friends, three generations removed.

Maria, my companion, and last love succumbed to cancer late in 1972. My only consolation was that I knew I would not be far behind her. I felt that, in spite of all my challenges and the many tragedies I had endured in my life, I was a lucky man. You see, as I shared with Mason, the challenges can make you a better man and strengthen your spirit, or they can break you. It's not that you won't falter, fall down, and despair. It's how you get up again. My heart may have been damaged, but it was never destroyed. I had loved and been loved. Soon I would see my three soulmates, my sons, and all those I had lost and missed in life. I was tired, and I wanted to go home.

The last time I saw my great uncle was a month before he died. I went to the hospital for my usual visit with him. Over the past two years, I'd come to look forward to seeing him and hearing all the tales of his complicated and challenging life. It helped me to mature and realize I had hardly lived compared to what he had gone through. He brought me outside of myself and my small perception of the world. I had so much of life yet, so much to look forward to, and much to overcome.

I sat in front of his coffin at the wake, with family and a few remaining friends paying their respects. I mourned him more deeply than I would have thought I could. It was as if once I'd lost him, I fully appreciated the gifts he had shared with me of himself and his life lessons. I remembered what he had told me when I visited him in the hospital that first time, a few years back: "A storm is coming." I now knew he meant for those words to strengthen me for what I would face personally, as well as what our race would continue to endure. I could not see it so clearly then, but he did prepare me for what was to come. He prepared me to be a man.

By the way, Virgil never wrote the book he wanted to write. He had known great literary figures and taught great literature throughout his life. His diaries held the key to his innermost thoughts about all that he lived and endured. He shared his gifts with me, a young, confused and angry boy who had the good fortune to know him and learn from him. In some ways, I see this as a collaboration between the two of us, between two very different generations who still face many of the same challenges both personally and in the world. But in the end, this is his story, and I am just his "pen."

The author encourages you to leave a review wherever you purchased the book or at www.thereluctantsoldier.com

Made in the USA
Middletown, DE
18 October 2023